# Bad Blood

# Bad Blood

## Arne Dahl

### Translated from the Swedish by Rachel Willson-Broyles

ISIS
LARGE PRINT
Oxford

First published in Great Britain 2013
by
Harvill Secker
one of the publishers in The Random House Group Limited

Published in Large Print 2014 by ISIS Publishing Ltd.,
7 Centremead, Osney Mead, Oxford OX2 0ES
by arrangement with
Harvill Secker
one of the publishers in The Random House Group Limited

CIP data is available for this title from the British Library

ISBN 978–0–7531–9284–9 (hb)
ISBN 978–0–7531–9285–6 (pb)

Printed and bound in Great Britain by
T. J. International Ltd., Padstow, Cornwall

# CHAPTER
# ONE

*Pain beyond words*, he thinks. *Now I know what it is.*

*Learn for life*, he thinks, and his gallows-humour laugh is silent. *Learn for death*, he thinks, and instead of laughter: yet another mute, infernal scream.

As the pain mounts its next attack, he knows with a kind of crystal-clear certainty that he has laughed his last laugh.

The pain is no longer deepening. With what he can still make out as a mixture of satisfaction and terror, he feels that its intensity has reached its peak, and he understands just what process is now under way.

The downward slope.

The graph of pain is no longer rising; it is levelling out, and beyond it he can glimpse the steep incline that will, with the inevitability of a playground slide, end in nothingness. Or — and he fights the thought — with God.

The images start to come to him; he knew they would. They come even as the pain increases to levels he couldn't have imagined in his wildest fantasies. He is surprised at the possibilities that have lain hidden within him all these years.

So they do exist.

While his entire being explodes in cascade after cascade, the pain seems more and more to shift from his fingers, genitals and throat to a place outside himself. It somehow rises above his body and invades his — and he can't help thinking of the word — his *soul*. All the while he tries to keep his mind clear. But then come more images.

At first he fought to maintain contact with the world, but now the world outside, beyond the small window, is nothing more than the giant aircraft lumbering past. Now and then the figure of his tormentor sweeps by, holding the deadly tools. Soon enough the roaring planes blend with the images, and now even the planes are transformed into shrieking spirits.

He can't control the images, how they come, their order, their structure. He sees the unforgettable interior of the labour room where his son has been born, but he hasn't been there himself; rather, as his son is born, he hears himself throwing up in the bathroom. But now he is there, and it is beautiful, odourless, soundless. Life goes on, clean and pure. He greets people he recognises as great authors. He drifts through elegant old corridors. He sees himself making love to his wife, and her expression is joyful in a way he's never seen. He is standing at a podium; people applaud wildly. More corridors, meetings, conferences. He is on TV, showered with admiring looks. He sees himself writing with a white-hot passion, he sees himself read book after book, pile after pile of papers.

But when the pain is interrupted and the rumble of the planes brings him back to the room, it strikes him that all he sees is *himself* reading and writing, not *what* he is reading and writing. During those brief moments when he can catch his breath, he wonders what this means.

It is clear now that the descent is starting. The pain no longer reaches him. He is fleeing his tormentor; he will be victorious. He even has the strength to spit on him, and the reply is a crunching sound and a slight increase in pain. Out of the darkness comes a roaring dragon, and it becomes an aeroplane that sweeps over a football pitch where his son is casting nervous glances at the sidelines. He waves to him, but his son doesn't see; he waves more frantically and yells louder, but his son only looks more resigned until he scores a goal for the opposing team, out of distraction or protest.

Then he sees the young woman next to the bookshelf, her impressed glances. They're walking along the large street, eagerly demonstrating their generation-defying love. On the other side: two completely motionless figures, his son and his wife, and he sees them and stops and gives the woman a deep kiss. He's running, working out. The little needle presses down into his scalp again and again, and finally his glorious thick hair is back again. His mobile phone rings during a debate at the book fair — another son. Champagne corks pop, but when he gets home, they're gone.

And he's reading again, and in a final burst of consciousness he thinks that something out of all he's read and written ought to fly past, but the only thing he sees is himself reading and writing, and in one last shining second of lucidity that makes him think he is truly dying, he realises that nothing he has read or written has meant anything. He might as well have done absolutely anything else.

He thinks of the threat. "No one will be able to hear you scream." Of how he didn't take the threat seriously. Because he suspected — a final burst of pain stops his last thought.

And so begins the end. The images come quickly now. It's as though there's no time.

He's walking in the protest march; the police raise their batons above him. He's standing in a summer pasture, the horse racing towards him. A little grass snake slinks into his rubber boots and winds its way between his toes. His father looks absent-mindedly at his drawing of the enormous snake. The clouds rush by above the edge of the pushchair canopy, and he thinks he sees a cat moving around up there. Sweet milk is sprayed over his face. The thick, pale green cord leads the way, and he travels through dark, fleshy canals.

And then he is no longer travelling.

Thinks somewhere: *What a sleazy way to die.*

# CHAPTER
# TWO

Paul Hjelm was convinced that there was such a thing as a motionless morning, and that this late-summer morning was one of them. Not a leaf was moving on the slightly wilted plants in the courtyard, nor a speck of dust in the office where he stood gazing outside. Extremely few brain cells were moving inside his skull. In other words, it was a motionless morning at police headquarters on Kungsholmen in Stockholm.

Unfortunately, the past year had also been motionless. Paul Hjelm was part of the police squad that had investigated the remarkable so-called "Power Murders", in which a serial killer had single-mindedly started to wipe out the elites of Swedish business and industry. Because the investigation had been a success, the group was made permanent as a special unit within the National Criminal Police, an auxiliary resource for "violent crimes of an international character", as the formal wording ran. In practice, they were tasked with keeping up with new forms of criminality that hadn't yet really reached Sweden.

And that was the problem. No other "violent crimes of an international character" had afflicted the country during the past year, so more and more internal criticism was being levelled against the existence of the A-Unit. It wasn't really called the A-Unit; that was just the name that had come up a year and a half ago when, in a state of panic, the group had been formed at short notice. For purposes of formality and justification, the group was now called "the National Criminal Police's Special Unit for Violent Crimes of an International Character". Because this name, in accordance with convention, was impossible to say without laughing, they continued to call themselves "the A-Unit", which was itself pretty comical, but at least it had a certain sentimental value.

But at this point, the group was close to being history. Idleness among civil servants was hardly in keeping with the times, and the group was slowly beginning to break up; it was given various bullshit tasks, and its members were being lent out all over the place. The group's formal boss, Waldemar Mörner, deputy commissioner of the National Police Board, worked like a dog, but it seemed that the story of the A-Unit would soon be over.

What the unit needed was a robust serial killer. Of a robust international character.

Paul Hjelm, staring stupidly and motionlessly at the motionless morning, watched a small leaf, one of the few that was already yellow, quiver and flutter to the courtyard's dreary concrete. He gave a start, which goaded him to pull himself together. He strode over to a flaking shaving mirror that was nailed to the wall in the generic office — and contemplated his blemish.

During the hunt for the Power Murderer, a red spot had broken out on his cheek, and someone very close to him had said that the blemish looked like a heart. That had been a long time ago. She was no longer close to him, and the person who had taken her place mostly thought it repulsive.

He looked back at the time of the Power Murders case with sadness and a sense of unreality. The case had brought a peculiar mix of professional success and personal disaster. And renewal, painful in the way renewal is always painful.

His wife, Cilla, had left him. In the middle of one of the country's most important murder investigations ever, he had ended up alone with the children out in the terraced house in Norsborg. This meant that the children had to drift around by themselves while he was sucked deeper and deeper into the case and found an ambiguous erotic release with a colleague. He still had trouble separating what had actually happened between them from what he had imagined.

But once the case was solved, the train of life returned to its customary rails, as he had put it in poetic moments. One car after another was pulled in from its siding and resumed its place on the main track until the Hjelm train was once again its old self. Cilla returned; family life went back to normal; the A-Unit, and not least himself, were declared heroes; the group was made permanent; he was promoted and was assigned regular working hours; a few of his colleagues became close friends; the female colleague found a new man; peace and quiet returned; and everything was fine and dandy.

The question now was whether he had got an overdose of peace and quiet, because suddenly one day, after the nearly six months it took to tie up the Power Murder case and come to a verdict, he realised that the mighty Hjelm train had been transformed into a little model railway set. Wide-open spaces and endless skies turned out to actually be the cement floor, walls and ceiling of a games room; and the train's speedy departure turned out to be nothing more than a perpetually recurring circle.

His first doubts about the purpose of the A-Unit's existence were accompanied by a whole series of further doubts. His return to the same old ruts felt more and more like a bad stage production of his daily routine. As though everywhere he went were poorly constructed, as though there were no solid ground under the railway tracks, as though the tiniest puff of air would blow it over.

Hjelm looked at himself in the mirror: about forty, with medium-blond, standard Swedish hair and a receding hairline. In general, his was hardly an appearance that attracted attention — aside from his blemish, from which he now removed a small flake of skin and onto which he rubbed a bit of skin cream. Then he returned to the window. The morning was still motionless. The small yellow leaf was lying still where it had landed. No breeze had descended upon the police headquarters courtyard.

What they needed was a robust serial killer, of a robust international character, thought Paul Hjelm as he slid back into his orgy of self-pity.

Sure, Cilla had returned. Sure, he himself had returned. But not once had they ever discussed what they'd really done and felt during their separation. At first he'd seen this as a sign of mutual trust, but then he began to suspect that it was a chasm they would never be able to bridge. And how were the children doing, really? Danne was sixteen now, and Tova would be fourteen soon, and sometimes when he caught their sidelong glances, he wondered whether he had used up all the store of trust they had in him. Had the strange summer almost a year ago left traces that would distort their lives long after his own death? It was mind-boggling.

And his relationship with Kerstin Holm, his colleague, also seemed to have entered a new phase. They ran into each other several times a day, and each time it felt more strained. Hiding behind their exchanged glances were abysses that hadn't been touched upon but that seemed more and more to demand attention. Not even his good relationships with his boss, Jan-Olov Hultin, and with his colleagues Gunnar Nyberg and Jorge Chavez seemed quite the same, as the little model train circled round and round in its stuffy room.

And then finally came the awful suspicion that the only thing that had changed was — him. Because he really *had* changed. He listened to music he'd never even considered before, and he found himself glued to books he'd never heard of. On his desk, a portable CD player lay next to a tattered paperback. In the CD player was John Coltrane's mysterious *Meditations*, one of the sax master's last albums, a strange mixture of wild improvisation and quiet reverence; and the book was Kafka's *Amerika*, the least renowned of his novels but in some ways the most curious. Paul Hjelm would never forget the chain of events that is set into motion when the young Karl lands in New York harbour, realises that he's forgotten his umbrella, and returns to the steamer. He was convinced that that kind of scene comes back to you when you're about to die.

Sometimes he blamed the books and the music for his metaphor of the model railway. Maybe he would have been happier if he still saw wide, open spaces and long, straight roads around him.

His gaze returned to the courtyard. The little yellow leaf was still there. Everything was motionless.

Suddenly and without warning, the leaf was lifted up into a spiralling whirlwind, and several more leaves were torn away, yellow ones as well as green ones; they performed a wild, multicoloured dance between the walls of police headquarters. Then the dance stopped as suddenly as it had started; the lone whirlwind continued invisibly on its way, and all that was left was a lonely pile of leaves on the drab cement.

The door was flung open. Jorge Chavez came in. The presence of this thirty-year-old dynamo of a desk mate always made Hjelm feel a decade older. But he could deal with it — Chavez was one of his best friends these days. He had come to the A-Unit from the precinct in

Sundsvall, where he had given himself the title of the only blackhead cop in Norrland. Actually, though, he was a Stockholmer, the son of Chilean refugees in Rågsved. Hjelm never really understood how Chavez had passed the physical requirements for entry to the police college; he was no more than five foot six. On the other hand, he was one of the sharpest policemen in the country — certainly the most energetic one Hjelm had ever come across. In addition, he was an elite-level jazz bassist.

Chavez's compact little figure slid to his end of the double desk. He took his shoulder holster from the chair, fastened it onto himself, checked his service pistol, and pulled on his summer jacket of light linen.

"Something's up," he said. "Full speed ahead down the corridor."

Hjelm copied Chavez's movements, "What do you mean, 'full speed ahead'?"

"Hard to define. But we're going to hear Hultin's voice within thirty seconds, for sure. Want to make a bet?"

Paul Hjelm shook his head. He looked at the CD player and the book on the desk, then at the pile of leaves in the courtyard, shook some life into himself, and jumped onto the locomotive. Time took on a new form.

A curt voice boomed over the intercom; it belonged to the A-Unit's operative director, Detective Superintendent Jan-Olov Hultin: "Quick meeting. Everyone. Immediately."

Hjelm pulled his leather jacket over his shoulder holster and he and Chavez half ran towards the room that had once gone by the name "Supreme Central Command" and that — he thought hopefully — might do so once again. On their way through the hall, a door flew open in Chavez's face, and Viggo Norlander hurtled out. Though he had once been the group's dependable rule follower, since the Power Murders Norlander had become their bad boy; he had replaced his old, worn-out bureaucrat suits with trendy polo shirts and leather jackets, and his slight mid-life flab was upgraded to a genuine six-pack.

The rest of the group was already assembled when Norlander and Hjelm tumbled in. Chavez arrived just behind them with a handkerchief to his nose. Detective Superintendent Jan-Olov Hultin surveyed him sceptically from the desk at the front of the unexceptional little room; he was sitting there like an owl, or rather like a bored secondary-school teacher who'd been forgotten by the pension board. His glasses were perched in their proper place, like a small, natural growth, on his giant nose. No newly kindled passion shone in his eyes, though something may have smouldered in their corners. He cleared his throat.

All the members of the select group were actually there; all of them had, as usual, clocked in early so they could go home early, and none had been loaned out to some strange posting elsewhere as punishment. Gunnar Nyberg, Arto Söderstedt and Kerstin Holm were already sitting up front. Nyberg and Söderstedt were of the same generation as Norlander, which meant they were a few years older than Hjelm and many years older than Chavez; Holm was somewhere between the latter two. She was the only woman in the group; a short, dark-complexioned Gothenburger, she was the third cog in the trio of brains, along with Hjelm and Chavez.

On the other hand, she had something very important in common with the group's purest bundle of energy, her office mate Gunnar Nyberg: both sang in a choir and weren't ashamed to be caught singing a cappella numbers in their office. Nyberg had a colourful past as a brutal, steroid-using bodybuilder, but nowadays he was a timid middle-aged man, a sloppily clad mountain of meat with a lovely singing voice who could still break out his old moves if necessary. During the investigation of the Power Murders, having already taken a bullet in his throat, he had tackled an accelerating car and put it out of action. Söderstedt, for his part, was one of the strangest group members, a Finland-Swedish, chalk-white former top lawyer whose conscience had caught up to him; he always worked apart from the others, following his own paths off the beaten track.

Norlander, Chavez and Hjelm took places in the row behind the trio. Hultin began in his customarily neutral voice, "A Swedish citizen has been murdered in the United States. But not just *anyone*, not just *anywhere* and not *by* just anyone. A relatively well-known Swedish literary critic was killed a few hours ago at Newark International Airport, outside New York. He was sadistically tortured by a serial killer whose activity goes back several decades. Up to this point, it has nothing to do with us."

Apparently there was time for one of Hultin's dramatic pauses, because what followed was that very thing.

"Our dilemma," he continued, "is that this serial killer is on his way here."

Another moment of silence, a bit more loaded.

"The information from the FBI indicates that the killer took the literary critic's seat on the flight. At this very moment he is on flight SK 904, which will land at Arlanda in just under an hour, at 08.10. All together the plane is carrying 163 passengers, and the police in New York have chosen *not* to inform the crew of the situation. At present we are in a state of uncertainty as to the identity of the perpetrator, which isn't so strange when you consider that he's been eluding the FBI for twenty years. But they hope to find out what name he's travelling under before the plane lands — I have an open line to a Special Agent Larner in New York. And so we need two parallel plans. One: we get the name in time, in which case there's a risk of a scuffle. Two: we *don't* get the name in time, in which case we have to try to pick out from among 163 passengers an elusive serial killer whose only known characteristics are that he is a white male, probably over forty-five years old."

Hultin stood and pulled the zip of his old sports jacket up over the butt of his pistol in its shoulder holster. He leaned forward.

"This whole thing is really quite simple," he said tranquilly. "If we fail, Sweden has imported its first real American serial killer. Let's avoid that."

14

He tromped off towards the waiting helicopter, leaving behind the following words of wisdom:

"The world is shrinking, ladies and gentlemen. The world is shrinking."

# CHAPTER
# THREE

The immense, irreplaceable calm that always appears comes in expanding waves of bliss. He knows he will never stop.

Outside, the tremendous emptiness stretches on, with the earth as a tiny, negligible exception. A magnificent speck of fly shit on the great white page of perfection, a protocol error that has likely destroyed the limitless divinity of the divine.

A thin sheet of Plexiglas separates him from the great, sucking holes of nothingness that his serenity makes him part of.

The peaceful rocking of the clouds drives the images away. They are far away now. He can even think about them. And at no point does the peaceful smile leave his lips.

He can even think about the walk down to the cellar. It isn't a series of images now — if it had been, he would have to conjure it away, smoke it out by the burning sacrifice — it's a story, with a logical, coherent structure. And even if he knows it will soon be lost again and will call on its sacrificial smoke, he is able to find pleasure in its sudden, crystal-clear perfection.

He is on his way.

He is on his way down the stairs he didn't know existed, down into the cellar he didn't know existed. The secret passage in the closet. The unforgettable, sweet-dusted air in the stairway. The silent cement stairs that seem to go on forever. The raw, clammy cold of the handrail.

The completely self-evident logic of the initiation. When eyes can be raised and steps can follow steps on the stairs down into the pitch black, the logic is indisputable. He has been chosen.

It has to come full circle. That is what has to be done now. Then he can begin for real.

The stairs lead on. Every trace of light vanishes. He feels his way ahead, step by step.

He allows himself to pause while the calm rocks him closer to relieving sleep. He follows the imperfect wing of the plane as it swings imperfectly out into the perfect swing of eternity.

Another light becomes visible, a completely different light, and it accompanies his last steps down the staircase. Like the frame of an icon around a darkness brighter than any light, the light shoots out from behind the door. A halo showing the way. A golden frame around a future work of art.

Which will now be completed.

He cracks open the door to the Millennium.

Outside the window, the Big Dipper slides into the Little Dipper, making an Even Bigger Dipper.

"Tonight we can offer you the special SAS Swedish-American drink for a long night's flight, sir," he hears a gentle female voice half singing.

But by then he is already asleep.

# CHAPTER
# FOUR

The A-Unit lifted off from the helicopter pad atop police headquarters at 07.23 on Wednesday, 3 September. The seven of them were crowded together. For a split second, Paul Hjelm thought that they were just imitating a unit whose time had come and gone, but the second passed, and he focused on his task, like everyone else.

He was crammed between the huge, faintly panting body of Gunnar Nyberg and the much thinner skeletal shell of Arto Söderstedt. Across from him, Kerstin Holm's small, dark body was squeezed between Viggo Norlander's now extremely fit late-middle-aged muscles and Jorge Chavez's youthfully unscathed compactness.

Between these two rows of people, Jan-Olov Hultin was crouching in a position that shouldn't have been possible for a man in his sixties — even if he was still a formidable centre back on their police league football team. And he had such an impressive pile of papers that it shouldn't have been possible to gather them up at such short notice. He coaxed his glasses up onto his monumental nose. The need to shout over the din from the helicopter caused his voice to lose a bit of its clinical tone.

"This is going to be complicated," he said. "The Arlanda and Märsta police are already at the airport. Hordes of armed officers have been rushing around in the international arrivals hall, threatening tourists with aggravated assault. I think I've got rid of them now. We're up against a man who'll stop at nothing. That much I've understood — he's a well-programmed murder machine, and if he starts to suspect anything, we're risking a bloodbath and hostages and an all-round worst-case scenario. In other words, we must act with great care."

Hultin paged through pieces of paper.

"There are more than 150 people on the plane, and we can't very well shove them all into some old hangar and check them one by one. We would probably effectively kill several of them. So instead, we'll have careful passport checks, done under our supervision of course; and we'll do extreme vigilance over all white middle-aged men — which will probably be quite a few people on a typical business-class flight.

"In addition, customs has provided us with digital cameras that allow the person who inspects passports to discreetly photograph each passport photo. The immigration officers won't be alone in their booths; you will be there behind them. You'll be practically invisible from the outside. I've got the number of passport control booths reduced to two, which will cause some disruption in the flow of people, but it makes it possible for us to have an overview of the flow. Kerstin and Viggo will be located in these two booths. I urge you to be meticulous, attentive and careful. Take action only in reaction to very strong indications; otherwise use the radio.

"The risk shouldn't be as great during the passage through the concourse from the gate to customs, which is critical in and of itself, because there's no exit there. It's a straight stretch through bars and boutiques. I've placed the Märsta police in the concourse, under the leadership of Arto. So you, Arto, will go up to the gate in question, where a gang of Märsta detectives will be waiting. Above all, make sure they remain invisible. Your task is to try to make sure that no one deviates off course on their way to the passport check. Place people in the toilets, in boutiques, in all accessible locations — there aren't many. The rest of us will be spread out around the terminal and outside. Because if anything is going to happen, it will happen there; everything indicates that that's the case. Arto's job is really just to herd the whole flock to passport control. Shepherd."

"Are there any other planes arriving at the same time?" Arto Söderstedt asked in his resonant, almost exaggerated Finland-Swedish accent, looking doubt-fully down at the E4 highway, which they were following like a helium-filled barge on the Danube River. "Black sheep," he muttered nearly inaudibly. Hjelm heard him and gave him a cutting side glance.

Hultin took another deep dive into the wind-whipped sea of paper.

"No other arrivals in the vicinity, no."

"And the armed guys?" Nyberg said.

"They'll be immediately accessible. But only if necessary."

"Säpo?" said Söderstedt.

Söderstedt was eager to bring up Säpo, the Security Police. The line between the unit's jurisdiction and Säpo's was incredibly narrow, which meant that there were frequent overlaps, violations of taboos, and conflicts. The way Säpo had horribly sabotaged the investigation in the Power Murders was fresh in everyone's mind.

"They'll probably be there," Hultin nodded with a sigh. "But since they never tell us much, we'll act as though they *weren't* there. Anyway, as you know, there's only one exit out of the arrivals hall, which divides into two parts like a T via the customs area, just inside the main entrance. We need one man on either side just outside: Gunnar, Jorge. Paul and I will try to look like non-police somewhere near the baggage claim, to get an overview of the arrivals hall itself. This means that there will be something of a four-phase control: first the gate, Arto with the other men; passport control, Kerstin and Viggo; the arrivals hall, Paul and me; and finally the exit, Gunnar and Jorge. Is this clear?"

"The placement is crystal clear," said Hjelm. "The question is how it will survive confrontation by hundreds of hung-over, jet-lagged passengers."

Hultin let this remark pass without comment. "All of it depends, then, on our being able to move quickly from Plan A to Plan B. If we get the name our man is flying under from the United States *before* the passengers get to passport control, then *that's* where we have to focus our attention, and then we have to take him on the spot. Is that clear? That's Plan A. But if he's changed identities in the plane, or if we're not told his name, then the responsibility that Viggo and Kerstin have in the booths increases radically. That's Plan B. As it is now, Plan B is in effect. But we haven't the slightest idea yet who the fuck he is. Right now it's . . . seven thirty-four, and at any moment" — his mobile phone rang with a silly Mickey Mouse ringtone, which Hultin suppressed with a swift grab — "Right. Special Agent Larner will call."

He answered the phone and turned away. The E4 ran on through exhaust-fertilised fields that were dotted here and there with a bravely struggling tractor. It was a crystal-clear day, shot through with indescribable sparks that portended autumn. *Summer is over*, Hjelm thought balefully. *Autumn over Sweden*.

An exceedingly misshapen complex of buildings towered in the distance, beyond the fields.

"Arlandastad, right?" Kerstin Holm shouted.

"Unmistakably!" Arto Söderstedt shouted back.

"About five minutes left," said Gunnar Nyberg.

"But why?" Hultin's jaw suddenly dropped. Then he listened for another moment and ended the call.

"No," he said, "they aren't having any success in getting the name. It seems the killer cancelled the flight in the murdered Swede's name, then immediately booked the empty seat in a fake name. So that's the name we'll have to go on, and I don't get why it's taking such a fucking long time to find who booked that last ticket. Plan B is in effect until further notice."

The helicopter turned away from the E4 and swung over the forests of Arlanda. They landed at Arlanda International twenty-four minutes before flight SK 904 from Newark was due, and five minutes later all members of the A-Unit had settled into position.

Chavez stationed himself inside the doors of the main entrance. Having ploughed his way through a crowd of soon-to-be and former tourists, he found a bench next to a Coke machine where he had a good view of his entire area of responsibility: the far half of the exit from the customs hall. He turned on his eagle eye. His level of ambition was, as usual, just above the maximum setting.

Some thirty seconds later Gunnar Nyberg arrived, a bit depleted by the helicopter ride. He sat down at a cafe table, his face covered in both cold and hot sweat, and turned towards Chavez and the other half of the exit. Needing extra energy, he ordered a bottle of sports drink, of a brand he recognised from his former career as a bodybuilder. As he downed the half-litre in one gulp, he realised that these days the drink was prepared with what was wrung out of left-behind workout clothes collected from all the world's gyms. It was possible that he restored his fluid balance; it was certain that he restored the balance of his nausea.

Between the two men, a quintet who were not entirely difficult to identify as officials trod, against the current, in through the customs area. Hultin stopped and exchanged a few words with the palpably nervous customs employees and joined the other four A-Unit members inside the arrivals hall. He placed himself last in a winding line to the currency exchange, where he had a good view of the hall. The others continued towards passport control, until Hjelm fell away and found himself standing and staring like an idiot at a baggage carousel that wasn't moving. Seldom has a policeman looked so much like a policeman, and the harder he tried not to look like a one, the more he did. When he felt the blue lights start circling on top of his head, he gave up the charade and was more successful. He sat down on a bench and paged through a brochure, the contents of which would remain eternally unknown to him.

At passport control, the remaining officers were met by a senior official who admitted Norlander and Holm into their respective booths, where they perched on small, uncomfortable stools in the shadows of the immigration officers. Their presence was hardly noticeable from the outside, and if it was, it probably wouldn't seem abnormal. They settled in, in anticipation of the coming rush.

Finally, Arto Söderstedt shoved his way through passport control and slalomed among stragglers up the escalator to the concourse. He didn't need to consult the arrivals board to identify the right gate. At gate 10, he found a collection of stubbornly recognisable men who were all but neon-blinking "police". Söderstedt called together the Märsta officers and assigned them more discreet positions. The toilets were the only truly secluded areas, so he placed one officer to each toilet and made sure that all the staff areas were properly blocked off. That left the duty-free shops, bar and cafe. He stationed an officer by the name of Adolfsson at the bar, where he managed to look completely out of place, which was an achievement.

Söderstedt sat down at gate 10 and waited. The concourse was still relatively empty. Scattered groups of passengers from earlier flights were wandering around.

A slight change in the state of things induced Söderstedt to push the loathsome little earpiece into his ear; he always felt as if it disappeared deep in among the creases of his brain. The fateful little word LANDED was now blinking after the notation SK 904 NEWARK on the arrivals board. Söderstedt looked to the right and through the large panorama window saw the plane roll by.

He pressed a button inside his belt, cleared his throat and said, "The game has landed."

He stood, straightened his tie, slung the bag over his shoulder and waited with his eyes closed. Children were snaking back and forth between his legs; parents were yelling, sometimes heart-piercingly and sometimes just piercingly. Experienced wearers of suits kept economy passengers at a distance with well-practised smiles.

He remained still. People hardly noticed him. He didn't attract attention. He never had.

Then the line started moving rather quickly. The blockage was sorted out, and he sauntered calmly through the fuselage of the plane, then along the metal jetway and through the swaying walkway.

He stepped into gate 10. He was here.

Now it would come full circle.

Now he would be able to start for real.

It was interesting to see how many faces one's brain could file away before they started to blur together.

Söderstedt found that his limit was as low as fifty. The stream of passengers arriving from Newark were mostly an anonymous, grey mass, and sure enough, most of them were middle-aged white men travelling solo.

He couldn't make out any signs of variation. The horde shuffled more or less as one down the concourse. Some slipped into a toilet; others stopped at a shop; still others bought sandwiches at the cafe — and had their appetites spoiled at the cash register. A few ended up in the bar and attempted to converse with the human waxwork Officer Adolfsson, who seemed about to pass out.

*A tourist attraction*, Söderstedt thought.

The first Newark travellers descended the stairs down to passport control.

"They're coming," he said out loud.

The words echoed in Kerstin Holm's ears like the declaration of peace after World War II. She had been mentally composing her letter of resignation from the police, inspired by the stealth-farting immigration officer in the gas chamber that was their booth. This wasn't what she was meant for. But then the first American faces peered in through the glass pane and blew away her sensations of odour. The immigration officer neatly guided each passport into a small, computer-connected camera device and discreetly photographed it. Each photo and name were immediately registered on a computer. If nothing else, they would have a picture of the killer.

Face after face swept by. In every smile and every yawn she tried to imagine a killer without a conscience. A persistent tic in the eye of a man who had been

**26**

extremely reluctant to remove his Ray-Bans *almost* convinced her to call Hultin. Other than that, all was utterly tranquil.

Viggo Norlander's booth experience was a bit different. He was the only member of the A-Unit who'd had a wonderful year. After the fiasco during the Power Murders, when he'd run amok and been crucified by the mafia in Estonia, he'd begun to work out. He got a hair transplant and turned once again to the fairer sex, which caused his stubborn bachelor life to take on new dimensions. His stigmatised hands had proved an asset in that respect. Unlike Holm's, the immigration officer in whose booth he had ended up was young and female, and he had flirted with her uninhibitedly. By the time the Americans arrived, *she* had practically finished composing her sexual harassment report.

But in a second Norlander forgot her — he was immediately on the ball. Pumped with adrenalin, he thought he recognised a serial killer in every passenger, and when he notified Hultin of his third suspect, a coal-black, eighteen-year-old junkie, he received such a sharp reprimand that it reminded him forcefully of his past, and he became more discerning in his judgement, as he put it to himself.

He had been sitting in browbeaten silence for a few minutes when a well-dressed man of about forty-five with a confident smile handed his passport over to the immigration official, who gallantly photographed it along with the name Robert E. Norton. When the man caught sight of Norlander over her shoulder, his smile vanished abruptly; he blinked and peered round uncontrollably. Then he snatched back his passport and dashed away.

"I've got him!" Norlander yelled into his invisible mini-radio. "He's getting away," he continued a bit inconsistently, then he threw open the door and raced out through the arrivals hall after Robert E. Norton. Norton ran like a man possessed, his bag thumping hard against his shoulder. Norlander ran like a man even more possessed. He sent women who were in his way sprawling; he stamped on children's feet; he broke duty-free bottles.

Norton stopped for breath and looked around in wild desperation. Hjelm jumped up from his bench, threw down the unread brochure and made a rush for Norton. The sight of the two charging policemen was too much for the American, who swung his bag above his head and flung himself towards an unmoving baggage carousel. He leaped like a tiger through the plastic ribbons that covered the opening of the conveyor belt. His tiger leap was immediately followed by Norlander's. Hjelm didn't take any tiger leaps; instead he carefully parted the plastic ribbons and stepped off into the baggage area, where he saw Norlander chasing Norton among piles of luggage. Norton threw a suitcase at Norlander, who gave a muffled growl, hurled himself at the man, took another suitcase to the face and tumbled over. Norton tore loose and headed back towards the conveyor belt. As Norlander rose on shaky legs, Norton came closer and closer to Hjelm, who had climbed back inside to await him. Norton ran straight into his arms, swung his bag and landed a direct hit. It threw Hjelm backwards, but it felt as though he turned in mid-air and was on top of the man. Norlander arrived and threw himself into the pile, bent Norton's arms beyond their physical limits, and planted himself atop him with his knees on the back of the man's neck. Hjelm, with one hand on his bleeding mouth, grabbed Norton's bag with the other and emptied it onto the floor. Among the sundry items that fell out was a small packet of hashish.

At that moment, Hultin's voice entered Norlander and Hjelm's ears: "I've got our man's name from the FBI now. Go immediately from Plan B to Plan A. He's travelling under the name Edwin Reynolds. I repeat: Edwin Reynolds. If the man who has been so energetically chased through the arrivals hall is *not* named Reynolds and doesn't seem to have anything to do with this case, release him immediately and return to your positions. Maybe we can still fix this."

Norlander and Hjelm immediately released Robert E. Norton to the Arlanda police, who had come to get him. They charged into the arrivals hall through a side door and returned to Norlander's passport control booth.

Hjelm took over. He thundered at the female immigration officer, "Fast as hell: Edwin Reynolds. Has anyone by that name passed through?"

A few quick stabs at the computer gave her the answer. "No. Randolph. Robertson. No one in between."

Norlander sank down onto his stool. Hjelm sank to the floor.

They pulled the door closed, caught their breath and licked their wounds. Maybe there was still hope. Barely half of the passengers had come through. If Reynolds hadn't been among those whom Norlander trampled down, he was still back there.

Thus reasoned the two heroes in the booth and, in a haze of testosterone, forgot the group's more oestrogenic member. Kerstin Holm's voice sounded in everyone's ear canals. "Eleven minutes ago an Edwin Andrew Reynolds passed my booth. He was among the very first."

It was quiet for a few endless seconds.

Then came Hultin's voice: "OK. Close passport control. Don't let anyone else out. Demand ID from everyone you see in the whole fucking airport. Discreetly, of course. Officially, we're looking for drug smugglers. We'll use everything we've got now. Get going. I'll arrange for roadblocks. Kerstin, do you have a photo of him? What does he look like?"

"The one I have is really bad. He may be blond. It's a terrible photo."

"And neither you nor the immigration officer remembers anything?"

"Unfortunately, no. He could have got pretty far in eleven minutes."

"OK. Get going — now."

Norlander exhaled in relief — his blunder hadn't been crucial after all. But Hjelm, as he stood up, thought Norlander's sigh was almost criminal.

They emerged from the booth just as Holm stepped out of hers. Her intensively searching gaze met theirs.

The white middle-aged men were everywhere. Armed men poured out of the airport's hollows like maggots out of a corpse and detained passengers where they were, demanding their passports.

Hjelm ran through customs. Out of the corner of his eye he saw Gunnar Nyberg being showered with passports from a cluster of white, middle-aged men. His baggy lumber jacket was unbuttoned.

Hjelm hurried outside and surveyed the congested pavement. An airport bus came over the crest. Taxis swarmed. It was impossible to get an overview.

He sprinted along the pavement. He questioned ten or so potential serial killers, who watched his mediocre running pace. They identified themselves without protest. As he skimmed their passports, his suspicion became a full-fledged thought.

He did another second of futile surveying. Suddenly Hultin was standing beside him. Each read his own thought in the other man's eyes. It was Hjelm who formulated the unavoidable conclusion: "He's out."

Hultin held his eyes for another moment and gave an unofficial nod that was contradicted by his stern injunction: "We have to go inside and continue. Don't stand here wasting time."

Hultin disappeared. Hjelm stayed there for a minute, wasting time.

He fingered his lips and was surprised by the blood. He turned his face up to the darkening sky and received a chilly sprinkle of rain.

Autumn had come to Sweden.

# CHAPTER
# FIVE

That afternoon the A-Unit reconvened in the room that had once been called "Supreme Central Command", whose quotation marks had become less and less ironic as the Power Murders investigation had gone on. Now a secret wish for a similar course of events whistled through the somewhat stale air. Otherwise the dominant atmosphere was relatively well-controlled fear; there was no question about the gravity of the situation.

Jan-Olov Hultin came out of the toilet absorbed in some papers that looked as though he had used them and forgotten to flush them. He settled into his well-worn armchair and, after ten seconds, began. "The results of the Arlanda debacle are discouraging. The only concrete result is three complaints against officers. Two are against Viggo."

Norlander's expression managed to combine shame with pride.

"The first complaint is from the immigration officer at passport control," Hultin continued without looking up. "She found your attention far too intense but says she'll be satisfied if you are reprimanded. As if we didn't have other things to worry about, Bonehead. The second complaint is in regard to a little girl you ran over while you were chasing the seriously drug-smuggling Robert E. Norton. You have a real flair for handling the fairer sex, one could say. Double bonehead. The third complaint is a bit hard to interpret. An officer from Märsta has been reported for having been, quote, 'out of control' in the concourse bar."

Arto Söderstedt laughed shrilly and abruptly. "Sorry," he said, calming himself. "His name is Adolfsson."

Since further clarification was not forthcoming, Hultin continued neutrally. "So, on to the essentials. Edwin Andrew Reynolds does not exist. Naturally, the passport was a fake. And despite the labourious efforts of our data technicians, the passport photo is still not helpful."

He turned the computer monitor round on the desk, to show an enlargement of a completely dark face. One could make out the shape of the face and a few contours; possibly he was blond. Otherwise it was unrevealing, and the man was anonymous.

"We don't even know if he used his own picture. They will accept ten-year-old photos, of course, and it's really not that hard to use a photo that has only some reasonable resemblance. In any case, customs' new photo devices were wasted — all the pictures they took look about the same. They're blaming this failure on the fact that the technology is brand new, and they didn't have enough time to prepare properly, and so on.

"It's a given that information about our man has gone out to hotels, Swedish Railways, airports, ferries, dungheaps, et cetera. I hardly think we should count on anything from those sources, but of course we will keep looking. One plus is that the media doesn't know anything, even though the TV cameras showed up quickly at Arlanda. I imagine you'll see the results tonight. Our most esteemed boss Mörner appeared and gave a statement, which guarantees some sort of quality TV, at least. Questions, anyone?"

"What happened with the roadblocks?" asked Gunnar Nyberg.

"The only thing we accomplished was a few hours of complete traffic chaos on the E4. The Arlanda traffic in every direction is quite simply too dense. In addition, it took a hell of a long time to set up the roadblocks. Only a true amateur would have been caught. We're trying to identify all the taxi and bus drivers who were working around Arlanda at the time in question, but as you know, deregulation has made the taxi traffic in Stockholm unmanageable, so we'll probably have to admit defeat on that point. Anything else?"

"Not a question, really," said Kerstin Holm. "Just some information. According to the data register, our man was number eighteen to pass through my passport control. I've tried to get my impressions in order, and I've talked to the immigration officer, but neither of us has any memory of him at all. Maybe something will come up eventually."

Hultin nodded and continued mysteriously. "To be on the safe side, I've made sure that *all deaths reported to the police* in the country, from now on, are reported *directly* to us, and the same goes for all suspected crimes against *Americans* in Sweden. If there's the least

34

suspicion of *foul play*, our brains must unanimously think: Could *this* have anything to do with our serial killer? This is *our* case now, even in an *official* sense, and it's our *only one*, and the *whole* unit is part of it, and it is *top-top secret*, and no one around you must even catch a whiff of the words *bestial-American-serial-killer-loose-in-Sweden*. Wherever you are, think: Could the serial killer have anything to do with this bus being late? Might he have any connection at all to this bike accident or to that man's incredibly bizarre movements or to your better half's increasingly loud snores? In other words, full focus."

They understood.

"I have kept in rather intensive contact with the authorities in the United States," Hultin continued. "Special Agent Ray Larner with the FBI has supplied us with a detailed account of last night's events and a brief profile of the perpetrator. Concerning the results at Arlanda, more information will be streaming in during the next few days. Here is the broad outline as it stands right now.

"The Swedish literary critic Lars-Erik Hassel was tortured to death just before midnight Swedish time in a cleaner's cupboard at Newark airport. It was a few hours before he was found. He had no ticket on him, but a flight to Arlanda that same night was found to be written down in his diary. In other words, it was likely that the killer had taken his ticket, but a person can't check in if the name on the ticket doesn't match the name on the passport, so they took a chance and checked with SAS to see if Hassel's ticket had been cancelled. Why steal the ticket otherwise? His wallet and diary and everything else was still there, after all. And they got lucky — they got hold of a ticket agent who remembered a late cancellation by phone, which was quickly followed by a late booking. But of course this all happened at night New York time, and in order to find the name of the person who booked last, they needed a data expert who could go into the computer and get exact booking times. They finally managed to tear someone matching that description from the arms of his sweetheart, and he dug up the name, after which it was delivered to us. Eleven minutes too late."

Hultin paused and let the A-Unit's slightly overloaded brains absorb this information.

"This caused us to face certain problems. The likely scenario is that the killer murdered Hassel, called in his name to cancel his ticket, then called again and booked the recently cancelled spot in his own fake name. What does this tell us?"

Since everyone realised that the question was rhetorical, no one was interested in answering it. Hultin complicated the laws of rhetoric by answering it himself, with another question: "The basic issue is, of course: Why Sweden? What kind of evil thing have we done for this to happen to us? Let us assume the following. A notorious serial killer finds himself in an airport. His intention is to flee the country, hence the fake passport. Maybe he can feel the FBI breathing down his neck. But in his excitement, his desire to kill is acutely intensified. He waits until a suitable victim comes close. He does his deed, finds the ticket and gets

**36**

it into his head that it's a good place to flee to; the plane is leaving soon, after all. But when he calls to book his seat, it turns out the plane is full. He knows, however, that one seat is definitely free. He takes a peek at the ticket, finds the difficult-to-pronounce name Lars-Erik Hassel along with a booking number, and calls to cancel, at which point a spot is vacant. What is wrong with this picture?"

"Spot the difference," said Hjelm. No one laughed.

"It is actually almost possible to find several," Chavez said with an unintentional but hardly career-boosting dig at Hultin, who didn't blink. "The most important part of your scenario, Jan-Olov, is the *coincidence*. If he truly didn't get the idea to travel to Sweden until *after* the murder, one might ask if he would really go to that much trouble to get to such an arbitrarily chosen country. The traffic to and from Newark is non-stop, after all. Why not just as well fly to Düsseldorf five minutes later or Cagliari eight minutes later?"

"Cagliari?" said Nyberg.

"It's on Sardinia," Hjelm said helpfully.

"It was just an example," Chavez said impatiently. "The point is, Sweden doesn't seem to have been chosen randomly at all. It feels a little extra unpleasant."

"And then one might ask," Kerstin Holm added, "if he would really risk first going up to the counter and getting a no, then calling in Hassel's name, and then returning to the counter a few minutes later and asking the same question, only to get a yes this time. A man who has been eluding the FBI for twenty years would hardly take such a risk of attracting attention and being directly linked to a corpse that could be discovered at any moment."

Hultin seemed thrilled by two such keen objections to his scenario and countered his opponents: "On the other hand, there is an obvious moment of risk in what he actually did. If they had got hold of a data expert eleven minutes earlier, we would have had him. It was far from an idiot-proof plan."

"I still think the evidence points to Sweden being his goal when he set out for the airport," Chavez persisted. "But when he arrives, it turns out the flight is fully booked. Then his plan takes shape. Why not combine work and pleasure? Somehow he locates a solo traveller to Arlanda, murders him in his usual, pleasurable way, and takes his place, even though this involves a definite but limited risk. The risk of discovery, on the other hand, is an important ingredient in a serial killer's enjoyment."

"Then what does that suggest?" Hultin asked pedagogically.

"That his desire to come here to Sweden was so strong that it caused him to take a risk that he probably wouldn't have taken otherwise. And in that case, he has a very definite goal here."

"Ice-cold calculation combined with impulsiveness and a craving for pleasure. Something to sink our teeth into . . ."

"There's nothing to indicate Sweden in his profile?" Arto Söderstedt wondered.

"Not according to the FBI." Hultin paged through the file. "Leaving the United States at all doesn't really fit with his profile. His history is as follows.

"It all started twenty years ago in Kentucky, where victims who had been killed in the same awful manner began to show up. The wave then spread all over the Midwest. It blew up in the media, and soon the notorious killer was going by the name the Kentucky Killer. Within today's deeply alarming serial killer cult, he's a legend, one of the original characters, and he's thought to have inspired many budding practitioners. He committed a series of eighteen murders in four years, then stopped abruptly for a decade and a half. Just over a year ago a new series began with exactly the same MO, this time in the north-eastern United States. Hassel was his sixth victim in this latest series, his twenty-fourth overall. His twenty-fourth *known* victim, I should probably add."

"A break of almost fifteen years," Kerstin Holm mused aloud. "Is it really the same person and not a — what's it called?"

"A copycat," said Hjelm, using the English word.

Hultin shook his head. "The FBI has ruled that out. There are details of the MO that have never been made public and that only a few authorities at the bureau know of. Either he's hidden his victims well for fifteen years, or else he quit and maybe settled down, before his craving for blood got the best of him once again. That's the FBI's scenario, anyway. That was why the bulletin went out for a white middle-aged man. Probability says that he was just under twenty-five when he began, so he's just under forty-five now."

"And 'white' is also based on probability, I assume?" said the chalk-white Söderstedt.

"Almost all serial killers are white men," said Kerstin Holm. "A much-debated phenomenon. Maybe it's some sort of hereditary compensation for the many hundreds of years of world domination that they are about to lose."

"Haphazard fascism" came flying out of Hjelm.

The A-Unit considered this expression for a few long seconds. Even Hultin looked contemplative.

"What kinds of victims were they?" Chavez asked at last.

Hultin leafed through the pages causing Hjelm to ponder the advantages of the Internet and encrypted email, something that wasn't too common yet. That was Jorge and Kerstin's domain. They were also the ones who looked most irritated when information was slow in coming.

"Let's see," said Hultin after a long pause.

Chavez groaned quietly, which brought him a look that could mean yet another stain on his work record.

"There's a lot of diversity in the victims," their wise leader said at last. "Twenty-four people of varied backgrounds. Five foreign citizens, including Hassel. Primarily white middle-aged men, to be sure, which an alert officer who's familiar with feminism could easily interpret as implied self-contempt."

"If it weren't for the fact that he wasn't middle-aged at all when he began murdering," Kerstin Holm countered promptly.

The icy chill in Hultin's long look could have been fatal. "Quite a few of them remain unidentified," he finally continued. "Even though the list of missing

**40**

persons in the United States is a book as thick as the Bible, the number still seems disproportionately large — ten out of twenty-four."

"Is *that* something that's changed?" Söderstedt asked alertly.

Yet another look from Hultin. Then he paged frenetically and got a hit. "All six victims in the second round have been identified. That means that ten of eighteen in the first round remain unidentified. A majority. Maybe some sort of conclusion can be drawn from that. However, I'm not ready to do that right now."

"Could it be the case that the MO itself has made identification difficult?" asked Hjelm.

Clearly their minds were sharp. Many of them had been waiting a long time for this very moment.

"No," Hultin answered. "The atrocities don't include torn-out teeth or chopped-off fingertips."

"What do they include, then?" Nyberg asked.

"Wait." Chavez was staring down into his overflowing notebook. "We weren't quite finished. Who *were* the identified victims? Does he concentrate on some particular social class?"

Hultin once again swung his mental machete through the jungle of paper. While he searched, he said, "Many of your questions will be answered by the complete FBI report, which Special Agent Larner is going to fax over this afternoon, but OK, we might as well anticipate the events . . ."

Then he found what he was looking for.

"The eight people identified in the first wave were relatively highly educated. He seems to have a weakness for academics. The six in the second wave were more varied. Maybe he's gone and become a democrat."

"Get to sex sometime," said Kerstin Holm abruptly.

A moment of bewildered silence ensued among the male audience. Then Hultin understood: "A single woman in the first group, out of eighteen. Two out of six in the second."

"There are a few differences after all," Holm summarised.

"Like I said," said Hultin, "perhaps he's become a democrat when it comes to sex, too. Let's wait and see what Larner has to say about it. He's followed the case from the very start. In the seventies, based on the MO, they narrowed it down to a group of, if not *suspects*, then at least *potential* perpetrators. It turned out to have certain similarities to a method of torture from, believe it or not, the Vietnam War. A specific and extremely unofficial American task force used it to get the Vietcong to talk without screaming. An utterly silent method of torture, tailor-made for the jungle. Since the existence of the task force was officially denied and brushed off as just another Vietnam myth, it was extremely difficult for Larner to get names. He hinted that he was stepping on quite a few tender and highly placed toes, and likely he was making a fool of himself and destroying his chances for promotion to boot. But slowly and surely, he tracked down the task force, which went by the disagreeable code name 'Commando Cool', and ferreted out the names of those involved. Above all, one person who could *almost* have been called a suspect crystallised: the group leader, a Wayne Jennings, from none other than Kentucky. There was never any proof, but Larner followed Jennings wherever he went. Then something unanticipated happened. Jennings got tired of the surveillance and tried to evade the FBI — and he got into a head-on car collision. Larner was there himself and saw him burn up."

"Did the murders continue after that?" Chavez asked.

"Yes, unfortunately. There were two more in quick succession, and then they stopped. Larner was blamed for having hounded an innocent man to death. There was a trial. He survived it, sure, but he fell in the hierarchy. And it didn't get any better for him when, after fifteen years of walking into a headwind, he realised that the killer had started up again. For just over a year now, Ray Larner has been back where he started with the elusive Kentucky Killer. I don't envy him."

"You should," said Söderstedt. "He isn't Larner's responsibility any more — he's yours. He's the one who's free, not you." Söderstedt paused, then continued maliciously: "You're taking over from scratch after twenty years of intensive FBI investigations that had resources equivalent to the Swedish GDP."

Hultin observed him neutrally.

"So what was so special about Commando Cool's modus operandi?" Gunnar Nyberg tried. "How did that literary critic die?"

Hultin turned to him with an expression that could have been interpreted as suppressed relief. "The point is that it's two different things," he said. "The serial killer makes use of what we can call a *personal application* of Commando Cool's method. The method is based on a single special instrument: specially designed micromechanical pincers that, when closed, closely resemble a terrifying cannula. A big syringe. It's driven into the throat from the side. With the help of small control wires, tiny claws unfurl inside the trachea and grip the vocal cords in a manner that makes it impossible for any sound to escape the lips of the victim. He or she is rendered completely silent. Even in a tight spot in the jungle with Vietcong soldiers in the bushes all over, you can see to a bit of refreshing torture.

"Once the victim is silenced, you can then heap on the conventional methods, best directed at fingernails and genitals, where small motions incur the most pain. And then you just release the grip around the vocal cords a tiny bit so that something like a whisper can slip out. The victim can reveal his secret, quietly, quietly. For this purpose, Commando Cool developed related pincers, based on the same principles as the vocal cord pincers, but these other ones were aimed at the central ganglia in the neck, which are tugged and pulled a little bit from the inside, at which point an appalling pain radiates up into the head and down through the body. The two holes in the neck with their associated internal injuries have been discovered on all twenty-four victims of the Kentucky Killer, and there have also been distinctive torture wounds on their genitals and fingers.

"Larner has been a bit secretive about what distinguishes the workings of our friend from those of the commando task force, but obviously it has to do with the design of the two micro-pincers. It's as though something like an industrial development process was used to make the pincers even more perfect for their atrocious purpose."

Hultin looked down at his lectern.

"I want you to restrain yourselves for a second now, so you can absorb all this," he said gravely. "Lars-Erik Hassel died one of the most horrific deaths a person can die. I would like you to think carefully about what we're up against. It doesn't resemble anything we've ever had to deal with in our whole lives. There's not an ounce of similarity to our good old Power Murderer. It isn't really possible to imagine such ice-cold indifference to other people's lives and such twisted pleasure at their suffering. This is a seriously damaged person of the sort that the American system seems to produce on an assembly line, and that they would have been welcome to refrain from exporting. But now he's here. And the only thing we can really do is to wait for him to start. It could be a long time; it could be tomorrow. But it will happen, and we have to be prepared."

Hultin stood to go to the toilet. As he left, he said to the dispersing group, "As soon as I receive Ray Larner's material, you'll get copies. The outcome of this case hinges on you all studying it diligently." He nodded at them and hurried towards his private, special door.

Jorge Chavez interrupted his departure: "How old is Edwin Reynolds, according to the passport?"

Hultin made a stiff face, dug through his pile of papers with his legs in a need-to-pee stance, and brought out a copy of the photographed passport page. "Thirty-two this year."

Chavez nodded. "Of course the passport was fake," he said, "but why choose to play fifteen years younger than he must, in all likelihood, be?"

"An element of risk, maybe," said Hultin against his better judgement, and rushed off with papers floating through the air.

Chavez and Hjelm looked at each other.

Hjelm shrugged. "Well, he could have bought or stolen a ready-made fake passport."

"Possibly," said Chavez.

But no one could really shake the feeling that something was wrong. Utterly wrong.

# CHAPTER
# SIX

There really wasn't anything they could do.

Naturally, there was a microscopic possibility that this was all coincidental, that the Kentucky Killer had been at Newark airport not to flee the country but only to look for a new victim; that poor Lars-Erik Hassel had cancelled his trip all on his own and had thrown his ticket away; and that just after that, a completely unrelated man with a fake passport had popped up with a last-minute booking. The combination of all these things, however, verged on the unbelievable. There was no real doubt that the Kentucky Killer had come to Sweden. The only question was why.

FBI Agent Ray Larner's more exhaustive report had come in. According to the timetable, the plane had taken off from Newark at 18.20 local time. At 17.03 a man who called himself Lars-Erik Hassel had called and cancelled his ticket, and at 17.08 an Edwin Reynolds had managed to get the extra ticket; thus he had waited five risky minutes so he wouldn't attract attention. Around midnight a cleaner had made the macabre discovery in a cupboard — just under two hours before the plane would land in Sweden. A few minutes later an Officer Hayden had appeared from the airport's local police station; he recognised the two small holes on the victim's neck and contacted FBI headquarters in Manhattan, which in turn contacted the Kentucky Killer specialist Ray Larner and got confirmation that it was a hallmark of the famous serial killer. After examining Hassel's belongings, Hayden had been smart enough to conclude that the murderer had in all likelihood taken a seat on the victim's flight to Stockholm–Arlanda. After a while he received verbal confirmation from the night staff at the SAS ticket counter that a ticket had been cancelled too late to have been rebooked, at which point the tired ground hostess also remembered that there had been a late booking. She could access only the passenger manifest, however, and not the specific data of *when* each person had booked. While the FBI frantically searched for someone who had access to that data, Hayden had contacted the National Criminal Police in Stockholm and ended up with Superintendent Jan-Olov Hultin via the head of the NCP. At that point, it was 07.09 in Sweden. Hayden swiftly faxed over all the material he had, and this turned into a portion of the pile of papers Hultin had brought along to the quick meeting before the helicopter ride to Arlanda.

Nothing in FBI agent Ray Larner's newly arrived, scrupulous report indicated any departure from what had been said earlier; nor did it indicate any imaginable ties to Sweden. Thus there was nothing they could really do, other than wait for the first victim, and that was unbearable.

Therefore they devoted themselves to mental preparation for the intensive burst of activity that lay ahead. They spent the rest of the afternoon on small tasks that not only gave them the illusion of meaningful work, the sensation of *doing* something, but also involved *individual* activity. Each of them seemed to need to digest the state of things on their own.

Hultin continued to collect and organise the material from the FBI. Holm returned to Arlanda to see if any of the staff had been struck by a flashback or a flash of genius, anything at all. The cabin crew of flight SK 904 would, they had heard, also be there, and she prepared herself for her speciality: conversations, interviews, interrogations. Nyberg returned to his usual routine: he set off for the underworld of Stockholm to sound out the situation there. Söderstedt shut himself up in his office and called all the places that he could in any way imagine might be sheltering this Reynolds, who was surely no longer called Reynolds. Chavez threw himself into the world of the Internet; what he thought he could find there was a mystery to the uninitiated. Hultin set Norlander to the task of scrubbing all the toilets in the police station with an electric toothbrush, which was viewed as a technical achievement within the noble art of punishment.

And Hjelm set out on his own assignment. Just as small as the likelihood that the Kentucky Killer had remained in the United States was the likelihood that the literary critic Lars-Erik Hassel's past had anything to do with the case. Nevertheless Hjelm set off for the large newspaper office that had been Hassel's workplace.

He allowed himself to walk there — a little habit that the relative idleness of the past year had permitted him to develop. He walked down to Norr Mälarstrand by way of Kungsholmstorg. The rainy weather from Arlanda, he couldn't help thinking, was biding its time, waiting in the wings, getting ready to sweep the city in autumn. But for now the sun was still shining, if more weakly with every day that went by. On the other side of Riddarfjärden, an enormous cat stretched out and purred contentedly in the white rays of late-summer sunshine: the head — Mariaberget — lapped Lake Mälaren's waters with the tongue that was Söderleden, while its body — Skinnarviksberget — twisted greedily and stretched down towards its elegant back legs, Långholmen, where the tail, formed by Västerbro, pointed the way to Marieberg and the newspaper complex.

The only thing Hjelm knew about Hassel was that he had been a literary critic. He had seen the man's name in the arts and leisure section of the big daily paper once or twice; other than that he was blank.

He wandered along Norr Mälarstrand and crossed Rålambshovsparken, where the *brännboll* players went stubbornly bare-chested, despite the goose bumps that were visible from a distance of twenty yards. How did the old *Farmer's Almanac* line go? Sweat the summer in; freeze in the winter?

At the newspaper building, the receptionist advised him with a well-practised apologetic expression that the lifts were temporarily out of order, and Hjelm found himself sweating the winter in as he trudged up the stairs. In the arts and leisure offices, the atmosphere was downhearted but bustling. Hjelm asked to speak to someone in charge and was supplied with a bundle of more or less aged issues of the arts and leisure section while he waited for the arts editor, who was rushing back and forth. He read the pages more carefully than he had in a long time and found a few articles by Hassel. He devoted just over half an hour to improving himself before the editor let him into his office, where the piles of books seemed to grow as he watched.

The editor stroked his grizzled beard, extended a hand and said briskly, "Möller. Sorry you had to wait. I'm sure you can imagine what things are like here right now."

"Hjelm," said Hjelm, removing a pile of papers from a chair and sitting down.

"Hjelm," said Möller, sinking down behind his cluttered desk. "Aha."

He didn't say more, but Hjelm realised that the old epithets "Hallunda Hero" and "Power Murders" were not so easily gnawed away by the tooth of time. Like all old heroes, he was confronted day and night by his insufficient heroism.

"I'm sorry for your loss," he said curtly.

Möller shook his head. "It's a bit difficult to understand," he said. "What actually happened? The information we've received so far is scanty, to say the least. What should we write in the obituary? We can't exactly pull out the old 'after a lengthy illness'. That much I've understood."

"He was murdered," Hjelm said mercilessly. "At the airport."

Möller shook his head again. "At the airport . . . Talk about bad luck. I thought New York was safe now. The New York model. 'Zero tolerance', 'community policing', and all that. For fuck's sake, that's why he was there!"

"What do you mean?"

"He was going to get a cultural perspective on the new, peaceful spirit of New York. I guess you could call it the irony of fate."

"Did he have time to write anything?"

"No. He was gathering impressions. He'd been there for a week and was going to devote the week after he returned home to writing the article."

"So the newspaper was paying for the trip?"

"Of course," said Möller, affronted.

"Was Lars-Erik Hassel on the permanent staff?"

"Yes. He had been on the editorial staff for almost twenty years."

"A baby boomer."

Möller glared at him. "That's a term we prefer not to use here. It's been corrupted by all manner of misuse."

Hjelm observed him for a moment, then couldn't help but argue a bit. "The article on the new, peaceful spirit of New York probably cost half a month's salary, say fifteen thousand kronor including taxes and fees, plus travel and board, another twenty thousand. All together, maybe more than fifty thousand kronor."

Möller's face darkened, and he shrugged. "You can't count it like that. Some articles cost more, some less. What are you getting at?"

"Did he have any contacts in New York? Friends? Enemies?"

"Not that I know of, no."

"Did you or anyone else on the editorial staff have personal contact with him during the past week?"

"I spoke to him once, yes. He had just been to the Metropolitan and was very pleased."

"And the visit to the Metropolitan was going to be included in the fifty-thousand-kronor article?" Hjelm sensed that he had to stop if he didn't want to lose Möller completely. He changed his tone: "We're going to need to speak to his family. What family relationships did he have?"

Möller sighed deeply and looked at the clock.

A younger, bald man came storming into the office and waved some papers. "Sorry to interrupt," he panted. "We're running out of time. Lars-Erik's obituary is almost finished, but what are we going to put as the cause of death? Should I forget about it? We have to put something, don't we?"

Möller gestured tiredly towards Hjelm and asked, "What can we write?"

"That he was murdered," said Hjelm.

The young man stared at him. "Nothing more?" he said at last.

"That should do," said Hjelm.

The man rushed out again. Through the windows in the office door, Hjelm watched him return to his computer and peck at the keyboard with the light touch of a professional butcher.

"Obituaries for the young are hard," Möller said tiredly. "When someone dies unexpectedly, you have to start from scratch. It takes a lot of hard work."

"And when someone dies *expectedly*?" said Hjelm.

"We have a store of obituaries."

Hjelm couldn't believe his ears. "You have a store of obituaries for *living* people?"

Möller sighed deeply. "It's clear that you're not particularly familiar with editorial work. Are we ever going to get this over with? Where were we?"

"Family relationships," said Hjelm.

"Lars-Erik had lived alone for several years. He had two marriages behind him, with one son from each. I'll get you the addresses."

Möller paged through a large address book, made a few chicken scratches, and handed the slip of paper to Hjelm.

"Thanks. How was he as a writer?"

Möller considered this question quietly. "He was one of the country's leading literary critics. An author could rise or fall on what he wrote. His byline on a piece always gave it a certain . . . aura. A superb and versatile critic, who didn't hesitate to be tough. And an underrated author."

"He wrote books too?"

"Not recently, but there are a few gems from the seventies."

"I skimmed some old arts and leisure sections out there and found several of his pieces. He didn't seem to like literature very much."

54

Möller rubbed his beard and peered through the window at the pale blue sky. "Literature today is beneath contempt," he said at last. "Positively beneath it. The young authors have completely misunderstood their vocation. In general, we don't write very much about literature any more."

"No, I saw that you prioritise reporting on society and film festivals and interviews with rock bands and official speeches at awards ceremonies and conflicts within various bureaucratic organisations."

Möller thrust himself forward, over the desk, and his eyes drilled into Hjelm's. "And what are you? A critic?"

"More like a bit surprised." Hjelm paged through his notebook. "I found an article in which a critic writes that critics read far too many books and that they ought to jog instead."

"Life is more than books."

"Well, that's certainly a truism. If I were to claim that I would be a better police officer if I spent less time on police work, that would be a breach of duty. Then there was an article about how authors today devote far too much time to sitting and pondering the mystery of life. I thought that was the whole point."

"It's clear that you know very little about this business," Möller muttered, staring out the window.

"And *you* write that the young ones are a gang of anaemic navel-gazers without direction. Here are some quotes from Lars-Erik Hassel's pieces: 'The question is if it's possible to get very much more out of literature'. 'Poetry and the visual arts alike seem to have had their day'. 'The great account of the present day that we were all waiting for never came; this is the tragic nature of literature'. 'Poetry seems to be nothing more than a game'. 'Literature has long been the most overrated art form of our time'."

When no response came from Möller, it was Hjelm's turn to thrust himself across the desk. "Was it not the case that one of Sweden's most influential literary critics didn't like literature at all?"

Möller's gaze was stuck up among the non-existent clouds. He was gone. His exhaustion seemed monumental. It extended right into the next life.

Because he didn't have much more to add, and because Möller was unlikely to lift a finger in the next half-hour, Hjelm decided to leave this site of human catastrophe. He stepped out into the editorial office and closed the door on the fossilised chief editor.

He walked over to the young man with the pecked-out obituary. He had stopped pecking and was now reading through the text on his monitor.

"Is it finished?" Hjelm asked.

The man gave a start, as though hit by a bullet. "Oh, sorry," he panted, once he collected himself. "Yes, it's finished. As finished as it can be, under the circumstances."

"May I have a copy?"

"It will be in tomorrow's paper."

"I would like to have it *now*, if it's possible."

The man looked at him with surprise. "Of course." He pressed a key, and a laser printer expelled sheets of paper. "It's always a pleasure to be read."

**56**

Hjelm skimmed through the text, which was signed Erik Bertilsson.

"In accordance with all the rules of the genre," said Bertilsson.

Hjelm peered up from the paper and zeroed in on him. "Rather than those of the truth?"

Erik Bertilsson gave what was, to an experienced interrogator, a very familiar now-I've-said-too-much look and fell silent.

"What kind of writer was Hassel, actually?" Hjelm said. "I've read a few rather strange pieces."

"Read the obituary," said Bertilsson resolutely. "All I have to say is there."

Hjelm looked around the editorial office. Isolated staff members were running around. No one seemed to be taking any notice of the police visit.

"Listen carefully, Erik," he said sharply. "I'm only trying to get an accurate picture of a murder victim. Any information that can contribute to the capture of the killer is of the utmost importance. What you say will stay within the investigation. It's not a matter of slandering someone publicly."

"Let's go to the stairs," Bertilsson sighed, standing up heavily.

They got to the empty stairwell.

Bertilsson squirmed as though he were standing in the flames of hell. After a moment he came to a decision, released his discomfort, and let out the ballast, a heavy chunk of frustration.

"It was an assignment to write this obituary, not my choice," he said with a glance over his shoulder. "And

I've never felt like such a hypocrite. Hassel was part of Möller's inner circle. They're the ones who make the decisions, quite simply, a clique from the same generation and with the same values, which they think are the same ones as in the golden sixties but in fact are the diametrical opposite. They rabidly try to ring in *the sign of the times*, and they happily follow the shallowest trends, but their willingness to let outsiders into their inner circle is non-existent. Hassel had power. He was allowed to write about whatever books he wanted, and he always chose things he didn't understand, just so he could cut those authors off at the knees. All his aesthetic convictions date back to the sixties, and they're based on the pretence that literature is, by definition, fraud. He wrote a theoretical Maoist manifesto and a few documentary novels in the seventies, but since then all his work has been based on raking people over the coals. It's almost impossible to count the promising authors he's single-handedly sunk."

Hjelm recoiled from the sudden, almost therapeutic oratory. He tried to change tack: "And privately?"

"After cheating on his wife for years, he left her for a young girl who allowed herself to be dazzled by his so-called refinement. He knocked her up immediately — but when it was time for the birth, he took off for Gothenburg in order to fuck himself silly at the book fair. When he got back to Stockholm, *she* had left with their newborn son. After that he spent most of his time picking up impressed young girls who didn't know that his refinement was just as transplanted as his hair. His performances at department parties and publishers' parties are legendary; you can't imagine them if you haven't seen one."

Hjelm blinked in surprise. He stared down at the obituary and compared Bertilsson's oral account of Lars-Erik Hassel's deeds with his written one. A truly sulphurous, infernal abyss opened up between them. "Perhaps you shouldn't have taken it upon yourself to write this." He waved the sheets of paper.

Erik Bertilsson shrugged. "There are assignments and then there are assignments. You just don't say no to some of them, if you want even a shadow of a career. And I do want that."

"But surely there must be some critics who are somewhat on the up-and-up?"

Bertilsson reprised his shrug. "Those are the ones who don't earn any money. You have no idea what a tough business this is. Either you're in or you're out. There's no in between."

Hjelm could have said much more but didn't. Instead he regarded Bertilsson for a moment. He thought of the revolutionary books he'd read in the past year and tried to find any connection at all with the two representatives of cultural life he had met today.

It was impossible.

He thanked Bertilsson and left him alone in the empty stairwell. Bertilsson didn't move.

# CHAPTER
# SEVEN

The long day trickled to its conclusion. Hjelm quite literally slipped into the Metro car on a banana peel. After executing a graceful ballet step on his left ankle, he sat down and thoughtlessly swore, and for the entire journey to Norsborg he found himself pierced by the burning glare of an old woman.

By the time they got to Mariatorget, he was able to ignore her. John Coltrane's hypnotic sax haze carried him to another world — or rather, as he preferred to think of it, deeper into this one. A thought disrupted his universe of pure sound: maybe Lars-Erik Hassel's character was not a completely negligible factor after all. Even if he couldn't accept Bertilsson's version as definitive, Hassel surely had quite a few skeletons in his cupboard, and conceivably they had risen again as vengeful spirits. Erinyes, he thought, and he was reminded of an earlier case. That it could in any way be connected with the Kentucky Killer was absurd, of course, but he left the door ajar, knowing from experience that as time went on, it was often through unclosed doors that the solution came creeping.

By six o'clock the A-Unit had had time to round out the day with one last meeting. Norlander was missing

— perhaps he had grown tired of scrubbing the toilets — but otherwise everyone was there. No one had anything new to contribute. Hultin had pieced together a whole lot about the Kentucky Killer that he would take home to go through. Nyberg had wasted his time in vain in the underworld, of course — no one there knew anything. Chavez said he would get back to them with possible news from the Internet world early tomorrow morning. Söderstedt had found tons of potential Americans in hotels and hostels, on Finland ferries and domestic flights; he activated a whole armada of foot soldiers around Sweden, all of whom drew a blank. Kerstin Holm's afternoon had been the most interesting, possibly because she *didn't* come up with anything.

No one in the large flight crew could place the name Edwin Reynolds, and no one was struck by even the most minuscule whiff of retrospective suspicion. Perhaps one could trivially conclude that he simply didn't stand out. An everyman, like so many serial killers. One might suppose that a man who, hardly an hour earlier, had carried out a bestial, tortuous murder would stand out in some way, perhaps not with large, wild eyes, bloody clothes and a dripping ice pick, but at least with something. The staff had no such recollections. But even that fact, after all, contained a certain amount of information.

Hjelm had compressed his rather baggy afternoon harvest into a synopsis that he was quite pleased with: "There are differing opinions on Lars-Erik Hassel's abilities."

At Skärholmen, Hjelm drifted out of the musical haze, opened his eyes, and looked over at the next seat. The woman's icy glare was still boring into him, as though he were the Antichrist. He allowed himself not to give a damn about her, fixed his eyes ahead, and was just about to close them when he saw Cilla on the opposite seat.

"Who's watching the children?" slipped out of him. He bit his tongue far too late and cried out in pain.

Cilla gave him a measured look. "Hi yourself," she said.

"Sorry." He leaned forward and gave her a kiss. "I was somewhere else."

She pointed at her ears with a scrunched expression.

He yanked out his earphones.

"You're yelling," she said.

"Sorry," he said again, feeling like a social wreck.

"The children are sixteen and fourteen, as you may recall. They watch themselves."

He shook his head and laughed. "I bit my tongue."

"Far too late," she said.

The ice was broken, by one of the little moments when they read each other's minds and overlooked each other's shortcomings; when the positive aspects of habit triumphed over the negative ones.

"Hi," he started over, placing his hand on hers.

"Hi yourself."

"Where have you been?"

"I bought a shower curtain at IKEA. The old one was mouldy. Haven't you seen those black spots?"

"I thought you had been throwing *snus* around."

She smiled. She used to laugh at his stupid jokes, but now she smiled. He didn't really know what that meant. That he wasn't as funny any more, or that she was worried that her teeth were stained brown from coffee?

Or was that what they called maturity?

He still thought she was beautiful: her blonde hair in its slightly dishevelled bob; the years that had gathered the right way, around her eyes instead of her waist; her gift for dressing sexily. And then her penetrating looks, too seldom in use these days.

He loved to be seen through; this was an insight he'd had late in life, but that's how it was. To be seen through is to be seen a second time, and that didn't happen so often. *Because first impressions last* — he hated that an advertisement was echoing through him.

"Something happened at work," she declared.

"We'll talk about it later," he said happily.

"What happened to your lip?"

"You'll have to watch it on TV."

They chatted a bit until Norsborg. He turned the job talk in her direction. She was a nurse on a rehab floor at Huddinge and was always ready with a heap of tragicomic stories. This time it was a brain-damaged patient who had urinated in the handbag of one of her colleagues; the woman didn't notice until she went to take out her SL card at the commuter train turnstile.

As they walked with their arms around each other through the outskirts of a neighbourhood that everyone considered to be a high-rise ghetto and that had once, what seemed like a very long time ago, been his workplace, and as the sun generously shared the nuances that had been well hidden during the day, and as a bit of summer warmth lingered in the air, and as the wasps buzzed in that dull, dying way, Paul Hjelm decided that this was what love looked like once you stepped into middle age. It could be worse.

They arrived home. Danne looked as if he'd been spilled onto the sofa; he was watching MTV. A social studies book with crumpled pages was open on the table. He was downing greenish soda. "It's past seven," the boy complained.

"I told you there was food in the fridge," said Cilla, who began to unpack a shower curtain with gold Egyptian hieroglyphs on a dark green background.

"We *ate*," said Danne without taking his eyes from the MTV screen. "What kind of fucking sludge was that?"

"Mexican fucking sludge," Cilla said calmly, holding up the new shower curtain she'd bought. Apparently she was awaiting a statement from her husband.

"What does it say?" he said.

She made a face and carried it to the bathroom.

He opened a beer and called, "Maybe it's Egyptian porn!"

Danne glared at him from the sofa.

After a few minutes she returned with the old shower curtain and showed him the horrible accumulation of mould: two small black spots down in the corner.

"What does this say about our household?" Cilla asked rhetorically, fingering the spots with disgust.

"That we take showers," said Paul Hjelm.

She sighed and crumpled the old curtain into an overflowing rubbish bin. Then she took out the remains of the Mexican fucking sludge, put the plastic container in the microwave, sat down in front of the TV and changed the channel.

Without a word, Danne took the remote and changed it back.

As Hjelm poured beer down his throat, he thought about how he had seen this scene before. Three thousand, four hundred, and eighty-six times. "What time is it?" he asked.

"Nineteen oh six and thirteen seconds," said Cilla. She had just countered her son by pushing the text-TV button. Now a dark curtain of letters fell down across the MTV-filled screen.

"In just under four minutes, the clock will chime," boomed the voice of the master. "I want to watch the local news."

The battle on the sofa continued in silence. Thus far it had been a game. He hoped it would remain so.

The microwave dinged. Tova came down the stairs and groaned when she saw the spectacle on the sofa.

"Hi," Hjelm said to his fourteen-year-old daughter.

"Hi," she said. "You're so late."

"Cut it out." He poured the Mexican fucking sludge onto two plates, dug out two spoons, poured two beers, and managed to balance it all as he brought it over to the living-room sofa.

"Isn't that a schoolbook?" he said to his son, who was attacking the pocket where Cilla had shoved the remote.

"Cut it out," Danne echoed, as he pulled out the remote and got MTV back. It was on a commercial break, so he gave in. The paternal hand snatched the remote, changed it to Channel 2, and turned up the volume. There was about a minute left before the local news.

Hjelm had time to ask, "How's school going?"

His son had just started upper secondary school, and Paul had devoted only a few wasted hours to trying to understand the school system. Danne was in something that went by the name "Programme in Social Sciences", and his lessons seemed decidedly simpler than the process of figuring out the curriculum.

"Good," said Danne.

The theme music of the local news came on, just as brief as his son's reply.

"Here comes some great television art," said Paul Hjelm. The rest of the family looked at him sceptically.

It came on right away. The anchorwoman spoke excitedly about a big crackdown on narcotics at Arlanda that morning — and about the dramatic assault of a top police officer in front of their cameras. Sensitive viewers were warned. Hjelm's expectations rose.

Then Waldemar Mörner, the deputy commissioner of the National Police Board and the A-Unit's formal boss, appeared on the screen.

His well-coiffed blond hair was impeccable, but he was breathing heavily, as though he had just personally chased some criminals through Arlanda. Presumably he had just tumbled out of the helicopter before he had

**66**

any idea of what had happened; perhaps he had been jogging on the spot inside the helicopter. Neither his breathing nor his ignorance stopped him from looking confident and efficient — or from lying with no inhibitions.

"Waldemar Mörner, deputy commissioner of the National Police Board," the reporter began. "What happened at Arlanda today?"

"The NCP acted on indications from the American police that a large quantity of narcotics would arrive at Arlanda today from the United States. I can't go into specifics on the action itself."

"Has anyone been apprehended?"

"At least one American citizen has been taken into custody in connection with smuggling narcotics, yes. We are expecting further apprehensions shortly."

A man in handcuffs was seen at the edge of the screen. Hjelm recognised the notorious drug smuggler Robert E. Norton, surrounded by four armed Arlanda police officers. As they watched, he managed to kick Mörner's backside, knocking Mörner over with a shrill cry. When he fell, he grabbed the microphone, so the reporter followed him to the floor. The microphone cord must, in turn, have been wound around the cameraman's legs, because he plunged to his face. Over the lengthy footage of Arlanda's ceiling, they could hear the camera man whimpering, the reporter moaning and Mörner's verbal gunfire: "Fuckinghellgoddamndildofuck."

The producer didn't cut until then; it wasn't hard to imagine his sadistic smile.

Yet it was too early for the anchorwoman in the studio. As the camera caught her, she shouted in a panic, "Am I really supposed to read this?" When she realised she was on the air, she pulled herself together and struggled heroically to keep her composure as she read "Fortunately, no one was seriously injured in the drug dealer's attack. Our reporter, however, suffered some oral injuries when the microphone, which had been pushed into his mouth, was removed."

On the sofa in Norsborg, no one was required to keep their composure. When the gales of laughter ebbed, Paul returned the remote control to Danne. He caught Cilla's glance. As she dried her tears and restored her face, her eyes were serious. She realised something was brewing.

They went to bed rather early; both had long days at work ahead. Danne was allowed to keep watching MTV; it wasn't an evening when they really had the energy to be responsible parents. Experience told them that he was probably doing his homework as he watched.

Neither of them could really understand how multitasking could be so quickly upgraded.

"What's going on?" Cilla asked with a flashing spark of attention as sleep tried to envelop her.

"Nothing yet," Paul said as he unpacked a few books onto the bedside table. "But the risk that something will happen has increased."

"And what about the wound on your lip?" she said more faintly.

"The TV celebrity," he snickered. "The one who kicked Mörner in the arse."

"Is it really all about drugs?"

"No," he sighed. "This thing kills faster."

She was already halfway into the realm of sleep. "A weapon?"

"Not exactly. It's best if I don't say more. But there's a risk that I'll have to put in some overtime. Good thing summer's over."

Then she was asleep.

He patted her cheek, then turned to the pile of books on the bedside table. On his way back from Marieberg he had stopped by the library at Fridhemsplan and looked up "Hassel, Lars-Erik" in the new computer system. He got hold of the Maoist manifesto from 1971 and two volumes of the somewhat later documentary novels.

The manifesto was unreadable — not for ideological reasons, but because it presupposed an understanding of the technical terminology of dialectical materialism. Hjelm didn't understand a word. And this was written by the man who later freely lambasted Swedish authors with accusations of elitism.

The documentary novels, though, were profoundly educational. The plot of one centred on a manor in Västmanland at the turn of the century. Step by step the reader could follow each class, from the landowner, whose inherited brutality was hidden behind fancy upper-class manners, to the oppressed farm labourers' heroic struggle for their daily bread. Hjelm was vaguely familiar with the concept. The problem was that everything was hyper-idealised. The message overshadowed the characterisations. The uneducated masses had to be schooled in politics. It was like a medieval allegory, an undisguised textbook in the true faith. The censorship of sleepiness was relentless.

The day on which one of Sweden's last levees broke ended with yet another assault on a police officer. Just as the living room clock struck midnight, Lars-Erik mounted a posthumous attack on Paul Hjelm: the right corner of *The Parasite of Society* struck his left eyebrow.

The Kentucky Killer's visit to Sweden entered its second day.

# CHAPTER
# EIGHT

Arto Söderstedt lived with his wife and five children in the inner city and thought it wonderful. He was convinced that the children thought it wonderful too, from the three-year-old to the thirteen-year-old. Every time he dropped them off at nursery and school, he found himself surrounded by self-tormentors who were convinced that their children's greatest dream was to have their own garden patch to romp around in. He often thought about the psychosocial mechanisms that caused the majority of inner-city parents to have a constant guilty conscience.

The suburban parents he met were different. All of them made an extreme effort to convince their friends that they had found heaven on earth. As a rule, upon closer inspection, the heaven that was suburbia turned out to consist of three things: one, you could let the children out in the garden and avoid being in their vicinity; two, it was easier to park your car; and three, you could grill outdoors.

The contradiction between thwarted conscience and inflated self-esteem often resulted in yet another family moving van heading north, south or west.

Söderstedt had seen the grass on both sides of the fence. When the A-Unit was made permanent, his family had moved from Västerås, with its private homes, to Bondegatan on Södermalm. Personally, he didn't miss the forced interaction with neighbours he had nothing in common with, nor the competition-orientated self-righteousness that came with homeownership, nor the fixation on the car, nor the enormous distance to everything, nor the useless public transportation system, nor the barbecue parties, nor the tranquil state of vegetation, nor the artificial proximity to nature, nor the predictable discussions about hoses, nor the lawn and the garden that sucked up more time than money, nor the architecture that lacked history and fantasy, nor the empty roads, nor the absolute lack of culture. And when it came to the children, he had produced a small list of arguments for use by inner-city parents when aggressive suburbanites pressed them up against the wall with accusations of child abuse. Memories of childhood follow a person throughout his entire life, and if these memories are of playgrounds, car parks and lonely roads rather than diverse building facades, church steeples and people, then that's a deciding factor. In the city the likelihood that a child will get a good education is greater, visits to the theatre and museums are considerably more numerous, access to activities is enormous, encounters with people of all sorts are legion. In general, in the city one's powers of observation and vigilance are developed in a way that lacks a counterpart outside.

72

What struck Söderstedt now, as he sauntered through this very city, was that this whole manner of thinking was dictated by a drummed-in guilty conscience.

What kind of societal stereotypes truly determined the picture of happiness?

Not, in any case, the five-room apartment on Bondegatan where the seven-person household was without doubt a bit cramped. The question was whether it really mattered that much.

Since Anja had taken care of the day's deliveries of their children, he permitted himself to walk from Söder to Kungsholmen; he had a feeling that it would be the last time he would be allowed that luxury for a long time. When he stepped into the police station on that beautiful early-autumn morning, he continued straight to the service vehicle pool and checked out a robust Audi. He pocketed the keys and stepped into the lift.

Arto Söderstedt caught a glimpse of himself in the lift mirror. He'd made it through another summer without getting skin cancer, he thought, looking for some wood to knock on. He had the kind of skin that only Finns and Englishmen have, the absolutely white-through kind that doesn't have a chance of turning anything other than red in the sun. It was the fourth of September, and he had just managed to take the crucial leap from SPF 15, the variety for newborns, to SPF 12.

Actually, he liked autumn best.

Except maybe not this autumn.

He had read up on serial killers in connection with the Power Murders, and as usual he found himself giving a few lectures to the group. Since then he had rationed them out. He was afraid that the time for rationing would soon be over. Sweden's last levee had broken, and violent crime of an international character, to cite a familiar source, had arrived. It would hardly be an isolated incident.

The fact was, he recognised the Kentucky Killer. He had read about him and vaguely remembered him. He had been one of the first in a long series of such killers.

There was something strange about his modus operandi, something that didn't really match up with the profile of a serial killer. Those terrifying pincers . . . he couldn't put his finger on it, but something was wrong. He needed to speak directly to Ray Larner at the FBI, but he didn't know how to get past Hultin. Certainly Hultin was the best boss he'd ever worked under, but he lacked Söderstedt's own insights into the grey areas of the workings of justice. Söderstedt had once been a defence lawyer, one of the most prominent in Finland, and he had defended the worst of the worst in the upper echelons. Then his conscience had rebelled; he'd quit, fled to Sweden, enrolled in police college at a slightly advanced age, and settled down as a policeman in Västerås. He had got it into his head that a lawyer's role as a vicarious criminal could be useful in this case. There had to be some sort of identification in order to catch a serial killer, he knew that.

So lost was he in his reflections about inner-city parents and serial killers that he didn't notice he was late. Which wasn't like him. So he was quite surprised to open the door to "Supreme Central Command" and find not only everyone already gathered there but Waldemar Mörner himself sitting at Hultin's lectern, drumming his fingers.

Because he hadn't had a chance to prepare himself for the confrontation, he burst into spontaneous peals of laughter. This didn't go down very well. Mörner looked audaciously fresh, unaffected by the incident at Arlanda, but Söderstedt's laughter caused him to put a small, permanent mental mark on Söderstedt's record. He wrinkled one eyebrow for a short but murderous second. Then he was himself again.

"I hope lateness won't become a habit for you, Söderstedt," he said sternly. "We're facing a task of a nature we have never come close to in modern times in this country. But *tempus fugit*, and we will too. Don't allow the four complaints from Arlanda to disturb your work; instead let's move forward with the extensive investigation."

"Four?" said Norlander.

"Currently," Hultin said neutrally.

Mörner didn't hear them but continued with glowing passion: "After extensive work in the upper echelons, I have persuaded them that this case should be entrusted into your warm hands, and I sincerely hope that you don't fall short of the confidence that I have placed in you. Inasmuch as a mustering of strength is needed, I urge you to develop expanded horizons and widened scopes. Your joint capital is firmly rooted in the visions of the management team, and the future looks bright. The light is visible at the end of the tunnel. Ahead of your great burden lies a fair reward. Seize the day, make the most of every minute, pull out all the stops. Work hard now, gentlemen. And lady, of course. Lady. The welfare of Sweden rests in your hands."

With these words of wisdom, Mörner departed, glancing at the clock.

The room fell silent. Language itself seemed to have become constipated. After this address, no word would be innocent. Any one might become a weapon of murder aimed at the heart of the Swedish language.

"With friends like that, who needs enemies?" Hultin said neutrally, grasping wisely at a proverb in order to normalise the linguistic situation. "I have spent the night with the Kentucky Killer," he continued.

"Then he ought to be easy to locate," said Söderstedt, who hadn't quite collected himself yet.

Hultin ignored him. "A summary has been distributed to your offices. There is an enormous amount of material, and somewhere in there is the hidden link to Sweden. My examination didn't turn up anything new, but if you have extra time, you can study it in detail. I'm afraid, however, that the killer will have to start up again for us to obtain any adequate clues."

"What if he's come here to retire?" Gunnar Nyberg asked. "Then we'd sit here twiddling our thumbs until we're retired."

The thought did not seem entirely repellent to Nyberg. He had been shot in the throat during the hunt for the Power Murderer. The industrious church vocalist had been close to having sung his last note. After six months' convalescence, he had returned to the

76

Nacka church choir; his bass had become deeper, taken on a more extensive tone, and these days he sang in jubilation, less at the benevolence of God, even if that were in his thoughts, than at the fact that he had a voice at all. For Nyberg, the Kentucky Killer's vocal cord pincers were identical to the devil's pitchfork. He ran the risk of becoming personally engaged in a way that he carefully avoided these days, in anticipation of his retirement. His problem was that that lay twenty years in the future.

"He came here with fresh blood on his hands," Hultin answered. "I don't think that's how a person ends his career. He could very well have slunk in completely unnoticed, but his craving got the upper hand. No, he has some sort of target —"

"That's something I've been thinking about," said the other church singer, Kerstin Holm. She was dressed in black as always, with a little black leather skirt of the type that Hjelm couldn't help reacting to. It suddenly threw him back in time to just over a year ago. Yesterday's feeling seemed to have opened the forbidden doors, and he found himself wondering how she really felt, who the new man in her life was, and what she thought of him now, afterwards. Their relationship had been intense but unreal. Did she hate him? Sometimes he imagined so. Had he left her? Or was she the one who had left him? Everything was still shrouded in mist. *Misterioso*, he thought.

He was abruptly brought back to reality by her words. "Serial killing is about being seen," she said thoughtfully. Her contributions always resonated in a slightly different way. A womanly way, maybe. "The victims are meant to see their tormentor and therefore their murderer. A person doesn't commit serial murders and then hide the victims. That would be something else. What are things like on that front? Has our man ever *hidden* a victim?"

Hultin flipped through pages again. "It doesn't seem like it, based on a quick look, but if you think it's important, you should investigate further."

"I think pretty much all of us have had a vague sense that something is a bit wrong. Not a lot, but a little. He is bestially bloodthirsty but takes a fifteen-year break. He brings a fake passport to the airport but hasn't booked a seat. He murders Hassel in the middle of the evening rush at one of the largest airports in the world without leaving a trace, but he doesn't hide the body. He has all the attributes of a classic serial killer, but at the same time there's a bit of a clinical hit-man professionalism to him. Does he really want to be seen? Or was he *telling* us where he was going? Can we also find a clue as to *why* he came here? We've discussed it before, but the combination seems not only dangerous but also wrong. Somehow."

It was that *somehow*, if anything, that everyone could get on board with.

"Does it have something to do with Hassel personally, after all?" Hjelm dared to ask. "I've looked at his Maoist writings from the seventies, and they're no trifling matter." He picked at his bandaged eyebrow. "Let's toy with the thought that the Kentucky Killer is KGB and that the wave of American murders is the result of Soviet imports. Hence the many unidentified victims. Did Hassel have some sort of information from the good old seventies that he couldn't be allowed to divulge? Was he just one in a series of security risks or traitors or double agents? Maybe we could check unofficially with Larner to see if that idea has come up before."

"In any case," Kerstin Holm replied eagerly, "that could explain the long break. He — or maybe a whole cadre — was quite simply called home sometime shortly after Brezhnev's death in the early eighties. The KGB decreased its activity then; that fits quite nicely. Then fifteen years later discontent spreads in Russia, the Communists make headway, agents are taken out of the deep freeze, and our friend is sent back to the United States to start afresh."

"He's finished with the American list and switches over to the Swedish one," Hjelm took up the baton of their relay. "He weighs the risks with professional precision: 'How can I get the message to the intended victims that I'm coming, without getting caught myself?' Because it obviously is a matter of *being seen*, but in a different way than we first thought; this is a matter of being seen by those who are to be punished. He's on a crusade; his goal is to strike fear in the hearts of all traitors. They must be informed that the state isn't dead, that it's never possible to flee the Soviet state; that it's in good health as a state within a state."

"On the other hand," Holm added, "he's aware that initially the message will reach only the police. That means he's now either waiting for the usual old leaks to start and for everything to come out, or else he's *aiming for the police* and, if that's the case, a very small group of police: just the ones he knows in advance will take up the case."

"If anyone here in the A-Unit, or higher up, has a past that is similar to Lars-Erik Hassel's," Hjelm continued, "then he should probably be on guard."

"And come forward," said Holm.

"Come out of the closet," said Hjelm.

It was quiet. Suddenly they had not only taken the leap to international politics and the aftermath of the Cold War — they had also dragged in the A-Unit personally. Could the Kentucky Killer really be that sophisticated?

Was he after one of them?

"What do we know about Mörner's background?" Hjelm said wickedly.

In among the suspicious, sweeping glances, he caught Kerstin's. It was the first time in a long time they'd exchanged pleased looks, which hid a great deal. She smiled a reserved and captivating smile.

Hultin did not smile. "Mörner is hardly a security risk for anyone other than himself," he said sternly. "Is there anyone else who feels like coming out of the closet?"

No one else felt like it.

Hultin continued silkily, "All due respect to speculations, but this one deserves the paranoia prize of the year. From the banal fact that the body was discovered before the plane landed, you are drawing the elegant conclusion that the KGB is targeting the

**80**

A-Unit, that the entire wave of serial murders in the United States is based on Soviet indoctrination, that the twenty-four victims, whom you have in no way investigated more closely, were Soviet traitors, that all of this has gone over the heads of the FBI, and that one of your close colleagues has had contact with the KGB. You really covered a lot."

"But wasn't it fun?" Hjelm said just as silkily.

Hultin ignored this rejoinder and raised his voice: "If this has anything to do with international political power plays, then we are a very, very small piece in the game. Neither Larner nor I have overlooked that risk. But if it is the case, it hardly looks the way you're describing it. We wouldn't be able to see more than the contours of it."

"Anyway, the point is," said Holm, "that there's a lot we can't see."

"Let's do this," said Hultin in a conciliatory tone. "You, Kerstin, take on the American victims: make a close study of who they actually were and what the FBI says about them, and see if there is any sort of link among them, or between them and Sweden. See if you can find anything from your point of view that the FBI might have missed from theirs. It's a hard nut to crack, so to speak, but blame yourself."

Hultin rummaged through his papers and seemed, for a second, to be as disorganised as they were. Then he pulled himself together. "This meeting was actually meant for Jorge, who spent the whole night surfing the Internet."

Chavez was sitting in a corner, exhausted. For a person who spent a lot of time on the Net, paranoia was always a temptation, and he appeared tempted. But also very, very tired.

"Well," he said, "I don't know if we can bear to listen to much more right now. But I've chatted for several hours with a group that is well hidden on the Net, namely FASK, Fans of American Serial Killers, a shady organisation whose website required some finesse and, I'll admit it, a financial contribution to get into. The Kentucky Killer goes quite simply by the designation K, and the crazies in FASK consider him to be a great hero. They knew that K had killed again but not, as far as I could tell, that he had made his way to Sweden, which probably indicates that their contacts, fortunately, don't go that high up."

"I hope you didn't leave behind a bunch of tracks that would lead here," said Hultin, who had only moderate insights into the Web.

"I was well disguised," Chavez said laconically. "Anyway, they had a whole bunch of theories about K that it might be good for us to be aware of. Most of them were crazy ideas like Kerstin and Paul's, but others were more sensible. Even they think there's some sort of professionalism involved. A few think he's high up in the military. Apparently there was a secret commander behind the Vietnam task force Commando Cool who was somehow directly below the president. His identity is unknown; that was the only thing Larner never caught, but in these circles he goes by the name Balls; apparently they've never seen *The Pink Panther*.

The rumour is that Balls personally invented the notorious vocal cord pincers, and that since then he has occupied a central position within the Pentagon. Larner's suspect, the guy with the country singer name, who died in the car crash —"

"Wayne Jennings. Not Waylon," corrected Hultin.

"Thanks. According to FASK, he was just Balls's henchman. The truly important operations in Vietnam were carried out under the personal leadership of Balls. Again, according to FASK. They're also convinced that Balls is K. Apparently he's a general at this point. According to the serial killers' cheerleaders, he stopped killing when he was transferred to Washington DC, and got Vietnam out of his blood, and he started up again when he retired. The reasoning itself seems pretty coherent, I think."

"But it can hardly be your Balls who's come here," Hultin said. "He was travelling with a thirty-two-year-old's passport."

Chavez nodded with as much enthusiasm as his exhaustion would allow.

"Exactly. That gives us a little perspective on the FBI's reasoning. The whole theory that the Kentucky Killer has come to Sweden actually rests on pretty flimsy grounds. It was a quick, smart conclusion under the circumstances, but it is based on something as trivial as Hassel not having a ticket on him. Then the speedy hypothesis became an axiom. We don't even know *when* Hassel was murdered. Our literary critic could very well have had some whim at the airport, thought of something else he had to do, and decided to stay another night or two. Maybe he called to cancel his own ticket, then threw it away. Maybe he stuck around for a while and had a few drinks. On the way to the toilet he was attacked and murdered. Meanwhile a young criminal with a fake passport arrived at the airport, maybe on the run from angry bookies or something, and wanted to get the first international flight he could find a seat on. The plane to Stockholm was going to take off in about an hour, and he hopped on. In which case, the Kentucky Killer never left the country. Does that sound unreasonable?"

Hultin looked around the room. Since no one else seemed willing, he raised the objections himself. He did so honourably.

"Aside from the fact that there are a few too many coincidences, it seems pretty bizarre that Hassel would have gone to the airport only to change his mind *once he was already there*, not bother to check in an hour ahead of time as is required, wait for at least half an hour, and then *call* to cancel instead of just walking up to the ticket counter."

"To my ears it sounds like classic alcoholic behaviour," said Gunnar Nyberg. "Maybe he arrived too late, wandered about aimlessly, realised he had missed the check-in deadline, thought that meant he'd missed the flight, and called the desk in order to avoid facing the contempt of the ground agent. Then he kept boozing at the airport and picked a fight with the wrong person. In which case, Jorge's hypothesis would work better."

"The problem," Hultin said coldly, "is that the autopsy didn't show any elevated alcohol levels in the blood. And no drugs. You would know that if you'd followed orders and read Larner's report."

"What happened to his luggage?" Nyberg asked, as if to confirm Hultin's theory that he had read inadequately.

"It was recovered next to him," Hultin said, "which bolsters the image of a cold-blooded murder. Not only did he silently carry Hassel into a cupboard in the middle of the rush of people at Newark; he also managed to get the luggage in." He sighed. "Let's try to apply some ice-cold logic here. The cancellation came seventeen minutes before departure. The employees obviously assumed that it was Hassel calling, and that he was calling from outside the airport. But if he was calling from outside to cancel, then why would he have gone to the airport? Because it's clear that he did: for one thing, the crime scene investigation shows that the cupboard was indisputably the site of the murder; for another, it wouldn't have been possible to carry a corpse in through a busy airport corridor. OK? So two possibilities remain. One: that he himself called from the airport, which is ruled out by its own absurdity, because in that case he (a) would have made it to the plane — after all, Reynolds did, and he arrived five minutes later — or (b) changed his mind on a whim at the last minute, and then why call at all — if he was sober? Why not just turn round and take a taxi back to Manhattan? And two: that someone else called in his name — and if so, then this other person had a good reason to do so, and the best reason seems, at the moment, to be that he wanted to get on the flight to Stockholm at any price. Hayden's intuitive hypothesis still seems to be a valid working hypothesis, if not yet an axiom."

"OK." Chavez was acting as though he had sniffed some ammonia during his break in the round. "It wasn't my hypothesis, anyway. Mine's based on Balls. If our man is now a retired general, it shouldn't be too big a problem for him to put down some false tracks; there would be lots of ambitious thirty-two-year-old officers at his disposal to use as less-than-scrupulous stand-ins. For some reason, Balls felt that now was the time to be rid of the FBI; maybe he thought Larner's persistence was becoming irritating. So then, what is the safest way to render the FBI harmless? You leave the country. The FBI is not the CIA; the FBI's domain is very distinct: within the borders of the United States. So if you carefully choose a country where the police have scanty resources, where the priorities are incomprehensible, where the directors are appointed with strange methods, and where the police are, to put it bluntly, likely to be bumbling, and you then murder a citizen of that country, steal his ticket home, and make sure that your stand-in is capable of suggesting that you have arrived in the country in question, then the FBI's conclusion is that you have got away. Just like Paul and Kerstin, I am of the opinion that there might be a message in the somewhat curious sequence of events at the airport, but that it is directed at the FBI rather than at Sweden, and that the entire Swedish part of this case

86

might well be faked. I have my doubts that he's here. The stand-in came in, switched passports and went back without leaving Arlanda, and waiting at home was a retired but far-from-powerless general who made sure the stand-in advanced a few steps in his career."

The A-Unit looked listless, as if about to hit a wall. So many hypotheses had whizzed around during the past hour that they needed fresh air. Viggo Norlander, the only one who had remained quiet, wearing a mental dunce cap after his own little sequence of airport events, got to summarise the whole thing: "In other words, we're pissing in the wind."

"That's exactly right," Hultin said good-naturedly.

# CHAPTER
# NINE

The day went by.

Another day or two went by.

A few more days went by.

Nothing happened. No headline sirens blared in the media. The A-Unit was allowed to work in undisturbed peace, which, in its own way, made their idleness even more frustrating. They quite simply had nothing to do, not even shoo away stubborn reporters, which at least would have brought a sort of bittersweet satisfaction.

All Swedish deaths that were reported to the police came trickling in — as did all the reports of Americans suspected of crimes. None of them seemed particularly promising as leads. If the Kentucky Killer hadn't abruptly adapted to Swedish circumstances and started surreptitiously murdering dementia patients, which someone seemed to be up to at the moment in a nursing home in Sandviken, then he was lying low. If he wasn't a twelve-year-old who had kicked a pregnant woman to the ground on the street so that her broken rib killed the foetus, if he hadn't raped and murdered a sixty-two-year-old prostitute and put her into a portable luggage trunk, stuck a one-year-old into a freezer, killed himself with nose spray, mistaken sulphuric acid for moonshine, or attacked his neighbour with something as strange as a recently sharpened rake. Officially, Nyberg was the one who kept track of the odd deaths; unofficially, the A-Unit didn't give a shit about them. Nyberg preferred to stick to the underworld, where he could terrorise old-guard small-time criminals in peace.

Things were about the same when it came to the potential criminal behaviour of visiting Americans. There Norlander was the one holding the non-existent reins; he thought it was taking an unusually long time for the mental dunce cap to wear off. A man who was unwise enough to call himself Reynold Edwins attracted Norlander's attention, more because of his name than because of his activities, which consisted of going round to primary schools in Malmö and picking up girls for porn films. Three American businessmen purchased sexual favours at porn clubs in Gothenburg and, when picked up, firmly maintained that it was illegal for this to be illegal. An unidentified American had had a forbidden key copied at a shoe repair shop in Gärdet; the owner hadn't called the police until afterwards, which resulted in charges being brought against him, too. Another unidentified American had been seen dealing hash on Narvavägen; apparently he had a bad map. A third naively exposed himself in Tantolunden and was assaulted by a women's football team. A fourth bought a sailing boat with thousand-kronor notes that had been badly photocopied; unfortunately the owner had been so drunk that it took him a day to realise it, and by then the American had already performed the unlikely achievement of driving the sailing boat through a shop window in Vaxholm.

And so it went, uninteresting through and through.

Chavez became more and more virtual; Söderstedt drove around in his Audi, personally investigating Americans staying in lodgings fit for both princes and paupers; and Hultin endured long, chaotic crisis meetings with Mörner and the national police commissioner, during which he entertained himself by thinking about what sort of wrenches the young Communist Mörner could conceivably have thrown into the works of the KGB.

Kerstin Holm worked intensively with the material from the FBI, but the descriptions of the victims from the 1970s had faded considerably, and the KGB hypothesis seemed less plausible. She noted with some interest that Hjelm was in her presence a bit more often than usual. They reasoned back and forth but never got further than they had in that single associative minute when they helped each other deliver a joint hypothesis that no one really believed.

Without his virtual office mate, Hjelm turned to Kerstin, and to his surprise, the very fact that he and Cilla were doing better than they had for a long time made him draw closer to Kerstin. There were so many things he wanted to ask her, but all that came out were indirect insinuations, such as when he played the tape of the interviews with Lars-Erik Hassel's two exes. First the ex-wife:

"You were together during his more political period, right?"

"Political . . . hmm . . ."

"He *did* take an active interest in the weaker members of society . . ."

"Well . . . I don't know . . ."

"An active, genuine interest."

"Yes . . . well . . . um . . . What are you getting at?"

"And then his interest in literature. Incredibly strong."

"Are you being sarcastic?"

It had been a catastrophe, and he very much deserved the stern side glance he received from Kerstin. Then he fast-forwarded the tape to the other ex, the young woman who had left Hassel before he had time to meet his second son:

"Has he seen his son since?"

"Yes . . . well . . . um . . ."

"Has he ever met him at all?"

"I don't think you could say he has. I'm not one hundred per cent sure that he knew he existed."

Rewind, and back to the first:

"Did he have any enemies?"

"Well, there are enemies and then there are enemies . . . You can't be a critic for that long without attracting someone's hatred, that's for sure."

"Anyone in particular?"

"Throughout the years there have been a few, three of them. And more recently I'm quite sure he received a steady stream of hate emails, all from the same nut job."

"Hate emails?"

"Hate letters via email."

"How do you know that? Did you still see each other?"

"Laban told me. They saw each other once or twice a month."

"Your son?"

"Yes. There was some kind of crazy person who sent him emails. That's all I know."

Then fast-forward again to the younger woman:

"How old is your son now?"

"Six. His name is Conny."

"Why did you leave him? It happened so quickly, after all. He didn't even have time to see his son."

"He had absolutely no desire to see him. My waters broke as he was packing to go to the book fair in Gothenburg. He called for two taxis, one to Arlanda for himself, one to Karolinska for me. Gallant, huh? Then he fucked around like a madman down there, while his son was being born. Maybe he had time to fertilise another one before the first one came out. Always a bun in the oven."

"How do you know that? That he — was so sexually active in Gothenburg?"

"One of his colleagues called me, actually. A woman. I don't remember her name."

"She called you? At the hospital? To tell you your husband was fucking around? So tasteful."

"Yes. No, not very — tasteful."

"Didn't you think it was a bit strange?"

"Yes, actually. But she sounded convincing, and besides, I could see when he left that it was over. He thought one kid was enough. Conny was an accident, but I didn't want to have an abortion."

"Can you remember what this colleague's name was?"

"I'm pretty sure her first name was Elisabeth. After that, I don't know. Bengtsson? Berntsson? Baklava? Biskopsnäsa?"

And rewinding again. Kerstin watched him rewind with raised eyebrows.

"Do you know if these hate emails are still on the computer?"

"No. The only thing I know is that Laban said that they upset Lars-Erik. I can't really picture it, but that's what he said."

"How old is Laban?"

"Twenty-three."

"Does he live at home?"

"He has an apartment on Kungsklippan, if you want to verify my statement, or whatever it's called. Laban Jeremias Hassel."

"What does he do?"

"Now don't laugh. [Pause.] He studies literature."

Hjelm pressed stop again and was just about to fast-forward when Kerstin pressed his very own stop button; it seemed necessary. "That's enough."

He stopped reluctantly and returned to the present. He sank down into the chair across from her and scanned the room. It was the office that Kerstin shared with Gunnar Nyberg, the choir room. Autumn light streamed in through its always-half-open windows. Sometimes they sat here and practised scales and sang in harmony, a cappella, he with his strong bass, she with her husky alto. Hjelm compared it to his own office, where Chavez surfed the Internet full time and where the conversation these days mostly seemed to involve football. He felt short of breath. He needed a little John Coltrane. And maybe he would be brave enough to return to Kafka, even though the worth of literature had been drastically devalued during the last few days.

But most of all he needed to tell Kerstin something. He wondered what it was.

"Can't you give me a summary instead?" she said.

He looked at her. She didn't turn away. Neither of them understood the other's look.

"Three things," he said professionally. "One: pay a visit to the twenty-three-year-old literature-student son, Laban Hassel. Two: find out more about the colleague Elisabeth Biskopsnäsa, or whatever she is called, the one who called the hospital and tattled. Three: check whether those threatening emails are still on the computer, either at home or at the newspaper office."

"Have you been to Hassel's home at all?"

"I swung by. No obvious KGB signs fluttering around like vampires. A tasteful, large Kungsholm apartment with a few bachelor touches. And exercise equipment. Do you want to take a peek?"

She shook her head. "There's something I have to check on. Try to get Jorge out into the sunlight."

He nodded, hesitated at the door for a second, and cast a quick glance at the tape player. Then he left it with her.

She regarded it for a while. She looked at the closed door, then back at the tape player.

She fast-forwarded to a point in between the passages that Hjelm had so frantically toggled. Paul had asked the ex-wife:

"Who is your new husband?"

"Surely that has nothing to do with this."

"I just want to know what you've got instead of Hassel. What you looked for instead. The differences. It might tell me a few things about him."

"I live with a man who works in the travel industry. We do well together. He works hard but leaves work at work and devotes his time to me when we're home. We have a normal life together. Was that the answer you were looking for?"

"I think so."

Kerstin Holm looked at the closed door.
For a long time.

★ ★ ★

Hjelm did get Chavez out into the sunlight. At a moment when his desk mate complained about increasing bum sweat, he jumped at the opportunity, and the two former Power Murder heroes left police headquarters to the hands of more permanently accomplished medallists like Waldemar Mörner. They hadn't been able to find out exactly what had happened with the complaint from the news reporter, who had received, quote, "massive lip injuries" when Mörner shoved the microphone into his mouth. Presumably the complaint had been considerably easier to digest.

Out on the street, yet another sparklingly clear late-summer afternoon offered up its services. Autumn had arrived in Arlanda, but it was delaying its appearance in Stockholm. The somewhat tired symbolism could hardly escape anyone.

Chavez could still comfortably wear his old linen jacket, which needed washing more than its camou-flaging grey colour cared to admit. He stretched his compact Latin body intensely as they walked along Kungsholmsgatan and crossed Scheelegatan.

"The Internet," he said dreamily. "Endless possibilities. And endless amounts of shit."

"Like life," Hjelm said philosophically.

They turned onto Pipersgatan, trudged up the hill, and started up the steep steps towards Kungsklippan, where the rows of houses tried to eclipse one another's views of Stockholm. Some stared out over City Hall and police headquarters — they were hardly the most attractive ones — while others cast covetous glances past Kungholms Church to Norr Mälarstrand and

96

Riddarfjärden; still others peered a bit disdainfully out over the muddle of the city and beyond, to upper Östermalm. Lars-Erik Hassel's son from his first marriage lived in one of these last.

They rang the doorbell. After a while a young man with a thin goatee, a sleeveless T-shirt and baggy trousers appeared.

"The cops," he said expressionlessly.

"Yes indeed," said the cops in unison, above their IDs. "May we come in?"

"I guess it would be shooting myself in the foot to say no," said Hassel Junior.

It was a little studio with a kitchen nook. A frayed navy blue window blind kept the sun at bay. A computer spread a bluish flicker across the walls closest to the desk; otherwise the apartment was coal black.

Chavez pulled the cord, and the blind flew up with a squeak that was strongly reminiscent of the one Mörner had produced when Robert E. Norton kicked him in the rear. "This isn't opened very often," Chavez observed. "With a view like this, maybe you should look outside once in a while." Beyond the window, Kungsklippan plunged down towards the junction between island and mainland.

"Were you working?" Hjelm asked. "Your mum said you study literature."

Laban Jeremias Hassel squinted at the sun and smiled with indoor pallor. "The irony of fate . . ."

"In what way?" Hjelm lifted an upside-down coffee mug from the tiny counter. He shouldn't have done it

— a whiff of the mouldy fumes nearly flung him across the apartment.

"My father was one of Sweden's leading literary critics," said Laban Jeremias, observing Hjelm's actions indifferently. "The irony is that I was born with a literary silver spoon in my mouth. But really, my interest in literature is a rebellion against my father. I don't know if it's possible to understand," he added quietly, lowering himself onto a thready, 1960s-style lavender sofa.

The furniture in the little apartment was both sparse and slovenly. Here lived a person without much interest in the outside world — that much was clear.

"I think I understand," said Hjelm, even if he couldn't really reconcile Laban's trendy appearance with the inner chaos that seemed to rule him. "Your view of literature is the exact opposite of your father's."

"He never understood the importance of improving oneself," Laban Hassel mumbled, contemplating a birch table that actually seemed to have rotted through. "Literature was and remained a decadent bourgeois phenomenon for my father. So he felt no need to learn about it. Just tear it apart. And that continued long after he himself had become the most bourgeois of the bourgeois."

"He didn't like literature." Hjelm nodded.

Laban lifted his eyes to him for a moment with surprise. "*I* do," he whispered. "Without it, I'd be dead."

"Your childhood wasn't happy," Hjelm continued in the same balanced, calm, certain tone. *A father's tone*, he thought.

*Or a mediocre psychologist's.*

"He disappeared so soon," Laban said, indicating that the situation wasn't new for him. Many hours of therapy, it seemed, were behind him. He started over. "He disappeared so soon. Left us. And so he became a hero to me, a personal myth of this great, well-known, unapproachable thinker. And as I began to read books, he became more and more interesting, with absolutely no participation on his part. I decided to wait to read his works until I felt ready. Then I would read them, and everything would be revealed."

"And was it?"

"Yes. But in the exact opposite way from what I had imagined. His whole cultural veneer was exposed."

"And yet you kept in touch up until the end?"

Laban shrugged and seemed to fall into a trance. Then it came out. "I waited and waited for him to reveal something important, something crucial from the past. But it never came. He always managed to keep up a raw-but-warm tone between us. It felt like stepping right into the AIK locker room. Disgusting guy talk. No chinks in the armour. I waited for them in vain. Maybe they were there at the moment of his death."

"If I understand you correctly, your contact was extremely superficial."

"To say the least."

"And still he confided in you that he had received threatening emails."

Laban Hassel kept his eyes on the rotting table. He seemed broken. "Yes."

"Tell us everything you know."

"I know just what he said — that there was someone terrorising him."

"Why?"

"I don't know. That was all. He just tossed it out in passing."

"And yet you found it worth telling your mum?"

Laban looked at him in earnest for the first time. It wasn't a look to mess with. It held a bottomless intensity that was rare among twenty-three-year-olds. That look set the unemployed but ready-for-action detective inside Hjelm into motion.

"My mother and I have a very good relationship," Laban Hassel said.

Hjelm didn't push him any further; he would need a new angle of attack before he returned. Because he would return. He and Chavez thanked the young man and left.

In the stairwell, Chavez said, "What the fuck did you bring me along for?"

"Kerstin thought you needed to get out in the sun," Hjelm said heartily.

"Not much sun in there."

"To be honest, I needed a sounding board, someone without any preconceived notions about Lars-Erik Hassel at all. So?"

They wandered down the stairs to Pipersgatan. The sun got caught up in some stubborn bits of cloud and cast the northern half of City Hall in shadow. The result was a strange optical double exposure.

"Right or left?" Chavez asked.

"Left," said Hjelm. "We're going to Marieberg."

They walked quietly down Pipersgatan. Down at Hantverkargatan they turned right, wandered past Kungsholmstorg, and stopped at the bus stop.

"Well," Chavez returned to conversing, "I wonder how Laban's literature studies are going."

"Check," Hjelm said.

The bus had almost made it to Marieberg before Chavez, calling on his mobile, managed to get past the switchboard at Stockholm University and reach the Department of Literature, whose telephone-answering hours were of the irregular variety. Hjelm followed the phone-call spectacle from a distance, like a director laughing covertly at the efforts of the actors. They were crammed into different parts of the overcrowded bus, Hjelm in the aisle in back, Chavez in the middle, leaning over a pram that was cutting into his diaphragm. Every time he half-yelled into his phone, the baby in the pram screamed back three times as loud, accompanied by the mother's increasingly acid remarks. By the time Chavez stepped off the bus at Västerbroplan, he had a vague idea of what hell was like.

"Well?" Hjelm said again.

"You are an evil person," Chavez hissed.

"It's a difficult line of business," said Hjelm.

"Laban Hassel was registered for basic studies in literature three years ago. There are no results listed in the register today. No courses at all."

Hjelm nodded. They had arrived at the same conclusion from different directions. He was pleased with the synchronicity.

They reached the newspaper building. This time the lift worked. They walked into the arts and leisure offices purposefully. If everything went well, this whole thing would be solved before the A-Unit's evening meeting.

Erik Bertilsson was leaning over a jammed fax machine. Hjelm cleared his throat half an inch from the man's red-mottled scalp. Bertilsson gave a start, looking as if he'd seen a ghost. Which, Hjelm thought, wasn't far from the truth.

"We could use a little help," Hjelm said with a neutrality that would have given Hultin's a run for its money. "Can you get us into Hassel's email inbox? If it still exists."

Bertilsson gaped wildly at the man upon whom he had unloaded his life's disappointments, and who he had thought was out of his life. He didn't move a muscle. Finally he managed to say, "I don't know his password."

"Is there someone here who knows it?" Bertilsson shuffled over to a computer ten or so yards away, where he exchanged a few words with an overweight woman in her early forties. Her long hair, which was hanging free, was raven black; her tiger-striped glasses were oval; her flowery summer dress was tight. She sent a long, frosty look over at the duo of heroes and returned to her computer.

Bertilsson came back and pecked in a password; Chavez observed the keyboard concert attentively.

*Access denied.* He hit the screen in an outburst of rage and returned to the woman. A short palaver played out that Hjelm and Chavez observed in pantomime. The woman threw up her hands and let the corners of her mouth fall — her entire massive form radiated indifference. Then she lit up with a flash of inspiration, stabbed her index finger into the air, and uttered a word.

Bertilsson came back and wordlessly pecked out the key to the electronic remains of the deceased.

"You can leave us now," Hjelm said, unmoved. "But don't leave the office. We'll need to talk to you some more in a bit."

Chavez felt immediately at home in front of the monitor, but no exhibition of professionalism was forthcoming. He dug around a bit in the in- and outboxes and consulted "deleted messages" but found only empty pages.

"There's nothing left here," he said.

"OK." Hjelm waved to Bertilsson, who arrived like a dog that has been punished into loyalty.

"Why are all of Hassel's messages gone?" Hjelm asked.

Bertilsson, looking at the monitor rather than at Hjelm, shrugged. "He's probably deleted them."

"No one else has cleaned them out?"

"Not that I know of. Either the whole mailbox and all the addresses should be gone, or else they should still be there. And that *is* probably everything. Maybe he was in the habit of cleaning it all out — what do I know?"

"There are no short-cuts?" Hjelm asked Chavez. "And no chance of finding out who deleted them?"

"Not from here," said Chavez. "Network trashes are hard to manage."

Hjelm had to accept this remark without understanding, like a true believer. He turned to Bertilsson again.

"Who is your colleague Elisabeth B something? Is she still in the office?"

"Everyone is still here," Bertilsson said, in a tone of *Everyone is always still here.* Then he roused himself: "You're talking about Elisabeth Berntsson, I assume."

"Probably," said Hjelm. "Is she here now?"

"She was the one I was just talking to."

Hjelm glanced over towards the black-haired woman, who was typing like mad. "What was her relationship with Hassel like?"

Bertilsson cast a nervous glance around, one that ought to have triggered the curiosity of anyone who wasn't asleep. But no one reacted. Möller, sitting behind his glass doors, was staring out the window. He didn't appear to have moved an inch since Hjelm's previous visit.

"You'll have to ask her," Bertilsson said resolutely. "I've said more than enough."

They walked over to the writing woman, who looked up from her computer. "Elisabeth Berntsson?" Hjelm said. "We're with the police."

She peered at them over her glasses. "Your names?" she said in a slightly hoarse smoker's voice, clearly experienced at this.

"I'm Detective Inspector Paul Hjelm. This is Detective Inspector Jorge Chavez. From the National Criminal Police."

"Aha," she said, recognising their names from the headlines. "That means there's more behind Lars-Erik's death than we're allowed to know."

"Can we go somewhere a bit more private?"

She raised an eyebrow, stood and walked towards a glass door. They followed her into an empty office that was a carbon copy of Möller's.

"Have a seat." She sat down behind the desk.

They found a pair of chairs sticking up among the mess of papers and took a seat.

Hjelm jumped straight in. "Why did you call the maternity ward at Karolinska Hospital during the book fair in 1992 to inform the mother of Lars-Erik Hassel's newborn son that her husband was engaged in sexual relations in Gothenburg while her son was being born?"

Her jaw ought to have dropped, but it remained as steady as her gaze. "Well, what do you know, *in medias res*," she said, not missing a beat. "Very effective."

"It ought to have been," Hjelm replied. "But apparently you've been expecting the question."

"Because you two are who you are, I realised that you would have ferreted it out." Had she said it in another tone, they could have taken it as a compliment.

"What was it? Revenge?" Hjelm asked abruptly.

Elisabeth Berntsson took off her glasses, folded them up and placed them on the desk. "No," she said. "Drunkenness."

"Maybe as a catalyst. Hardly as a reason."

"Maybe, maybe not."

Hjelm switched tactics. "Why did you delete all of Hassel's emails?"

Chavez pointed out, "That wasn't very difficult to trace."

Hjelm gave him a look that he hoped would not be too easily interpreted as grateful.

Elisabeth Berntsson, however, seemed to have other things on her mind. An inner battle was being waged behind the naked concentration on her hardened face. Finally she said, "The sexual relations you were talking about took place primarily with me. Larsa needed something a bit more solid than that twenty-year-old. It was practically over already; all I did was hurry the process up a little. A catalyst," she said with a sardonic touch.

"And then? Was it the two of you forever and ever amen?"

Berntsson snorted. "Neither of us was particularly interested in forever and ever amen. I suppose we were both too scarred by the downsides of cohabitation. And had developed a taste for the alternative. One-night stands are really nothing to sneeze at. Me, I lead an active social life and want to be free to do what I want. And Larsa's tastes were probably more in the vein of . . . the younger age groups. For me, he was a decent lover and a more or less reliable part of my life. Like a TV show, maybe. Same time, same channel. And I do mean channel."

Hjelm made a quick decision. "Did he let you read the threatening emails?"

"I got tired of them. They were all different variations on the same theme. An almost unbelievable amount of persistence. A fixation. Someone had found a scapegoat he could lay all his life's frustrations on."

"He?"

"Everything suggested it was a man. Male language, if that makes sense."

**106**

"How many were there?"

"There were only scattered sprinklings of them for the first six months. During the past month, they accelerated into a veritable flash flood."

"So it's been going on for just over six months?"

"About that."

"How did Hassel react?"

"At first he was pretty shaken up. But when he realised that they seemed to be written mostly for therapeutic purposes, he became more thoughtful. As though he were pondering his past actions and what he was being punished for. But later, when they started to come more frequently, he got scared again and decided to fly the coop for a while. That's how the New York idea was born."

Hjelm didn't comment on the cost of this escape. Instead he said, "Can you describe the contents of the emails in greater detail?"

"Very explicit descriptions of how evil Larsa was and, above all, what would be done to his body. They said nothing about what wrong he had actually committed. That was what made him nervous, I think: that the source was so vague."

"Who do you think it was?"

She fingered her glasses, turning them at different angles on the desk. Then she finally said, "It must have been an author."

"Why?"

"You've read what Larsa wrote."

"How do you know that?"

"Möller told me. Which means you know that he didn't mince words about things he disliked. That was what made him stand out as a critic. That was how he built up his nationwide reputation. But when you do that, you hurt people. And sometimes when people are hurt, they never get back on their feet. Bad blood always comes back round."

Hjelm wondered at her strange final comment. Was she quoting someone?

"Did the sender write like an author?" he asked.

"A fallen author. Yes."

Hjelm usually didn't touch his cheek in public, but now he scratched his blemish absent-mindedly. A small flake of skin floated down towards his trouser leg. Elisabeth Berntsson watched it expressionlessly.

He gave Chavez a meaningful glance, then said, "So we're back where we started: why did you delete all of Hassel's emails?"

"I didn't."

Hjelm sighed and turned to Chavez. His partner had had enough time to fabricate a story, but Hjelm wasn't sure he was in on the plan; after all, they'd got a little rusty.

Chavez was in. "We arrived here at the editorial office at 15.37. At 15:40, Bertilsson asked you about Hassel's password. At 15.41, he entered it; it was wrong. He went back to you, and you came up with the correct password at 15.43. We got into Hassel's inbox at 15.44. By then everything had been deleted. I found the time stamp of the deletion: 15.42, two minutes after you had learned what we were doing and given us the wrong password."

Chavez had done his homework and had outdone his teacher by a mile: *if you're going to lie, lie in great detail*.

Elisabeth Berntsson stared deep down into her desk.

Hjelm leaned towards her. "If you weren't the one who wrote them, then why delete them? To salvage Larsa's reputation? Hardly. Where were you on the night between the second and third of September?"

"Not in Newark," she said quietly.

"Have you been going around hating him all these years? How did you have time to write all this hate mail? Did you do it during working hours?"

Elisabeth picked up her glasses, unfolded the earpieces, and settled them onto her distinguished nose. She closed her eyes for a moment, then opened them to meet Hjelm's. The gaze he saw was a completely new one.

"I suppose you could say I loved him. The hate mail was about to break me."

"So you hired a hit man to make the pain end?"

"Of course not."

"But he told you who he suspected was behind them, right? And you deleted everything to protect his murderer. Sort of strange behaviour towards the dear departed, isn't it?"

Now she looked determined, but not in a self-confident way; rather, she was determined not to speak at any price. She wasn't going to say anything more.

But she said enough: "It's private."

Then she broke down. It was unexpected for everyone present, including herself, but the repressed sadness came tumbling out in long, sweeping waves.

When they stood up, Hjelm realised he liked her. He would have liked to place a comforting arm around her, but he knew the comfort he was capable of offering wouldn't go very far. Her sorrow was much deeper than that.

They left her alone with her pain.

In the lift, Chavez said, "A pyrrhic victory — isn't that what it's called? Another victory like that, and I'm done for."

Hjelm was silent. He told himself he was planning his next step. In reality, he was crying.

*Bad blood always comes back round.*

In the taxi to Pilgatan, they didn't say much. "It's lucky she didn't check the times," said Chavez. "I was at least five minutes off."

"I don't think she was planning to let us leave without a confession," said Hjelm. Then he added, "You did an excellent job."

He didn't have to tell Chavez where they were going. On their way up the stairs of the stately building on Pilgatan, between Fridhemsplan and Kungsholmstorg, he said, "You remember the password, don't you?"

Chavez nodded. When they arrived at the top floor, Hjelm took out a set of keys and unlocked the three locks on the door marked "Hassel". They stepped into a gym; the entire enormous hall had been converted into an exercise room.

Apparently, in a previous life, Lars-Erik Hassel had been an alchemist on the hunt for the fountain of youth.

They walked past modern glass vases and ceramic pots and arrived at a computer on an antique desk in the middle of the living room.

Chavez turned it on and settled into the grandiose easy chair that functioned as a desk chair.

"Do you think he has a personal password?" Hjelm asked, leaning over the seated hacker.

"No, not at home," said Chavez. "If he does, we might have a problem."

Hassel did have one. The computer blinked out a scornful ENTER PASSWORD.

"I guess we'll try the same one." Chavez typed in the letters L-A-B-A-N.

The scornful blinking of the computer halted. They were in.

"Strange for a father and son to live so close to each other," Chavez said as the computer coughed to life.

Hjelm peeked out through the window towards the beautiful old council building, which seemed to shiver in the shadow of the clouds. If the window were placed at a slightly different angle, he could have looked straight up at Kungsklippan.

Autumn seemed to arrive in just an hour. Heavy clouds rolled up. Wind whined through the elegant gardens of the council building, tearing both green and gold leaves from the trees. A few raindrops spattered the windowpane.

While Chavez pecked at the keyboard, Hjelm explored Lars-Erik Hassel's apartment thoroughly. Not only was it a bourgeois turn-of-the-century flat, Hassel seemed to have wanted to return it to its original condition. In the living room, each detail seemed modelled on a Biedermeier aesthetic. He had a hard time associating this almost ironically exaggerated bourgeois taste with the critic who despised literature.

"Well, look at that," Chavez said after a while. "I don't even need to go into his trash. He has a folder called 'hate'."

"I thought he might." Hjelm came up to the computer. "Are the emails there?"

A gigantic list unfurled across the screen. At the bottom left corner it said "126 items", and the 126 files were numbered.

"Year, date, time," said Chavez. "Complete records."

"Look at the first one."

The message was short but to the point.

You evil bastard. Your body will be found in eight different places, all over Sweden, and no one will know that this head belongs with that leg; this arm with that cock. And they don't, either. See you. Don't look over your shoulder.

"Dated the end of January," said Chavez. "The most recent ones are from the twenty-fifth of August."

Hjelm nodded. "The same day Hassel went to the United States."

"He didn't save any after that, of course. If more emails showed up when Hassel was in the States — and it's probably pretty important to know whether this bully kept threatening him while he was gone — they disappeared when Elisabeth deleted them. If the author of the emails *is* the murderer, or hired the murderer, then he ought to have realised that this was the final threat."

"Let's look at it."

The writer's style had, without a doubt, evolved during the past months. The very last saved email read

You tried to change your email address again. There's no point. I can see you; I can always see you; I will always be able to see you. I know you're going to New York, you evil bastard. Do you think you're safe there? Do you think I can't reach you there? Death is on your heels. You will be found in every state, with your cock in deep freeze in Alaska and your bowels rotten with shit in the swamps of Florida. I will tear out your tongue and split open your vocal cords. No one will be able to hear you scream. What you have done can never be undone. I am watching over you. Enjoy the Metropolitan. I will be there, on the bench behind you. Don't look over your shoulder.

Hjelm and Chavez looked at each other and saw their own thoughts reflected back. New York, the Metropolitan: a striking knowledge of details. Still, such information was relatively easy to come by.

But splitting the vocal cords and "No one will be able to hear you scream" — things were heating up.

How had the writer known a week before it happened that Lars-Erik Hassel's vocal cords would be taken out of commission and that no one would be able to hear him scream?

"Didn't someone suspect that this had nothing to do with the Kentucky Killer?" Chavez said self-righteously.

"Go back a bit," Hjelm said. His focus had narrowed considerably.

A random selection of the 126-file-strong "hate" folder flew by:

You evil bastard. You are the most bourgeois of the bourgeois. Your repulsive remains will rot in small silver jars and then be distributed to your cast-off mistresses one by one, and they will be forced to masturbate with your deceased organ.

You tried to change your email address. Don't do that. There's no point. One day the source of all the excrement you produce will be exposed. Everyone will be able to see the defective digestive system of your rotten soul. Your intestines will be wound round the glass cock on Sergels Torg. All will be revealed. Those intestines held the only intellect you ever had. Never look over your shoulder.

I am going to slit the throat of your little son. His name is Conny, and he'll be six years old soon. I know where he lives. I have the code to their door. I know what school he goes to. I'm going to fuck his cut-open throat, and you will be called to identify your son, but because you've never seen your son, you won't recognise him. You will deny both head and body. It has happened before. Your whole cultural veneer will be exposed.

There are cracks in your rotten wall. At the moment of death you will see them. They will overwhelm you when I torture you to death.

They had read enough.

"Are there any disks here?" asked Hjelm.

Chavez nodded and saved the whole "hate" folder onto one of them.

"What do you say?" Hjelm asked.

"The choice of words seems familiar." Chavez put the disk into his pocket. "What would the scenario look like? Was he so personally familiar with the Kentucky Killer's habits that he could copy them perfectly? In that case, where did he get the information?"

"Wouldn't your Fans of American Serial Killers have it? And he seems to be familiar with computers."

"So he found out exactly when Hassel's trip back to Sweden was booked and waited for him at the Newark airport? The rest was a coincidence?"

"Or the opposite: he planned it in great detail. Strictly speaking, Edwin Reynolds could have been Laban Jeremias Hassel."

Chavez was quiet for a moment, sorting through his impressions. Then he summed it up: "He arrives at Newark from Sweden on an earlier flight, waits an hour or so at the airport, strikes, and comes back with a false passport. It's entirely possible. Although he might just as easily have hired a professional."

They considered this scenario.

"Shall we go?" Hjelm asked at last.

Chavez nodded.

They passed through the deserted neighbourhood via Hantverkargatan and cut diagonally across Kungsholmstorg and up Pipersgatan; it was like coming full circle. Or tying up a sack. The rain whipped at them sideways.

They reached the stairs, climbed up to Kungsklippan and went into the building. Outside the apartment door, Chavez took out his pistol and said, "She may have warned him."

Hjelm drew his service weapon too and rang the bell.

Laban Hassel opened the door right away. He stared expressionlessly into the barrels of the pistols and said quietly, "Don't make fools of yourselves."

Their scenario collapsed like a house of cards. Laban Hassel was either extremely cunning or completely harmless.

They followed him into the darkness; the blinds were down again, and the computer screen emitted its listless light. Chavez raised the blinds again; this time there was no sun to stun them. Laban hardly blinked as the pale light filtered into his eyes — it was as though he were beyond all earthly reactions.

He took a seat at the rotten table. Everything was familiar, yet everything had changed. The two police

**116**

remained standing and kept their service weapons up. Laban let himself be frisked without protest.

"Elisabeth Berntsson from the newspaper called," he said calmly. "She thought I should run away."

" 'Don't look over your shoulder,' " Hjelm quoted as he took a seat and put his pistol into his holster.

Laban Hassel gave a crooked smile. "Eloquent, isn't it?"

"Did you kill him?" Hjelm asked.

Laban raised his eyes, stared intensely into Hjelm's, and said, "That is a very, very good question."

"Is there a very, very good answer?"

But Laban said no more. He just looked fixedly at the table and kept his mouth shut.

Hjelm tried again. "What happened in January?"

Absolute silence.

Another attempt: "We know that you registered at the university three years ago but didn't complete a single course. Perhaps you were able to cheat your way into student loans for a while. But for the next two years — what did you live on then?"

"CSU," said Laban Hassel. "Cash Support for Unemployment, I think it means. Then it ran out."

"In January this year," said Hjelm.

Hassel looked at him. "Do you know how demeaning it is to apply for welfare? Do you know what it's like to be openly distrusted and then meticulously investigated? Do you know what it feels like when they find out that your father is too well known and well-to-do for you to qualify for welfare? It's not enough that he's been

**117**

hanging over me like a repressive shadow all my life —
now because of him, I can't even get money to survive."

"That added to your hatred."

"The first threat was spontaneous. I just vented on
the computer. Then I realised that I could send my
outburst as an email. Then it became an *idée fixe*."

"Why did you threaten your half-brother Conny?"

The look on Laban Hassel's face could not be
described as anything other than self-loathing. "That's
the only thing I regret."

"Cut the throat of a six-year-old and fuck the severed
throat?"

"Please stop. I wasn't threatening the boy, only my
father."

"Have you met Conny?"

"I see him now and then. We're friends. His mother,
Ingela, seems to like me. We're almost the same age. Do
you know when I saw her for the first time?"

"No."

"I was probably about fourteen, fifteen. I was out
walking with my mum along Hamngatan. And as if it
weren't bad enough to be out walking with your mum
at that age, we caught sight of my father on the other
side of the street. With Ingela. He saw us, but far from
being embarrassed by the seventeen-year-old at his
side, he started crudely making out with her in the
middle of the street. Mum and I got a private show."

"Was that before the divorce?"

"Yes. Sure, all our relationships were hellish at home,
but from the outside we still looked like a family. That
day ripped the veil from the illusion."

"Hellish in what way?"

"People seem to think that it's much worse for children if the parents argue rather than shutting up and pretending to be friends. But that's the worst kind of hypocrisy, because children can always see through it. Our house was dominated by an icy silence. Hell isn't warm, it's cold. Absolute zero. I went frostbitten through the polar landscape of my childhood. And besides that, he could go missing at any time: football matches he promised to come to but never showed up at, always the same thing. And then he'd come home only to freeze the whole fucking apartment."

"You have literary talent," said Hjelm, "I can hear that. Why waste it on hate letters to your dad?"

"I think it was an exorcism," Laban said thoughtfully. "I had to get that bastard out of my blood. That cold bastard. But I might as well have chosen not to send that shit to him."

"It could have been a novel."

Laban looked into Hjelm's eyes and blinked intensely. Perhaps some sort of connection was forming between them.

"Maybe," he said. "On the other hand, I wanted to see how he'd react. I wanted to see if I could notice anything in him when we met. Maybe I also had some sort of vain hope that he would confide in his son. If he had hinted that he was being threatened even once, I would have stopped right away, I'm sure of that. But nothing. He showed no trace. He spouted the same old, tired jargon every time we met. I don't even think he ever considered that the evil that the letters accused him of committing had to do with his role as a father."

"I'm not so sure of that," said Chavez from over by the window. "Do you know what the password on his computer was?"

Laban Hassel looked over his shoulder.

"Laban," said Chavez. "L-A-B-A-N."

"Why do you think Elisabeth Berntsson called you?" Hjelm asked. "She was prepared to take the blame herself in order to keep you out of it. Why do you think she suspected you?"

"Why do you think your father saved all your emails in a folder called 'hate'?" Chavez asked. "Every single file we looked at had been accessed at least ten times."

"*You* were waiting for *him* to take the first step," said Hjelm. "And *he* was waiting for *you* to."

Laban seemed to disappear into himself again, but they didn't let him go completely. "What happened a month ago?" Hjelm asked. "Why did you suddenly start firing off more emails?"

Laban slowly raised his eyes; it seemed like an enormous, purely physical effort. His gaze fastened on Hjelm.

"That was when I got close to Ingela. She told me about Conny, about his birth, that he had never even wanted to see him."

"'Got close to'? How close?"

"I decided to murder him for real."

Hjelm and Chavez held perfectly still. Hjelm tried to formulate the right question, which ended up being "You started piling on threatening emails with the intent of murdering him?"

"Yes."

"And in the last one, you let him know that you knew about his New York plans and that you were going to kill him in a way that would make it impossible for him to scream out his pain? Do you know how he died?"

"He was murdered."

"But the details?"

"No."

"He was tortured to death, and his vocal cords were cut so that no one could hear him scream. When did you go to New York?"

"I haven't —"

"When? Were you there waiting for him, or did you arrive just as the plane was about to take off?"

"I —"

"How did you learn about the Kentucky Killer's MO?"

"Where did you get the Edwin Reynolds passport?"

"How did you sneak past the police at Arlanda?"

Laban Hassel gaped into the crossfire.

Hjelm leaned forward and said emphatically, "Where were you on the night of the second and third of September?"

"In hell," Laban Hassel said almost inaudibly.

"Then you must have run into your father there," said Chavez. "I don't think any living person could come closer to hell than he was right then."

In the dramaturgy of investigative techniques, Laban should, at this point, either have broken down or clammed up. What happened was something in between. His lips hardly moving, he said to the table flatly, "I can't understand it. I had almost made up my mind to take that step, and then he died. Then someone else murdered him. It was completely crazy. Or rather completely logical. Divine justice. A desire so strong that it materialised. It couldn't be a coincidence; it had to be fate, a fate as grotesque as life itself. A message from above. And only now, now that nothing can be taken back, do I realise that I never would have killed him. And that I didn't even want to. On the contrary, I only wanted to punish him. I wanted to talk to him. I wanted to get him to show some tiny trace of remorse."

The room was quiet for a moment. Then Hjelm repeated, "Where were you on the night between the second and third of September?"

"I was in Skärmarbrink," Laban whispered, "at Ingela and Conny's place."

And Chavez repeated: "What happened a month ago? How close to Ingela did you get?"

"Very close," said Laban calmly. "Too close. It's not enough that I slept with my brother's mother, not enough that she slept with the son of her son's detested father, and that these insights slugged us hard in the face. We were also confronted with something we had in common, something horrible with the same root cause, and that was what caused me to make my decision. That was what made me send more and more letters. By then it was mutual."

"And what was it that you had in common?"

Laban Hassel bent his neck way back and stared up at the ceiling. "We had both been sterilised."

Hjelm looked at Chavez.

Chavez looked at Hjelm.

"Why?" they said in unison.

Laban got up, walked to the window and opened it.

Dusk had fallen. Rain clouds swept across the city, borrowing a bit of street light now and then. A gust of autumn blew through Laban's hair and into the musty room.

"Bad blood always comes back round," said Laban Hassel.

# CHAPTER
# TEN

It's time.

He's on his way.

Now it will begin.

He moves silently through the empty cottage. The bag is resting over his shoulder. It rattles slightly in the dark.

He stops at the window next to the front door. He hears a weak, drawn-out, hollow cry as the autumn winds whine through the round hole next to the lock.

He raises his eyes from the hole in the pane of glass and takes in the night's autumn storm, which heaves great sheets of rain across the pitch-black landscape. When he steps out onto the porch and the rain whips his cheeks, it is another wind he feels.

It is dry, dry as a desert. It sweeps down from Cumberland Plateau and whistles through the ice-cold house.

Through the night, he sees the shadow in the closet as a darker darkness. He follows it.

He wanders through the rain. It doesn't exist. All that exists is a target. A darker darkness.

He gets into the beige Saab and drives away. The roads are more like paths. He carefully avoids the flood-like rivulets and balances on the banks of the river until the first lights of civilisation colour the bands of rain, and he discovers the stairs behind the secret door that catches the arm of a jacket. He takes the first step, and the next. The lights disappear; the dusty-sweet scent comes, the same one that is thick in the car that is just turning out onto the big road. Occasional headlights sweep by. The illuminated facades of buildings take shape around him. There are nuances to the darkness now: he can not only *feel* the ice-cold, damp handrail; he can *see* it too, see it as a hazy band hurtling down towards the abyss in an endless, snake-like copycat of the stairs, which crunch with sand; and the skyscraper towers, strangely alone, at the entrance to the city. He sees it, a bit to the right, and drives along the street with the green swath in the middle. He doesn't know its name, just knows the street, knows the number of steps, the exact number of steps down to the light-framed door that he can almost see now, a tiny glimmer at the very bottom. He knows exactly where each correct movement ought to happen, and then he turns round the stadium with the old clock tower, and he's very close. Forest again; he is balancing at the edge of civilisation: complexes of buildings on one side, forest on the other, a nocturnal jungle that he drags himself through until the contours of the door are visible. Like an icon frame around a darkness that's brighter than any light, the light shoots out from behind the door. A halo that shows him the way.

He enters to the right. Dimly lit contours of ships give faint illumination to the rows of empty offices and warehouses. Otherwise, nothing.

He stops the car in an empty car park and walks with even, distinct steps down to the water. The rain is flung from side to side; it can't get to him. Now he can tell it's a door; the light is coming from inside it. Not a sound can be heard. A few steps left. Something makes a clinking sound behind him. The key clinks softly in the lock. He turns it, pulls open the heavy door, closes it behind him and opens the bag. He places a hand towel on the floor just inside the door and stands there dripping. Then he changes shoes, puts the wet towel and the wet shoes back in the bag, takes out a torch, and climbs down the stairs, the back point of a solitary cone of light. He stops in front of the door with the glittering halo swarming around it. He stands there. He can't breathe.

He lets his torch sweep through the cellar. Nothing has changed. The junk in one corner, the collection of carefully stacked boxes in the other and the empty surface a bit further away; the always well-scrubbed cement floor with the drain and the heavy cast-iron chair. He pushes his way behind the furthest row of boxes, sits down with his back against the cold stone wall, turns off his torch, and waits.

He loses contact with time. Minutes pass — or seconds, or hours. His eyes adjust to the darkness. The image of the humid cellar develops slowly. The door appears clearly, above the stairs, about ten yards away. His eyes do not leave it.

Time passes. Everything is quiet. He waits.

Then a key is pushed into the lock. Two men step in, one older and one younger. He can't make out their features. They converse quietly but intensely in a foreign language as they walk down the stairs.

Suddenly something happens. It goes so quickly. The older man presses something against the throat of the younger one. He immediately loses consciousness. The older man drags him over to the heavy cast-iron chair, takes a number of leather straps out of a case, and binds the man's legs, arms and body. Then he bends down to the case again.

That is when he opens the door and everything is revealed. The light streams out. He steps into the Millennium.

The older man lifts a large syringe out of the case and, with an experienced hand, guides it into the unconscious man's throat from the side. He adjusts a few small knobs on the upper part of the mechanism.

He gives a start behind his boxes; he is close to knocking them over.

Then the older man lines up a series of surgical instruments on the cement floor, in careful order. Furthest to the right is another large syringe-like gadget.

Finally he pats the unconscious man on the cheeks, harder and harder until he starts to shake. His head is stabilised. Intense jerks course through the restrained body, but the chair remains completely still. There is not a sound to be heard.

The older man says a few toneless words and bends down towards the second syringe. When he leans to the side to inject it in exactly the right spot, a faint light comes in from an unknown source and illuminates his face. For one second, it is completely clear.

That is when he truly gives a start. A box falls.

The older man stands stock-still. He places the syringe on the floor and starts to move. He's approaching fast.

It's time, he thinks, and steps out of his hiding place.

# CHAPTER
# ELEVEN

The minibus imitated the gliding flight of a bat through the rainy night. Its night vision was turned on; its perception of space was perfect.

Although maybe bats don't glide.

And was it really night vision they had?

He wished he hadn't had that last whisky.

"Where the hell are we?"

"Damn, Matte broke down up there."

"Fuck, isn't that the leaning tower? Did you drive us to Spain, you bastard?"

"Italy! Italy! I long for Italy, the lovely beaches of Italy . . ."

"Shut up!"

"It's the gas tower — the only thing that's leaning is your head."

"The leaning brain of Skarpnäck."

"The leaning minibus of Frihamnen. What curve-taking skills!"

"Where the fuck are you going? Matte!"

He looked over his shoulder.

It was an awful mess back there. It would take the whole morning to clean up after them. The bottles were mixed up with their bandy sticks, and the hazy figures seemed to be throwing themselves on top of each other in a cluster of snakes.

"Gärdet," he said. "You live there, Steffe. As you may recall."

"But you drove *around* all of fucking Gärdet! We shouldn't have let you drive."

"Says the man who blew the driving test six times."

"Come on, try to go the right way. I know you're from Nynäshamn, but you must have been to Stockholm once or twice."

"Or heard of it."

"The king lives there. Maybe that'll help."

"Does he really live in the palace? Or is it Drottningholm? Trick question."

"What the hell? Are you going to send him fan mail?"

" 'Dear King, can you send a lock of Victoria's pubic hair to a pining bachelor with roots in the working class of Säffle?' "

"Take a right. A right, you moron!"

"Dumbass!"

He got tired of it all and turned left out of pure spite. A general bellow spread through the minibus.

"Psycho!"

"Dipshit!"

"Idiot!"

The minibus glided on along a little dark road that split into four; he randomly chose one of them, and it seemed like the bus might be stopped at any second by a sudden iron fence and a severe Latino border guard with a cigar in the corner of his mouth.

That didn't happen. Instead, he could see a Volvo station wagon fifty yards away. Fumes were rising from its exhaust pipe. The car was blocking the road.

He braked until they were almost standing still. They were thirty yards from the car when he saw a man next to it. His head was covered by a balaclava. He shoved something into the back of the car, threw himself round the side and roared away with shrieking tyres. When the smoke settled, Matte noticed something lying on the ground. A large package with alarming contours.

Three of the guys who were somewhat sober leaned forward, above him.

"What the fuck was that?"

"A burglary?"

"Fucking hell! What have you got us into, Matte? Let's split."

He let the bus slowly glide up to the blanket-wrapped package. The headlights made the rain come alive. It whipped at the blanket.

He stopped the bus and went out into the storm. They followed him. He bent down and started to unwrap the blanket.

A face stared up at him. Chalk-white, with surprising facial features under the ruptured eyes. The rain beat against the eyeballs. The eyelids made no effort to avoid the drops.

They recoiled and stared silently at the white face that stuck out of the dripping blanket, shining through the night.

"Shit!" someone whispered.

"Let's split," someone else whispered.

"We can't just leave him," he said.

Someone grabbed the lapels of his jacket and brought his face close. "Yes. We can. Do you hear me, Matte? This has nothing to do with us."

"You've been drinking," someone else said soberly. "Think of the consequences."

They went back to the minibus. The mood was different now.

He remained standing there for a moment, observing the corpse with reluctant fascination. It was the first time Matte had seen a dead person.

He returned to the driver's seat. The bus was dripping with rain that would eat its way into the upholstery and make it mould. But that was the furthest thing from his mind as he turned the key in the ignition.

# CHAPTER
# TWELVE

Gunnar Nyberg lived in a three-room apartment in Nacka, just one street away from the church where he would much rather be, singing loudly. When his bed had collapsed a few nights ago, he saw it as an omen. He awoke with two microscopic pincers driven into his throat. They grasped his vocal cords; he would never be able to sing again. It took a long time to get them out — not out of his throat but his head. He lay there among the wreckage of his bed and let the pincers fade away. Sharp, broken planks were sticking up around him. It slowly dawned on him how lucky he'd been. He started to laugh. It was several minutes before he was able to stop.

His near-accident resulted in two concrete actions. For one, he started a diet. It was hardly the right time, with the Kentucky Killer running riot outside his window, but his need for it had become more and more acute, and the collapse of his bed was the last straw. For another, he bought a new bed, specially designed for overweight sleepers; it was looking the truth in the eye, he thought, pulling himself together.

In this specially designed bed for the overweight, a classic bachelor dream about intensely horny young women was interrupted by a horrible ringtone. It had been a long time since he had received a night-time phone call, and it took a long time for him to realise what it was. At first he thought it was, strangely enough, his ex-wife. Had something happened to Gunilla? When he heard a police voice echo through the receiver, it struck him that he was probably the last person who would be contacted in that case.

"Is anyone there?" the police voice said for a second time.

Nyberg got some life into his voice, which he thought sounded like a threshing machine: "Nyberg here."

"This is the Stockholm police," said the voice. "We have standing orders that so-called 'suspicious deaths' must be reported directly to you. Is that correct?"

"I don't really know what it means, but that's correct, yes."

"We have a murder in Frihamnen that can probably be classified as such."

Nyberg's reaction was immediate. "Does the victim have two holes in his neck?"

"Are you awake?" the police voice said suspiciously. "Vampires belong in dreams."

"Just answer the question."

"I don't know," the voice said tersely.

Nyberg obtained directions, hung up, shook some life into himself, pulled on his customary sloppy clothes, got his apartment key and car key, dashed — he thought — down the stairs, and drove off in his old Renault.

He had the rain-whipped streets to himself. He tried to think about the Kentucky Killer; about the little pincers that, with one simple motion, could rob a person of her most unique outward feature, her voice; and about the series of similar American influences, but it didn't really work. His awakening had forced onto him the thing he was trying to repress most of all.

During the early 1970s, Gunnar Nyberg had been Mr Sweden, an internationally recognised bodybuilder; he was also on active duty with the Norrmalm police and had a certain amount of contact with what would later be called the Baseball League, the most ruthless cops in the history of the Swedish police. But by then he had already moved to Nacka and shelved the steroids. And lost his family.

He had been a truly rotten bastard. When he thought of it, he always had to close his eyes, which actually worked very well out on the empty Värmdöleden.

Everything poured through him when he closed his eyes for just a second . . . all the abuse, all the patience he'd lost before anything even happened, all those steroid attacks of extreme rage.

About a year ago he'd started speaking in schools pretty regularly. He was an early victim of the side effects of anabolic steroids, and in his work he saw each day how their abuse was increasing out on the streets; he could sniff out a steroid user immediately. His pastor had asked if he might consider helping out, and with great reluctance he had gone to the first school and spoken. But they listened; even though most of his muscle mass had gone to the fat that broke his bed, he was still an impressive figure. He kept a low profile and showed frightening pictures while talking in a matter-of-fact voice, and possibly someone somewhere had abstained from using steroids thanks to him.

But the veil of penance was thin. Behind his eyelids came what he knew would come — it always did. The last time he abused his wife, he split — no, burst — Gunilla's eyebrow, and her frightened look, and the frightened looks from Tommy and Tanja, settled in his brain forever. He knew that those memories still existed. The family had moved to Uddevalla to get as far away from him as possible. He hadn't seen them for over fifteen years, not once. If he had run into his children on the street, he wouldn't have recognised them. His life had closed up around a giant void.

He had to stop the car.

*I sing for you!* he shouted without making a sound, as though pincers were clamping his vocal cords. *Don't you realise I sing for you?!*

But no one heard him, no one in the world.

He drove slowly out onto Värmdöleden again, rounded the long curve at Danviksklippan, and crossed the Danvikstull bridge in the pounding, smacking, striking rain.

Then he was there. He didn't know how it had happened; it was as if the last few miles were gone, blown into the great void.

When he'd gone some way into the port warehouse district, he saw the familiar blue lights rise, sweeping through the rain clouds. He followed their signal, drove slowly in on the narrow roads, and stopped the car at the blue-and-white stripes of the police tape.

There were three police cars there, and one ambulance. And Jan-Olov Hultin.

He was standing under an umbrella in the middle of the soaking-wet collection of police officers, and even in this weather and this situation, he was managing to look through a bunch of papers.

Nyberg sneaked in under his umbrella, but three-quarters of his body didn't fit. "What have we got?" he said.

Hultin looked at him neutrally over his owlish glasses. "See for yourself."

"Holes in his neck?"

Hultin shook his head.

Nyberg sighed heavily. He walked over to a bundle of blankets in the middle of the narrow road. A white face with dead eyes looked up at the black-as-night skies. The rain struck the irises relentlessly.

Nyberg bent down and took mercy. He closed the eyelids and, crouching, studied the body.

It was a man of about twenty-five. A young man.

It could have been Tommy, he thought.

Then he shuddered. Maybe it *was* his son. There was no chance he would recognise him.

Nyberg shook his uneasiness away, a giant bulldog in the pouring rain.

He looked at the exposed throat. No marks. But right where his heart would be, in a perfect pattern, were four bullet holes. Very little blood had run out. Death must have been instantaneous.

Groaning, he pulled up his heavy body and returned to Hultin, whose papers were still dry under the umbrella.

"Does this really have anything to do with us?" Nyberg asked.

Hultin shrugged. "It's the most promising thing so far. There are certain details."

Nyberg waited for him to continue. There was no point in trying to get under Hultin's umbrella; the last dry spot on his own body had disappeared.

"At three twelve a security guard from the company LinkCoop called the police and reported a break-in on their premises. By then the police were already on their way. Because just before that, at three oh seven, emergency dispatch got a call from an anonymous man in a telephone booth at Stureplan. Want to hear?"

Nyberg nodded.

Hultin bent down into one of the police cars and popped a cassette into the stereo. At first there was a crackling sound. Then an agitated male voice: "The police, please."

Then silence and crackling again and a woman: "Police."

"There's a corpse in Frihamnen," the excited voice hissed.

"Where, exactly?"

"I don't know the name of the road. A narrow road, some way in, near the water. He's in the middle of the road. You can't miss him."

"What is your name, and where are you calling from?"

138

"Forget that. A guy in a balaclava was shoving a similar bundle into a car. We surprised him. He drove away really fucking fast."

"Make of car, number plate?"

Then just the crackling sound and then silence.

Hultin popped out the tape and put it back in his inner pocket.

"And that was all?" said Nyberg.

Hultin nodded. "It could be a double murder. And the balaclava might indicate a certain amount of professionalism."

"That's still quite far from our man," said Nyberg. "Is the security guard here?"

Hultin nodded and gestured. They pushed their way through the throng of police. The ambulance crew moved the corpse up onto a stretcher; out of the corner of his eye, Nyberg could see that it was as stiff as a board.

They made their way round a few rows of buildings and arrived at a sentry box in front of a row of warehouses that belonged to LinkCoop; an almost bizarre logo was blinking spiritedly, in four colours, above the entrance, in glaring contrast with the faint light that floated out through the rain from the sentry box.

They stepped into the microscopic sentry box, dripping water. A uniformed guard was having coffee with three police officers, also in uniform.

"My, what a well-guarded guard," said Nyberg.

"Out in the rain," said Hultin neutrally.

The three officers went off with their tails between their legs.

The guard rose quickly and stood to attention. He was a young man, apparently in his twenties, with a nearly shaved skull and genuinely pumped-up muscles. The scent of steroids struck Nyberg's very sensitive olfactory organ with force. As the guard stood there at attention, he recognised the type: a commando or ranger background, solid training in the hierarchy, substantial use of steroids, possibly a few rejected applications for officer and police training, a not entirely tolerant attitude towards immigrants, homosexuals, people on welfare, smokers, civilians, women, children, people . . .

Gunnar Nyberg had to be careful not to throw stereotypes around as heartily as his imagined stereotype did.

The guard presumably spent his nights here, along with an extensive selection of men's magazines, Nyberg thought, sinking deeper into the swamp of stereotypes. He would have liked nothing better than to glimpse a CD of Schnittke's *Requiem* and the magazine *Modern Art Forum* in the quickly closed desk drawer; unfortunately, what swept by under the experienced hands of the guard was the porn mag *Aktuell Rapport*.

Hultin paged through his bone-dry papers. "Benny Lundberg?"

"Present," Benny Lundberg said distinctly.

"Sit down."

The guard followed orders and took his place at his worn desk in front of eight television monitors, all of

**140**

which displayed the pitch-black interiors of warehouses. Hultin and Nyberg pulled up stools, already warmed by police backsides, and sat. The rain beat on the little booth intensely.

"What happened?" Hultin asked curtly.

"I was going on my usual three o'clock rounds, located a door on one of our warehouses that had been broken into, went in, found the warehouse in disarray and called the police."

"End of story," said Nyberg.

"Yes," said Lundberg seriously.

"Was anything stolen?" Hultin asked.

"I can't answer that. But boxes were lying all over the place."

"What kind of boxes?" Nyberg asked without much interest.

"Computer equipment. LinkCoop is an import-export company in the computer industry." Lundberg sounded like he was reciting something he'd memorised.

"Shall we look at the warehouse?" Hultin said with about the same amount of interest as Nyberg.

The guard led them through the rain towards the LinkCoop buildings. They took a left at the entrance with the absurdly blinking logo and approached one of many doors on a loading dock alongside the building. The blue-and-white plastic police tape was already in place.

They looked for stairs but found none nearby, so they had to heave themselves up; it took some time. Inside the forced door were the same three police officers who had recently been having coffee in the sentry box. Perhaps they should have expected that their superiors might be on their way.

"You sure don't like rain, boys," Nyberg observed, surveying the building. It was a classic warehouse; boxes of various dimensions were stacked on well-marked shelves. Many of them were on the floor now. Computer equipment peeked out of some of them, a bit jumbled. Very little seemed to have been stolen.

"Maybe they had other things to do," Nyberg said aloud.

Hultin gave him a quick but expressionless glance and turned to Benny Lundberg. "Is this exactly how it was when you came in?"

Lundberg nodded and cast a furtive glance at the three unfortunate fellows, who were still standing inside the door, at a loss since no orders had been forthcoming.

Hultin and Nyberg dutifully poked around the large warehouse, then thanked Lundberg and went back out into the autumn night.

"Two unrelated incidents?" said Nyberg.

"Hardly," said Hultin.

"A dispute between burglars about the division of loot?"

"Hardly," Hultin said, with little variation.

"At three oh seven our anonymous tipster calls about the body. Five minutes later, the steroid stereotype Benny calls about the break-in. The time is now four oh six and ten seconds, beep. Where's the connection?"

"You'll have to talk to LinkCoop tomorrow."

"Today," Nyberg corrected him, wondering whether there was any point in going home and sleeping for two hours.

"You look like you need those two hours," said Hultin telepathically.

He himself appeared to be thoroughly need-free as he made his way dry-footed through the rain towards his Volvo Turbo.

# CHAPTER
# THIRTEEN

To claim that progress had been made would certainly have been a lie — and yet something had changed during the night. The atmosphere in "Supreme Central Command" had been, if not transformed, at least upgraded.

Arto Söderstedt had taken the liberty of using an official car to transport his five children to various nurseries and schools; nowhere would the extra miles around Södermalm be reported. Paul Hjelm still hadn't signed out an official car but took the Metro from Norsborg, undisturbed by the rush-hour traffic, and listened to music for as long as possible.

Jorge Chavez, however, got stuck in the traffic from his bachelor's studio in Rågsved, where he had returned after having rented a room in town. Every morning he found himself experiencing the same infantile surprise at the extent of the traffic; it was as though cars were becoming more and more central to people's lives, as though the distinct metal borders were replacing the increasingly diffuse borders of self-identity. Every morning he promised himself he'd leave his old BMW home the next day; every morning he broke his promise. It was like an ineffective magic spell.

Gunnar Nyberg had gone home; he lay down with his clothes on in his bed for the overweight, slept like a clubbed seal — and woke two hours later like a completely *pulped* seal. He felt as though an aggressive Norwegian had lost his head during seal clubbing and kept going until all that was left was a nine-foot-square steak tartare. He finally ceased fantasising about his similarities to small, cute, white, threatened baby seals, joined the line of cars on Värmdöleden along with all the other sourpusses, and decided that his right to be a sourpuss was superior to that of his fellow drivers.

Viggo Norlander had defied the long working hours and gone to King Creole for a last-chance pickup at three in the morning. It had worked, but somewhere inside himself he began to realise the advisability of getting to know the lady in question a little bit before the act was allowed to commence. The fact was, tonight's lady turned out to have had the sole goal of becoming pregnant; immediately after the fait accompli she pulled on her clothes and rushed through the door fertilised and happy and spitting in the face of menopause, leaving behind a detective inspector who felt as if he had lost his mind. It took him half an hour to find it. On the morning bus from Östermalm, he fell into a trance-like fantasy about an unknown, successful son who tracks down an old bachelor cop father at the nursing home.

Kerstin Holm moved in mysterious ways from her new two-room apartment somewhere in Vasastan; possibly burned by a few collapsed relationships with colleagues, she kept a distance between her private life and her work life. But that was nothing compared to Jan-Olov Hultin, the man without a private life. Rumour had it that he lived with a wife and without an empty nest in a villa somewhere north of the city and that he played intercompany football with startling brutality in the Stockholm Police Veterans team, but it was impossible to find out more than that. He *was* his job. He was like a god — pure presence, pure action — or like a father figure viewed through the eternally selective eyes of a five-year-old.

Sure enough, by the time they all arrived at "Supreme Central Command" from these various directions and experiences, each sensing the heightened atmosphere, he was already there.

The rain continued its ravages outside. At least, since rain always had a certain dampening effect on crime, fewer false leads would be scattered about.

The item they discussed by way of opening the meeting was the false lead of Laban Hassel. Hjelm and Chavez's quick summary filtered out the unfathomable tragedy: a father-fixated son threatens the absent father to get attention, then turns to his half-brother's mother in a half-incestuous relationship, where they both discover they've taken their ability to procreate out of the game because of the father, who is murdered in almost the same way that the threats had described.

It sounded like the synopsis of a soap opera that they were pitching to the director of programming at a commercial television channel. The director of programming replied with an awful tone of rejection: "And he didn't do it?"

**146**

"No," they said in unison.

Hjelm added, "But we'll keep that door open."

"OK. Gunnar?"

Sullenly and laconically, Gunnar Nyberg recounted the night's events in Frihamnen.

When he was finished, Söderstedt said, disenchanted, "It sounds about as promising as the flasher in Tantolunden." Targeted by their stares, he elucidated, "The one who got beaten up by the women's football team."

"In any case, we'll keep that door open as well," Hultin said.

Despite the rather worthless reports and the lack of responses, the atmosphere remained heightened. Somewhere in what had been said lay the potential for more.

"Who was he?" said Chavez. "The body in Frihamnen?"

"Unidentified," said Hultin. "The fingerprints didn't tell us anything. A classic John Doe, as the Americans like to call their unidentified bodies. About twenty-five, medium-blond, nothing more. The autopsy didn't tell us anything. Four shots to the heart can probably be considered reason enough to die. Otherwise he was hale and hearty."

"Hale and hearty, he lay on the autopsy table," Söderstedt said indifferently, counting on being ignored, as he was.

"We're looking around Frihamnen for any vehicle he might have left behind," Hultin continued. "Gunnar will go to the company, LinkCoop, to discuss the break-in. We'll send the fingerprints to Interpol for examination, and some people whose next of kin are missing will come to look at the body. Viggo can go to the pathologist and get a statement. Otherwise we'll keep on with what we were doing before."

What they were doing before was, in practice, waiting. Considering the circumstances, it was surprising that all of them left with renewed hope. No one could explain it as anything other than an *intuition*, and intuition was really the only thing they had in common; it had been the decisive characteristic when, once upon a time, Hultin had handpicked them.

Even Viggo Norlander, whose task could once again be seen as suitable for a dunce, felt uplifted — which couldn't be explained by his lingering conviction that his genes were, at this very moment, being perpetuated. Sure, he was being forced to spend the rest of the day with more or less desperate next of kin who would probably never find their loved ones, but even he was sucked into the slightly indefinable sphere of hope.

He stopped by his office to retrieve his trendy but slightly dirty-old-mannish leather jacket. Up until the Russian mafia had nailed him to the floor in Tallinn, he had always worn a pretty respectable civil-servant suit at work, and he had in general been a respectable police officer with faith in the system, the hierarchy of command and the social order. He had been brought up in a different world from the one he was part of now; this fact had become more and more obvious during the Power Murders, and it was that insight that had led him to take the desperate measure of setting

**148**

aside all the order he'd had so much faith in and going alone to Estonia to solve the case. The stigmatisation he had suffered there would never leave his extremities. The robust strikes of the hammer had emphatically ended the era of faith in his life. Never again would he trust anyone other than himself. And never again would he really trust himself. Instead he took refuge in sex, which had never seriously interested him; his pot belly, his bald spot and his civil-servant suit all disappeared. He changed to polo shirts and the leather jacket he'd just fetched from the office.

His office mate, his former adversary Arto Söderstedt, had sat down at the computer, but his gaze was far off in the nasty autumn weather. They were good friends these days, not least because they hadn't the slightest thing in common and thought that excellent grounds for friendship. A little affirmative nod was enough, as Norlander picked up his leather jacket. He then made his way through the corridors and down to the garage under the police station, where his service Volvo was parked. He got behind the wheel and came out onto Bergsgatan, which closely resembled the Torne River just after the ice has melted. An autumn flood was streaming down towards Scheelegatan, but Norlander fought his way upstream towards Fridhemsplan so he could continue on towards Karolinska Hospital.

In the not-too-distant future, he would turn fifty. Nearly thirty years ago, he had been married for a few incredibly misery-tinged years; since then all relations with the opposite sex had lain fallow, only to bloom now, in a fifty-year-old's crisis of uncritical one-night stands. Up until the night before, he had attributed it to repressed horniness; now he began to suspect that he was hearing the ticking of his biological clock. An endless line of forefathers extended back in time from him to Adam himself, and each of them was tapping on his successor's shoulder, and the tapping was magnified into a demanding, biological tick-tock-tick-tock, and the line of men lifted their thunderous voices in unison and said, "Do not let it stop here. Do not break the line of descent. Do not be the last one." And if he hadn't even come close to thinking about being a father, not once, it was now the only thought that prevailed: he *would* become a father, he *wanted* to become a father, he *had* to become a father. And all because of that strange woman, almost his own age, who had swept into his bachelor pad on Banérgatan like a spring breeze, allowed herself to be fertilised, and disappeared out into the autumn storm. It had all happened in fifteen minutes. Now she was carrying his life inside her. About that, he was sure. The more he thought of it, the more certain he became that he had seen it in her even then.

The arrangement was ideal. His genes would live on, the line of men would cease tapping his shoulder — and he wouldn't even have to take part in the difficulties of fatherhood. At most, he would be looked up by his Nobel Prize-winning son, who would suddenly realise where his exceptional gift had come from, and who would invest all his intelligence and a great deal of his enormous capital into contacting his father before he died so that he could fall to his knees and thank him for everything.

A honking truck brutally yanked him back to reality, or rather to the correct half of the street, just in time for him to make the turn to the pathology department at Karolinska, where the unknown body awaited his glorious arrival.

Viggo Norlander wandered through corridors that were much like those at the police station, made his way down to the notorious basement, and was welcomed by a none-too-warm nurse. There he stood before the legendary medical examiner Sigvard Strandell, a man of at least seventy-five, infinitely distinguished and infinitely slovenly — a combination that, within the medical profession, only researchers and pathologists could allow themselves to be; the risk that their patients would complain was minimal. Everyone called him Stranded; he had become stuck in this job as soon as he'd started. His speciality was hackneyed corpse jokes, one of which was immediately forthcoming: "Norlander, of all people. Are you here for a follow-up?"

"You know why I'm here," Norlander said in a measured tone.

Stranded jangled a small plastic bag and its contents and handed it to Norlander. "His belongings. Travelled light, as they say. Otherwise I have nothing new to add. A sound and healthy young man, whose last meal probably consisted of hamburgers of the fattier sort. With honey on them, strangely enough. The death probably occurred between midnight and three in the morning; it's not possible to be more exact. Four shots right into the heart and out again. Immediate death. His watch is still ticking, though — unfortunately." He pointed at the plastic bag.

Norlander was shown to a spot next to a desk outside the cold chamber and supplied with copies of autopsy reports; there he awaited the visits from potential next of kin.

Six of them showed up. First came an older couple, Mr and Mrs Johnsson, whose son-in-law had disappeared a few weeks earlier. Norlander's papers said that the son-in-law had run off with the daughter's not-insignificant fortune to Bahrain, where he had procured a harem that would have been a bit pricey to run, so the viewing was merely a formality.

The Johnssons' faces went from hope to despair when they saw the dead man, and they shook their heads; nothing would have made them happier, it seemed, than to be reunited with their son-in-law in these environs.

It was with the Johnssons that Norlander saw the corpse for the first time. It lay there, in the ice-cold, stripped-bare room with refrigerator doors along the walls, and seemed to glow white in the horrid, naked fluorescent light. He was immediately struck by the ordinariness of the young man. He had not a single distinguishing feature. If someone were to draw a specific individual and send a copy into outer space with the *Voyager* as an example of a male *Homo sapiens*, this youngster would have been made for the role, thought Norlander with astonishment.

Next came a couple of experienced visitors whose sons had disappeared as small children in the 1970s. They had never given up hope and never made peace or accepted a *fait accompli*. Norlander shared their sorrow; their lifelong powerlessness and protracted grief moved him deeply.

Then came a long period of waiting. Norlander skimmed the difficult autopsy report and emptied the man's possessions from the plastic bag. There were three things: a fake Rolex that, sure enough, was still keeping time; a long tube of ten-kronor coins; and a shiny key that seemed to have been made very recently. Nothing more. It told him nothing. And so it seemed quite fitting.

After that came two women, in quick succession, who had male family members who had disappeared the night before. First was Mrs Emma Nilsson, whose junkie son was to have come home from detox but never showed up. Norlander could have told the middle-aged woman that the dead man wasn't her son, but still he led her, with her prematurely crooked back, to the body. In the seconds while it was pulled out of its cooler box, fear was mirrored in the unfathomable darkness of her eyes. Once she saw the corpse and shook her head no, she seemed liberated, almost happy; there was still hope.

It was a different story with Justine Lindberger, a young, dark beauty with the Ministry of Foreign Affairs whose equally young husband and co-worker Eric hadn't come home the night before. While the cooler box was opened, she waited, paralysed with fear, radiating desperation, convinced that the corpse would be her murdered husband — and when that turned out not to be the case, she broke down and wept. Norlander's attempts to comfort her were beyond awkward; he had to call in personnel from psych, who gave her an injection of a rather heavy sedative. When Norlander sat back down at the desk, his body was trembling.

Last up was Egil Högberg, an old rapids-shooter from Dalsland who'd had both legs amputated. He'd been driven down from the nursing home in his wheelchair by a young female aide.

"My son," he said to Norlander in a toothless, quavering voice. "It must be my son."

Norlander did everything in his power to ignore Högberg's monstrously bad breath. The gum-chewing aide just rolled her eyes. He let the odd couple into the room and opened the cooler.

"It's him," Högberg declared calmly, placing his rheumatic hand on the dead man's icy cheek. "My only son."

The aide tapped Norlander lightly on the shoulder, and they left Högberg alone with the dead man. Norlander closed the door.

The aide said, "He doesn't have a son."

Norlander looked at her sceptically and peered through the window at the elderly man, who was now laying his cheek against the corpse's.

"He gets unmanageable," she continued, "if he doesn't get to come down and look at the new bodies.

154

We don't know why, but it's best to let him have his way."

Norlander didn't take his eyes from the old man.

"Presumably he's preparing to die," said the aide.

"Or?" said Norlander.

"Or else he's an old necrophile," said the aide, blowing a big pink bubble.

It was quiet for a moment. Then someone said, "Or else he wishes he had a son."

After a while, Norlander realised that he'd said it himself.

He opened the door. Egil Högberg looked up from the corpse and sent his crystal-clear gaze straight into Norlander's. "The line of descent is broken," he said.

Viggo Norlander closed his eyes and kept them shut tight for a long time.

# CHAPTER
# FOURTEEN

The first thing that struck Gunnar Nyberg was the contrast between LinkCoop's headquarters in Täby and its warehouses in Frihamnen. The only link between them was the vulgar logo that blinked in all the colours of the rainbow as though advertising Stockholm's most lavish brothel.

At closer glance, the 1980s-style two-storey building was a well-camouflaged skyscraper that had prophesied the conclusion of the decade by falling over. The luxurious atmosphere inside the company gates had more in common with a golf club than with a factory building. LinkCoop didn't manufacture anything; the company was merely a link between east and west, as advanced computer equipment made in a variety of places streamed in from the east and out towards the west and vice versa. Nyberg didn't really understand how this enterprise could be as profitable as the building suggested it was. On the other hand, economics was not his strong suit, and he felt some trepidation about the terminology that he would soon have to face.

Nyberg drove his Renault past a security gate that was disguised as a vehicle reception, then headed towards the main building. He obstinately parked across two handicap spots, because he couldn't imagine that anyone with a handicap worked at LinkCoop; the spots were the only two empty ones and reeked of artificial political correctness. Striding through the overzealous rain, he couldn't see a single vehicle in the car park that had cost less than 200,000 kronor. Either the cleaners and receptionists used public transport, or there was a hidden lower-class car park somewhere, along the lines of a good old kitchen entrance to a gentry flat.

In other words, Gunnar Nyberg was properly worked up as he loped through the autumn storm, fat jiggling, and arrived at the main entrance. Once he was inside the automatic doors, he shook off the water like a walrus on amphetamines. The twin receptionist beauties had clearly been forewarned, for their only reaction to this antibody in their bloodstream was a tandem smile of the kind that could soothe even the most inflamed of souls.

"Mr Nilsson is waiting for you, Mr Nyberg," they said in unison.

Mr Nyberg stared at them. Was this Villa Villekulla? Was Pippi Longstocking's horse waiting in the wings?

He collected himself, returned the smile, and accepted what tonight's dreams would have in store. That was apparently the duo's mission: to supply the customer's subconscious with a positive image; LinkCoop would be present at even the most intimate moments.

The exquisitely beautiful duo were separated, however, as one of the receptionists led him through the sober rooms, his impressions of which were unfortunately diminished by the tempting dance of the miniskirt. In only a matter of seconds, Nyberg had been transformed from a radical champion of the working class to a drooling dirty old man — the result of some carefully planned PR work.

*The seduction of capitalism*, he thought helplessly.

Finally they reached a door, which opened the instant they reached it. The security system must have been perfect. A thoroughly elegant middle-aged woman appeared, nodded curtly to the receptionist, noticed Nyberg's wandering eyes and shook his hand firmly. "Betty Rogèr-Gullbrandsen," she said, "Mr Nilsson's secretary. Please follow me."

*Pippi Longstocking herself*, Nyberg thought inappropriately, *downgraded to Mr Nilsson's secretary.* He followed Betty Rogèr-Gullbrandsen into a gigantic room where the only piece of furniture was a large desk. It was empty except for a well-designed computer and an equally well-designed telephone, on which she pressed a button and said: "Detective Inspector Gunnar Nyberg from the National Criminal Police is here."

"Send him in," replied an authoritative, distortion-free voice from within the keypad.

Betty Rogèr-Gullbrandsen gestured towards a door at the far end of the room and sat down at the computer without conferring upon him a single further look.

**158**

Nyberg stepped into the CEO's office, which was about twice as large as the secretary's atrium. The whole room — it was sacrilege to call it an office — had a well-balanced, utterly showy unshowiness; a splendid, crystal-clear, pure style. An impeccably dressed man in his forties stood behind a gleaming oak desk and extended his hand. Nyberg took it. His handshake was firm, to say the least.

"Henrik Nilsson, CEO," said the man distinctly.

"Nyberg," said Nyberg.

Henrik Nilsson pointed at a chair in front of the desk, and Nyberg took a seat.

"I don't believe I said either 'detective inspector' or 'National Criminal Police' when I announced myself out there," said Nyberg.

Henrik Nilsson smiled self-confidently. "It's Betty's job to have all available information."

"And to show it," Nyberg said, but was ignored. He was used to it.

"National Criminal Police," Nilsson said. "That means that you think there's a link between the banal break-in at our warehouse and the corpse outside it."

"It's likely."

"And furthermore, it means that the corpse isn't just any corpse, but a corpse of national concern. And furthermore, that LinkCoop has somehow been dragged into a national murder case, which we would prefer not to happen. In other words, we're at your service."

"Thank you," Nyberg said, instead of saying what he bit away from his tongue. "Was anything stolen?"

"A great deal was destroyed. Nothing stolen. The door has to be replaced. Otherwise we came out relatively unscathed this time."

"This time?"

"Our goods are so theft-prone that they're hard to insure these days. We've had a few break-ins recently. The goods are sold to the east."

Nyberg thought for a moment, then said, "So the guard ought to have been on alert?"

"Without a doubt."

"Then how did it happen that he didn't see the crime being committed on his monitors? Even your Betty out there could see me walk from reception up here to her custom-designed computer."

Henrik Nilsson shook his head. "You'll have to speak to our chief of security about that. It's his responsibility."

"I will. But first I'd like some information about the company. You buy computer equipment from west and east and sell it to east and west. Is that the business concept?"

"The best one there is today," said Henrik Nilsson, not without pride. "As long as the trade routes between east and west are as blocked as they still are, the kind of link we provide plays a crucial role."

"And when the blockade is lifted?"

Nilsson leaned forward and fixed his gaze on Nyberg. "It never will be. It's a fluctuating branch of commerce. Old businesses collapse; new ones are always springing up. The only constant is us."

"What kind of computer equipment is it?"

"Everything."

"Even military?"

"Within the boundaries of the law, yes."

"And was it military equipment that was in the warehouse that was broken into?"

"No, that was regular computers. Taiwanese WriteComs. I've compiled the information for you in this folder, a complete list of what was stored in that warehouse. As well as information about the company. You can get someone with experience to look at it, of course."

Nyberg ignored the sarcasm and took the elegant, burgundy leather folder. The company logo that adorned the front was toned down into a single colour — gold. "Thanks," he said. "Then there isn't much more to ask. I just want to speak to your chief of security."

"Robert Mayer," said Nilsson, who stood and extended his hand again. "He's waiting for you. Betty will show you the way."

Once again Betty popped in at exactly the right second, herded Nyberg out of the monumental CEO room and into the corridor, walked past a few doors and stopped outside the furthest one. After a few seconds of embarrassing delay, a broad man in his fifties opened the door. He could probably be considered a rather typical chief of security at a high-risk company: former police or military, sunburned, weather-beaten face, close-cropped hair, sharp eyes, handshake as firm as a rock. Since the former Mr Sweden had had enough of firm-as-a-rock handshakes, he answered with one that was even firmer; he couldn't help it.

"Robert Mayer," said Robert Mayer with slightly raised eyebrows and a slight accent. It wasn't German, as Nyberg had expected, but Anglo-Saxon.

"Nyberg," said Nyberg. "Are you an Englishman?"

The eyebrows went up a millimetre or so. "I'm originally from New Zealand, if that is of interest." Mayer made a slight gesture, and they stepped into the first of the chief of security's rooms: a relatively small nook where the walls were covered in monitors. They sat down at the desk.

Nyberg decided to skip all the chit-chat. "How did it happen that the guard, Benny Lundberg, didn't see the break-in happening on his monitors?"

Robert Mayer, behind the desk, didn't seem to lack the ability to concentrate. "It's simple," he said. "All together, our storage at Frihamnen is made up of thirty-four buildings of various sizes. We have monitor coverage on only eight of them, the most important ones. Maintaining thirty-four monitors would require us to post at least two more guards, which, with round-the-clock observation, would involve at least six full-time positions, many of them with odd working hours. Along with the cost of materials and installation, the extra cost would far exceed the potential returns. The building where the break-in occurred, in other words, doesn't have monitor coverage."

*A straight answer*, Nyberg thought, and shifted tactics. "How well do you know Benny Lundberg?"

"I suppose I don't really know him, exactly, but it's hardly possible to find a more dedicated guard."

"Mr Nilsson pointed out that you've had a number of break-ins down there recently. What happened with those?"

"There have been eight break-ins in the last two years, which isn't a catastrophe, but it isn't acceptable, either. Three of them were stopped by our security guards, Lundberg among them; two failed for other reasons, while three were truly devastating pro jobs. It was after the last one that we got our own guards instead of relying on security companies. Since then we've done well."

"So Lundberg has been on staff for — only a year?"

"A bit more than a year, yes. Since we switched over. And that's another reason everyone's thinking it was an inside job, if that's what you're fumbling for: not a single successful break-in has occurred since we got our own squad of guards. The boys do an excellent job."

"What was stolen during the 'successful' break-ins?"

"I've put together a file." Mayer handed him a folder bearing LinkCoop's gold logo, which gave Nyberg a sense of déjà vu. "It contains copies of our police and insurance reports from all eight break-ins. All the information is there. You can get someone with experience to look at it, of course."

Gunnar Nyberg observed the man in front of him. Robert Mayer was the perfect chief of security, a rock that a company could lean on, professional, clear-sighted, experienced, hard as nails, cold as ice. The steel-blue eyes met his, and he sensed that his bodybuilder handshake had not been forgotten. For a second he wondered what Mayer had actually done when he was in New Zealand.

Then he relaxed. There was nothing more to add.

He wondered what a chief of security earned.

*The seduction of capitalism*, he thought, and bade farewell to Robert Mayer.

# CHAPTER
# FIFTEEN

When Jan-Olov Hultin returned on the well-worn path from the toilet, he found a nervous man in his forties standing outside his door. His first thought was that the Kentucky Killer had quite coolly walked into police headquarters to stick his tongs into his neck. The man's strangely clear, green eyes calmed him, however; he looked more like a humiliated school student outside the headmaster's office.

Having realised this, Hultin could curse the security procedures down at reception a bit more level-headedly.

"Can I help you?" he asked calmly.

The green-eyed man gave a start. His fingers fumbled along the knot of his tie as though they had a life of their own.

"I'm looking for someone who's working on the murder in Frihamnen," he said uncertainly. "I don't know if I'm in the right place."

"You are." Hultin let the man into his office.

As the man sat down on the practically unused visitors' sofa, Hultin waited for him to speak.

"My name is Mats Oskarsson," he said. "From Nynäshamn. I called on the night of the murder."

"At three thirty-seven from a telephone booth on Stureplan," Hultin said neutrally.

Mats Oskarrson from Nynäshamn blinked a few times. His eyes looked like a starboard light with battery problems.

"I don't really know when it was, but it was from Stureplan."

"Get to the point," said Hultin. "You've already done enough to obstruct our investigation."

By this point, Oskarsson had been degraded to a primary school student. "The others didn't think I should call at all."

"What others?"

"On my bandy team. Stockholm Lawyers' Bandy Club. We'd had a late away game up in Knivsta, and we were on our way home."

"Let me see if I understand," Hultin said mildly, and little did Mats Oskarsson suspect how ominous this mildness was. "A gang of the guardians of the law were on their way home from a bandy match at three in the morning, ended up in Frihamnen, witnessed a murder and intended to keep it from the long arm of the law. Is that correct?"

Oskarsson stared down at the table. "It was late," he said.

"Late on earth," Hultin said even more mildly.

"I beg your pardon?" Oskarsson asked.

"Are you a lawyer?"

"A tax lawyer at Hagman, Grafström and Krantz, yes."

"And you were the one driving the car?"

"Yes. A Volkswagen van."

"Do you want me to try to reconstruct the chain of events?" Hultin asked rhetorically. "You played bandy, got creamed, drank it off, lost your way in Frihamnen of all places, ran into a murderer who had left a body behind, realised you were all shit-faced and decided to hell with it all. Then you were struck by a pang of conscience, maybe after having dropped off the whole gang to avoid any digs, and called from a telephone booth at Stureplan, even though you all surely had pockets stuffed full of mobile phones, but of course you wouldn't want to leave behind any traces in the registry. Were you driving drunk?"

"No," said Oskarsson. His eyes were drilling green holes in the desk.

"Yes, you were," Hultin said, still mildly. "You called even so, and now you're here. I'm sure you're basically a conscientious person, unlike your law colleagues in the ball club, and that the only reason you could have had for calling anonymously was that you were driving drunk. But of course, that's not something that can be proven."

"No," Oskarsson said, with unintentional ambiguity.

Time for a change of tone. Hultin bellowed, "Spit it all out now, the whole fucking story, and we'll see if I can save you from being charged."

Mats Oskarsson sighed and spat it out with a lawyer's precision. "It was a few minutes past two thirty. The man was a bit taller than average, rather powerfully built, and was wearing black clothes and a black balaclava over his face. He was driving a ten- or twelve-year-old dark blue Volvo station wagon with a number plate that started with B. He had just loaded a bundle of blankets into the boot and was about to load the other one when we interrupted him."

"So it was more than half an hour before you called?"

"Yes. Unfortunately. I'm sorry."

"Me too. If that information had been reported immediately, there wouldn't be a raving serial killer running loose in Stockholm today. I hope your daughters are his next victims."

Hultin didn't usually go too far, even in his most agitated moments, but his firmly rooted distrust in the guardians of the constitutional state caused him to go over the limit. "A raving serial killer." He had to smooth things over. "Do you remember anything more than the B in the number plate?"

"No," Oskarsson mumbled.

The man didn't have more to say. Hultin could have given him a thorough lecture on the corrupt legal practices in the buy-and-sell world of Swedish jurisprudence; on how the Western democracies were gradually selling out the constitutional state; on how laws that were established to protect citizens were being transformed into market games and low-odds competitions between high-cost old-school lawyers and recently graduated low-budget prosecutors; and on how a whole busload of lawyers hadn't for one second considered setting aside their own egos in order to catch a double murderer. But Mats Oskarsson had shown at least the beginnings of moral courage, and in addition he seemed already pounded into the ground by the contents of the non-existent lecture. He slunk towards the door. He had just opened it when he heard Hultin's subdued "Thanks".

For a split second, Hultin met the man's clear green gaze. It actually said more than a thousand words.

Jan-Olov Hultin, now alone, stretched his legs out under the desk, emptied his consciousness and let his eyes sweep over the walls of his office. For the first time in a long time, he was struck by the room's anonymity. There was not a single trace of him in here. It was purely a workroom. He hadn't even taken the pains to put up a photo of his wife. When he was at work, he was one hundred per cent policeman, maybe even a little more. The rest he kept to himself. Not even after the success with the Power Murders had he let anyone in. He didn't really know why. The intercompany football wasn't a secret any more. One night Hjelm and Chavez had popped up on the AstroTurf field at Stadshagen and seen him in action. Unfortunately, the Stockholm Police Veterans team had been playing Rågsved Alliance, which had a sharp attacker named Carlos, and Hultin had clipped Carlos's left eyebrow with a thundering header, so the blood gushed out. Carlos's last name was, unfortunately, Chavez. He didn't know whether Jorge had informed his father that it was Jorge's boss's skull that had transported him across the street to St Göran's Hospital.

His short, weak smile was interrupted by the ringing of a phone.

"Yes," he said into the receiver. "Yes. Yes. I understand. Yes."

**169**

Then he thought for a few seconds as his finger hovered over the internal telephone's keypad. While he thought, he dialled Kerstin Holm's number.

"Kerstin, are you there?"

"Yep," came Holm's alto, in a reproduction that didn't do it justice.

"Are you busy?"

"Not particularly. I'm trying to familiarise myself with every detail of the FBI's material. It's a huge volume."

"Can you run a check on a dark blue Volvo station wagon, model years, say, eighty to ninety? The number plate should start with a B. We've got a better witness report on Frihamnen."

"Hell, that's great! Of course." She hung up on him before he had time to hang up on her.

His finger hovered again. Söderstedt? Nah. Norlander, who would be back by now? No. Was Nyberg back from LinkCoop? Nah. Chavez? Not alone.

His hesitation, he knew, was more of the democratic than the realistic sort. He dialled Hjelm's number. "Paul?"

"Yes."

"Come see me. Bring Jorge."

It took thirty seconds.

"Is the Laban Hassel story over and done with?" he asked as they stood there like schoolboys. Why was everyone always standing in front of him like schoolchildren?

"Yes," said Chavez. "We've tried to find a basis for bringing charges, but we might as well admit that we don't really want to charge him. We can only hope things go well for him and Ingela. Despite their sterility."

**170**

"OK, then. I've just received information about a clue in Frihamnen. A car that doesn't seem to belong to anyone has been found a few streets from LinkCoop's warehouses. A beige Saab 900. Two things make it interesting. One, it was completely clean, with not a fingerprint anywhere, neither inside nor outside. And two, it's registered to Andreas Gallano. Does that name mean anything to you?"

"Gallano," said Hjelm. "Repeat offender down in Alby, right?"

"Right."

"Yeah, yeah, Andreas Gallano. I had a few confrontations with him during my time in Huddinge. Quite a bit of violence, as I recall. He's way up in the chain of drug distribution, but still a classic street hooligan. No conscience. We put him away once for assault and battery and once for selling drugs."

"Oh yeah!" Chavez exclaimed. "He escaped from Hall Prison."

"That's right," said Hultin. "He was in Hall for assault and battery again until just over a month ago. He and three violent criminals escaped through the kitchen. A bold plan."

Hjelm and Chavez nodded. It had been a noteworthy escape.

Hultin looked at them. He tried to inventory his intuitions one by one. "It must have something to do with this, right?" His question mark was nearly an exclamation point.

They nodded.

"Gallano's car, left behind, without fingerprints, a break-in, two bodies," Hjelm summarised, and concluded, "Oh, yeah."

"The body wasn't him, was it?" Chavez asked.

"If it were, the fingerprints would have screamed it out," said Hjelm. "But he must have played some part in the drama."

"The only thing we don't have any indication of is the Kentucky Killer," Hultin mumbled.

"Except hunches," said Hjelm. "Latest address?"

"Same as ten years ago."

"We'll take it."

The duo were on their way — Chavez's BMW got to play police car. They raced wordlessly through the rain-soaked city and came out on Essingeleden. Riddarfjärden seemed to have risen to biblical-flood proportions. It would gush up over the city at any moment, and who, in these times, would have received forewarning to build an ark?

No one, Hjelm thought misanthropically, sitting beside the violently accelerating Chavez. Not a single one of us would be forewarned by God. We would all drown in the same sticky sludge and be swallowed up by the angry earth, and from out in the universe, the earth would look exactly the same. A negligible little disturbance in the balance of eternity, nothing more.

He raised his eyes from his morass of pessimism and launched a vain attack against evil. It felt as though they were tilting at windmills.

No passers-by out on the E4 could have told Alby from Fittja or Norsborg from Hallunda. The crazy

172

buildings climbed sky-high, brutally similar along the hills, as in a self-fulfilling prophecy, they had filled up with criminals. The building was the result of the same social-building spirit that had once planned to level Gamla Stan to the ground so that Le Corbusier could build a row of glass-and-concrete palaces.

But no one knew better than Paul Hjelm that this place also contained an inaccessible alternative culture, with small-scale everyday heroism, infinite inventiveness and a continuous battle against all odds. He had been stationed here for all of his working life up until the remarkable change just over a year ago, when, instead of being booted from the force, he was transported to inner-city mode, more specifically A major, A as in the A-Unit, major as in success.

His transfer had come in large part thanks to Erik Bruun, his old chief at the Huddinge police, whose contacts with his former colleague Jan-Olov Hultin had been crucial, and it was outside his office that they now stood. Hjelm had succeeded in walking past his former colleagues unnoticed and knocked on Bruun's door. The light system on the doorpost shone yellow as in "wait", and Hjelm was seized by apprehension. Bruun's light was never yellow as in "wait".

They waited in the hallway for three excruciating minutes, under continual threat of discovery, before Hjelm had had enough and barged in.

The Bruun room, once covered in health-injurious rings left behind by smoke, was now bright yellow. The wallpaper paste didn't seem to have dried yet.

Behind Bruun's desk sat a forty-year-old man in a suit and tie, his chestnut-coloured hair brushed back over the beginnings of a bald spot. As they entered, his hand moved instinctively in the direction of his service weapon.

"Where is Bruun?" Hjelm demanded.

The man refrained from drawing his pistol, but he kept his hand at the ready. "It says to wait out there, in case you can't read."

"It says wait, and it says Bruun. Where is Bruun?"

"Who are you?"

"Hjelm. I worked here once. Under Bruun. Where is he?"

"Hjelm. Aha, the man who was kicked upward."

"Exactly. Where's Bruun?"

"Hjelm, well — not long ago I sat down and went through your file. I hope you're not here to get your old job back now that the A-Unit has packed it in. There's no room for you here."

"Where's Bruun?"

"There's no room for heroes and mavericks here. It's time to clean up. Close up the ranks a little."

"Where's Bruun?"

"I guess you'll have to brush off the old uniform, then, and get ready for a good old time on patrol."

Hjelm had had enough. He did an about-face and nearly ran into Chavez, who was waiting at the door. Behind him he heard: "Bruun had a heart attack a week ago. Just thinking about how this office looked ought to be enough to cause one."

Hjelm did another about-face. "Is he dead?"

174

The man at the desk just shrugged. "I have no idea."

Hjelm had to leave immediately; otherwise time on patrol would have seemed like utopia. He went downstairs to the break room.

It was as though no time had passed. Every mug and sugar cube seemed to be in the same place as they had a year and a half ago. And every cop. They were all sitting there: Anders Lindblad and Kenneth Eriksson, Anna Vass and Johan Bringman. And there was Svante Ernstsson, who had been his partner for over a decade. They had been best friends; now it had been many months since they'd spoken.

"Well, look at that," Ernstsson said with surprise. "A special visitor."

Their handshake was firm and almost ridiculously manly.

"First off," said Hjelm, "is Bruun dead?"

Ernstsson looked at him gravely, then burst into a smile. "Just a scratch, as he said himself."

"Who's the clown?"

"New chief inspector, Sten Lagnmyr. A stain on our department. Instead of Bruun we got a real brown-noser. With a taste for yellow, to boot."

"This is Jorge Chavez, by the way. Sorry. My new colleague."

Chavez and Ernstsson shook hands. Hjelm was struck by a strange vision — for a split second, he saw Cilla and Kerstin shaking hands. He pulled himself together. "We're not here to socialise ourselves, as Lena Olin said, but to get some help. Do you have any more active investigations going on about our old friend Andreas Gallano?"

Ernstsson shrugged and raised a curious eyebrow. "Not more than what you'd usually have on a fugitive."

"Do you know if he's here at all?"

"What is this all about?"

"The murder in Frihamnen."

Ernstsson nodded and stopped being stubborn. "We have no indication that he's returned; that'd be pretty stupid after escaping from Hall. His apartment was empty and undisturbed. There was six-month-old milk in the fridge. As usual, we're overloaded with work, and he's not a top priority. We were going to start working on it next week."

"I'm going to make sure that Hultin takes care of Lagnmyr — then you can help out a bit more officially. Is it still best to go through, what was his name, Stavros?"

"Stavropoulos. No, he died. Overdose. Gallano had to get new contacts and fought his way into a new gang with slightly greater resources, synthetic drugs. We got him through a dealer, Yilmaz. We still have pretty good means of investigating him, if you're not too worried about privacy protection."

"It'll all work out. What could we get from Yilmaz?"

"Gurra gets his junk there. You remember Gurra?"

"Hell, yes!" Hjelm exclaimed. "Crazy Gurra. Childhood friends."

"If anyone has any idea where Andreas is, it would be Gurra. For old times' sake," Ernstsson added a bit ambiguously.

**176**

"How should we go about this?"

"Yilmaz distributes in a pretty good place, stakeout-wise, so we've let him be. The old storeroom of the ICA that shut down. We just lie there on the upper floor and look right down. Ideal."

"It's not possible to get hold of Gurra some other way?"

"He keeps out of sight. This is best."

"Right away?"

Ernstsson shrugged. "Let's just do it," he said briskly.

Jorge Chavez was trying to get an idea of the partnership between Hjelm and Ernstsson. Had it been like his and Hjelm's was now? Had they been close to each other? Did their teamwork work as well? He observed them as they all waited in the filthy old upper floor of the ICA store. Wasn't there something hesitant, even guilty, about the way Hjelm related to his former colleague, something strained in their body language? But then how coloured was his own view?

Their stakeout position was slightly strange. They really could have peered straight down through the floor and observed Yilmaz's law-defying transactions, but that would have meant lying on the floor with their cheeks in rat droppings and syringes, hour after hour. It was a bit simpler, they found, to tape a miniature camera to the hole and observe the spectacle on a monitor. It was in front of this monitor that all three were now crouching.

A steady stream of customers passed through Yilmaz's hardly hidden pharmacy. It was like a cross-section of society, from peculiar relics of the 1960s trying to escape their overdoses in unfathomable ways to fresh-looking middle-class kids on their way to raves; from prostitutes with advanced Aids to executive secretaries on secret missions. If Hjelm felt a pang of nostalgia for his old workplace, it had long since passed.

Yilmaz was sitting like a pasha on an old chest freezer and, with great control, fishing the orders up out of another one. To his drug customers, he was God. His goodwill meant the difference between heaven and hell. He found pleasure in waving the keys to the pearly gates for a few seconds.

Hjelm hated every one of those seconds, not only because the line of the downtrodden was endless but also because time crept on and Gurra was conspicuous by his absence. Yilmaz's visiting hours would be over soon, and the day would be wasted. Three hours had passed. It was already afternoon. The dampness sucked itself deeper and deeper into the rotten building. The steady stream of customers began to subside.

Yet another young middle-class boy showed up to treat himself to some small, colourful pills with funny figures imprinted on them. He was about sixteen or seventeen and strode self-confidently up to the pasha on the freezer. In the background, a friend was waiting with his hands in his pockets and his shoulders hunched. He stood with his back to the camera and stamped his feet nervously while his buddy extended his hand to Yilmaz. Then the friend threw a short, ultra-nervous glance over his shoulder — at which point Hjelm saw his face.

It was more than enough for Hjelm. His body contracted into an incredible convulsion that threw him sideways, and he vomited straight out. Even as it happened, his reaction surprised him. Shame and guilt rippled through him. He saw the procession that is said to pass before the eyes of the dying. His whole life as a father passed by, and he saw every false step, every wounding shot that he had inflicted upon his son over the years.

When he looked up after thirty seconds, transfixed, and stared past his astounded colleagues, Danne was still there, standing with his back to the camera. His friend's transaction had been temporarily interrupted. A truly rock-bottom junkie came in and fussed at Yilmaz.

"It's Gurra," Svante Ernstsson whispered.

Hjelm didn't give a damn. He stood up so violently that his chair flew over, and he took off. All the eyes on the lower floor looked straight up at the camera. Before Yilmaz could close his shop, Hjelm charged downstairs, drawing his weapon. Not until they saw him do so did Ernstsson and Chavez think to follow him.

The massive bodyguard who had been standing beside Yilmaz was now sprawled flat on the ground. Hjelm dug a large western-style revolver out of the man's waistband and tapped its barrel lightly against Yilmaz's forehead. Chavez took over and kept a gun trained on Yilmaz and the bodyguard. Gurra tried to slink away unnoticed, but Ernstsson yanked him to the ground.

Hjelm walked over to the teenager, who was in the process of stomping the colourful pills into the rotten wood floor. He grabbed the kid's collar and pulled his deathly pale face close until there were only a few fiery inches between it and his own. "Your face is engraved on my corneas, you bastard." His nose told him the kid was pissing himself in his grip. He let him go. The kid collapsed, sniffling.

Hjelm then turned to his son, who was cowering in the doorway, gawking in astonishment. His jaw was moving, but no words came out.

"Go home," said Hjelm neutrally. "And stay home."

Danne took off and disappeared.

His friend stared wildly. "Get out of here," Hjelm ordered, and the kid scrambled away.

Hjelm then turned to Gurra, who was lying under Ernstsson with his back in the rat crap. Somewhere behind the practised sneer he could see genuine pallor.

"Andreas Gallano," Hjelm said, with emphasis on each syllable.

"What the fuck are you talking about?"

Hjelm bent over. His facial expression was nothing to mess with, Gurra noticed. "Try again," said Hjelm softly.

"I haven't seen him since he went in."

"But?"

"But he . . . well . . ."

"It's simple. Speak and live. Keep silent and die."

**180**

"Yeah, yeah, what the hell, he thinks he's so fucking fancy now anyway. He has a secret cabin somewhere up north. Riala, I think it's called. I have the address. In my address book."

"I'm surprised," Hjelm said, fishing damp, folded papers from Gurra's inner pocket. "Not only do you have an address book, it contains the address of an escaped criminal."

"Encoded," Gurra said sophisticatedly. "It's listed under Eva Svensson."

Hjelm tore out the page with Eva Svensson's address in Riala and put the address book back in Gurra's pocket.

He heard sirens in the distance; Ernstsson had called for backup. They shoved Gurra into the freezer corner next to Yilmaz and the bodyguard. "Have you got this, Svante?" Hjelm said, already on his way.

"Keep an eye on them," Ernstsson said to Chavez, then took Hjelm aside. "You ruined our best stakeout spot, Pålle," he said, a dash of disappointment in his voice.

Hjelm closed his eyes. This hadn't occurred to him, even for a second. "I'm sorry," he said quietly. "The circumstances were a little special."

Svante Ernstsson stepped back and looked at him. "They've actually managed to change you." Then half turning, he added, "I hope it works out with Danne."

Hjelm nodded heavily.

"Now get out of here," said Ernstsson. "I'll take care of this. Lagnmyr's gonna love it."

Hjelm remembered to contact Hultin from the car. The detective superintendent promised, without having received more than an outline of the course of events, to contact Sten Lagnmyr and try to salvage the situation. As for everything else, Hjelm was at a loss.

Chavez felt petrified. It had all gone so fast, all of it. He had seen sides of Paul Hjelm that he'd never seen before, but that wasn't unpleasant. Not until they reached Skärholmen did it occur to him that the teenage boy must have been Paul's son. He decided not to mention it. "Aha" was all he said. Hjelm turned to him expressionlessly, then went back to being out of it.

They avoided Stockholm. These days one could easily get from the southern to the northern suburbs without passing Go. Still, the price had been high.

Around Norrtull, Chavez began to organise his thoughts. Without having exchanged a word with Hjelm, it was clear that they were on their way to Riala, in Roslagen, between Åkersberga and Norrtälje.

Judging from the police atlas, the address belonged to a cabin in an isolated forest.

"Are we going to do it alone?" said Chavez.

He didn't receive an answer. Hjelm just stared out the window.

"Are you ready for this?" Chavez said a bit more sharply.

Hjelm turned to him with the same blank facial expression. Or was it resolute?

"I'm ready," he said. "And we're going to do it alone."

"If we look at it rationally, then Frihamnen could have been a drug deal. And in that case, of course, a whole lot of shit might be waiting for us up in Riala. Gallano's cabin, for example, could be a centre for his new drug syndicate."

"Then why would they leave the car in Frihamnen, completely wiped?"

"Maybe he was the other body, the one in the car. Our unknown body could have been a foreign companion. Maybe they were superfluous and were weeded out. But the cabin could have tight security."

"That could be," said Hjelm, "completely rationally. But let's be completely irrational. Here's a piece of paper and a pen, and I'll take some paper and a pen. We'll write down what we think we'll find up there, fold up the papers and put them in our pockets. Then we'll compare them later."

Chavez laughed and wrote something. Hjelm was back.

They placed the pieces of paper in their pockets.

Then Hjelm disappeared again. His gaze dissolved in the unending cascades of rain.

Fatherhood. How incredibly easy it was to inflict irreparable wounds. A random word, a moment of indifference at the wrong time, too hard a grip on an upper arm, demands, not enough demands. If the parents have a rotten relationship, what's best — silence, constant fighting, divorce? An icy hell, like the one Laban Hassel would always be frozen in? Or the white-hot, crackling, absurd hell of fighting? Last summer the Power Murders, the separation — how had their absence affected the children at their most sensitive age? And how much of their behaviour was inherited?

The banner of biology waved grandly nowadays. It didn't seem to matter any more what people were subjected to; everything was pre-programmed in their genes. This ought to have given Paul Hjelm some comfort: maybe it wasn't his fault that his son associated with drug dealers. Maybe there was a gene for drug abuse that made his upbringing irrelevant. But he refused to believe it. Somehow or another Danne's behaviour was his fault, but how? What the fuck was the problem? That he hadn't been able to change nappies without throwing up? That he chose to converse in relatively masculine jargon? That he was a policeman? What the fuck was it?

He knew that there wasn't *one* answer. That was one advantage of his job. For each case there was one answer, one guilty person. Your focus narrowed, filtering out anything ambiguous and complicated.

The rain poured down.

Two hunters travelled north on Norrtäljevägen.

Two pieces of paper burned in two pockets.

Riala had a small business area, but the district was spread out across a large region in heavy pine woods, and the map took them further and further from the main area. In the end, the road was nothing more than a cow path through virgin forest.

"Stop here," Hjelm said with his eyes on the police atlas.

**184**

Chavez stopped the car.

"Two hundred yards or so. Up the rise and then to the right. It's isolated."

Chavez nodded, took out his service weapon, checked it and put it back into his shoulder holster. "Do we dare leave the car unlocked?" He grinned.

Hjelm gave a weak smile and hurled himself out into the pouring rain. It was past five o'clock. The waterlogged skies were made more ominous by the suggestion of dusk; the forest lay in a dense gloom.

Hunching slightly, they ran through the autumn storm. The crowns of the trees danced above their heads and released copious needles, which the rain carried through their hair. A bolt of lightning lit up the forest with piercing clarity. For a fraction of a second, the trunks of the trees were separate from one another; when the thunder came, hard and heavy, only a few seconds later, they merged again.

The cabin was wedged among trees up on a hill; if they hadn't known it was there, they probably would have missed it. It was small, brown and dark. From where they stood, not a single sign of life was visible.

They made their way up to the door, their weapons raised, ready.

Next to the door was a glass pane with a round hole in it. Hjelm pressed the door handle down silently. The door was locked.

He extended his hand through the hole in the glass pane and turned the lock. Then he kicked the door open, and they rushed in.

Even before Chavez found the light switch and the light blinded them, the stench struck them. They exchanged glances. Both knew immediately what it was.

They searched around the cabin; it didn't take long to get through the living room, the kitchen nook and the tiny bedroom. Everything was empty, unused. Had it not been for the hole in the glass and the stench, they would have put their pistols away.

There was another door, just next to the sink. Hjelm cracked it open carefully. A dark cement staircase led down to a cellar. There was no light switch. Keeping close to each other with their weapons raised, they trod carefully down the stairs.

They could see nothing. Then they were down. The stench intensified.

They felt their way along the ice-cold stone wall. Finally, Chavez found a light switch.

A naked, faint light bulb on the ceiling lit up.

In a chair sat Andreas Gallano.

His eyes stared lifelessly at them. A pain that was beyond words remained in his eyes.

In his bare neck were two small holes.

They went back upstairs. Hjelm sat on the floor and, his hand trembling, dialled Hultin's mobile number. Meanwhile Chavez leaned over the sink and splashed water on his face. Both of them still had their service weapons in hand.

Chavez stared out into the loud darkness for a moment. A flash of lightning lit up the forest. It looked horribly insignificant.

He sat down next to Hjelm. The crash of thunder came. He moved a bit closer. Hjelm didn't move away. Their shoulders were rubbing. They needed it.

Almost simultaneously they fished their pieces of paper out of their pockets and, with effort, unfolded them.

Chavez's read "Corpse with holes in its neck". Hjelm's read "Neck-perforated stiff". They smiled weakly at each other.

Such good teamwork.

# CHAPTER
# SIXTEEN

*Retired*. He tried the word in his mouth a few times on his way down to the boathouse. He still hadn't really got used to it.

A life full of activity. Always in a tight spot. The conference rooms. The meetings. The trips. That suppressed jubilation when the contract was signed.

He missed it all. It was a fact that was impossible to run away from.

Now there was only the boat. His wife had been dead for many years; he hardly remembered her, a vague fluttering somewhere on the edges of the landscape of his past.

Everything was fixated on the boat now. His pride and joy. A fine old two-masted wooden yacht of the classic and tragically forgotten brand Hummelbo. From 1947, in superb condition.

But only because it was so well cared for.

Twice a day he went down to the boathouse. He had turned into the boat club's unpaid guard.

Not even the worst autumn storm could stop him. It didn't usually look like this in September, did it? Had the greenhouse effect started to show its ugly mug? He rejected the thought — he didn't believe in it. An infantile fantasy of the green movement. They were always blaming industry and cars. Didn't they understand what industry and cars had done for the Western world? Did they want to live without them? By the way, how much shit did Greenpeace's old ships release?

But the storm was irrefutable. He fought his way down towards the Lidingö coast and entered the boat club's grounds with the help of a robust set of keys. Another couple of keys got him out on the pier.

He could hardly see his own hand in front of him. He was standing right next to his Hummelbo yacht before he could see it at all. Every time the same little jolt of happiness and pride coursed through him. His life in a nutshell.

He checked the locks. The chain was in place; the trap — which resembled a bear trap — was in its place. He got down on his knees, hunched forward, and let his hand slide across the well-polished stem.

Such a pleasure.

He bent a bit further forward, and his hand slid along the stem until it reached the waterline. He caught something in his hand. The persistent rain meant that he couldn't really see what it was. Sticky. Like seaweed.

Seaweed? But he had cleaned the stem of seaweed as recently as this morning.

He got a good grip on the bunch of seaweed and lifted it upward.

And stared into a pair of open eyes.

He immediately let go of the body and screamed.

As the body splashed back down into the water, he noticed two small red holes in the pale white neck.

Vampires in Lidingö?

# CHAPTER
# SEVENTEEN

Viggo Norlander was back on his dunce task, but he hadn't realised until now that it had nothing to do with dunces. Quite the opposite: it was important work, and he had been placed there because of his competence.

He had arrived at his spot in the pathology department before the new corpse did, which he considered to be of merit. This time, unfortunately, he wasn't alone.

He didn't really understand how it had happened, but several of the unpleasant morning's visitors were already present.

The Johnsson couple were there, the ones who dreamed of finding their son-in-law in the morgue at Karolinska instead of in his Bahraini harem. The old rapids-shooter Egil Högberg, accompanied by a new aide, was there, ceaselessly repeating "My son, my son". And Justine Lindberger, the young civil servant from the Ministry of Foreign Affairs, was there, intensely missing her missing husband. Norlander did his best to cool down the heated atmosphere.

By the time old Sigvard Strandell peeked out of the loathsome cold chamber and gave Norlander a quick nod, the latter had already decided to prioritise Justine Lindberger.

She appeared to have collected herself after the morning's breakdown, but Norlander made sure that there were still medical personnel on site.

He led her carefully into the cold chamber. Unlike the unidentified corpse from Frihamnen, the new body had not yet been placed in a cooler box; it was lying on a gurney in the middle of the room, covered by a sheet. Strandell was there to make sure that no damage was done to his future working material. It was he who pulled the sheet aside for Justine Lindberger.

This corpse was a man almost as young as the previous, unidentified one. The dark hair gave a ghostly contrast against the whitish-blue face, slightly swollen from its stay in the water — and it had two small holes in the neck.

Justine Lindberger squeaked, nodded, and ran out into the hallway. The staff outside were ready, caught her up and gave her an injection. Before it took effect, Norlander had time to ask the unnecessary question: "Do you recognise the dead man?"

"It's my husband," said Justine Lindberger faintly. "Eric Lindberger."

And then a gradually developing mist brought her long, horrible day to a merciful end.

# CHAPTER
# EIGHTEEN

Supreme Central Command finally lost its quotation marks. The clear indication was that the whiteboard had been set up behind Hultin's desk. It was time for brainstorming. The markers lying there seemed to be simmering with impatience.

The case had let out a giant blob of ketchup. First came nothing, then nothing — and then everything. So far perhaps only a little of America's favourite condiment garnished the Swedish bread. Perhaps the sandwich would soon be covered in sticky red sludge.

In any case, the Kentucky Killer had begun. Two definite victims had, in the course of a few hours, been added to the probable one. Things had been set in motion, possibly in escalating motion.

It was after nine o'clock at night. Everyone was there. No one even thought of complaining about the unreasonable working hours.

Jan-Olov Hultin was rummaging through his papers, then found what he was looking for, stood, grabbed a marker and got the meeting going.

"So," he said evenly, drawing squares and arrows on the whiteboard, "at eight ten on the third of September, the Kentucky Killer arrived in Stockholm under the name Edwin Reynolds after having murdered the literary critic Lars-Erik Hassel at Newark International Airport outside New York during the night. After his arrival, it seems he promptly went to Riala in Roslagen; the degree of decomposition of drug dealer Andreas Gallano's body suggests that he was murdered just over a week ago, which matches up quite well with the Kentucky Killer's arrival in Sweden. Andreas Gallano had escaped from Hall and apparently taken shelter in a cabin that, by way of various fronts, belongs to a tax evader named Robert Arkaius, who had once been Gallano's mother's lover. What happened in the cabin we don't know, other than that the Kentucky Killer put Gallano to death with the method he is in the habit of using. There is reason to believe that he then lived there for over a week with an increasingly stinking corpse in the cellar. That he almost immediately made his way to such a perfect hiding place indicates previous contact with Gallano or his drug syndicate. This must be verified.

"Then what happened? Here it gets complicated. Gallano's beige Saab is discovered near the site of a double murder. Of course, it may have been there for a long time, for completely unrelated reasons, but for the time being, all signs indicate that, the night before last, on the twelfth of September, the Kentucky Killer took Gallano's car to Frihamnen. There with his usual pincers he murdered two more people: an as-yet-unidentified man, whom we'll call John Doe as the Americans do, with four shots to the heart; and a thirty-three-year-old civil servant with the Ministry of

Foreign Affairs, Eric Lindberger. Just as Hjelm and Chavez were finding Gallano, Lindberger's corpse was discovered at a Lidingö boat club by the retired executive Johannes Hertzwall. Eric Lindberger has the same vampire bite on his neck as Gallano and Hassel did. An examination by Strandell has shown that he died at about the same time as John Doe; that is, less than twenty-four hours ago, and the boat club is situated a reasonable distance from Frihamnen. So it is extremely likely that Eric Lindberger is the corpse that was seen being shoved into a decade-old dark blue Volvo station wagon with a number plate that starts with B by a man with a balaclava at two thirty in the morning."

Hultin paused. His students were like lit light bulbs, in front of the horribly expanding diagram on the whiteboard.

"May I suggest a scenario?" he continued. "The Kentucky Killer goes to Frihamnen to commit a pair of seemingly well-planned murders. He travels there in Gallano's car, but has another one waiting.

"He commits his crimes in some deserted cellar, wraps the victims in blankets and starts to load them into the second car. Then he's surprised by a gang of lawyers who are lost, brandishing bandy sticks and bottles of vodka. That means that he has time to load only one of the bodies — Lindberger. He leaves behind the other, our unidentified twenty-five-year-old John Doe. Convinced that his car has been reported to the police, he thinks he has to get out of there quickly and

195

hurries to Lidingö, where he dumps the victim rather carelessly and scrams."

"In this scenario," said Gunnar Nyberg, "you're assuming that the break-in at LinkCoop's warehouse doesn't have anything to do with the murders."

"I can't get a failed break-in at a warehouse to fit. Does anyone here have an opinion? . . . No? No, I think it's an irrelevant event. One thought, of course, is that the break-in failed because the burglars happened to witness a considerably worse crime and got out of there."

"Or maybe this," said Kerstin Holm thoughtfully. "You're probably right that it was a well-planned crime, but only for Lindberger. Sure enough, the poor guy had a visit from the pincers in the neck. But if the Kentucky Killer shot someone in the heart, too, then that's the first time he's broken the pattern. It could be that our John Doe is the *burglar*, and that he happened to see the murderer as he was dragging his victim, and was discovered and shot. I would bet the Lindberger murder was planned, but the John Doe murder wasn't."

Hultin nodded calmly. "Back to basics, then. Why did the Kentucky Killer come to Sweden? He obviously knew Gallano in some way, but was Gallano the *reason* he emigrated? Once he'd done what he came to do — murder Gallano — wasn't the rest just a matter of continued bloodthirstiness? That after nine claustrophobic days of increasing corpse stench, his desire became too strong, and it was time to kill again? Or was Gallano more of a means than an end? Was Eric Lindberger the real target? The strange murder location would suggest

196

it — you don't just go down to the deserted Frihamnen at night to search for victims. No, he *knew* Lindberger would be there. So Eric Lindberger must also be carefully investigated."

"Of course, it's not at all certain that Eric Lindberger *was* there," said Kerstin Holm. "He could have been *taken* there. The killer could have randomly chosen him as a victim in the city, chloroformed him, and taken him to a deserted place with suitable buildings. Or perhaps they planned to meet for one reason or another, and Lindberger went along willingly. Both the victim and the location might very well be random."

Hultin nodded; he was getting used to his scenarios being torn to shreds. Was he starting to lose his edge? Was it time to hand the controls over to his first officer? And Kerstin Holm (who many years later would actually *become* his successor) was very much a first officer at present.

"We need to find the site of the murder," he said. "There must be hundreds of places just in the area near where we found John Doe."

"Well, LinkCoop is closest," said Nyberg, remembering his visit to Täby.

Hultin gathered his strength. "The problem is, we know too little about the Kentucky Killer," he said. "You have the best idea of what's up, Kerstin. Isn't there a lot missing?"

"If we're going to have a chance of finding the Swedish link," she said, "we'll probably have to go to the United States and consult the FBI and Ray Larner. That's my assessment. It's not at all certain that the

Americans would recognise a Swedish link if it jumped up and bit them on the arse. They hardly know where Sweden is. Swiss watches and polar bears in the street . . ." Holm paused. "He's slipped through our hands this time, thanks to your lost lawyers. We can investigate Gallano, the drug syndicate, Lindberger, the Ministry of Foreign Affairs and LinkCoop all we want, but I think the only reasonable path is the American one. We have to know who he is and what he's doing in Sweden. Once we understand these things, we can catch him. We can't otherwise."

"Now it's been confirmed that he's here," said Hultin. "It wouldn't have been possible for us to waste the taxpayers' money on a visit to America before it was certain. Now it is. And now we have quite a bit to work with — and, for that matter, to offer the FBI. Tomorrow I'll ask Mörner for permission to send a pair of you to the United States. One would be the person who knows the material best. That's you, Kerstin. And the second would be a more, hmm" — he mumbled, giving Hjelm a sidelong glance — "a more action-orientated person."

Hjelm gave a start. Against his will he was being yanked away just as things were starting to move. He had just discovered a horribly tortured and rotten corpse in a basement in the wilderness; tonight when he went home, he would have to find out whether his son was a junkie; and now he was being given notice of a trip to the United States. Along with Kerstin, of all people. It was too much.

"Lagnmyr is out to get you," said Hultin expressionlessly. "It's a good opportunity to get away."

"I'm going to the United States?" Hjelm said, confused. "And what the hell is Lagnmyr?"

"Svante Ernstsson bore as much of the brunt as he could," Hultin continued, unperturbed, "but Lagnmyr saw right through him. I don't think he even knew about the stakeout spot before you ruined it, but he doesn't like you, that much is for certain. So go to the United States. Tell Larner about your KGB theory. I'm sure that'll go down well."

"But I can't go to the United States," Hjelm continued, still confused. "It's all happening here."

"We'll see what happens with Mörner." Hultin tried to smooth things out. "Pack a bag anyway. The provisional division of labour this evening is as follows: Paul and Kerstin go to the United States, Jorge takes on Gallano, Gunnar works on LinkCoop, Viggo takes John Doe, and Arto takes Lindberger and the Ministry of Foreign Affairs. Does that sound reasonable?"

No one spoke. It was getting late, after all.

"One more thing," said Hultin quietly. "We can't keep this from the media any longer. It's begun — they're going to whip up the mood and hunt for headlines. Swedes are going to install hundreds of thousands of extra locks on their doors; they'll procure thousands of weapons, legally and illegally; and security firms will do great business. So far American serial killers have been an exotic but distant threat, but all at once we're coming a great deal closer to the American social climate. The last breath of relative innocence is going to disappear in a tornado of general mistrust. Everyone will be looking over his shoulder."

Hultin leaned forward across his desk.

"The devil is here, ladies and gentlemen, and even if we catch him, no exorcism will be able to drive out what he brought with him."

# CHAPTER
# NINETEEN

His only protection against the rain a borrowed police umbrella, smartly stamped with abundant police logos, Paul Hjelm wandered through the Norsborg night. The rain seemed here to stay. The pitch-black sky warned of the biblical flood, as he thought more and more often.

What was happening to Sweden, that little country in the sticks, up by the Arctic Circle, whose populist movements had once conceived of the first democracy that truly extended down into the ranks of the people, but that had never brought it to fruition? The country had finagled its way out of the horrors of World War II, kept all its skeletons in the cupboard, and ended up with a fabulous competitive advantage compared to all other European countries. For that reason, it could play the self-righteous world conscience until other countries, or at least those unhampered by intrinsic sluggishness, caught up; and then Sweden would see the end of not only the world's highest standard of living but also of its status as the world's conscience. Swedes' strange, naive, deterministic conviction that everything would work out for the better meant that during the 1980s they, more than any other people, surrendered themselves to international capital, and they let it run more freely there than anywhere else.

The inevitable downfall brought a decisive collapse of all political control over the fickle whims of computerised capital. Everyone had to pay to clean up the mess — except business. As the country neared bankruptcy, its large-scale companies were maximising their profits. The burden of payment was placed on households, on the health care system, on education, on culture — on anything that was fairly long-term. The slightest suggestion that business ought also to pay for a tiny, tiny bit of the mess it had made was met by unanimous threats of leaving the country.

All at once the whole population was forced to think of money. The soul of the Swedish people was filled to bursting, from all directions, with financial thoughts, until only small, small holes were left unfilled — and there, of course, nothing long-term could find room. There was room only for lotteries, betting and shitty entertainment on television; love was replaced by idealised soap operas and cable TV porn; the desire for some sort of spirituality was satisfied by pre-packaged New Age solutions; all music that reached the public was tailor-made for sales; the media stole the language and made themselves the norm; advertisements stole emotions and shifted them away from their proper objects; drug abuse increased considerably.

The 1990s were the decade when capitalism test-drove a future in which the hordes of lifelong unemployed had to be kept in check so they didn't revolt. Numbing entertainment, drugs that didn't require a lot of follow-up

202

care, ethnic conflicts to give rage an outlet, gene manipulation to minimise the future need for health care, and a constant focus on the monthly act of balancing one's own private finances — would it take anything more to ruin the human soul that had developed over the millennia? Was there still dangerous ground somewhere, where a free, creative and critical thought could be suppressed and redirected before it had time to flower?

The Power Murders had been a reaction, but a *directed* reaction. Blindly striking, conscience-free violence hadn't yet shown up in this country, that extremely frustrated and ice-cold, sympathy-constipated reaction against everything and everyone. But now it had begun. Everything would change — and that was logical. One can't be choosy about what is imported from the rulers of the universe. If one chooses to import an entire culture, then the dark sides will come along too, sooner or later.

Through the impenetrable deluge of water, Paul Hjelm glimpsed the illuminated contours of a city-planning project that was meant to destroy the last remnants of human dignity. He stopped, closed his umbrella with the illusory insignia of the police, and let the torrents wash over him. Who was he to cast the first stone?

He squeezed his eyes shut. What was left of the simple private ethics that functioned when one wasn't seen, when people did good without needing to show it? Of do unto others as you wish them to do unto you? Was it all in ruins?

He had planned to end the day by checking out a service car, but now that he was suddenly on his way to contemporary culture's place of birth, he wouldn't need one. So he had taken the Metro home again. And now, having wandered through Norsborg, he set himself in motion. He ran. He ran through the volumes of water with his umbrella folded under his arm. He needed to run until exhaustion filled his entire soul and pushed everything else away. He did so by the time he reached the door of his terraced house. There he stumbled into the hall, panting alarmingly. It was dark, past eleven o'clock. He could see a faint light coming from the living room: it wasn't the television light for once — more like a small, flickering flame. He stopped in the hall until his breathing returned to normal. He pulled off his leather jacket and hung it up in the overcrowded hall. Then he turned the corner.

Danne was sitting in the living room waiting. No MTV, no comic book, no video game. Just Danne and a little flame.

Paul rubbed his soaking-wet eye sockets hard before he could attempt to meet his son's eyes. It still wasn't possible. They were boring deep into the table next to the little tea light that glimmered in an icy grotto of glass.

He walked over and sat down on the sofa next to his son.

A few minutes passed in silence. Neither of them knew how to begin, so no one began.

Finally Danne whispered, as though his voice had been cried away, "He just dragged me along. I didn't know where we were going."

"Is that a fact?" Paul Hjelm said.

204

Danne nodded. It was quiet for another moment.

Then the father placed an arm around his son's shoulders. He didn't recoil.

Becoming an adult just means being able to hide your uncertainty better.

"I've seen it too often," Paul said quietly. "Do it just a few times, and you ruin your life. You can't let that happen."

"It won't."

First had come the sight of the sky, the sun, the moon, the forest, the sea. The first human gaze saw all of this. Then came fire, which first scared people to death but was soon tamed and became man's companion. The little flame in front of them became a campfire. The clan gathered around it. It was a matter of survival of their blood. They remained in front of the ancient sight, and it brought out the memory of blood.

*Bad blood always comes back round.*

They stood up. Their eyes met.

"Thanks," said Paul, without knowing why.

They blew out the flame and walked upstairs together. As Paul opened the door to his bedroom, Danne said, "You were awfully . . . tough today."

"I was scared out of my mind."

He felt paradoxically proud as he fumbled his way through the pitch-black bedroom. He didn't shower or brush his teeth; he crept right into the bed next to Cilla. He needed her warmth.

"What was happening with Danne?" she mumbled.

"Nothing," he said. And meant it.

"You're cold as ice," she said, without pulling away.

"Warm me up."

She lay still and warmed him. He thought of his upcoming trip to America and all its potential complications. All he really wanted was for things to be as simple as this: children to delight in and a woman to warm himself with.

"I'm going to the United States tomorrow," he said, testing her a little.

"Yes," she said, sleeping.

He smiled. His umbrella was closed, and he was dry. For the time being.

# CHAPTER
# TWENTY

Arto Söderstedt didn't usually miss the sun. He was a lover of nuance, and as a newcomer to Stockholm, his manner of enjoying the city fell in a grey zone between a tourist's superficial fascination and a native's experienced gaze. The sun promoted both types of relationships, but the more profound pleasure of the newcomer required a certain degree of cloudiness, enough that the colours could come into their own without being flattened by the distorting light of the sun. That his theory might have something to do with his own sensitivity to the sun was not something he'd reflected on.

But now he'd had enough of clouds. He was standing in one of his favourite places in the city and could barely see his hand in front of his face, and he definitely couldn't see either Operan or the Arvfurstens Palace, home to the Ministry of Foreign Affairs. That was where he was strutting off to now, under his silly Bamse cartoon umbrella, which he had grabbed at home by accident; he could visualise his next-youngest daughter's face staring up into a heavenly arch of police logos. As he climbed the venerable steps, he had to admit that he truly missed the sun.

He wasn't the envious type, but he felt a bit aggrieved that he hadn't been considered for the trip to the United States; he *was* the serial killer expert, after all. Instead he was now treading the monotonous paths of fieldwork all the way to the reception desk at the Ministry of Foreign Affairs.

The receptionist informed him in a reserved tone that Justine Lindberger was off sick, that Eric Lindberger was deceased, and that a day of mourning had been announced for the entire ministry. Söderstedt found it unnecessary to tell her that this information was superfluous, not only because he was working on the case but also because his eyes were open. After all, the story had appeared in every single morning paper and news broadcast. Not even a sleepwalker could have missed the fact that the dreadful Kentucky Killer had come to Sweden, nor that the police had known about it for almost two weeks without saying a word or giving citizens a chance to protect themselves. Söderstedt had counted eight pundits who demanded that all responsible officials' heads roll.

"Did the Lindbergers work in the same department?"

The receptionist, a distrustful woman in her fifties, was sitting behind glass and looking like a work by a modern Velázquez, a thoroughly true-to-life but still incredibly mean depiction of a dying class. Söderstedt realised that, after all was said and done, he preferred this languishing, contrary sort of receptionist to today's streamlined version.

The woman was paging with obvious reluctance through a folder. After a great deal of toil, during which she almost groaned audibly, she answered, "Yes."

*An exquisite answer,* Söderstedt thought. "Who is their closest supervisor?"

More groaning, toiling, and effort. Then: "Anders Wahlberg."

"Is he here?"

"Now?"

*No, the first Tuesday after the Ascension Day before last,* Söderstedt thought, but said with an ingratiating smile, "Yes."

Then she began again the customary procedure of extreme effort; in this case it consisted of pushing two keys on the computer. After this almost superhuman amount of work, the woman was unable to answer with more than an absolutely breathless "Yes".

"Do you suppose I might be able to speak to him?"

The look she gave him was the sort that had once met plantation owners with ox whips. The slave was once again forced to demean herself. She pressed no fewer than three buttons on an internal telephone and, with the last remnants of her anguished voice, said, "The police."

"Oh?" an indifferent male voice rasped out of the telephone.

"Is it OK?"

"Now?"

"Yes."

"Yes."

As a result of this inspiring dialogue, Söderstedt wandered through one chandelier-lit corridor after another. He got lost twelve times. Finally he found the venerable door behind which the department's deputy director general, Anders Wahlberg, kept himself. He knocked.

"Come in" came a thunderous voice.

Arto Söderstedt opened the door into an elegant atrium with a mute secretary and then entered an even more elegant office with a view of the Stockholm Sound. Anders Wahlberg was in his early fifties and wore his corpulence with the same tangible pride as he did his mint-green tie; it looked like Arto's youngest daughter's bib after a full-blown food fight.

"Arto Söderstedt," said Arto Söderstedt. "National Criminal Police."

"Wahlberg," said Wahlberg. "I understand it's about Lindberger. What a story. Eric couldn't have had a single enemy in the whole wide world."

Söderstedt sat on a chair opposite Wahlberg's candelabra-adorned mahogany desk. "What did Lindberger work on?"

"Both of the spouses concentrate on the Arab world. They have primarily devoted themselves to business with Saudi Arabia and have worked with the embassy there. They're young and promising. Future top diplomats, both of them. We thought. Is it really an American serial killer?"

"It seems so," Söderstedt said curtly. "How old are they? Or were?"

"Justine is twenty-eight; Eric was thirty-three. Dying at thirty-three . . ."

"That was the average age of death in the Middle Ages."

"Certainly," said Wahlberg, surprised.

"Did they always work together?"

"Essentially. They had slightly different concentrations with their business contacts. In general, their tasks were the same: to facilitate trade between Sweden and, first and foremost, Saudi Arabia. They had close cooperation with industry representatives from both countries."

"Different concentrations?"

"Eric worked primarily with the big Swedish export firms. Justine worked with the somewhat smaller ones. Simply put."

"Did they always travel together?"

"Not always, no. They made lots of trips back and forth and weren't always synchronised."

"And no enemies at all?"

"No, absolutely not. Not a single problem. Irreproachable and solid work, in general. Cash cows, you could have said, if it didn't sound so vulgar. Justine was to have travelled down there one of these days, but I'm assuming she won't be able to now. The plan was for Eric to be based at home for a few more months. Now it will be home base forever and ever amen."

"Do you know what Justine's trip 'one of these days' was about?"

"Not in detail. She was going to brief me today, actually. Some kind of problem with new legislation about small business trade. A meeting with Saudi government representatives."

"And with the best will in the world, you can't imagine that Eric's death was because of anything other than randomness or fate?"

Anders Wahlberg shook his head and looked down at his desk. He seemed on the verge of tears.

"We were friends," he said. "He was like a son to me. We had booked time to play golf this weekend. It's inconceivable, horrible. Was he — tortured?"

"I'm afraid he was," said Söderstedt, realising that his sympathetic tone sounded false, so he changed to a harsher one. "I'm sure I don't need to remind you how important it is that we catch this murderer. Is there anything else you can remember, professionally or privately, that might be of significance? The tiniest little thing could be important."

Wahlberg shoved his sorrow behind the mask of a true diplomat and appeared to think it over.

"I can't think of anything. Between you and me, they were probably the only truly happy couple I know. There was a natural affinity between them. I don't have any children of my own, and I'll miss Eric as I'd miss a son. I'll miss his laugh, his natural integrity, his humble composure. Shit."

"Can you think of any reason for him to have been at Frihamnen at two thirty in the morning?"

"No. It sounds crazy. He hardly ever even went out for a beer after work on Fridays. He always went straight home to Justine."

212

"I need to take a peek at his office. And if you could make sure that all his data files are copied and sent to me, I would be extra grateful."

Anders Wahlberg nodded mutely and stood. He took Söderstedt out into the corridor and stopped in front of Lindberger's door. Then he disappeared back into his den of sorrow.

Söderstedt took a few steps. The door to the right of Eric Lindberger's was Justine's. The spouses lived and worked literally side by side. He went into Eric's office.

It was smaller than Wahlberg's, it lacked the secretary's atrium, and the view wasn't of the Sound but of Fredsgatan. There was a connecting door into his wife's office; he checked and found it unlocked.

The desk contained a moderate jumble of work papers, nothing more. A wedding picture showed a very young, dark Justine and a slightly older but just as dark Eric. They were smiling the same broad smile, and it didn't seem nearly as pasted-on as the genre invites; it was professionally practised but natural nonetheless. The happy couple gave the impression of belonging to a higher class of citizen by virtue of birth and force of habit, with full knowledge of all its etiquette. Neither of them appeared to have fought particularly hard for their career; on the contrary, both seemed born to be diplomats.

But perhaps he was reading too much into a standard photograph.

As for the rest of the room, Söderstedt found some notes written on everything from official Ministry of Foreign Affairs stationery to yellow Post-its, as well as a rather thick planner; he hunted for the correct term, *fax* something, *Filofax* — was that it? In any case, he collected everything, put it into his briefcase, and took it with him as he opened the connecting door and slipped into Justine's office. It was all but identical to her husband's.

He inspected her desk, too. It was decorated with the same wedding photo, or rather another from the same series. Their smiles were a bit less pronounced, and there was something less self-sufficient in it; a vague sense of unease hovered over them, a disturbance. The minor difference between the photos spoke to Söderstedt's extremely well-developed sense of nuance.

Just as in her husband's office, in Justine's there were many notes scribbled on various pieces of paper, on the desk and in the drawers, which he rooted through even though the act could hardly be characterised as legitimate. He copied the occasionally cryptic notes and fished an identical Filofax out of a desk drawer. He peered around the room and spotted what he was looking for, a small photocopier, and he nervously copied a month forward and a month backwards in the planner; that ought to be enough.

He packed the copied notes and the photocopies into his briefcase, next to what he had already confiscated, and put Justine Lindberger's Filofax back where he'd found it. Then he returned to Eric's office, stepped out into the corridor and went down the stairs. He nodded cheerfully at the receptionist, who looked as if she'd been eating dog shit, opened his glorious Bamse umbrella and rushed out into the pouring rain.

214

He'd had to park his service Audi on the other side of Gustav Adolfs Torg, over by Operan, and now he ran straight across the square with his briefcase glued to his body to keep it dry; the Bamse umbrella barely protected more than his head.

He jumped into the Audi and opened the briefcase. He skimmed through the pale copies of Justine Lindberger's planner so that he would have a few trump cards in his hand when he met the recent widow; he hoped he wouldn't have to use them.

Then he turned the car out along the Stockholm Sound, drove past Operakällaren, crossed Blasieholmen and Nybrokajen, drove up Sibyllegatan, and took a right onto Riddargatan at the Army Museum; the stupid hot-air balloon that had been filled with tourists and raised up and down all summer was still there, but it looked deserted in the rain.

Partway up the hill he stopped, did a seriously illegal parking job outside the unloading dock of a boutique, and rushed into a doorway where, sheltered from the rain, he pressed the intercom button next to the names ERIC AND JUSTINE LINDBERGER.

After four rings he heard a faint "Yes?"

"Justine Lindberger?"

"Not the press again, I hope?"

"The police. Detective Inspector Arto Söderstedt."

"Come in."

The lock buzzed and he went in, climbed six lift-free flights of stairs, and found Justine Lindberger standing in the door. Viggo Norlander hadn't been exaggerating when he described her delicate beauty in fairly unpoetic terms.

"Söderstedt," he panted, waving his police ID. "I hope I'm not disturbing you too much."

"Come in," she said again. Her voice was weak from crying.

The apartment looked about as he had expected: elegant through and through, high-class but not flashy — rather, austere and subtle. He fumbled internally for adjectives.

In the living room Justine Lindberger offered him a spot on the leather sofa, which seemed unused. Of course, it was comfortable to the point of immediately inducing sleepiness. Opposite a low, lemon-shaped glass table, she sat down on the edge of a stylish Windsor chair. A glass door led to a balcony that looked out on Nybroviken and Skeppsholmen.

"I'm sorry for your loss," he said quietly. "Have the media been difficult?"

"Yes, I've been feeling horribly pressed."

It never bodes well to start off with a misunderstanding, so he refrained from quibbling over the meaning of the word *press*. In addition, he had to decide quickly whether to use the informal version of the pronoun *you* or the more formal one. He decided on informal: "Can you think of any reason at all for your husband's murder?"

"No." She shook her head and scrupulously avoided meeting his eyes, as she had since he arrived. "If it's a serial killer, I guess it was just by chance. The most awful kind imaginable."

"There's no other possibility? It's not something connected with your contacts in the Arab world?"

"Our contacts have been utterly peaceful."

"You were supposed to go to Saudi Arabia on Friday. What was that all about?"

She finally met his gaze. Her dark brown eyes were brimming with sorrow, but for a split second he seemed to see a deeper sorrow there, a guilt even deeper than the survivor always feels towards the dead partner; all the unfinished things that would forever remain unfinished, everything a person ought to have said but had always put off. It was something more than that, he was certain of it, but her eyes moved away before he had time to define it.

"It was about details of some new Saudi import laws — the consequences for small Swedish businesses. What could that have to do with this?"

"Most likely nothing. I just have to get a clear picture of the situation. For example, is there anyone who would profit if you were excluded from the meeting?"

She nodded heavily, then met his gaze again; there might have been a tiny new spark in her eyes. "Do you mean that it might *not* have anything to do with — what was he called — the Kentucky Killer?" She spat out the word.

"I'm trying to find possibilities other than pure chance," Söderstedt replied mildly.

"My job is to facilitate the business activity of Swedish companies in Saudi Arabia, at the expense of domestic and other foreign companies. For the time being, I'm the only person who is completely familiar with the situation, and my absence could potentially mean a certain competitive advantage for companies from other countries."

"Which sectors are affected by these new Saudi laws?"

"Primarily the machine industry. But the changes in question are far too small to motivate anyone to commit any sort of crime, least of all murder."

Söderstedt nodded. "How would you describe your relationship with Eric?"

"It was very good," she said immediately. "Very, very good. In all ways."

"Isn't it difficult to work alongside your husband?"

"On the contrary. We share an interest. Shared. Past tense!" she shouted, then suddenly stood and ran to the bathroom. He heard the tap running as ferociously as on an upper-class Japanese toilet.

Söderstedt got up and started walking around the apartment. It gradually dawned on him that it was much larger than his first impression had led him to believe. He walked and walked, but it never ended, and then he was suddenly back where he'd started. Three doors led out into the stairwell; the Lindberg home encompassed the entire floor, which had originally been divided into three apartments. He counted at least ten rooms. Three bathrooms. Two kitchens. Why two kitchens?

Employees of the Ministry of Foreign Affairs, he knew, had a good basic salary and their daily allowance nearly doubled it, but an apartment like this must have cost tens of millions of kronor. Likely a substantial

**218**

amount of family capital had been invested from both sides.

He sat down, and when she came back, he looked as though he hadn't moved. Her face was reddish, as if it had just been scrubbed. Otherwise everything was the same.

"Please forgive me." She returned to the edge of the white Windsor chair.

"No problem," he said grandly. "You don't have any children?"

She shook her head. "I'm only twenty-eight. We still had plenty of time."

"This is a pretty big apartment for two people."

She met his gaze, immediately on the defensive. "Shall we stick to the point?" she asked cuttingly.

"I apologise, but we do need a clear picture of the circumstances of the inheritance. What are they? Do you inherit everything?"

"Yes. Yes, I inherit everything. Do you think I tortured my own husband? Do you think I let him suffer for an hour of hell while I stuck horrific pincers into his neck?"

*Now, now,* he thought. *Smooth things over now.*

"I'm sorry," he said. "I apologise."

It wasn't enough. She had risen to her feet again and was half shouting, the panic in her voice rising. "Small people like you can't have the slightest idea of how much I loved him. And now he's dead — gone — gone forever. Some fucking lunatic has tortured my beloved and thrown him into the sea. Can you even imagine what ran through his head during that last horrible hour? I know that the last thing he thought of was me; I have to find solace in the fact that it gave him comfort. It must have. It was my fault that he died! I should have died, not him! He died in my place!"

Halfway through the torrent of words, Söderstedt was at the telephone. He was about to call for an ambulance when Justine Lindberger suddenly went quiet and sat down. To be sure, her hands were still twisting around in her lap, but she was calm enough to announce, "I took a few tranquillisers in the bathroom. They're starting to work now. Continue."

"Are you sure?"

"Yes. Continue."

Söderstedt returned a bit clumsily to the sofa. Now he too was sitting on the edge of the furniture. "What did you mean by saying you should have died instead?"

"He was a happier person than I am."

"That's all?"

"It's not just that. It would have been enormously fortunate for the world if I had died instead."

Söderstedt thought of the minute difference in the wedding pictures on the couple's respective office desks and was secretly happy for hitting the nail on the head. "Can you expand on that a little?"

"Everything was so easy for Eric — he floated along without a care in the world. I don't do that. Not at all. I don't want to say more than that."

Söderstedt decided not to push her, out of concern for her condition. Instead he asked, "Can you think of any reason why he would have been at Frihamnen at two thirty in the morning?"

"None at all. I don't believe he went there on his own. He must have been taken there."

He changed tack, partly because he was flustered: "What is the situation like in Saudi Arabia now?"

"What do you mean?" she asked, surprised.

"In regard to fundamentalism, for example."

She eyed him somewhat suspiciously but answered professionally: "It's there. But for the time being, it doesn't cause any hurdles for business. The government keeps it in check, often with rather tough measures."

"What about the women? Aren't there a few compulsory veils?"

"Don't forget that fundamentalism is a popular movement, and what seems compulsory to Western eyes may not always be so. We're a little too quick to believe that our norms are the only correct ones. There are actually still considerably more people who wipe their arses with their left hand than there are people who shake hands with their right."

"Of course," said Söderstedt, bracing himself. "But isn't it the case that the Gulf War had a much different effect than intended? The Americans concentrated their efforts against Saddam Hussein, who is more of a secularised dictator; they uninhibitedly murdered civilians, women and children; they kept Saddam in power; they united the Muslims; and they threw so many resources at Saudi Arabia, for the sake of oil, that a large portion of that money benefited Saudi fundamentalism. Saudi fundamentalism is, after all, the richest and best-organised system in the Arab world, the spider in the worldwide net, and it's been supported to a great extent by American funds. Isn't that ironic?"

Justine Lindberger stared in amazement at the strange, chalk-white, slender Finland-Swedish policeman who was candidly airing his political theories. At last she said in a measured tone, "Maybe you ought to become a politician."

"No, thanks," said Arto Söderstedt.

# CHAPTER
# TWENTY-ONE

The biblical flood refused to end. The rain's eternally drumming gloom drowned out every spark of clarity, and dampness found its way into every corner and rotting, mouldy hole. It seeped rapidly into the core, into the very source, a shaking, roaring inferno, the birthplace of the biblical flood; a deeper darkness, thoroughly incomprehensible. And then the plane came out the other side, to clarity, serenity, light; to the broad view that made the earlier darkness seem so small, distant and understandable.

Paul Hjelm wished life were like a plane taking off in an autumn storm.

Or at least that this case were like that.

The sun was as blinding as darkness for the snow-blind. It lit up the tops of the pitch-black masses of clouds and made them shine with a Renaissance-bronze colour, like Rembrandt's backgrounds.

He couldn't tear himself away from the play of colours; colours had been missing for so long. In real time, the autumn storm had been going on for only a few days, but real time had nothing to do with it — the rain had erased all his memories of summer in one fell swoop. His memory had stopped with the Kentucky

Killer's arrival in Sweden, which swept everything that had come before into darkness.

He hoped that the successive encounters with the sun that would come during the flight would mean a clear sort of non-time; the plane would land at approximately the same time it had taken off. If it didn't crash.

He was scarcely afraid of flying, yet those seconds when the acceleration ceases and the wheels leave the ground always caused him a deep thrill, as he unconditionally put his life in the hands of a stranger.

Only after fifteen minutes of losing himself in pure fascination did he even think of turning to Kerstin Holm. When he did, she was still there. He recognised the expression he had never seen on himself, but which, after the fact, he realised he must have had. When the drinks trolley went by, they exchanged something like a normal glance, but they were still far from words.

Here the serial killer had sat, maybe in this very seat, staring out not into the blinding sun but into the equally blinding darkness. What had he thought about? What had he felt, experienced? He had just murdered a person — what had flowed through his darkened soul?

And why had he come to Sweden? In the answer to that question, after all, lay the solution to this strange and elusive case. He tried to recap it roughly. In the late 1970s, a man starts to murder people in the American Midwest, in a manner reminiscent of a torture method used by a special task force in Vietnam called Commando Cool. The victims, eighteen of them in four years and primarily in Kentucky, have mostly remained

224

unidentified. Most of the ones who are identified are academics, both foreign and American. The FBI focuses on the special task force's squad leader, Wayne Jennings; possibly they also try to find Commando Cool's unknown commander, who goes by the name Balls. Jennings dies in a car accident after sixteen murders have been committed. Two more murders follow; after that there's a timeout for more than a decade.

Then the murders start again. All signs point to the same perpetrator. This time he is active in the north-eastern United States, especially in New York. And this time the victims are all identified, and they come from very different backgrounds. The pattern seems more random this time. After the sixth murder in the second round, the twenty-fourth overall, the murder of the Swede Lars-Erik Hassel, the killer suddenly leaves the country and arrives in Stockholm on a fake passport. There he goes to drug dealer Andreas Gallano's secret cabin, about forty miles north of Stockholm, which, according to the latest information, is free of fingerprints and fibres, meticulously cleaned. About a week later, he sets off from the cabin in Gallano's Saab, leaving behind Gallano, who has been murdered in the serial killer's distinctive method. Probably the killer leaves the cabin at night. He goes to Frihamnen, where he murders two more people: Erik Lindberger of the Ministry of Foreign Affairs, and a still-unidentified twenty-five-year-old. Lindberger has been tortured to death in the same way, but the unknown man, the John Doe, is shot to death. This is the only known occasion when the murderer deviates from his usual method and uses a firearm. Presumably he changes now-patriotic cars, from the Saab to a ten-year-old dark blue Volvo station wagon with a number plate that starts with B. There's been no sign of him since.

How the hell did it all fit together?

"How the hell does all this fit together?" said Kerstin Holm, her first words since the plane had taken off from Arlanda and set course for New York. She and Hjelm were apparently on the same wavelength.

"I don't know," said Paul Hjelm.

Then it was quiet.

The sun shone blindly, as though it belonged to no particular season, outside the trembling Plexiglas aeroplane windows; it could just as easily have been a winter sun as a summer one — but it was an autumn sun. They found themselves in a detached moment. It was a journey through time, the only possible kind. Time passed and no time passed. It was a place for contemplation.

He would have liked to have a whisky and soda and listen to music and read a book. All of that would have to wait.

Should he use the time to develop hypotheses, then? No, those would have to wait. This was more a time to establish openness, a critical receptiveness, to all the information and impressions that would come streaming towards them in the new world. They would have to keep the questions coming without trying to answer them too quickly. For there were so many questions.

Why does he kill? Is it for the same reasons before and after his break? Why did he take a break for almost fifteen years? Is it really the same killer? Why does everyone feel there's something wrong with the image of him as a classic serial killer? Why was Lars-Erik Hassel murdered at the airport? Why did the murderer go to Sweden? Why did he use a thirty-two-year-old's passport if he is over fifty? How did he find Gallano's cabin in Riala? Why did he change cars in Frihamnen? Was it because he *wanted* Gallano's corpse to be traced via his car? After all, Lindberger's corpse was easy to find, too. Does he, like most serial killers, want to display his art for an audience? Why did he murder Lindberger, an employee of the Ministry of Foreign Affairs? What was Lindberger doing in Frihamnen in the middle of the night? Where was he murdered? Is the failed break-in at the computer company LinkCoop's warehouse connected to the case? Why did the killer shoot John Doe instead of torturing him? Who the hell is this John Doe, who can't be found in any international registry? Are we asking the right questions?

The last question was perhaps the most important. Was there a link between all these questions, something you couldn't see until you got up high enough and looked down at the darkness in the crystal-clear sunlight, and then it would be obvious?

Right now it didn't feel like it.

But at least they were on their way.

# CHAPTER
# TWENTY-TWO

A wasp had come into the room to die. How it had survived the storms of the past few days was a mystery. Perhaps, more dead than alive, it had managed to hide from the madness in some musty hole but hadn't died there. Instead it had come out with its stinger drawn, ready to wound even in the last moments of its life. A doomed survivor with all its senses but the sixth gone: the sixth sense, that of a killer.

The wasp made a few wobbly rounds of the fluorescent tube light up on the ceiling, as unaffected by heat as it was by light. It buzzed suddenly; it was no longer the usual drone of a wasp but was duller, more aggressive. Then it rushed downward, a last kamikaze attack with its stinger raised. It came closer.

Chavez executed a mercy killing. A precise backhand using a yellowed issue of *Expressen* sent the body into the corner under the churning old dot-matrix printer; the stinger stuck straight up from the crumpled body. The body would almost certainly lie there until next year, when a light spring breeze would reveal it to be a collection of dust that stuck together only out of habit.

228

As he stared at the wasp, he had a lightning-like but wordless insight. For a split second he thought he saw the core of the case, crystal clear.

Then reality returned and concealed his clarity with a data list that was growing and curling up on itself, on the floor over the wasp. A shroud of everyday, routine work enveloped the detective's stroke of genius.

The printer stopped printing. Chavez got up, tore off the list, tore at his hair, and observed his own future as though in an utterly trivial crystal ball. The list of dark blue Volvo station wagons with number plates that started with B and that were registered in Sweden was long, surprisingly long. He was bored with this task before he'd even started.

He would start by crossing out all those Volvos that were older than fifteen and newer than five years old. After that he would concentrate on those in the Stockholm area. That would bring the cars down to a manageable number — sixty-eight.

Jorge Chavez threw the list down onto his desk and picked up a list he had made himself. There he wrote, as point number three, "The Volvo shit". Point number one was "The cabin shit": to return to the nightmarish cabin in Riala in full daylight to assist the industrious technicians, who, to their vociferous surprise, had not found a single strand of hair at the site of the murder and therefore were continuing their intensive search. Point number two was "The Hall shit": to go to Hall and talk to Andreas Gallano's fellow inmates and go through his belongings, which he had left behind after his escape a month ago.

Chavez had drawn Gallano in the lottery, and as if that weren't enough, the damn Volvo had been assigned to him, too. This was the work he'd inherited from Kerstin, and he couldn't help harbouring an envious grudge; he and Hjelm could damn sure have been of much greater use to the FBI. They were, after all, the ones for whom things had been moving along; first with Laban Hassel, then with Andreas Gallano.

He wondered, in his not-entirely-peaceful conscience, what he had done to earn the dunce cap. *He* hadn't run over small children at Arlanda or groped chicks in the passport check. *He* hadn't taken off for Tallinn on a purge à la Charles Bronson and ended up on the floorboards like a fallen version of the only begotten son. And yet here he sat with the worst job of all while that nobody Norlander was gathering up the few brain cells he had and destroying the next most stimulating job: taking on John Doe. That job demanded the right man — and Norlander was definitely not that man.

Chavez's modest request for a change had brought him two things: an icy look from Hultin and a list of two hundred dark blue Volvos.

He turned on the coffee-maker with the tip of his toe and watched the spout until the first drop hit his freshly ground Colombian beans. Then he gazed across the desk, where Hjelm was conspicuous by his absence.

*The man with the golden helmet*, Chavez thought maliciously. The fake Rembrandt. Perhaps the most admired of the master's paintings, and it turned out to have been done by an anonymous pupil.

He missed him already.

Then he gave a deep sigh, artfully poured the coffee while the hot water was still bubbling, and dived into the Volvo inferno.

The future was not his.

# CHAPTER
# TWENTY-THREE

The non-time had passed. The hours that didn't exist no longer existed. They landed at Newark in a boiling-hot noonday sun that embraced the entire unending system of runways; from up in the sky, they had glittered in the sun like an inexperienced fly fisherman's tangle of lines.

Paul and Kerstin hadn't exchanged many words during the flight, not only because they had been contemplating the case; the disruptions in their relationship seemed to keep spreading — although neither of them thought much about it.

They were shepherded through passport control and had to wait more than half an hour for their luggage. After clearing customs, they finally entered the enormous arrivals hall, where a crowd of people were holding signs with the names of their unfamiliar arriving guests. After a few minutes, they realised that a sign in the hand of a tall suit-clad man, with the Lewis Carroll-inspired text "Yalm, Halm", must be directed at them. The renowned comedy duo of Yalm & Halm politely greeted the gigantic man, whose name they made out as Jerry Schonbauer, and who shepherded them to a slightly calmer part of the arrivals hall.

Waiting there was an equally well-dressed but slightly less stiff and slightly less FBI-like black man in his fifties. As the enormous Schonbauer took his place in the hierarchy just behind him, the black man extended his hand with a genuinely welcoming smile. "Ray Larner, FBI. You must be officers Yalm and Halm from Stockholm."

"Paul Hjelm," said Yalm.

"Kerstin Holm," said Halm.

"So he's started again now?" said Larner with a regretful smile. "A pair of fresh eyes is probably what this case needs."

"It's basically a matter of adding our information to your vast archive of knowledge," said Kerstin with gently ingratiating humility.

Larner nodded. "As you know, I've devoted a great deal of my professional life to this character, and yet I still don't know what he's up to. He is the most mysterious of all our serial killers. With most of them, you can come up with an approximate motive and psychological profile pretty quickly, but K deviates from almost all the usual norms. You will have seen my report, of course."

They nodded. Larner called the Kentucky Killer "K", as did the diehards in FASK, Fans of American Serial Killers, with whom Chavez had Internet contact. They shivered a joint shiver.

Jerry Schonbauer picked up their luggage, which hanging from his fists looked like toiletry bags. As they started walking, Larner asked them, "What do you say to the following schedule? We'll drive you to the hotel so you can freshen up after your journey. Then we'll have a late lunch at my favourite restaurant. And then we'll start work. But first" — he nodded at Schonbauer, who was drifting with their bags towards an exit glimmering in the distance — "a little guided tour of Newark International Airport."

Larner took them up the stairs to the check-in hall. They wandered for quite some time through an indoor landscape that never seemed to change; even the steady stream of travellers remained static.

Finally they stopped at a small door amid the sea of people. Larner pulled out a bunch of keys, slipped one in and yanked it open. It was a cleaner's cupboard, large model: fluorescent lights on the low ceiling, clean, whitewashed floors, and shelves with meticulously arranged cleaning equipment — rags, brushes, buckets, towels. They made their way around the shelves to a more open area with a chair and a desk with a few old sandwiches on it. On the wall above was a tiny window through which one could see the giant bodies of arriving and departing planes sweeping past.

This was where Lars-Erik Hassel spent the last hour of his life.

And what an hour.

Hjelm and Holm looked around the cupboard. There wasn't much to see. It was a clinical place in which to die a clinical death.

Larner pointed at the chair. "We've taken the original chair, of course. Aside from Mr Hassel's bodily fluids, there wasn't a trace on it. There never is."

"Never?" said Kerstin Holm.

"When we began, of course, there weren't any real possibilities for DNA testing." Larner shrugged. "But judging by the six murders in this new series, we probably weren't missing anything. The closet is spotless. Like he's superhuman. K."

This last word was just a letter, but his tone took it to astronomical heights.

"Nine," said Kerstin Holm.

Larner looked closely at her and nodded.

As they left the cupboard, Hjelm lingered for a few seconds in the open area. He wanted to be alone there. He sat in the chair and looked around. So sterile — such an American brand of sterile efficiency. He closed his eyes and tried to imagine just a tiny bit of the horrible, silent pain that these walls had encircled, tried to make some telepathic contact with Lars-Erik Hassel's suffering.

It didn't work.

It was there, but it was beyond words.

Agent Schonbauer drove with a practised hand through chaotic traffic of abnormal dimensions. Larner sat next to him, talking to Hjelm and Holm in the back seat: about the late-summer heat in New York, about "community policing", the city's new and successful model for fighting crime, about the structure and strange priorities of the Swedish police system, about the autumn storm in Stockholm, and extremely superficially, about the FBI and the Kentucky Killer. Throughout, Hjelm watched Larner, whose body language said something different from what the official, dark FBI costume projected. His controlled, cheerful relaxation and smooth, exact motions seemed to beg forgiveness for his get-up. Hjelm amused himself by comparing expected and actual appearances. First and foremost, he had not expected Larner to be black; embedded in that assumption, of course, was a whole package of prejudices. But he hadn't expected him to be so alert, either, after all the setbacks with K: the futile search twenty years ago; the pursuit of the apparently innocent Commando Cool leader Wayne Jennings, which had ended in Jennings's death; the resultant lawsuit and Larner's demotion; and then the reboot, when everything started up again. But Larner seemed detached, as if he were watching the spectacle with an indulgent smile. He seemed to possess the divine gift of being able to separate his professional and personal lives; he radiated, in some way, a happy home life.

They entered the gigantic Holland Tunnel, passed under the Hudson River, and came out on Canal Street, then turned left into SoHo. They drove up Eighth Avenue and arrived at a small hotel by the name Skipper's Inn near Chelsea Park. Because a free parking spot was as rare as a Swiftian utopia, they were dropped off on the pavement after being informed that Larner would return in an hour and a half. They climbed the stairs to the peculiarly long, narrow building that was crammed like a turn-of-the-century relic between two considerably glitzier Manhattan complexes of pearly glass.

They were given adjoining rooms, each with a window facing out onto West 25th Street, and thus took up a quarter of the sixth floor of this lodging house, which actually succeeded in feigning resemblance to an English inn — or rather, several inns stacked on top of one another. Their rooms were small and cosy, with a rustic touch, if you could ignore the roar outside the non-functional, quadruple-paned windows. Although the air conditioning was spurting air at full force and was competing with the racket from the street, it wasn't able to cool the room below body temperature.

Hjelm lay down on the bed, which rocked precariously. He had never been to the United States before, but there were two things he associated with the country: air conditioning and ice. Where was the ice? He got up and went over to the minibar. The top half of the small fridge was a freezer, and sure enough, it was filled with ice cubes. He took a few, returned to the bed, and let the ice cubes balance like horns on his forehead until they fell to his ears.

How he had longed for the sun in the Stockholm rain! Now he longed for the Stockholm rain. *The grass is always greener*, he thought, clichéd; his brain felt mushy.

In American films, New York was either sparkling with hysterical but happy Christmas snow, or it was boiling like a cauldron in the midsummer sun. Now he understood why. In mid-September, the happy Christmas snow was months away.

He made his way to the shabby but *amicably* shabby bathroom. There was a shower in a grungy little bath, and he made use of it, without preparing toiletries or a change of clothes — he just went straight in, satisfied that he'd remembered to take off what he was wearing. When he was finished, he didn't dry off but went over to the sink and drank from it. After five gulps it struck him that perhaps he shouldn't drink the water, and he spat and sputtered. The last thing he needed was to get a juicy case of travellers' diarrhoea.

He looked at himself in the bathroom mirror. In keeping with the style of the room, it was properly cracked. His reflection somewhat split, he met his own gaze a bit cubistically. The blemish on his cheek was the same as ever, but he gave thanks to various creators that it had at least stopped growing. For a while he had worried that it would end up covering his whole face.

Why did Kerstin's presence always make him think of that blemish?

He wandered into the bedroom, naked, and by the time he covered the twelve feet, he was dry; when he lay down on the bed, the sweat began to return. He lay there and pondered his male organ. He considered masturbating — that was always a way to make oneself feel at home — but the circumstances weren't right. Instead, he practised an appropriate breathing method, as strength-preserving as possible, and quickly fell asleep.

In his dream, just at the right moment, Kerstin popped in. He was in a different hotel room. He was sleeping in his sleep and dreaming in his dream. Or rather, in his dream, he found himself in a state between dream and wakefulness. Then she came in.

From nowhere, her small, dark figure sailed through the room. In his dream they had talked about sex earlier that evening, a bit tipsily, but openly, maturely, modernly. It didn't have to result in anything.

He had happened — if you could call it *happened* — to mention his favourite fantasy, and now she was lying beside him and masturbating, just a few feet away. His subconscious had pedantically stored the memory of each of her movements, and for a year it had drawn them forth at night, every little singularity in the way she touched herself, every caress; and a whole collection of his desires and longings were interspersed with every movement. Then there was a knock, and she drew her hand down through the triangle of hair like a harrow; there was a knock, and she slowly, slowly spread her legs; there was a knock, and she caught hold of . . .

There was a knock.

He shot straight up in bed and looked down at his erection.

"Paul?" a feminine whisper came through the door. "Are you awake?"

"Yes! I'm naked!" He was almost awake. "Awake!" he called a bit louder, hoping that the door was resistant to Freudian slips. "Is it time already?"

"Not really," said Kerstin. "Will you let me in?"

"Hold on," He was finally awake. His erection was still awfully stiff. He came up with a white lie: "I'm in the shower, wait a minute!"

Why couldn't he work with this woman without making her into a sex object? Was he not a grown man?

He thought he had a relatively healthy view of equality and women's rights and all that, but lust was a tyrant that would always live on. If anything, he thought, he was making her into a sex *subject*, but where the fuck was the limit?

Ridiculously, his erection didn't give up. He laughed at himself. What a fool! And the fool had to make a choice: put her off, and risk burning up the last vestiges of their built-up trust, or else be honest — and risk burning up the last vestiges of their built-up trust.

He teetered on the brink for a few seconds, then: "I've got an erection."

"What the hell are you saying? Let me in."

He grabbed a towel from in the bathroom and wrapped it around himself. It looked so pathetic that it no longer *was* pathetic by the time he reached the door and turned the key. She stepped in, clad in an elegant, tight little black dress.

"What did you say?" she asked the more or less presentable newly showered person.

"I was in the shower," he said, gesturing awkwardly. "I didn't think it was time yet."

"But you're dry," she said sceptically.

"The heat. Everything dries right away."

"It *isn't* time yet," she said in a more professional tone, and sat down on the edge of the bed. "I just thought we could talk through our strategy."

"Strategy?" He bent over the suitcase on the other side of the bed. His towel wasn't on tightly, so he had to hold it with one hand and undo the straps of the suitcase with the other. It wasn't all that easy.

240

"That looks hard," she said maternally, turning away. "Let go of the towel. I promise not to look."

Relieved, he let go of the towel, took out fresh clothes and put them on. "Why do we need a strategy?"

"It's the FBI we're going to meet. They're going to see us as the country cousins on a visit to the big city. They'll consider it to be their primary task to make sure we don't get run over or robbed and murdered or become junkies. We have to know exactly what we want to do here and stand firm. They're the ones who are going to supply us with tasks, not the other way round; the killer is on our turf. So what is it we're actually doing here?"

He took out a narrow purple tie and started to tie it. "We're going to fish for clues and see if they've missed anything."

"But we can't put it that way . . . Are you going to wear that?"

He looked down himself. "What?"

"We probably shouldn't look more countrified than we are. We are from a big city, after all, even if it is a small one."

"What's wrong?" he said, mystified.

"What colour is your shirt?" she said pedagogically.

"Blue," he said.

"It's closer to azure. And your tie?"

"Purple?"

"Do those go together?"

He shrugged. "Why not?"

"Come here." He obeyed her. She untied the tie and started to unbutton his shirt.

*Control yourself*, he ordered his unruly nether regions. "What are you doing?" he asked calmly.

"Since I'm assuming you only have one tie with you, we'll have to change the shirt. What have you got?" She rooted around in his suitcase and took out a white one. "This'll have to do." She tossed it to him.

"No," she said, changing the subject abruptly, "we can't present it as though we're here to correct their mistakes. That might be a sensitive subject — if not for Larner, then for his superiors."

"So we ought to focus on the Swedish stuff?" he said, buttoning his shirt.

"I think so, yes. But first and foremost we ought to share *our* information liberally. It could be that they'll be able to add something, of course, but above all it's a goodwill gesture. If we lay our cards on the table, maybe we'll get a few cards back."

"So our strategy is, one: unconditionally blurt out everything we have, and two: say we want to go through the material to try to find a Swedish connection."

"And assure them that we're here to work on it *only* from a Swedish perspective. We won't step on any toes. We'll be diplomatic. Can you handle that?"

He ought to have felt insulted, but this was the first thing she'd said that approached a personal remark. "Yes."

"As you know, I've gone through all the material we've had access to pretty carefully. I don't know how complete it is, but Larner seems to have latched on to Wayne Jennings a little too early. When Jennings disappeared from the scene, all the ideas disappeared,

242

too. There's not a single tiny hypothesis among the material from after the break. Maybe I'm being unfair, but Larner seemed to give up after his failure with Jennings. Now he's just collecting facts. It feels like there should be a lot more to do, not least with the later portion of the case."

He nodded. Even with his considerably scantier knowledge of the details, he saw that the American side was at a loss when faced with the Kentucky Killer's return after fifteen years.

"So you don't think we ought to mention the KGB theory?" he said seriously.

"We can hold off on that for a bit," she said, just as seriously.

Ray Larner's lunch consisted of a magnificently authentic pasta carbonara at a little restaurant annexe called Divina Commedia on 11th Street. Paul and Kerstin were surprised to see the meal served with Loka brand bottled water, but as people said, the world was getting smaller. Larner was on top form and talked exclusively about the art of Italian cooking; he waved off everything else as irrelevant. A long and painfully prestige-loaded argument over whether the world's best olive oil came from Spain or Italy ended in a thrown game when Kerstin suddenly remembered her diplomatic strategy and let Italy win. Hjelm countered with Greece but scored no goals. Australia got a few unexpected points from a neighbouring table.

"When I retire, I'm moving to Italy," Larner said loudly. "The privileges of a retired widower are endless.

**243**

I'm going to die with my mouth full of pasta, olive oil, garlic and red wine. Anything else is unimaginable."

It was no exaggeration to say that he deviated from the stereotypical image of an FBI special agent.

"So you're a widower?" Holm said with soft sincerity.

"My wife died about a year ago," Larner said, chewing good-naturedly. "Fortunately the sadness is followed by an almost rash feeling of freedom — if you don't kill yourself or become an alcoholic. And that's almost always what happens."

"Do you have any children?" Hjelm asked.

"No," said Larner. "We talked about it up until I took on K. He robbed me of all my faith in humanity. You can't bring children into a world that can create a K. But that's a line of reasoning you've heard before."

"I have," Hjelm said. "Had children, that is."

"You had no K then. Wait and see if you have any grandchildren."

"Children were born despite Hitler," said Holm.

Larner was quiet for a moment, then leaned towards her. "Do you have kids, Halm?"

She shook her head.

"What I'm going to show you this afternoon" — Larner leaned back in his chair — "will keep you from doing it for all time."

Zero tolerance was a term that played an important part in New York's new spirit. A euphemism for intolerance, it worked extremely well. Quite simply, the police were ordered not to tolerate any behaviour that fell outside the bounds of the law. Committing the

244

slightest offence meant that one would immediately be taken into custody. The theory behind it was a sort of vertical domino effect: if the little criminals fall, the big ones will too. It was based on the idea that those who commit serious crimes also commit a great many minor ones, and that's when it's possible to catch them.

As a federal officer, Ray Larner was outside the operations of the state police and hence this project. Although he worked in the heart of New York, he observed its workings at a distance. His candour, of which they had already seen ample proof, never extended an inch into controversial territory. Yet something in his tone of voice grated a bit as he described the results of the New York spirit alongside Jerry Schonbauer in the FBI car. Did a trace of a grim view of the future surface in his intonation?

A few years ago, law enforcement had been forced to do something about the state of things in the largest city in the United States. Crime had run amok. There were countless murders. The police and the justice system were at a loss and faced a choice between a long-term path and a short-term one, prevention and punishment. Unfortunately, they had let the situation become so acute that they really only had one alternative. It was too late to equip people with enough self-esteem that they would see an alternative to drugs and easy money. Not only would that approach take too long, but it would also require a break with a centuries-old tradition. The best solution seemed to be a synthesis that would unite the short term with the long term: prevention by punishment.

"Community policing" turned out to be more successful than expected. Suddenly there were police on every corner, and in the rankings of the world's most murder-heavy cities, New York fell from a pole position to almost last place. The decent citizens — that is, the somewhat well-to-do — were of course thrilled. Once again you could jog through Central Park without getting a switchblade between your sixth and seventh ribs; you could take the subway without needing ten seats. In general, it was once again possible to move around the city.

But how high a price did the city pay? First and foremost, it required an absolute acceptance of the status quo. The thought that criminals could better themselves in one way or another vanished. The city was no longer interested in making sure people didn't become criminals — it just wanted to banish them once they had. In the past the prevention side had at least managed to snap up a few crumbs of resources, but now the whole tiny pie was allocated to the punishment side. No one in his right mind spoke any longer of America's old central idea — *equal opportunity* — and the vision of a melting pot was transformed into a sheer myth; nowhere were people so separate as in the United States. The new police strategy — to be able to show up anywhere, at any time — without a doubt carried historic baggage. The question was whether inequality was already so severe that the police state was the only available method of upholding law and order.

In addition, there had been an uncomfortable shift in the view of human rights when it came to the death penalty. Thirty-eight of the states had capital punishment, and recently the country had seen an unprecedented increase in the number of death sentences handed down and carried out. The latest stroke of genius was the policy according to which no one who opposed the death penalty on principle could be permitted to serve on a jury in a trial where the death penalty was a possible sentence. This "death-qualified jury" quite simply disqualified any liberal layperson from the legal process and paved the way for rash and hasty verdicts. The fact was that the crime rate was no lower in states that had the death penalty than in the minority that still resisted it. So the most important argument for the death penalty — that it was a deterrent to crime — was lost, and the only remaining argument in its favour was the victims' desire for retribution. Revenge.

Larner's neutral demeanour when he explained this situation rivaled Hultin's. The question was, did it conceal as much anger? Or did Larner — as Holm had suggested — quite simply dedicate himself to the collection and reporting of facts?

Hjelm was about to query Larner on his opinion of the death penalty — the test that, in his opinion, constituted a fundamental dividing line between two sorts of people. But just then, the car reached the top of the Brooklyn Bridge. Larner cut short his own explanation and said, "Look out the back now."

They turned round, and Manhattan, bathing in sunlight, stretched out its fabulous cityscape before their eyes.

"A strange kind of beauty, isn't it? Every time I drive this way I think about the eternity of beauty. Would our forefathers also have found it beautiful? Or would they have thought it disgusting? Is there such a thing as eternal beauty?"

The sight was overwhelming. Hjelm didn't return to the question of the death penalty. The view of Manhattan had, in some strange way, opened the door to the city, and he eagerly awaited their arrival at the FBI's New York field office.

Schonbauer drove them to the end of the Brooklyn Bridge, then turned the car round and drove back the way they'd come; apparently he had brought them there only for the sake of the view. They followed the bridge back and headed to the majestic City Hall, turned down one of Manhattan's few diagonal streets, Park Row, which bordered City Hall Park, came out onto Broadway, passed City Hall again, and after a few cross-streets arrived at Federal Plaza, where a garage door opened and they glided in.

This was the FBI's Manhattan headquarters, 26 Federal Plaza. The bureau also had local offices for Brooklyn-Queens, on Long Island, and at JFK.

The foursome strolled through corridors that did not much resemble the ones in police headquarters on Kungsholmen. Everything was bigger, cleaner and more clinical. Hjelm wondered if he would be ever able to work here — the place seemed immune to the wild kind of thinking that he considered his speciality.

Hjelm soon stopped counting the number of security doors they went through with the help of various cards and codes. Schonbauer acted as gate boy while Larner rambled on, uninterrupted, spouting information of the sort one might find in a brochure: the number of employees, the departments, the nature of basic training, the expert groups, everything but what was relevant.

Finally they approached one last security door, which opened on its monumental hinges, and then they were standing before a system of corridors that belonged to the serial killer squad at the FBI's New York division. Larner's and Schonbauer's names were inscribed on two adjacent doors. Schonbauer went into his office without a sound, and the rest of them stepped into Larner's.

"Jerry's going to prepare a little multimedia show for you," Larner explained, sitting down at his desk. The office was small and lived-in, Hjelm noted gratefully; it had at least a shade of the personal touch. The walls had bulletin boards instead of wallpaper, it seemed, and tacked up on them were all kinds of notes. Behind Larner stood a whiteboard, and the familiar pattern of arrows, rectangles and lines could have been mistaken for Hultin's.

"Well, here we have everything in concentrate." Larner followed Hjelm's gaze. "Twenty-four rectangles with tortured bodies. Forty-eight holes in twenty-four necks. A sober outline of the un-outlineable. Gruesome terror reduced to a few blue lines. What else can we do? The rest of it, we carry inside us."

Hjelm looked at Larner. Without a doubt, the FBI agent carried a great deal inside himself.

"One question first," said Larner calmly. "Is it true that you think he shot one of the victims?"

"It seems so," said Hjelm.

"If it is, it changes in one blow the minimal psychological profile we've scraped together."

"On the other hand," said Kerstin Holm, "your original theory was that he was a Vietnam veteran. They aren't usually too far from firearms."

Larner made a face. "You know what happened to that theory."

"Of course," said Holm, and Hjelm almost thought she blushed. A diplomatic faux pas in her first remark. He could tell that she was cursing herself. But she didn't seem to want to give up. "Could you explain why you let all the other members of Commando Cool go?" she asked. "They weren't analysed in the material you sent to Sweden."

Larner stretched and gathered the information from the considerable archive in his brain. "The group seems to have been made up of eight members, all specially trained. Its focus was torture in the field — a somewhat brutal way to put it, I suppose. Once someone explained to me that its more official purpose was 'active-service collection of information', but I got the sense that they invented this term specifically for me — it was never the plan that even a tiny crumb of information would leave the inner circle."

"Who was in the inner circle? Was it the military in general?"

Larner gave her a sharp look. "Military intelligence."

250

There was more on his mind, she noticed. "That was all?" she prompted.

"Commando Cool — just the obnoxious name suggests it wasn't meant to become public . . . Anyway, Commando Cool was somehow directly below Nixon. It was established during his administration, toward the end of the war, and you get the impression that it was done out of desperation. Publicly its role was said to be military intelligence, but other powers were at work behind the scenes."

"The CIA?" Holm seemed to have left her diplomatic mask at the hotel.

Ray Larner swallowed and gave her a look that indicated that their relationship had changed — not necessarily for the worse.

"With many layers of top-secret stamps, yes, possibly. You have to understand how tense the relationship between the CIA and the FBI is. And if it in any way gets out that I've said this, I can forget ever having a pension. My personal phone has been monitored, and I can only hope there aren't any bugs in this room. They're always a step ahead of me. But you understand, I've already said too much. Try to forget it."

"Already have," said Holm. "We're just here to find links to Sweden. Nothing else will end up in our reports."

Larner regarded each of them for a minute, then nodded briskly. "It had eight members," he resumed.

"What about Balls?" Kerstin interjected recklessly.

Larner burst out laughing. "Have you been consulting FASK? Fans of American Serial Killers, on the Internet?"

They looked at each other.

"Follow me." Larner leaped to his feet and rushed out into the corridor. A few offices down, he knocked on a door marked BERNHARD ANDREWS and ushered them in.

A seemingly out-of-place young man in his early twenties, with jeans and a T-shirt, looked up through round glasses from a huge computer and smiled broadly. "Ray," he said cheerfully, holding out a printout. "Yesterday's haul. A cotton executive in West Virginia, a golf club in Arkansas and a couple other little goodies."

"Barry," said Larner, taking the list and scanning through it, "these are officers Yalm and Halm from Sweden. They're here about K."

"Aha," said Bernhard Andrews jovially. "Colleagues of Jorge Chavez?"

Their jaws dropped.

"Born in Sweden in 1968," Andrews continued. "In Ragswede, right? To Chilean parents with left-leaning associations."

"It's called Rågsved," Hjelm said, bewildered.

"Chavez was in the FASK site a week ago," Andrews explained smugly. "He had a good but slightly transparent disguise. He put up a hundred and thirty dollars of taxpayers' money to get in. A little development aid from the Swedish people to the American tax coffers."

They gaped at him, their jaws rattling against their kneecaps.

"Barry's a hacker," said Larner calmly, "one of the best in the country. He can get in anywhere. We were lucky to grab him. Also, he's FASK."

"Fans of American Serial Killers," said Andrews. "Nice meeting you."

"Barry set up FASK as a way to attract potential serial killers." Larner waved the printout. "No matter how hard they try to disguise themselves, he catches them. We've caught three with FASK's help. I would venture to say that Barry is the country's most obscure hero."

Bernhard Andrews smiled broadly.

"So Balls doesn't exist?" said Kerstin Holm, who was quicker on the uptake than Hjelm.

"I got it from *The Pink Panther*," said Andrews. "The expert in disguise whom Inspector Clouseau hires and who survives every bombing attack. When it comes to serial killers and their fans, the only thing that's certain is that they have no sense of humour. Humour seems to be the antidote to everything."

"He used the name Balls to fish out a protest from someone who knew better," said Larner. "But so far we haven't had a bite."

They said goodbye to Fans of American Serial Killers, who gave them another broad smile and waved.

In the corridor, Larner said, "Very little is as it seems in the world today."

He led them back to his office and sat at his desk. "I didn't think you had ethnic minorities in your police corps," he said, putting his finger precisely on a Swedish sore spot. "But not even Chavez can be told about FASK. Barry is one of our most important secret weapons in the fight against serial killers."

He pulled out a drawer and took out a few sheets of paper, laid them on the desk, and placed an FBI pen on each sheet.

"It's not that I don't trust you, but my superiors have prepared these papers for you. It's an oath of confidentiality that, if broken, will result in penalties in accordance with American law. Please read through them and sign them."

They read. The small print was difficult to interpret. Both Hjelm and Holm felt an instinctive aversion to putting their signatures on such ambiguous papers, but diplomacy reaped yet another victory — they signed.

"Excellent," said Larner. "Where were we? Commando Cool. Eight members, no Balls. The team leader was the very young Wayne Jennings, who was already a veteran when they netted him — twenty-five years old and with six years of war behind him and God knows how many dead. All the best and most formative years of his life spent in the service of death. Twenty-seven when the war ended, thirty when K began to be active. Returned after the war to his dead father's farm in eastern Kentucky, at the foot of the Cumberland Plateau, if that means anything to you. Didn't do much farming, just lived on his veteran's pension. He was without a doubt the most likely suspect; according to statements, he was very skilled at handling the pincers. The third body was found just thirteen miles from his home.

"As for the others in Commando Cool, three died in the final stages of the war. Besides Jennings, there were four left; you'll find their names in the complete material, which you'll have access to. One came from Kentucky, Greg Androwski, a childhood friend of Jennings's, but he fell apart and died a junkie in 1986. He was alive during K's four years in the Midwest, but he was pretty worn down and quite unlikely to be a killer. Completely destroyed by Vietnam.

"Three left. One came to New York, Steve Harrigan, who became a stockbroker and was one of the wizards of Wall Street during the 1980s. Another went to Maine: Tony Robin Garreth, who makes his living taking tourists on fishing tours. Both were pretty safeguarded against suspicions. The last one, Chris Anderson, moved to Kansas City and sold used cars."

"Swedish background?" said Kerstin.

Larner smiled faintly. "Four generations back. His great-great-grandfather came from someplace called Kalmar, if you've heard of that. Anderson was actually number two on our list, Jennings's second-in-command, just as icy, just as destroyed by the war. But his alibis were a tiny bit better than Jennings's. And Jennings was nastier — that was my main argument, just based on a feeling, that is. I managed to push the whole thing pretty far."

"How sure were you, really, about Jennings?"

Larner leaned back in his chair with his hands on the back of his neck. He deliberated for a moment. "Completely," he said. "One hundred per cent." He fished a thick folder out of an old-fashioned filing cabinet that stood next to the whiteboard.

Jerry Schonbauer peeked into the room. "It's ready," he said.

"Five minutes." Larner tossed the folder to Holm, who opened it. A small bundle of photographs unfolded like a fan. The first one was a portrait. Jennings in his thirties, a young, fresh-looking man with light blond hair and a broad smile. But he also had a steely blue coolness in his eyes, which sharply divided the picture into two parts. Kerstin held her hand over the upper part of his face and saw a happily smiling young person; but when she moved her hand to the lower part, she saw the icy gaze of a man who was hard as nails.

"That's it," Larner said almost enthusiastically. "That's exactly it. When we first visited him, he was pretty amiable, really pleasant — the lower half. As we persisted, we saw more and more of the upper half."

They looked through the rest of the photographs. A teenage Jennings in uniform, Jennings slightly older in a circle of identical field uniforms, Jennings with a big tuna fish, Jennings pointing a Tommy gun at the camera with a fake attack face, Jennings at a dance with a beautiful Southern woman with two first names, Jennings with a small child on his lap, Jennings with a Vietnamese prostitute — and then Jennings roaring with laughter as he presses a pistol to the temple of a grimacing, naked, kneeling Vietnamese man who is pissing himself in a deep hole in the ground. Holm lifted it up towards Larner.

"Yes, that," he said. "It's like it makes you forget the others. It's a fucking awful picture. I would get a lot of money if I sold it to *Time* magazine. I don't understand how he could keep it. We found all of these pictures when we raided his house after he died."

"What happened when he died," Holm said, "exactly?"

"Well," Larner began, "at the end we had him under surveillance twenty-four hours a day —"

"For how long?" she interrupted.

"It had been going on for a month when he died."

"Were any murders committed during that time?"

"The bodies were usually found in a state of decay that made them hard to date. But all sixteen that preceded his death had been found by then. It was one reason I was so persistent, even though every imaginable authority was against me: the longer we watched twenty-four hours a day and no new victims were found, the more likely it was that he was the murderer. May I continue now?"

"Of course," said Holm, ashamed. "Sorry."

"I tried to be there in the car as often as possible, and I was there that day, the third of July 1982. It was broiling hot, almost unbearable. Jennings came rushing out of the house and yelled at us; he'd been doing that for the last few days. He seemed at the end of his rope. Then he rushed over to his car and tore off. We followed him north along a county road for maybe ten miles, at a crazy speed. After a while, a bit ahead on the road, past a long curve, an incredible cloud of smoke rose up. When we got there, we saw that Jennings had crashed head-on into a truck. Both vehicles were ablaze. I got as close as I could and saw him moving a little in the car, burned up."

"So you didn't see the collision itself?" said Holm.

Larner smiled again, the same smile of understanding and indulgence that had become characteristic of their relationship. Hjelm felt a bit like an outsider.

"I know why you're persisting in this, Halm," said Larner. "No. We were a few hundred yards back, and there was a curve in the road. And no, I didn't see his face as he burned up. Did he fake the accident and flee the scene? No. For one thing, there was nowhere for him to go, just flat, deserted earth all around, and no other vehicle was in the vicinity; and for another — and this is crucial — the teeth from the body in the car were his. I had to spend a great deal of time convincing myself that he actually died in that car.

"But he did. Don't believe anything else. Don't do what I did and get stuck on Jennings. It destroyed any chance of moving forward on this case. I can't even come up with a sensible hypothesis any more. K remains a mystery. He must have been sitting somewhere, laughing out loud, while I harassed a tired, unemployed war veteran and drove him to his death. Then, just to show me how wrong I'd been, he killed two people within six months; both of them died long after Jennings did. And then vanished into thin air."

Larner closed his eyes.

"I thought I was done with him," he said slowly. "I kept working on the case, going through every little detail with a fine-toothed comb for several years after the eighteenth and final murder. More than a decade went by. I started working on other things, chasing racists in the South, taking on drug traffickers in Vegas,

258

but he hung over me the whole time. And then that bastard started again. He'd moved to New York. He was mocking me."

"And you're dead certain that it's him?"

Larner touched his nose, tired. "For security reasons, we make sure that only a very tiny number of agents know the crucial details of each case. For K, it was me and a man by the name of Camerun. Don Camerun died of cancer in 1986. Not even Jerry Schonbauer knows this particular detail — I'm the only one in the bureau who does — it's about the pincers. It's the same pincers, and they're inserted in the same, exact, exceedingly complicated way. Because it's your case now, you two will also be given access to the description; I strongly recommend that no one else learns about it."

"What happened with this Commando Cool character who moved to New York?" Holm persisted. "The stockbroker?"

Larner laughed. "Apparently all of my old thoughts are floating in the air and you're catching them, Halm."

"Kerstin," she said.

"OK, Charstin. You're absolutely right, Steve Harrigan isn't mentioned in the report I sent you. But I've checked up on him. He's in the complete material that you'll get to look at. Harrigan is a billionaire, always on the go. He's been abroad during each and every one of the six murders in the second round. And he is definitely not in Sweden now. So now that considerably more than five minutes have passed, let's join Jerry in the showroom and watch a movie."

He led them through the corridors and into an auditorium that, sure enough, resembled an actual cinema. The giant man was sitting on a table up front, below the screen, dangling his feet. His trouser legs were slightly pulled up, exposing a pair of extremely hairy calves above the regulation black socks. When he saw them, he hopped down and showed them to seats in the front.

"Jerry had just come in from the Kentucky office, when the second round started," Larner said, wiggling into one of the sleep-inducing chairs. "He's a damn good agent. Took Roger Penny alone, if you've heard of him. Go ahead, Jerry. I'm gonna take a nap. It's awful at first, but you'll get used to it."

The lights went down with a dimmer function; it really did feel like a cinema.

The special effects did, too. Unfortunately, they were not Hollywood brand.

"Michael Spender." Schonbauer's bass accompanied a picture of a man whose only whole body part was his head, under which two conspicuous red dots shone from his neck like lanterns. His head was canted backwards, white and swollen. He was naked. The look in the dead eyes had retained the same horrible pain as Andreas Gallano's. The nails on his hands and feet had been ripped away, the skin had been cut from his trunk in narrow stripes, and his penis had been split down the middle from glans to base and lay open, two bloody rags, one on each side of his groin.

Their nausea was abrupt and mutual. They very nearly had to run from the room.

"Spender was the first victim," Schonbauer continued expressionlessly, "a computer engineer at Macintosh in Louisville. Found by a berry-picker in the woods in north-western Kentucky about two weeks after his death. Went missing from his workplace after lunch on September fourth, 1978. Was discovered on the afternoon of the nineteenth, sixty miles from his home town. Worked on the development of the first big Apple computer."

The next victim was unidentified, a large man with Slavic features. The picture was a bit more stomach-friendly. He was partially dressed, but his fingers and genitals were disfigured.

"Looks a bit Russian," Hjelm said, thinking of the absurd KGB theory.

"Without a doubt," said Schonbauer. "As soon as it was possible, we sent the fingerprints to the Russian police, but it didn't result in anything. We don't have any information at all, except that he was found in southern Kentucky about two months after Spender. In an old outhouse near a deserted farm. He had been dead for over a week."

The next picture showed another unidentified victim. A thin, fit white man in his sixties, naked, disfigured in the same way as Spender. The picture was gruesome. It was dusk, there was a dim light above the treetops, and the only thing that gleamed was the body, sitting straight up on a rock in the woods. Rigor mortis. The arms were sticking straight out from the body, as though they had been lifted by an inner, irresistible force; the bones were sticking straight out of the hands, like nails that had been driven out from the inside. The eyes stared, openly accusing.

Hjelm didn't get used to it; on the contrary, he felt even closer to throwing up.

They rolled on, a terrible cavalcade of the remains of suffering. It was beyond the limits of human comprehension. The very quantity made the crimes even more gruesome. Slowly but surely, the extent of the case became clear to them — the incredible accumulation of human suffering. Holm cried out twice, silently; Hjelm felt her shoulder lightly nudging his. He cried out once too, but more loudly.

"Do you want me to stop?" Schonbauer asked calmly. "I couldn't make it all the way through till my third try. I'm pretty used to it now."

Larner was snoring audibly next to them.

"No, keep going," said Hjelm, trying to convince himself that he had recovered.

"We have so many of them," Schonbauer said in a subdued voice. "So incredibly many serial killers, and no one can really understand a single one of them. Least of all themselves."

In the end their defence mechanisms kicked in, and although they never started snoring, they slowly became indifferent. Like a horrible conclusion, Lars-Erik Hassel woke them up. He was sitting on his chair with shredded fingers, sprawling in all directions; his genitals were a swamp of half-floating remnants. Through the small window in the background, they could see part of a large aircraft.

His head was craned back; he stared at them upside down, his pain mixed with disgust, his suffering with paradoxical relief.

*Maybe*, Hjelm thought, *he was relieved that it wasn't Laban*.

The lights came up again. Schonbauer returned to the table and sat with his legs dangling once again like a teenage girl's. Larner awoke in mid-snore with a start and snuffled loudly. Hjelm rolled his shoulders. Holm was sitting stock-still. No one looked at anyone else for some time.

Larner stood, yawned, and stretched until his compact body creaked. "And now, do you two have some dessert for this party?"

Kerstin handed over the Swedish folders wordlessly.

Larner opened them, skimmed through the pictures, and gave them to Schonbauer, who would soon add them to the series of images. Then he got up to leave.

Kerstin and Paul thanked Schonbauer, who gave a curt nod, and they all followed Larner out. Walking through the corridors, they came to a door without a name on it. Larner opened it. They stepped into an empty room.

"Your workroom," he said with a gesture. "I hope you can work together."

The office looked exactly like Larner's, minus all the signs of life. The question was how much of their own they could offer. The desk had been pulled out from the wall and furnished with two chairs, one on each side. Two computers rubbed shoulders on the desk next to a telephone and a short call list. Larner picked it up.

"My number" — he pointed — "Jerry's number, my pager, Jerry's pager. You can always get hold of us. Below are names of the files in question, descriptions of them, personal passwords, and guest passes with codes so you can get in, but only in here. Locked doors are doors that you don't have admittance to. You have no reason to leave this corridor, nor any possibility of doing so. Bathrooms, women's and men's, are a few doors down. There are a couple of cafeterias — I recommend La Traviata two floors down. Any questions?"

No questions. Or an endless number, depending on how you looked at it. None were asked, in any case.

"It's 6p.m. now," Larner continued. "If you like, you can work for a few hours. I stay till about six. Unfortunately I'm busy tonight, otherwise we could eat dinner together. Jerry has offered to eat with you and show you around town, if you'd like. You can let him know.

"So all that's left is to wish you good luck. You don't need to worry about getting into the wrong things on the computers — they're customised for you, and everything confidential is elsewhere. Contact me or Jerry if problems or questions come up. Bye."

He disappeared. They were alone.

Holm rubbed her eyes. "I don't actually know if I can handle this," she said. "It's midnight Swedish time. Shall we accept Swedish time and go back to the inn?"

"Maybe we shouldn't leave right away," said Hjelm. "We have to continue being diplomatic."

264

She sensed a slightly sarcastic bite and smiled. "Yeah, yeah, curiosity got the better of me, I admit it. My strategy went to hell."

"CIA —"

"OK, OK, rub it in. I made the judgement that he wouldn't be angry."

"I don't think he was. More like relieved. What do you think?"

"I don't know. But I understand why he got stuck on Jennings."

"But he's right that we have to think past him."

"Are you sure?"

They looked at each other. Their jet lag, combined with the overdose of impressions, made them giggle foolishly. Their exhaustion was about to get the better of them. Hjelm liked the irresponsible stubbornness that had fallen upon them; their defence mechanisms were starting to be taken out of the game.

"Shall we say to hell with Schonbauer's tour?" he asked.

"Can you be diplomatic and let him know in a nice way?"

"You're the diplomat."

"In theory. This is in practice. You were much better at it than I was."

"I was just absent-minded," he said, dialling Schonbauer's number. "Jerry, this is Paul. Yalm, yes, Yalm. We're going to try to work on this as long as we can manage, and then we'll let our jet lag take over. Can we put our tour of Manhattan off until tomorrow? Good. OK. Bye."

He hung up and exhaled. "I think he was relieved."

"Good," said Holm. "Should we get an overview of what we have and let the details wait? I've had enough details for today."

The computers contained all the necessary information. Detailed lists of all the victims. Folders with all the crime-scene investigations. Folders for every individual case investigation. Expert psychological profiles of perpetrators. Folders with all the autopsy results. Folders with all the press cuttings. Files with descriptions of weapons, FYEO.

"What does that mean?" Hjelm asked.

"For your eyes only. This must be where he has the top-secret details that connect the first round with the second."

They glanced through the files; an incredible amount of information. How the hell could they add to this enormous investigation even a tiny bit? It seemed hopeless enough to motivate them to stop working. They turned their computers off after the countdown "one potato two potato three potato four!" and felt blissfully frivolous.

"Do you think we can run away from the FBI?" said Kerstin Holm.

Of course it would have been an experience to get out and see New York by night, but they weren't disappointed that they'd declined Jerry Schonbauer's offer. They enjoyed a quiet dinner in the hotel restaurant instead. It was 2 a.m. in Sweden, nine o'clock local time, when they came down to the lobby and

**266**

looked for the restaurant *in* the restaurant. It was, in other words, very small.

Skipper's Inn continued to play at being an English inn. What the restaurant lacked in variety and elaborateness, it made up for in quality. They chose one of the two possible entrées, beef Wellington, and a bottle of Bordeaux in an unfamiliar brand, Château Germaine. They sat at a window table and got at least a small, indirect view of Manhattan's street life. The little restaurant, where they had been the first guests, filled up, and soon all twelve tables were occupied.

Paul Hjelm was struck by another sensation of déjà vu. Last time they had sat alone, enjoying a quiet dinner in a restaurant in an unfamiliar place, the consequences had been unmistakable. He squirmed slightly, thinking of Cilla and the children and the sense of family that they had so strenuously won back. He thought of the extreme temptation that the woman on the other side of the table still represented, of how she invaded his dreams and remained a pressing mystery. She had put on a modest but noticeable amount of make-up and had changed into a little black dress with tiny straps that criss-crossed her otherwise bare back. She was so small and thin, and her face seemed smaller than usual within the frame of her dark, slightly messy bob. Had she tidied herself up on purpose?

He couldn't help saying, "Do you remember the last time we sat like this?"

She nodded and smiled, incredibly attractively. "Malmö."

That husky Gothenburg alto. Her duets with Gunnar Nyberg echoed in his ears. Schubert lieder. Goethe poems. Was he trying to get away or to get closer? When he opened his mouth, he didn't know what his next step would be. He let it happen.

"That was one and a half years ago," he said.

"Soon," she said.

"You remember?"

"Why wouldn't I?"

"You know . . ."

The social wreckage bobbed on the surface. He tried to force it down and said abruptly, "What was it that happened?"

She could interpret that as she wished. She was quiet, then said at last, "I had to go another way."

"Where to, then?"

"As far as possible from work. I was close to quitting."

"I didn't know that."

"No one knew besides me."

*Not even him?* He thanked his creator that he didn't say it.

"Not even him," she said.

He didn't question it. She could go whatever way she wanted or needed to.

"After you and your agonising over decisions, I planned to live without a man," she said quietly. "I needed time to think. Then I met him, a silly coincidence. He kept calling at work, too, so soon everyone knew I had a new man. What no one knew was that he was sixty and a pastor in the Church of Sweden."

Hjelm said nothing.

With her eyes on her fork, she poked distractedly at the half-eaten beef Wellington. "No one thinks you can have a passionate relationship with a sixty-year-old pastor in the Church of Sweden. But that's what it was. That's the only kind of relationship I seem able to handle these days."

She looked out to the crowds of people on West 25th Street. "He'd been a widower for twenty years," she continued in the same toneless voice. "The pastor in the church where I sang in the choir. He cried when I sang, came up, and kissed my hand. I felt like a schoolgirl who finally got some attention. I was a daughter and a mother at the same time. After a while, out of that, a woman was reborn."

She continued to avoid his gaze.

"There was so much unfinished in that man, but he finished a little of it with me. He carried so much quiet and lovely life wisdom — I don't know if it's possible to understand — an ability to enjoy the little gift of every day. If nothing else, he taught me that."

"What happened?"

She finally looked at him for a split second, her eyes slightly veiled but very much alive. "He died."

He took her hand and held it, unmoving. Both looked out onto the street. Time nearly stopped.

"He was already dying when we met," she continued quietly. "I didn't realise that until now. He had so much life in him and wanted to pass it on. Give a farewell gift to the living. I hope he got a little bit of me to take with him. Some passion, if nothing else."

He had stopped thinking of how he ought to act and just listened. It was nice.

"It went quickly. He was actually supposed to go through his third round of chemotherapy. He didn't bother — he chose one last period of health instead of a fight to the finish. I kept a vigil over him for a week, every day after work. That was last spring. It was like he just shrank up. But he smiled almost the entire time. That was strange. I don't know if it was the giving or the taking that made him happy. Maybe just the exchange. As though he had received one last insight into the mysteries of life and could await the big mystery without fear."

She turned to him for another split second, as if to make sure he was listening. He was. She turned away again.

"I don't know," she said. "Those pictures today . . . you think you can prepare yourself, but you can't. You think you've seen everything, but you haven't. It's like there were different deaths. My pastor friend was in pain, too, horrible pain, but he smiled. There were no smiles here, just the horrific faces of suffering, like a frieze of horrible medieval pictures of Christ, made to strike terror into the viewer. A warning. Like he's trying to warn us away from life, as medieval prelates were. And he almost succeeds."

"I don't know," Hjelm tried. "I don't really see a message in what he does. I think looking at those bodies is more like being confronted with waste

**270**

products, remainders, industrial waste, if you know what I mean. It feels like the mechanical, industrial deaths of Auschwitz. If anything can ever feel like that . . ."

Now she looked into his eyes. She had got what she needed. There and then, in her deep, distressed, empty eyes, he saw the spark ignite again. The fabulous inexhaustibility of her eyes.

He wondered what she saw in his face. A clown who runs around trying to hide his erection? He hoped there was a trace of something more.

"Maybe they're not incompatible," she said, and her new-found energy didn't erase her thoughtful tone. "Expressing contempt for life and clinical perfection in one and the same action. It *is* one and the same action, after all."

They sank into pondering. The professional and the private blended uncontrollably into each other. Nothing in this life was isolated.

He sensed that it was his turn. He took her hand again.

She didn't resist.

"Was what we had before just sex?" he asked without quavering. "Is there such a thing as 'just sex'?"

She smiled grimly and kept hold of his hand.

"There probably isn't," she said. "And in any case, what we had wasn't that. It was — confusing. Too confusing. I had just got out of a hellish relationship with a man who raped me without understanding that that's what he was doing. He was a policeman, you know that much, and then I ended up with another policeman who was the complete opposite. Hard-boiled and full of bright ideas as a cop, tender and awkward privately. The pictures got all mixed up. I had to get away from it. You fled back into the bosom of your family. I didn't have anything like that, so I fled in my own way."

"In one way, life is easier than ever," said Paul. "In another, it's harder."

She looked into his eyes. "How do you mean?"

"I don't really know. I have this feeling that the walls are closing in around us. We've cracked open the door, but now it's being closed again. And the walls are beginning to creep in." He was searching for words, but it was going slowly. He was trying to formulate things he had never formulated before. "I don't know if it's comprehensible."

"I think it is," she said. "You actually have changed."

"A little bit, maybe," he said, and paused. "Just a little on the surface, but it has to start somewhere. Our inherited patterns of habit break us down before we even get a chance to *start* living. I haven't gone through any revolutionary outer changes, as you have; it's actually been a pretty uneventful year. But a few new possibilities have opened up."

She nodded. The conversation died away but seemed to be continuing inside them. Their eyes drifted away into nothing. Finally she said, "I'm starting to understand how important it is that we catch him."

He nodded. He knew what she meant.

They left the restaurant and walked hand in hand up the stairs. They stopped outside his room.

"What should we say?" she said. "Seven?"

He sighed and smiled. "OK, breakfast at seven o'clock."

"I'll knock on your door. Try not to be in the shower."

He chuckled. She gave him a kiss on the cheek and went to her room. He remained standing in the corridor for a few minutes.

# CHAPTER
# TWENTY-FOUR

They came, they saw, they conquered — their jet lag. But hardly anything else. Their focus narrowed, cutting out all of New York, targeted at two computers on a desk.

Sure enough, there was a gigantic amount of material, thousands of pages with impressive detail that extended to ten-page interviews with truly unimportant people, like those who had found bodies and neighbours of neighbours; pedantically scientific comparisons with earlier and contemporary serial killers; immensely elaborate maps of the crime scenes, socio-political analyses by university professors, autopsy reports that made note of the victims' incipient gum problems and developing kidney stones, extremely carefully executed crime-scene investigations, and Ray Larner's labouriously compiled description of Commando Cool's actions in the South East Asian jungles.

It probably wasn't the right place to start, but Hjelm picked the last item. If Larner had got hold of the truth, which was in no way certain, President Nixon had created Commando Cool by direct order, after he received information about the steadfastness of the NLF soldiers who had been captured in the field; they

274

tended to die before they had time to talk. What was needed was a small, secret, active-service, mobile group of torturers with combat experience, even if the word *torturer* was, of course, never mentioned. The task of creating it went to military counter-intelligence — and here Larner had placed quite a few question marks — which collected eight top men, each one younger than the last, and forced the operation into existence. It was in constant use during the final stages of the war. Where the pincers came from was uncertain, and Hjelm read "CIA" between Larner's lines.

He opened the top-secret file about the pincers. There they were, in black and white: to the left a photograph of Commando Cool's vocal cord pincers; to the right a sketched reconstruction of K's pincers. Their function was the same in principle, but the differences were striking. K's pincers were of an advanced, refined design, which seemed to have undergone some sort of industrial process of improvement. Scrupulous descriptions of their function followed: how the micro-wires moved through the tube with the help of miniature wheels, penetrated the throat, and fastened themselves around the vocal cords with small barbs, putting the vocal cords out of commission. A slight turn of one of the two small wheels then made it possible for whispers to force their way out. When they had forced their way out, all one had to do was turn the wheel again and end the job, in complete silence. The version on the right, K's, was designed so that it was easier to make a puncture correctly. But Commando Cool had never used it during the war; it kept using the older model to the very end. The differences between the sets of pincers meant two things: one, that it was not at all certain that K was someone from Commando Cool; and two, that the horrible invention from the Vietnam War had been further developed. Why? And by whom? There were no hypotheses in Larner's report.

After this came the second pincers, the pincers of pure torture, the one that twisted and prised at the cluster of nerves in the neck. This one had changed, too; someone had located new points on the nerves that were capable of increasing the pain even more, thus making the pincers even more effective. Here, too, the file provided a scrupulous description of the exact progression of pain, how it shot down to the back and shoulders and then up into the brain itself, resulting in explosive attacks.

The point was that the same pincers had been used in the first and second waves; they weren't just identical models — certain characteristics of the wound formation indicated that the *exact* same pincers were used, and this was invoked as justification for saying that the perpetrator was the same. K.

If the pincers were the result of an industrial improvement process, then many people must have been involved in the task of development, whether it was military counter-intelligence or the CIA or something else. But at this very point, where a considerable number of further suspects could have been sifted out, Larner had hit a wall of silence. Had he and the hacker, Andrews, invented Balls because he suspected that there

276

actually *was* a Balls, a secret commander who would have been promoted all the way up into the Pentagon to effectively choke off all access to information? How had Larner obtained the information about the members of Commando Cool when he hadn't got anything else?

He called Larner and asked.

"All that was a strange process," Larner answered on the phone. "It took a lot of bribes and string pulling and veiled threats. After running into every wall imaginable, I worked my way to an anonymous official who, for several thousand dollars, copied the entire top-secret file on Commando Cool for me. Everything ought to have been there, but the only thing it contained was a list of the group members. The military just didn't have the rest of it."

"Was that when you started thinking CIA?"

Larner chuckled. "I guess I had been thinking that the whole time," he said, and hung up.

Kerstin pulled up the list of victims and printed it out. The macabre inventory contained the sparsest amount of information imaginable: name, race, age, job, place of residence, site of discovery and approximate time of death.

1) Michael Spender, white, 46, civil engineer at Macintosh, resident of Louisville, found in NW Kentucky, died around September 5, 1978.
2) Unidentified white male, 45–50 years of age, found in S Kentucky, died in early November 1978.

3) Unidentified white male, approximately 60, found in E Kentucky, died around March 14, 1979.

4) Yin Li-Tang, Taiwanese citizen, 28, resident of Lexington, biologist at University of Kentucky in Lexington, found on campus, died on May 9, 1979.

5) Robin Marsh-Eliot, white, 44, resident of Washington DC, foreign correspondent for the *Washington Post*, found in Cincinnati, Ohio, died in June or July 1979.

6) Unidentified white female, about 35, found in S Kentucky, died around September 3, 1979.

7) Unidentified white male, about 55 years of age, found in S Illinois, died between January and March 1980.

8) Unidentified Indian male, about 30, found in SW Tennessee, died between March 13 and 15, 1980.

9) Andrew Schultz, white, 36, resident of New York, pilot for Lufthansa, found in E Kentucky, died October 1980.

10) Unidentified white male, about 65, found in Kansas City, died December 1980.

11) Atle Gundersen, white, Norwegian citizen, 48, resident of Los Angeles, nuclear physicist at UCLA, found in S West Virginia, died May 28, 1981.

12) Unidentified white male, 50–55, found in Frankfort, Kentucky, died August 1981.

13) Tony Barrett, white, 27, resident of Chicago, chemical engineer at Brabham Chemicals, Chicago, found in SW Kentucky, died between August 24 and 27, 1981.

14) Unidentified white male, 30–35, found in N Kentucky, died in October or November 1981.

15) Unidentified white male, 55–60, found in S Indiana, died January 1982.

16) Lawrence B. R. Carp, white, 64, resident of Atlanta, vice president of RampTech Computer Parts, found in his home in Atlanta, Georgia, died March 14, 1982.

[Death of primary suspect Wayne Jennings, July 3, 1982]

17) Unidentified black male, 44, found in SW Kentucky, died October 1982.

18) Richard G. deClarke, white, South African citizen, 51, resident of Las Vegas, owner of a Las Vegas porn club, found in E Missouri, died between November 2 and 5, 1982.

[Nearly fifteen-year break]

19) Sally Browne, white, 24, resident of New York, prostitute, found in the East Village, Manhattan, died July 27, 1997.

20) Nick Phelps, white, 47, resident of New York, unemployed carpenter, found in SoHo, Manhattan, died November 1997.

21) Daniel "Dan the Man" Jones, black, 21, resident of New York, rapper, found in Brooklyn, died between March and April 1998.

22) Alice Coley, white, 65, resident of Atlantic City, New Jersey, on disability, found in her home, died between May 12 and 14, 1998.

23) Pierre Fontaine, white, French citizen, 23, resident of Paris, tourist, university student, found in Greenwich Village, Manhattan, died July 23–24, 1998.

24) Lars-Erik Hassel, white, Swedish citizen, 58, resident of Stockholm, literary critic, found at Newark International Airport, died September 2, 1998.

25) Andreas Gallano, white, Swedish citizen, resident of Alby, drug dealer, found in Riala, died between September 3 and 6, 1998.

26) Eric Lindberger, white, Swedish citizen, 33, resident of Stockholm, civil servant with the Ministry of Foreign Affairs, found on Lidingö, died September 12, 1998.

27) Unidentified white male, 25–30 years of age, found in Stockholm, died September 12, 1998.

Could no other conclusions really be drawn from this list, other than those that Larner had drawn? She was struck by a short, brutal suspicion that Larner hadn't put all his cards on the table.

She turned to the psychological profile. A group of experts had made an attempt to explain the fifteen-year gap. Apparently it hadn't been simple; she perceived that they had had differences of opinion that they tried to bring into line with one another, and the result was fascinating. She wondered why the profile hadn't been part of what Larner had delivered to Sweden.

The first murders, according to the group of experts, suggested a rather young man's hatred of authority, personified in an older, well-educated man. His inferiority complex turns into delusions of grandeur when he is able to silence the voices that have kept him down and possibly denied him admittance to the university. It makes the inaccessible accessible, and it makes them feel the same pain he felt. He can even control how much of the pain they express; all he has to do is turn a wheel. Because wasn't that how they had behaved towards him, denying him the opportunity to speak, keeping him, with one fell swoop, from the higher education that would have made it possible for him to understand and express his suffering? His behaviour is a distorted variation on "an eye for an eye"; his retaliation imitates what he feels he has been subjected to. He wins back the power. The great number of victims indicates not that he is becoming increasingly bloodthirsty — there is no real acceleration — but rather hints at the degree of oppression he has experienced. It takes eighteen deaths for him to get his nose above the water so that he can take his place in human society. For perhaps his bloodthirstiness gradually *diminishes*, and he reaches equilibrium; the murders have a truly therapeutic effect. He reaches the point where he feels he has attained a balance in status between himself and authority, and then he can stop and work his way to a position of authority himself. That is what he does during these fifteen years.

He gets the upper hand. Perhaps he has managed to get an education and become a leader or boss. But naturally his past has not left him unscathed. Now he has become the oppressor himself; *that* is what he trained to be. And then he cracks down on those who are weaker. His hatred of authority is revealed as envy — he was envious of their power. And now he is the one who strikes first; he pokes out the first eye, instead of just getting revenge. He plays a decisive role. His actions no longer only *reflect* those of the more powerful, he *is* more powerful. And this can go on forever.

Thus the Kentucky Killer is likely a white man in a position of power who has had to fight his way up against all odds. This was the gist of the expert group's report.

Kerstin Holm once again neglected to be diplomatic and called Larner.

"Ray, Kerstin here. Halm, yes, Halm, dammit." This last word was in Swedish. "I'm wondering why we didn't have the opportunity to read the expert group's psychological profile earlier."

"Because it's bullshit," the phone reverberated.

"What do you mean? There are a lot of aspects we haven't thought of in here."

"I was in the group of experts. I agree that it's a coherent narrative. It works. But the story swallowed up the troublesome objections from the police officer in the group. The desire to create unity forced the most fundamental fact to the side."

"And what's that?"

"K's professionalism."

"What do you mean?"

"K isn't trying to even out any positions; it's not a process but rather an ice-cold series of exterminations. He leaves no red-hot evidence behind, only frostbitten remains. The corpses are ruins, not buildings."

She didn't say anything — she recognised the argument. She thanked him and hung up.

"He agrees with you," she said.

Paul Hjelm, who had just been scrutinising the delicate line between the pincers, gave a start. "What are you talking about?" he said, irritated.

"Nothing," she said, and tried to press on through the material.

It didn't really work. She called Larner again and got straight to the point. "Is it really professionalism in the second round?"

"As you have surely noticed" — his voice remained patient — "I have very little to say about the second round. I don't understand it. It is the same professionalism, the exact same course of action. The victims are what has changed character."

"But why?" she nearly shouted. "Why did he go from engineers and researchers to prostitutes and retired people?"

"Solve that, and you've solved the case," Larner said calmly. "But is the distinction really that clear-cut? After all, you've recently had literary critics and diplomats and drug dealers die. Both kinds, one might say."

"I'm sorry," she said remorsefully. "It's just so frustrating."

"When you've worked on it for twenty years, you'll see what frustration is."

She hung up and reluctantly went on. The difficult thing was *not* to come up with hypotheses, to resist venting them and just get to work. To expand their horizons instead of narrowing them. To wait for the right moment.

They devoted the whole day to getting a reasonable overview. As well as the evening. Their tour of Manhattan would have to wait yet another day.

The next day they began to narrow their focus and take a fine-toothed comb to the thousand pages to find possible Swedish threads. Why had the killer gone to Sweden? Somewhere in these pages was the solution.

Hjelm took upon himself the investigation of the eleventh victim, the Norwegian, the nuclear physicist Atle Gundersen; there might be something there. He contacted UCLA and tried to find potential Swedish colleagues from the early 1980s; he contacted the family in Norway. He burned up half a day but drew a blank.

Holm turned to the descendant of Swedes in Commando Cool, Chris Anderson. She even called him. He sounded exhausted. He had been grilled many times and was sick and tired of it. Vietnam was far away now; weren't they ever going to let him bury the memories that still haunted him at night? They had done terrible things, but it was war, and they had worked almost directly under the president, so what could they have done? No, he didn't know exactly how the chain of command and the issuing of orders had worked; it should be in the reports. Yes, he had been close friends with Wayne Jennings, but they had drifted apart after the war. And now Anderson had no contact at all with the land of his forefathers — he didn't even talk to his parents.

They searched on, intensely. As soon as any tiny, burning question appeared, Larner threw his patiently smothering blanket over the flame. He seemed to have thought of everything after all. They began to re-evaluate his work. The lack of hypotheses and ideas seemed more and more to be because there were none to find. He had kept a cool head and hadn't let wild hypotheses take over in the absence of sensible ones.

Moving forward without having any clues to follow was the most difficult balancing act in their line of work.

And yet they felt — and they talked a lot about it, talked too much in general, were on their way to becoming friends instead of lovers — that all they needed was one small, crucial piece for the whole puzzle to become coherent; they felt frustratingly close without having the slightest reason for such a feeling.

"There's something we've missed," Paul said one evening in the hotel restaurant. By now they had no thoughts of placing their bodies anywhere but at the FBI building, in the taxi, or in the hotel. It was becoming a routine. He kept acceptable amounts of contact with Cilla and his family in Sweden; at first, before he knew how it was going to go with him and

Kerstin, he hadn't felt very motivated to call — something had held him back. But as they became more and more like pure police officers, his uneasiness fell away, and his conversations with Cilla felt completely normal. He missed her sometimes — when there was time.

"What do you mean 'missed'?" Kerstin said, biting into a braised fillet of cod. "We miss things all the time. The more we find, the more we miss."

Paul watched her sip her wine. Had he got so close to her that she had stopped being beautiful? He contemplated her larynx as the wine ran down. No, he hadn't. But perhaps his lust had found an alternative route that hadn't been on his map earlier. He was treading upon virgin territory — and the intractability of fucking metaphorical language.

"I always have the feeling that we *don't* need to know *more*," he said.

"Then what are we doing here?"

"Looking for the little surge of impulse that runs through it all and brings it together."

"You romantic." She smiled.

Had he seen that smile so often that it had stopped being captivating? A ridiculous thought.

They stopped counting the days, simply swam like two fish in an aquarium. One early morning, Larner appeared in the door. He was worked up, and with his service weapon in place under his armpit.

"Are you tired of this?" he called, exhilarated.

Four square eyes looked at him sceptically.

"What do you say to some real police work? Want to be foreign observers at a raid on a drug den?"

They exchanged a glance. Maybe that was what they needed.

"OK," Larner said as they half ran through the corridor behind Jerry Schonbauer; the floor shook substantially, as though his steps had transplanted the fault line from the west coast to the east. "We're on loan to ATF. They don't really know what do with us now that you guys are working on K. The rest of the state's serial killers are in other hands. We're going to a crack house in Harlem — you'll have a chance to stare American reality in the eye. Come along."

They were out on the street. Big black American cars drove up, and Hjelm and Holm threw themselves into one of them alongside Larner and Schonbauer, all four in the back seat. The two agents pulled on jackets with luminous yellow letters on the back: ATF, Bureau of Alcohol, Tobacco and Firearms. Like a funeral procession out to prevent the gravesite from being stolen, the caravan forced its way through the New York traffic and reached northern Manhattan, the hopeless neighbourhoods, the sacrificed and buried neighbourhoods. The building facades became more and more dilapidated; finally it looked like a bombed-out city. Shadows of Dresden. The faces in the streets became darker and darker, till finally they were only black. It was a terrible but logical transformation, a gradual transition from the white downtown to the black Harlem. There was no possibility of trying to explain it away. That was just how it was.

287

The cars stopped in a well-mannered line. Equally well-mannered lines of ATF-clad experts poured out with weapons drawn, then ran through a ragged, burnt garden, ravaging what plants were there.

"Stay back," Larner said, joining the ravagers. They gathered in a more or less invisible line along the pavement on the next block. All eyes were on one single building, a ramshackle house, one of two buildings that remained in the rubble of the neighbourhood. It was already surrounded by a well-organised series of ATF men with sub-machine guns. They were everywhere, pressed up against dirty stucco walls that seemed to crackle in the desert-like sun. The asphalt quavered. It was silent and desolate amid, instead of black faces, black jackets with yellow letters. A few pigeons flapped up and flew around the house in strangely rising circles, as though aiming for the sun. The sole streak of cloud broke up before their eyes.

Everyone was in position, as in a photograph, a still image. Then all at once, everyone moved, streaming into the ruin, an army of superior ants intent on taking over the disintegrating anthill. Finally Hjelm and Holm were alone on the street, a vulnerable duo of foreign observers who might at any moment be dragged into a doorway and given a liberal taste of American reality. They heard sporadic gunshots from inside the house, muffled, somehow unreal, as though Hollywood had supplied some sound effects. A few sub-machine-gun rounds. Individual shots. A minor explosion. It only took a minute, then silence. A figure popped out the door, black with a black jacket, and waved in their

**288**

direction. It took a moment for them to realise that it was waving at them, and even longer for them to realise that it was Larner. They made their way over to him.

"Come on," he said, waving his pistol. "This is reality."

Inside a light haze of dust met them, crystal-like, with the sun dazzling through it — it stung in their throats. Gradually they realised that the cloud that they were breathing in was drugs — crack. Big black men were lying on the floor with their hands behind their heads. The bodyguards, disarmed. Two were without their hands on their heads; their torsos were half lying against the walls, their legs and spines at strange angles. Blood oozed out of an open wound, drop by drop, looking increasingly viscous until the last drop hung in the air and seemed to be sucked back in.

They went up to the first floor. Room after room looked like one chemistry lab after another, with shattered flasks, overturned bottles, flickering Bunsen burners — and thicker clouds of dust. A dead body lay among the shards on a table, shot to pieces, segmented, half covered in white dust that became pinker and pinker until it finally turned to red and ran into a body upon the body. People were on the floor here, too, with their hands on the backs of their necks. All was silent. The calm after the storm. The silence of the storm warning.

The next floor, the second. Chemistry workshops here too, with different devices. Packs of plastic bags with white contents, half open, the dust still rising, like a mist sliding over a lake. Hands on necks. A dead

**289**

person half hanging out the window, a piece of glass like a shark's fin straight up through the trunk. Windows were opened. The cloud of dust was carried out over the city. Drugged pigeons cooed audibly. A white wind swept through the house, reaching well-wrapped bundles of dollars in the room furthest in, the inner room. The paper band around one bundle was torn; the wind caught the green notes, and they whirled about the room, were seized.

The room spun. A brown spot spread out around a prostrate jeans-clad backside. They were all the way in, in the very innermost room. Larner smiled, and his smile seemed to split his head. Half his skull flew up eighteen inches and then fell back. His skin was drawn down from his head, his skull flopped around, his skin was sucked back up.

Hjelm staggered towards the open window and greedily inhaled the dirty but uncrystalline air.

"You'll be drugged for a few seconds," said Larner. "It'll pass."

Holm sat down on the floor next to the window and hugged herself. Hjelm leaned out through the window, tried to find stability, to focus his eyes. Everything was flying around. The still image was heaving behind them. The silence died. People were being moved out, with shouts and bellows. They didn't see it.

A pair of pigeons descended unexpectedly from the sky and landed gently on the slightly lower roof of the neighbouring building. Hjelm stared at them as they sat placidly on the ridge of the roof. A fixed point in the spinning world.

"You have to avoid inhaling for a while," Larner said behind him. "You learn from your mistakes. Trial by error."

He was punishing them — Hjelm realised that now. He kept his eyes on the pigeons. They flew off some way and pecked at something, then took off again but stayed within sight. He followed their flight; they were doing aerobatics, mimicking each other precisely. When they reached the stinking crater of the crack house, they swept upward, then glided down through the filthy air and stopped on a windowsill on the top floor of the building next door. The window shone like gold in the sun. Hjelm looked through the dirty but golden windowpane and saw a man and a boy. As if in slow motion, the father lifted his hand and struck his son, a classic, traditional box on the ear, several times, using exactly the same motion, as though a minute in time were being repeated again and again, just for him, demanding his attention, and each image ended up on top of the last in a fabulous multiple projection. The son's expression after the blows, peering up at his father, inexhaustible. It was like Laban Hassel, looking up at his father; like Danne, looking up at his; then Gunnar Nyberg's children, looking up at theirs. Finally K. The very last in the bunch, K looking up at K.

*Bad blood always comes back round.*

"Holy shit!" he yelled.

Holm staggered over and saw that he had it.

"This is it!" he yelled again, like an idiot.

The collective glares of the ATF men ate into the back of his neck. He didn't give a damn.

"What is it?" Holm shouted in a strange, muted voice.

"The impulse," he said with sudden calm. "Clear as a bell."

He turned abruptly and went over to Larner, who was regarding him with deep scepticism.

"I've got him," he said, his eyes boring into Larner's.

Then he rushed down the stairs. Larner looked at Holm, bewildered. She nodded, and they rushed after him. He was outside on the street with Schonbauer, who had just shoved a substantial drug manufacturer into one of the black cars.

Schonbauer got into the driver's seat in one of the other cars; Hjelm hopped in, and Holm and Larner scrambled into the back. They drove off. Hjelm didn't say a word.

"What are we doing?" Larner said after fifteen minutes.

"Looking at a picture," said Hjelm.

They said no more on the way back to the FBI building. When they arrived, they reached the corridor, and Hjelm got to Larner's office ahead of the others. He grabbed Wayne Jennings's thick file and flipped through the photographs. He found the horrible picture of Jennings and the Vietnamese man and placed it to the side. Then he held up the photo of Jennings with a child on his lap.

"Who is this?" he asked.

"Jennings's son," Larner said, surprised. "Lamar."

Hjelm placed the picture on the desk. Jennings was dressed like a cowboy, minus the hat: jeans; a red, white and blue flannel shirt; and sandy-brown snakeskin boots. He had his hand on his son's head, but he wasn't smiling; his face was expressionless, and the ice-cold blue gaze penetrated the camera. You might almost get the impression that he was pressing his son's head down, as if to hold him in place. The son was perhaps ten years old, just as blond and blue-eyed, but his eyes hardly seemed to see. Upon closer examination, one could make out an absentness in them, as if he were only a shell.

"This is K," Hjelm said. "Both of them."

His manic state ending, he shed the dramatic persona and became a policeman again. He cleared his throat. "What happened to Jennings's family after he died?"

"They lived in the same place for a few years. Then his wife killed herself. The boy ended up in an orphanage and then with foster-parents."

"How old was the boy?"

"He was eleven, I think, when Jennings died."

"He must have seen it."

"What are you talking about?"

Hjelm ran his hand through his hair and collected himself. "He must have seen it. He must have seen his father in action."

He took a deep breath.

"That explains the difference between the first and second rounds, and it explains why he went to Sweden. The first round was Wayne Jennings's work, just as you thought all along, Ray. They are executions, professional jobs — we can come back to why. But the second round is the work of a seriously damaged person. It is the work of his son.

"He must have surprised his father, while he was torturing someone, when he was around nine or ten. It destroyed him — what else could it have done? We have to assume that it was the culmination of a hellish childhood of abuse and iciness, the whole shebang. When his father dies, the son gets his hands on his pincers; he's seen him do the worst with them, the most nightmarish deeds imaginable, and he knows every little movement. They become heirlooms, but he doesn't know what to do with them; he's no murderer, he's the murdered. Then at some point something happens. I bet he somehow finds out . . . that his father is alive.

"I'm convinced that Wayne Jennings is alive, that he faked that car accident. It took some resources, but he had a lot of resources behind him. He went underground and committed another couple of murders, mostly, I think, to punish you, Ray, for your stubbornness and in order, so to speak, to posthumously prove his innocence. Murders number seventeen and eighteen resulted in your ending up in a trial.

"Then Jennings flees the country. The wave of murders stops. Jennings's so-called widow kills herself; either she knows that her husband is the Kentucky Killer and has known it the whole time and can't take it any longer, or else she works it out and kills herself in horror. Much later when their son is an adult, he finds out his father is alive, and he realises that even his

294

mother's suicide was the work of his father. In addition, he now has a culprit to blame for his own suffering.

"He is already broken, beyond all hope; now he becomes a murderer as well. His are crimes of insanity; he's letting off steam or murdering for lust, we don't know which, but he's practising, too: practising for the real murder, the only important murder, the murder of his father. Somehow, he finds out that his father is living abroad — in Sweden — and decides to hunt him down. He somehow obtains an address in Sweden — it's a hidden cabin some forty miles north of Stockholm. He travels there with a fake passport. What happens next is unclear — but in any case, we don't have just one Kentucky Killer in Sweden, we have two."

Larner sank down into his chair, closed his eyes and thought.

"I remember that boy so well," he said slowly. "He seemed pretty disturbed — you're right about that. Always sat in his mom's lap, never said a word, seemed almost autistic. And it would explain an awful lot. What do you think, Jerry?"

Schonbauer sat on the desk, dangling his legs; apparently this was his thinking position. He was silent for a bit while his legs were swinging. The table creaked alarmingly.

"It's a long shot," he said. "But it might be worth looking into."

"It might be easy, too," said Holm. "Do you have a phone book?"

Chuckling, Larner threw an enormous phone book up onto the desk.

Holm paged through it. Then, without asking permission, she tore out a page. "There's one Lamar Jennings in New York," she said. "In Queens."

"Let's go," Larner said.

On the way to the car, Larner led them into an area with quadruple safety locks and triple PIN codes. Out of a large metal cabinet he took two complete shoulder holsters and tossed them to the Swedes.

"Special permission," he said. They strapped themselves in for a journey into the heart of darkness and followed Larner out to the car.

It was a nondescript apartment building in an immense, fortress-like row of identical buildings on a cross-street of Queens's enormous Northern Boulevard. The neighbourhood was poor, but not dilapidated; a slum, but not a ghetto. The stairwell was dark and cluttered. Pieces of junk were strewn around the stairwell; no one had cleaned here for a long time.

They crept up the stairs, flight after flight. The stairwell became darker and warmer, bathed in a stagnant, dusty, dry heat. They were dripping with sweat.

Finally they were standing outside a door that bore an ordinary nameplate reading "Jennings".

All four of them drew their weapons. Their jaws were tense, their breathing suspended. They feared for the welfare of their souls more than their bodies. They were on their way into the lion's den. What gross distortions of human life would they encounter in there?

Schonbauer rang the bell. No one answered, and they heard no movement inside. He carefully pulled on the door handle. Locked. He looked at Larner, who nodded slightly. Schonbauer kicked the door in, causing splinters to fly. One kick was enough. He rushed in; they followed as if he were an enormous shield.

No one was home. The meagre light that followed them in through the busted door was the first light that had been there in a long time. As their eyes grew accustomed to the dimness, the room's contents emerged slowly — it was perplexingly empty, naked, blank. The air was still and hot. Motes of floating dust swirled in pirouettes. There were no human skins hung up on the wall, no rotten heads on stakes, no signs of the devil at all, just a bare studio apartment with a shabby desk and bed, an empty kitchen nook and an empty bathroom. A black venetian blind was pulled down over the only window.

Larner raised it. The sun sent in its unfiltered rays. But the almost obscene light unveiled few signs of life, Lamar Jennings's American legacy.

Hjelm glanced over the desk's bare surface and saw a pile of ashes and half-burned paper that had eaten its way into the wood. Maybe, in a final task, Jennings had intended to set the apartment on fire. A farewell fire. Hjelm reached for the remains of paper in the pile.

"Don't touch anything," Larner stopped him, and put on a pair of plastic gloves. "You two are still observers. Jerry, can you check the neighbours?"

Jerry left. Larner considered the pile of ashes.

"Was he planning to start a fire?" Hjelm said.

"I don't think so," Larner said, touching the paper remnants lightly. "It's something for the crime-scene techs to get their teeth into. Must not be moved a fraction of an inch."

He took a mobile phone out of his pocket and punched in a number.

"Crime techs, first unit," he said briskly. "One forty-seven Harper Street, Queens, eighth floor. ASAP."

He put the phone back in his pocket. "Go around to the other side of the desk, carefully," he continued. "The tiniest breeze could cost us a word."

Hjelm moved carefully. Larner pulled out the top desk drawer. It contained a single object, but that was plenty. It was a portrait of Wayne Jennings, wearing a youthful smile. A pin nailed the photo to the desk drawer through the man's throat, as if he were a mounted butterfly. It hardly seemed an exaggeration.

Larner chuckled mildly and shook his head. "It's for me," he muttered. "Twenty years. How the hell did you do it? I saw you burn. I saw your teeth."

He pulled out another drawer. In it were several torn-up pieces of paper, small fragments a quarter-inch wide. A date was visible on one of them.

"A diary?" said Hjelm.

"He's left just enough for us," said Larner. "Enough to give us a hint of the hell he lived through. But no more."

They found nothing else in the apartment, nothing at all.

Jerry Schonbauer came back in with a small, nearly transparent old woman who came up to his hip. They stopped in the doorway.

"Yes?" said Larner.

"This is the only neighbour I've found who knew anyone lived here at all," said Schonbauer. "Mrs Wilma Stewart."

Larner walked over and greeted the old woman. "Mrs Stewart, what can you tell us?"

She looked around the room. "This is exactly how he was," she said. "Expressionless, anonymous. Tried to avoid being seen. Reluctant to say hello. I invited him for a cup of tea once. He declined, not politely, not impolitely, just said no thanks and left."

Larner made a small face.

"What has he done?" said Mrs Stewart.

"Do you think you could help us make a portrait?" said Larner. "We'd be very grateful."

"He could have murdered me," she said quietly and insightfully.

Larner gave her a small parting smile, and Schonbauer escorted her to the door.

In the hallway, they met a small army of crime-scene technicians. One of them approached Larner, standing in the doorway. "We'll take it from here," he said briskly.

Larner nodded.

He waved the Swedes over. "Now we have to wait," he said, "as though we haven't done enough of that." They all began working their way down the eight flights of stairs.

A few flights down he turned to them. "The devil's lair never looks like you expect," he said.

# CHAPTER
# TWENTY-FIVE

When two heads that were not usually the cleverest were put together, something new was born. Viggo Norlander was working on John Doe; Gunnar Nyberg was working on LinkCoop. At a certain juncture, their labouriously struggling thoughts met, and the world took on a new shape.

At first Norlander got nowhere with his unknown body. He had incredibly little to go on. He sat in his office and read through the autopsy report, time after time.

Directly opposite him sat the considerably more swiftly working Arto Söderstedt, who had obtained his very own whiteboard and was playing mini-Hultin.

"What the hell are you working on?" Norlander said, irritated.

"The Lindbergers," Söderstedt said distractedly, continuing to draw.

"Do you need a whiteboard for that?"

"Hmm, need . . . He left behind a lot of notes that have to be sorted out. And she had some, too . . ."

"She? You swiped *her* notes?"

Söderstedt looked up with a scornful smile. "Not swiped, Viggo. A policeman never steals. Just as a policeman never harasses female immigration officers and never runs down little girls."

"Idiot!"

"A policeman never steals. He makes copies." He continued to fill in his squares.

"Like that's any better," said Norlander.

Söderstedt stopped again. "It's much better. Not least because you can compare what you've copied with what she chooses to share. The difference is what's essential. As soon as I'm finished with this, I'm going to ask to look at her planner and see if she's removed anything. *Comprende?*"

"That's a grieving woman, for fuck's sake! Leave her alone."

Söderstedt put down his marker. "Something feels wrong about them. They're in their thirties and live in an enormous apartment in Östermalm — eleven rooms, two kitchens. Both of them work at the Ministry of Foreign Affairs and are gone half the year. In Saudi Arabia. If they're up to something in the Arab world, and if it has anything to do with Eric's death, then she is quite possibly the next victim. I'm not trying to harass her, Viggo. I'm trying to protect her."

Norlander made a tired face. "Then put her under watch."

"It's still too vague. I have to work it out. *If* I get the chance."

Norlander threw out his arms. "I'm very fucking sorry," he said.

He tried to return to the autopsy report but couldn't. Thoughts of his unknown son, who was only just coming into being, wouldn't let go. He stared out through the window.

It was late afternoon; soon it would be time to go home. Outside the darkness was thick; rain was still drowning Stockholm. He thought of the flood in Poland a year or two earlier, the one that had contaminated the Baltic Sea. How much rain would it take for Lake Mälaren to run over?

The door flew open, and Chavez put his head in. "Hi, middle-aged white men," he said cheerfully. "How's it going?"

"Hi, swarthy young man," Söderstedt replied. "How's it going with you?"

"Incredibly badly. I was just at Hall sniffing Andreas Gallano's old underwear. What are you two doing?"

"I'm trying to work out John Doe," Norlander said grimly. "*If* I get the chance."

"OK, OK," said Chavez, closing the door. He continued through the hallway till he reached Hultin's door. He knocked, heard an indefinable mutter, and stepped in.

Hultin pushed his owlish glasses up towards his forehead and scrutinised him coldly.

"Have you heard anything from the United States?" said Chavez.

"Not yet," said Hultin. "Leave them alone. How's it going?"

"I've just returned from Hall. None of the other prisoners had anything useful to say; no one knew whether Gallano had contacts in the United States. And that new drug syndicate he's supposed to have belonged to is invisible — no one knew anything about that, either. Here's a list of what he left behind when he escaped: underwear, a few reminders from various authorities, electric shaver, and so forth. A total failure. Then I went to the cabin in Riala, talked to the techs. They've given up now, I think, incredibly frustrated that they didn't find a single clue. Except what was in the fridge, and here's a list: butter, a few packages of *tunnbröd*, hamburgers, cream cheese, honey, parsley, mineral water, bananas."

Hultin sighed and took off his glasses. "And the blue Volvos?"

"It will take some time. There are sixty-eight dark blue Volvo station wagons with number plates that start with B in the greater Stockholm area. Thanks to the rank and file, forty-two of them have been inspected and eliminated. I myself have looked at eight, and they were clear. If that isn't a contradiction in terms. Two that are still missing are fairly interesting: one belongs to a company that doesn't exist, at an address that doesn't exist; the other belongs to a habitual criminal by the name of Stefan Helge Larsson. We haven't had time to look at the other twenty-four yet, because I had to go to Norrköping."

Hultin observed his frenzy neutrally. "Proceed."

"I'm on it," said Chavez, and rushed out into the corridor.

Outside the two middle-aged white men's office, he couldn't resist the temptation to yank the door open and yell "Boo!"

Söderstedt drew a broad line straight across the whiteboard.

Norlander jumped almost two feet. He threw the autopsy report at the door, but it was already closed.

"Fucking idiot," he muttered as he bent down to pick it up. Söderstedt chuckled as he carefully erased the line.

Norlander once again opened the autopsy report. Four shots to the heart, each one of which would have been immediately fatal. No bullets were left behind, probably nine-millimetre calibre. The victim was generally in good shape. He had some old scars, probably from razors along his wrists, that were at least ten years old, and some even older circular scars spread out over other parts of his body. "Cigarette burns?" Stranded had written in his sprawling, old-man handwriting. How had the old devil missed the computerisation of the world? What planet did he live on?

Clothes. A blue T-shirt with no print. Beige lumber jacket. Jeans. Tennis shoes. Dirty white socks. Boxer shorts. None of that told him a thing.

He switched his attention to the man's possessions. How many times had he dumped the contents of the little plastic bag onto the desk? Apparently often enough to get a frown out of Söderstedt.

A fake Rolex, a roll of ten-kronor coins, a key. The key seemed very new. He turned it over and over.

It was a pretty substantial door key. Its lock must be much bigger than you would find on a regular door, a safety lock of some sort; but it was hardly possible to say more than that. The key said "CEA" and "Made in Italy" and could have been made in any shoe repair shop anywhere.

But did shoe repair shops really manufacture such large safety keys?

Somewhere in the back of his head, a diligent brain cell went on the loose. Hadn't he, at some point during this case, run into this very thing, just in passing, something that flickered in the corner of his eye? On one of the dunce jobs, perhaps? Yes, sure as hell, at the very beginning of the case, he had been in charge of all the idiotic reports of "crimes committed by Americans in Sweden". One American had exposed himself and got beaten up by the women's football team, another had copied thousand-kronor notes in Xerox machines — and another had copied a forbidden key at a shoe repair shop. Could that incident be connected with this key?

Norlander turned to the computer with an intensity that made Söderstedt look up in surprise. He dug into his archive, feeling like a hacker. He found the case, with a reference to the fraud squad of the Stockholm police. Why the fraud squad? After enough hard work to put an end to any hacker aspirations he harboured, he came to a minuscule document from the uniformed police. There it was. It had been the fourth of September. A little shoe repair shop on Rindögatan in Gärdet. The owner, Christo Kavafis, had copied an illegal key from a plasticine original, was seized with remorse, and was then stupid enough to report the whole thing to the police. He was arrested, but the case was dropped for lack of priority.

Norlander didn't have all the threads clear in his mind, but it was time for action. He grabbed his leather jacket and rushed out into the corridor. As he passed Gunnar Nyberg's door, another stubborn brain cell in the back of his head started to dance. He stopped. That computer company — what was it called? And the key — weren't they connected? He approached the door and took it right to the head.

Nyberg came out and stared at the crouching, swearing Norlander.

"Just the man I was hoping to run into," said Nyberg, perhaps unaware of the double meaning of this expression. "Didn't your John Doe have a key on him? I wonder if we should test it out down at LinkCoop's warehouse. Something about that break-in still seems mysterious."

Norlander forgot his pain in a flash and held the key up to Nyberg's face, as though he were trying to hypnotise him.

"I'll drive," said Norlander.

Nyberg followed him willingly. The two stout men half jogged through the corridors, and the local seismograph registered an unexpectedly high reading on the Richter scale.

They reached the basement and drove out in Norlander's service Volvo, which he had been refusing to return for four years, and set out for Frihamnen.

That was the planned destination, anyway. But they got stuck in traffic as soon as they got down onto

Scheelegatan. It was the middle of rush hour, and it seemed to get worse every day. Shouldn't the sky-high unemployment levels mean that fewer people had reason to be in the city at five thirty, the time when they gave up?

"Let's stop and eat," said Nyberg.

"Weren't you on a diet?" said Norlander.

"Yes. Past tense," said Nyberg.

Norlander parked in a highly illegal spot on Kungsbroplan. They ran through cascades of rain into the closest restaurant. It was called the Andalusian Dog and was so pleasant that they nearly forgot their urgent business. Norlander dug into some Mexican fucking sludge. Nyberg gulped down four baked potatoes with *skagenröra*.

"You could diversify a little, you know," said Norlander.

"It's skinny food," Nyberg said, with half of his fourth portion in his jaws.

By six thirty they were full, and the traffic had become a bit lighter.

"Dammit, he's probably closed by now," Norlander exclaimed, standing.

"Who?" said Nyberg.

"The shoe repair. On Rindögatan."

"We'll take our chances and drive by. It's on the way, after all."

They took their chances and drove by. Kungsgatan to Stureplan, Sturegatan to Valhallavägen, Erik Dahlbergsgatan to Rindögatan.

"Lidingövägen would have been better," said Nyberg.

"Lay off," said Norlander. "But umbrellas would have been good."

It was pitch black, as if it were the middle of the night; actually it was only quarter to seven. The shoe repair shop was a short way up the long hill of Rindögatan. There was a faint light coming from the little workshop. They hurried out into the pouring rain and pounded on the window, where old soles and keys from the 1960s were lying and collecting dust.

A small Greek man in his sixties peeked discreetly out the window. He gaped in fear at the dripping, pounding Nordic giants. *Polyphemus*, he appeared to be thinking. *Two of them*.

"Police," Norlander mimed, showing his ID. "Can we come in for a minute?"

The Greek opened the door and, with a small gesture, let the cop-Cyclopes in. On the ancient work table lay an open book under a small, weak shoemaker's lamp. The man walked over to it and held it up. It was in Greek.

"Have you heard of Konstantin Kavafis?" he asked.

They stared at him like idiots.

"Never has the modern Greek language sounded so sweet," he said, stroking the cover of the book. "He lifted us up to the level of the ancients. I always sit here for a while after closing time and read him. A poem a day keeps senility away. He was my grandfather's uncle."

"So you're Christo Kavafis?" Norlander said briskly.

"That's right," said Kavafis. "To what do I owe the honour?"

"A few weeks ago you copied a key from a plasticine original, right?"

Kavafis turned pale. "I thought I was free." He felt the threat of grievous bodily harm nibble at the back of his neck. *My name is No One,* he seemed to be thinking.

"Yeah, yeah, you *are* free, don't worry. Tell us about it."

"I have already told about it."

"Do it again."

"A young man who spoke English with an American accent came in and asked to get a key made from a clay impression. I knew it wasn't legal, but it was such a challenge. I don't come across that many challenges in my work, so I couldn't resist. Then I regretted it and called the police, and they came and arrested me. I was in jail for the night. I haven't been that scared since the civil war. All my memories came back."

"What did he look like? The American?"

Kavafis shook his head. "It was a long time ago. Ordinary. Normal. Young. Pretty blond."

"Clothes?"

"I don't remember. Grey jacket, I think. Tennis shoes. I don't know."

Norlander took out the key and held it up to Kavafis. "Is this the key?"

The Greek took it and turned it over. "This might be it. It was one like this."

"Can you come up to see us tomorrow and help us try to get a picture of him? It's very important."

Kavafis nodded.

Norlander fished out his wallet and took out a dirty business card, which he gave to the Greek. Then they said goodbye.

Kavafis looked hesitant. "I wonder," he said, "if I don't remember one more thing. He paid in ten-kronor coins. Out of a long roll."

Nyberg and Norlander exchanged glances. They had been right. John Doe was an American. He had made a clay impression of a security lock. He had gone to a shoe repair shop in Gärdet to get a key made. Then he had been shot in the heart. Why? Where? In the rush to get going, they couldn't really get all the threads to come together, but they had to get to Frihamnen; they knew that much.

It was almost seven thirty when they reached the sentry box outside of LinkCoop's warehouses. It was pitch black, the heavens were wide open and they had no umbrellas. They had at least thirty-four doors to test. They didn't hesitate.

Tonight it wasn't Benny Lundberg sitting in the sentry box but another of the guards. Nyberg went over and waved his police ID in the air.

"We need to take a look at the premises in connection with the break-in," he said to the cracked window hatch. "Isn't Benny working?"

"He's on holiday," said the guard.

"How long has he been gone?"

"A few days. Since the break-in."

"Strange time for a holiday." Nyberg felt a twinge of suspicion.

"I know," said the guard. He could have been mistaken for Benny Lundberg. The stench of steroids trumped the perpetual ozone scent of the storm. "He took a holiday in August, so it is a little odd. He travelled somewhere. Out of the country, I think. Was it the Canary Islands?"

Nyberg nodded.

Norlander came jogging up after having parked the car round the corner. They entered the grounds and walked to the door where the break-in had taken place. Thick planks were nailed up across the door as a temporary repair job. Nyberg heaved himself up onto the loading dock and inserted the key. It went in. But it didn't turn in the lock.

"Right kind, anyway," he said. "I guess we should start from the left."

They followed the loading dock past the series of doors up to the far end of the large warehouse. There were about as many doors to the left of the entrance as there were to the right. There ought to be more on the back of the building as well. Mayer, the chief of security, had talked about thirty-four units; after testing ten doors it felt like considerably more. They were soaking wet. The torrents of rain were splendidly combined with loathsome gusts of wind. Two cases of pneumonia sailed through the air, searching for their rightful owners.

The key fitted in all the locks but was never the right one. They reached the entrance and began to work their way through the other half. It felt more and more hopeless. A fool's errand. And a voluntary one, at that. They were doing overtime that they didn't know if they dared to put in for. Couldn't they have waited until tomorrow?

They approached the end of the row. By the time they came to the last door, they were resigned.

"What do you think?" Nyberg held the key a few inches from the lock.

"Aren't there any doors on the other side?"

"That remains to be seen," said Nyberg, who inserted the key. He turned it. It was the right one. "Ha ha." Laughing, he pulled the door open a few inches.

It was violently kicked the rest of the way open, straight into his nose. He tumbled over. A black-clad figure in a balaclava jumped over him and raced along the dock in the pouring rain. Norlander drew his pistol and set off after him. Nyberg got up, his hand to his face. He roared. He felt the blood welling between his fingers. He was about to throw himself after them when he turned to the storage unit.

Looking down a set of stairs, he saw Benny Lundberg, the guard. He was naked and tied to a chair. Blood was streaming from his shredded fingertips. A needle was threaded through his genitals. And out of his neck stuck two gently quivering syringes.

Gunnar Nyberg stiffened. His own pain vanished immediately. He took his hand from his face and let the blood flow out of his nose. He went down the stairs. He was trembling. A small, bare light bulb radiated a ghastly glow over the macabre scene.

312

Benny Lundberg was alive. His eyes had rolled back; only the whites were visible. Spasmodic jerks passed through his face. Convulsions were ripping through the pumped-up body. White foam bubbled out of his mouth. No hint of sound.

Gunnar Nyberg was looking at pain beyond words.

His large body shook. What could he do? He didn't dare touch the horrible pincers in Lundberg's neck. Any movement could have disastrous consequences. He didn't even dare to unfasten the leather straps around his arms and legs. What would happen if Lundberg convulsed and fell to the floor? The only thing he could do in the way of a small attempt at care was to pull the long needle out of his male organ. He did so.

Then he got his mobile phone out of his inside pocket, and, with concentration, managed to dial the number. He didn't recognise his own voice as it asked for an ambulance. "A doctor has to come too," it said. "A neck specialist."

Then he bent towards Lundberg. He placed his hand on the shaking cheek. He tried to speak comfortingly to him. He embraced him. He tried to be as brotherly as he could.

"There, there, Benny, take it easy. Help is on the way. You can do it. Hang in there, Benny. There. Everything is OK. Nice and easy."

The spasms and twitches began to subside. Benny Lundberg grew calmer — or was he about to die in his arms?

Gunnar Nyberg realised he was crying.

★　★　★

Norlander ran after the man in black. He was in good shape these days, and he was gradually gaining on the man. But the man was quick and lithe. He threw himself down from the loading dock and kept running, past the sentry box. Just as Norlander ran by, the guard peered out. "Call the police!" he bellowed as he ran.

The man in black dashed into a side street and vanished from sight for an instant. Norlander approached the spot. He saw the man disappear behind a building about ten yards away. Without thinking, he ran that way. His weapon was dangling from his hand. The man in the balaclava peeked out and shot at him.

Norlander threw himself forward into the mud. He checked himself out for a second, then was up again. His pistol was muddy. He tried to wipe it off as he ran. He raced up to the corner and carefully peered round it. It was empty back there, an alley. Crouching, he ran to the next corner and peered round it. Empty again. Up to the next corner. Peer around it carefully.

One step was all he heard behind him, a faint splash. Then an incredible pain on the back of his neck. He fell into the mud like a pig. He was nearly unconscious. He looked up into the rain clouds. Everything was dancing. The man in black was staring down at him through his balaclava. He couldn't make out his eyes. The only thing he could see was the silencer on the barrel of the pistol that was pointed at his face.

"Get out of here," the man hissed. "Beat it."

Then he was gone. Norlander heard a motor start up. He stood and peered round the corner of the building. He was dazed. The world was spinning. He could vaguely see the contours of a car in the middle of the centrifuge. Maybe brown, maybe a jeep.

Then he fell down into the sludge.

# CHAPTER
# TWENTY-SIX

The sun in New York had become as insane as the rain was in Stockholm. Time was out of joint. All that was missing was for horses with two heads and jackdaws with beaks sticking out of their arses to be born.

It was excessively hot. Not even the FBI's hyper-modern air conditioning could combat it. Hjelm could have testified that Eenie meenie miney moe didn't work either. He was bored; he felt as if he had been stopped mid-step.

They waited. Waiting never promotes tolerance for irritation. Everyone was irritating everyone else. Even Jerry Schonbauer had a fit and tore off his soaking wet shirt, causing his buttons to fly off. When one of the buttons knocked the contact lens out of Holm's left eye, he resumed his timid self and begged for forgiveness.

"I didn't know you wore lenses," Hjelm said after a while.

" 'Wore' is right." She examined the two pieces of the contact, which were stuck to her thumb and index finger respectively. "Now you'll get to see me in glasses."

She took out her right contact and threw it away. Then she dug out a pair of classic round glasses and secured them on her exquisite nose. To avoid bursting into confidence-shattering peals of laughter, he concentrated on being irritated with the heat.

It didn't work. He burst into laughter.

"Look at that funny bird," he said unconvincingly, pointing out the window.

"I'm glad I can be of service," she said sulkily, pushing the glasses up towards her forehead.

They had been to visit the young computer expert Bernhard Andrews, who hacked his way into every branch of the Internet on the hunt for Lamar Jennings. Maybe he would find a photo. But as expected, he was nowhere. Not one single tiny directory could produce anything at all on Jennings; he had kept himself out of the monitoring systems of society for twenty-five years. The only thing that turned up was his birth certificate. It seemed that he hadn't existed since his birth.

Mrs Wilma Stewart had failed miserably to create a portrait of Lamar Jennings. As the image took shape on the computer screen, the old woman had shaken her head time after time. "Thicker lips . . . Thinner lips, I said, young man . . . Listen here. I said thicker lips."

The heat claimed another victim. She nodded off in front of the computer and promised to come back later and try again.

Finally the crime techs dropped off the first of the materials they had finished processing from Lamar Jennings's apartment. They had attempted to reconstruct the pages of Lamar Jennings's diary from the remains they had found and made four copies. Each of the four took one and began reading. Schonbauer sat on Larner's desk, dangling his legs, clad in a ridiculous string vest that had been revealed after the shirt catastrophe. Larner sat in his chair with his legs on the desk beside Schonbauer. Yalm & Halm sat in visitors' chairs at a respectable distance from each other.

The fragments were incoherent, like key words out of a life story. Apparently Larner had been right in saying that Lamar Jennings had left just enough to indicate the depths of his pain. Each fragment bore a small amount of information.

"don't know why i'm writing, pleading? am i trying to stop myself before i have time"

"a grave in the great perfection of futility"

"the old neighbour woman wanted to have me for tea, said no, thanks, would have vomited on her, got permission to"

"they are so small, they don't want to understand how"

"stronger and stronger. Why do they get stronger and st"

"in the middle of the night, shadow in the closet, it's stuck, invisible hinges"

"reduced to nothing, less than zero, there is a life under zero"

"in passing, the glow of a cigarette, can already hear the sizzle, can already smell the stench, but i can never predict the pain, only"

318

"April 19. What power they have now, can't resist any longer"

"grandma dead. OK. A package came. Just crap, except for a letter. Going to read it soon. The handwriting is worrying."

"earth a grave, people maggots, where is the corpse? is it the dead god we eat up?"

"stairs out of nothing in nothing, like a dream. Comes in flashes now, like it travels inside me, like i'm being driven toward a goal"

"just go there, say i'm sick, try to get help"

"if the images can become a story"

"July 27. Who am i trying to kid? There is only one help. The Aztecs killed in order to live. Human sacrifices. I"

"follow the shadow, the arm of a jacket has got caught, a door, stairs"

"theletterislyingthereimwaitingicantitwontwork"

"Grandma dead. Try again. Grandma dead. OK."

"The light behind the door like the frame of an icon, a darker darkness, have to get out, have to plead"

"the stairs straight down, can't follow, only flashes"

"the cellar the cellar the cellar"

"sick SOB at the bar, Arkaius, fucking name, bragging bragging bragging, tons of houses all over the world, suck him off, dead as a doornail, need the address now, reward"

"open the letter, read, i knew it, it was impossible for him to be"

"open the door, into the light. Chaos, have to get
  out, have to"
"glow of a cigarette, our little secret, our little hell"
"why us in the middle of all this perfection, the
  tiniest mollusk is more adapted to life on earth,
  can't feel pain"

As they read, they sneaked glances at each other.

When they were all finished, Larner said, "This is
why it didn't all fit together. This is a classic serial killer
of the more intellectual sort, incredibly wounded, very
intelligent. It couldn't be reconciled with the early
coldness. I ought to have realised. On July twenty-
seventh we have a date. On July twenty-seventh, 1997,
the prostitute Sally Browne was murdered in
Manhattan. That was Lamar Jennings's first murder. It
starts there: 'The Aztecs killed in order to live'. Any
other thoughts?"

"Arkaius," said Kerstin Holm. "Robert Arkaius is a
Swedish tax exile. He owns the cabin where Lamar
committed his first murder in Sweden. Apparently he
got the address in exchange for sexual favours. Arkaius
couldn't return to Sweden anyway. Of course, he didn't
know that his former lover's son, Andreas Gallano, had
holed up there after he'd escaped from prison."

Larner nodded mutely.

Schonbauer said, "That must have been after he
opened that letter and found out that his father was in
Sweden, when he had already started the murders. He
goes out and looks for Swedes in sketchy bars in order
to get his hands on a good place to stay in Stockholm.

Sex doesn't seem to have anything to do with it, other than that. The trauma seems to have occurred before puberty."

"Our reconstruction of his profile," said Larner, "is quite close to the one you've already done, Yalm. As a child, he is abused by his father — that's probably the glowing cigarettes we see. Sure enough, the culmination comes when he goes down some stairs and opens that door and sees his professional murderer of a father at work. After that, he is never the same again. Then comes blow after blow. His father dies, his mother commits suicide after a few years, possibly because of that letter that reaches her in some unknown way and ends up in an untouched box at his grandmother's house. When his grandmother dies, the letter ends up in the hands of the now-twenty-four-year-old son in New York, where he — as the apartment indicates — lives half outcast from society. It confirms what he's suspected all along: his father is alive. His tormentor still exists; he hovers over him and possesses him.

"His repressed images of the past start to return, moving in a certain direction, 'like it travels inside me, like i'm being driven toward a goal'. Finally the images drive him down to that door. He opens it and is confronted with the most repressed image of all, his father above a victim who's foaming at the mouth, with the micro-pincers in his neck. He has to get rid of it, and that can only happen with homeopathic magic: like pleads to like. He has the pincers; now he can use them. The image in his memory is exact; he knows exactly what to do. As soon as the images appear, he must go out and kill. It calms him: 'if the images can become a story'. The murders make the lightning-like, hard-hitting pictures into a more easily handled story.

"But as you said, Yalm, at the same time it's about preparing himself for the big, decisive murder. He has to get rid of his father, he must die by his own methods, the very ones that haunt him. He's finally got hold of the address of a safe house in the Stockholm area — it's time. Apparently the letter has revealed that his father is in Stockholm, and even more important, it's revealed what he calls himself — otherwise the whole project is hopeless. The techs have to be finished with the burned letter soon. If we're lucky, the name will be there.

"Anyway, he gets a fake passport under the name Edwin Reynolds and goes to Newark airport. Annoyingly, the next flight to Stockholm is fully booked. It's not really a catastrophe, but somehow he happens to stumble upon Lars-Erik Hassel. Maybe the images came to him again in the airport; maybe he decides to kill two birds with one stone: getting his hands on a ticket, and simultaneously getting rid of the images and having a peaceful flight; avoiding six hours of inferno might be worth the relatively minor risks. Hassel somehow reveals himself as a traveller to Stockholm who hasn't yet checked in, which means his seat can be made available. Jennings gets Hassel and his luggage into the janitor's closet and does his deed; maybe he uses sex as a temptation again. Then he snatches Hassel's ticket, calls and cancels in his name, books himself the seat with Reynolds's name, and has a nice, calm flight.

"Presumably he has no idea how close you are to catching him at Arlanda. All he has is carry-on luggage — he just goes right through, gets in a taxi, stops somewhere on the way and buys some food, and goes straight to the cabin. Your drug dealer happens to be there, but by now Lamar Jennings is a practised killer. He gets in easily and murders the drug dealer; the sight now and then of the body in the cellar is enough to keep the images at bay as he searches for his father and plans the best way to deal with him. What happens next is your business."

No one had any objections. That was surely how it happened.

In the meantime, Hjelm's thoughts had gone in a slightly different direction. "Was there a cellar on Wayne Jennings's farm?"

Larner looked at him. He had expected to be able to catch his breath after his account, but now he had to make a sharp turn-around. "There was a small cellar, yes. But it was a sort of rec room, a cosy room with a fireplace, and we checked it several times. It wasn't the scene of the murder."

"Who lives there now?"

"I seem to recall that it went round and round in the media for so long that it became unsellable. After his wife died, it was left to rot. It's deserted."

"There's something about a closet that Lamar apparently wants to tell us. A shadow in the closet at night, a door that's got caught on 'the arm of a jacket', then the stairs. Might there have been another cellar, a secret one? The very origin of the entire story of the Kentucky Killer?"

Larner thought it over, then picked up the phone and dialled a number. "Bill, how long is the letter going to take? OK. I'm going to Kentucky. Jerry will hold down the fort here."

He hung up and looked at them urgently. "Well, are you coming?"

They flew to Louisville, Kentucky, in a flash. At the airport, an FBI helicopter was waiting to carry them eastward. A tall mountain range towered up in the distance.

"Cumberland Plateau," Larner said, pointing.

The helicopter landed at the edge of a tobacco field, and Larner and three bundles of muscle from the FBI, along with the two Swedes, jogged through the field and out onto the country road alongside. A grove of tall, unidentifiable deciduous trees lent shadow to a decaying farm out on the wilderness land; there wasn't a neighbour for miles.

Seen at a closer distance, the farmhouse looked haunted. Fifteen years had left their mark. Houses always seem to do their best when inhabited — otherwise they wither. Wayne Jennings's farm had withered. It didn't look as if it had felt very well from the start, but by now it had reached a state of complete abandonment. The front door was crooked and warped, and it took the efforts of the collective FBI muscle mass to tear it open, which was the same as tearing it apart.

They entered the hall. The house hadn't been airtight. Everything was covered in a thin layer of sand. Each step was followed by a small, rising puff of sand. They passed the kitchen; dishes were laid out under the layer of sand, as though time had stopped in the middle of a regular day. They passed the stairway that led down to the small cellar; Hjelm cast a glance down the steps. Three beer bottles stood on a small table. The sand had glued itself along their edges; they were like three pillars of salt. They entered a room with a bed. A few disintegrating posters were still clinging to the wall: Batman, a baseball team. A book lay open on the desk: *Mary Poppins*. On the pillow sat a threadbare teddy bear, covered with sand. Kerstin lifted it up; one leg remained on the bed. She blew it off and studied it. Her heart seemed about to break.

They went from Lamar's room to his parents'; it was furthest off towards the wide-open spaces, which stretched on, flat, towards Cumberland Plateau. Larner pointed at the double bed; in the place of one pillow there was a large hole; down was still floating in the sandy air.

"This is where Lamar found his mother one hot summer morning," he said quietly. "A shotgun. Her head was almost completely blown off."

They went back out into the hallway and through the next door entered a guest room, which had its own entrance from the terrace.

"It has to be here," Larner said.

He went over to the cupboard and opened the door. The assembled FBI forces stepped in with sturdy tools and instruments of measurement. They pulled a microphone along the wall. "Here," said one of the FBI men. "There's empty space behind here."

"See if you can find the mechanism." Larner moved back. They kept looking; he sat down on the bed, where the Swedes were already sitting.

"You can probably put that down now," he said.

Holm stared down at the teddy bear that was sitting in her lap. She placed it on the bed. Sand had run out of the hole at the leg until it was just a fake shell of skin. She held up the scrap.

"The things we do to our children," was all she said.

"I warned you," said Larner.

It took time, almost fifteen minutes of intense, scientific searching. But finally they found a complicated mechanism, behind a piece of iron that had been screwed into place. Apparently Wayne Jennings hadn't wanted anyone to make their way down there after his so-called death. But his son evidently had — and had retrieved his pincers.

A thick iron door slid open inside the cupboard; Hjelm even thought he could see the jacket arm that had got stuck one night and kept the door from closing again as it should. He walked over to the door to the guest room and crouched down, simulating the view a ten-year-old would have. Lamar had stood here; from here he had seen the shadow glide into the cupboard, and then he had followed. The thick metal door hadn't closed properly.

Larner went into the cupboard and pulled open the door; the mechanism was a bit rusty and creaked in a way it surely hadn't twenty years earlier. He turned on a powerful torch and disappeared. They followed him.

The narrow stone staircase had an iron handrail. Sand crunched under their feet as they made their way down the staircase, which was surprisingly long. Finally they came to a massive, rusty iron door. Larner opened it and shone his powerful torch around.

It was a shabby cellar, cramped, almost absurdly small, a concrete cube far below ground in the wilderness. In the middle a large iron chair was welded to more iron in the floor; leather bands hung slack from the armrests and chair legs. There was also a solid workbench, like a carpenter's bench. That was all. Larner pulled out the drawers under the bench. They were empty. He sat in the iron chair as the little concrete cube filled with people; the last FBI man didn't even fit and had to stand on the stairs.

"These walls have seen a lot," said Larner.

For a second Hjelm thought he had made contact with all the suffering that the walls guarded: a wind that was simultaneously hot and ice-cold went through him. But it was beyond words.

Larner stood and clapped his hands. "Well, we'll do a complete crime-scene investigation, but there's no doubt that this is where most of the Kentucky Killer's victims met their long-awaited deaths."

They went back upstairs — claustrophobia wasn't far off.

What had happened when ten-year-old Lamar had stepped into the torture chamber? How had Wayne reacted? Had he beaten him unconscious? Threatened him? Did he try to comfort him? The only person to ask was Wayne Jennings himself, and Hjelm promised himself and the world that he would ask him.

For he was becoming more and more certain that if father and son confronted each other in Sweden, the father would be victorious. He would kill his son for a second time.

They took the helicopter back to Louisville and caught a flight back to New York. The whole foray had only taken a few hours. It was afternoon at JFK, a long, hot afternoon. They took a taxi back to FBI headquarters, where they found Jerry Schonbauer sitting with his legs dangling, leafing through a pile of papers as though nothing had happened.

But it had.

"Good timing," said Schonbauer. "I've just received a preliminary crime-scene report, including a preliminary reconstruction of the burned letter. That's the only thing of interest. The rest of the investigation didn't turn up anything — the apartment was completely clean. Here are your copies of the letter."

It had been possible to make out the date: April 6, 1983. Almost a year after Wayne Jennings faked his death. It was a letter he wouldn't have needed to write nor, presumably, been *able* to write. That he had done it anyway revealed a trace of humanity that Hjelm didn't really want to see.

"When did his wife kill herself?" he asked.

"The summer of 1983," said Larner. "Apparently it took a few months for her to understand the extent of the whole thing."

**328**

The envelope had been among the burned remains. The Stockholm postmark had been clear. The address was that of the farm; apparently Wayne Jennings had been relatively certain that the FBI wasn't reading his widow's mail a year after his death.

What could be reconstructed read as follows, with the technicians' comments in brackets:

Dear Mary Beth. As you can see, I'm not dead. I hope one day to be able to expla [break, burned] see you in another life. Maybe in a few years it will be p [break, burned] have been absolutely necessary. We were forced to give me this dis [break, burned] pe that you can live with this knowledge and [break, burned] ucky Killer is me and yet it's no [break, burned] now go by the name [break, cut out] ty that Lamar is better off without me, I wasn't always [break, burned] lutely must burn this letter immedia [break, burned]. Always, your W.

"Lamar didn't want to give us the name." Larner put down the letter. "Maybe he did want to give us the rest — it depends on how seriously we should take this half-failed incineration. But he didn't want to give us the name — he cut it out before he set fire to the letter."

"A loving husband," said Holm.

"What does it actually say here?" said Hjelm. "'The Kentucky Killer is me and yet it's not' — is that how we should interpret it? And: 'We were forced to give me this — disguise'? 'We'?"

"That could mean Jennings was a professional killer, employed by someone else," said Larner pensively. "Suppose, in the late seventies, it was suddenly necessary to get a great number of people to talk — engineers, researchers, journalists — and a whole cadre of unidentified people, probably foreigners. They called in their torture experts, who may have been on ice since the Vietnam War. They had to disguise the whole thing as the actions of a madman. The serial killer was born. And the consequences were plentiful."

It hung in the air. No one said it. Finally Hjelm cleared his throat. "CIA?"

"We'll have to attend to that bit." Larner sighed. "It won't be easy."

Kerstin and Paul looked at each other. Maybe the good old KGB theory hadn't been so far off target after all. Maybe it *was* top-level politics. But it was the *victims* who were KGB. Maybe.

"If I were you," said Larner, "I'd look closely at Sweden's immigration register for 1983. The last victim died at the beginning of November 1982. The letter was written from Stockholm in April 1983. Maybe you'll find him listed among the immigrants during that interval."

An FBI man looked in. "Ray, Mrs Stewart has come up with a picture."

They stood in unison and followed him. Now they would find out what Lamar Jennings looked like.

★ ★ ★

Chief inspector Jan-Olov Hultin looked sceptical. "'Get out of here'?" he said. "'Beat it'?"

"That's what he said," said Viggo Norlander.

He was lying in a hospital bed at Karolinska, dressed in a bizarre hospital gown. He had a large compress on the wound in his neck and still felt a bit groggy.

"So in other words, he spoke Swedish?" Hultin ventured pedagogically, bending down towards the once-again-defeated hero.

"Yes," Norlander said sleepily.

"You don't remember anything else?"

"He was dressed all in black. A balaclava. His hand didn't shake so much as a fraction of an inch when he sighted me with the pistol. He must have missed on purpose when he fired. Then he took off in a pretty large car, maybe a Jeep, maybe brown."

"This is an insane serial killer with many lives on his conscience. And he's shot people before. Why didn't he kill you?"

"Thanks for your support at this difficult time," Norlander said, and passed out.

Hultin got up and went over to the other bed in the hospital room.

In it was yet another once-again-defeated hero. Both of his bundles of muscle had been flattened by the same man; that didn't feel so great.

Gunnar Nyberg's bandage was more extensive. His nasal bones were cracked in three places; he found it incredible that such small bones could be cracked in so many places. But his soul hurt much worse. He knew that no matter how hard he tried, he would never get that horrible image of Benny Lundberg out of his mind. He would probably die with it before his eyes.

"How's he doing?" he asked.

Hultin sat in the visitor's chair with a little groan. "Viggo? He's recovering."

"Not Viggo. Benny Lundberg."

"Aha. Well, the latest news isn't good. He's alive, and he'll survive. But his vocal cords are seriously injured, and the nerve paths in his neck are one big mess. He's on a respirator. Worst of all, he's in a state of extreme shock. The perpetrator literally terrified him out of his wits. He pushed him over the line of sanity, and the question is whether there's any way back."

Hultin placed an incongruous bunch of grapes on Nyberg's table. "Your clear-headedness saved his life," he said. "You should know that. If you'd tried to pull out the pincers, he almost certainly would have died right away. That neck doctor you got there struggled for over an hour. He had to operate at the scene. It was good that it was you and not Viggo who went in; I guess I can say that now that he's out."

Hultin looked into Nyberg's eyes. Something had changed. "Are you OK, by the way?" he said quietly.

"No, I'm not OK," said Gunnar Nyberg. "I'm furious. I'm going to put a stop to this guy if it's the last thing I do."

Hultin was in two minds about that. Certainly, it was excellent that Nyberg was coming out of his recent apathy towards work and his longing for retirement; but a furious Nyberg was like a runaway steam engine.

"Come back as soon as you can," Hultin said. "We need you."

"I'd be back already if it weren't for this damn concussion."

"That's something we've got plenty of right now," Hultin said neutrally.

"If we hadn't stopped to eat, we could have saved him," he said bitterly.

Hultin looked at him for a moment, then said goodbye, and stepped into the corridor. Before he stepped out into the evening's downpour, he opened an umbrella with police logos, which kept the deluge in check until he reached his turbo Volvo, the only privilege of his rank that he accepted.

He drove through the pitch-black city, up St Eriksgatan, then Fleminggatan and Polhemsgatan, but at this moment he was an unfit driver. Mixing facts with intuitions as he was, he was a grave danger in traffic; fortunately, though, the night-time traffic was non-existent. Why Benny Lundberg? What had the security guard seen or done that night? After all, Hultin had been there and talked to him that same night, and everything had seemed normal. And yet there must have been something strange about that break-in. Immediately afterwards Lundberg had taken holiday time and was later discovered half murdered by the Kentucky Killer, who had spoken Swedish, flattened two solid, professional policemen, and refrained from killing Norlander even though he'd had him in his sights. If they hadn't had the background information on the killer, Hultin would have immediately thought: inside job, a criminal cop.

He went into the dark police building. Everything was still. The rain's uninterrupted rumble had been absorbed into the background noise; when the rain stopped sometime in the future, something would feel wrong, like a disturbance in the normal state of things.

He arrived in the A-Unit's corridor. A little light was shining — he realised where from. Chavez hopped out from his office and rushed up to his boss.

"Come take a look at this shit," he said, as hyper as a seven-year-old.

Jan-Olov Hultin wanted to think, not look at shit. He had been doing quite enough of that during the past few weeks. He felt like a grumpy old man — which, it struck him, he was. He followed Chavez without protest.

In Hjelm's place at the desk sat a small older man with Mediterranean looks. His face was illuminated by the large computer monitor in front of him.

"This is Christo Kavafis," said Chavez, "the locksmith. I took the liberty of bringing him in. Christo, this is Jan-Olov Hultin, my boss."

"My pleasure," said Christo Kavafis.

Hultin nodded and looked with surprise at Chavez, who hurried over to the Greek man.

"I was struck by a flash of genius when I heard that John Doe's key allowed admittance to the site of the murder," Chavez said eagerly. "Everything seems to indicate that the American who got into Sweden under the name Edwin Reynolds looks — like this." He

**334**

turned the computer monitor a quarter of the way around.

Hultin stared into the face of the Kentucky Killer. It was John Doe, their unidentified body.

He was silent for a minute. The pieces were starting to fall into place. "So there are two Kentucky Killers," he said.

"Now there's just one," said Chavez.

Hultin picked up his phone and dialled Hjelm's number in the United States. It was busy. Very strange — the number was to be used solely for this purpose.

Kerstin and Paul approached the computer monitor above Wilma Stewart's small, nodding head.

"That's just what he looked like," said the old woman. "Just like that. Lamar Jennings."

Kerstin and Paul stared into the face of the Kentucky Killer.

It was John Doe, their unidentified body.

Hjelm took out his mobile phone and dialled Hultin's number in Sweden. It was busy. Very strange — the number was to be used solely for this purpose.

Hultin didn't give up. He called again. This time he got through.

"Hjelm," Hjelm answered on the other side of the Atlantic.

"John Doe is the Kentucky Killer," Hultin said abruptly.

"One of them," said Hjelm.

"I'm looking at composite of him right now."

"Me too."

Hultin gave a start. "I just tried to call."

"Me too."

Hjelm had difficulty getting everything straightened out. Hultin kept talking instead of explaining.

"Norlander and Nyberg almost got him. The second one. He speaks Swedish."

"He's lived in Sweden since 1983. How close did they get?"

"Close enough to take a licking, both of them. In LinkCoop's warehouse. He had Viggo in his sights but didn't kill him. Is he a police officer?"

"Sort of. We'll talk about that later. So he's free?"

"Yes, but just by a hair. We have the pincers. And a half-dead guard."

"Benny Lundberg?"

"Yes. Unfortunately, he's probably going to be a vegetable. Can you explain all this?"

"There are two killers, Jennings father and son. The son went to Sweden to kill the father. Their roles were reversed."

"So it *was* Wayne Jennings . . . that means he's alive?"

"He's been living in Sweden for fifteen years. It's his son Lamar who's dead; we know that now. That explains why he shot John Doe without torturing him. Presumably Lamar was waiting in ambush and saw his father Wayne torturing Eric Lindberger. It turned into a horrific déjà vu. The son discovered the father and got shot. It's likely that Wayne Jennings doesn't even know it was his son he shot."

336

"So Wayne was the one who was surprised by the bandy-playing lawyers."

"Yes. There are two different perpetrators for the Swedish victims. Hassel and Gallano were chosen at random, one for his plane ticket and the other for the cabin. John Doe was their murderer — Lamar Jennings. Lamar was murdered in turn by Wayne, also randomly. What we have left is Lindberger. His death is not random; Wayne doesn't kill at random — he's a professional."

"Professional killer and 'sort of' a police officer? Your insinuations reek of —"

"Don't say it. But it's right."

"OK. I need everyone at full capacity now. It sounds like you're starting to wrap it up. Can you two come home?"

"Now?"

"If possible."

"OK."

"Say hi to Larner, and thank him."

"Absolutely. Bye."

"Bye."

Hjelm hung up and stared at the phone. The unit had been close to getting Wayne Jennings. Norlander and Nyberg, of all people.

"Did you hear?" he said to Holm who was leaning over him.

"Yes," she said. "He goes to Sweden to avenge a 'life under zero', as he wrote, once and for all. He prepares extremely carefully, locates his father, follows him, and waits for the right moment to strike. Then he wavers somehow — and he's killed immediately. A second time. By his father. Who doesn't even know it. There's some horrible irony here."

"Don't think about it too much. We're going home. Now. To get him."

She nodded.

They went to see Larner and explained the situation.

"So he threatened him?" His tone was measured. "He had your colleague in his sights but refrained from shooting him. A professional through and through, you have to admit."

"Yes," said Hjelm. "But we're going to get him."

"I'm actually starting to believe you will. You came sweeping in here like cousins from the sticks and solved the case in a few days. I'm feeling really old and rusty. But you lifted a burden from my shoulders."

"It was pure chance," said Hjelm. "And you were the one who solved the case — don't think otherwise. Your stubbornness got him to leave; you were the one who drove him to flee the country. That he then forgot an old truth is another matter."

"And what old truth is that?"

"Bad blood always comes back round."

# CHAPTER
# TWENTY-SEVEN

The next morning, strangely enough, everyone in the A-Unit was in their place. Only two should have been present, besides Hultin: Chavez and Söderstedt. But the old, experienced comedy duo Yalm & Halm arrived straight from the airport with red eyes, and at the back sat a fresh duo: everyone's favourite bandage-skulls, NN; it would have taken a lot to keep Norlander and Nyberg on the bench now.

Hultin didn't look like he'd been celebrating any triumphs of sleep, either, but his glasses were where they should be, and so was his sharp look.

"A lot has happened," he said. "We're nipping at his heels. Has everyone had a chance to take a look at the summary I put together last night with the help of a little conference-calling across the Atlantic?"

"I've accidentally pulled out that phone they have in the armrests a lot of times, but this was the first time I used it," Hjelm said sleepily.

"Have you had a chance to look through it?" Hultin repeated.

Everyone appeared to nod, if a bit sluggishly here and there.

"Then you know what our main task is: to find out Wayne Jennings's Swedish name. Besides that, the questions are, one: Why has he been using a warehouse at LinkCoop to carry out his business? Apparently it was a habit; otherwise his son wouldn't have copied the key. Two: Why did he torture Benny Lundberg, the security guard? Three: How does the failed break-in at LinkCoop relate to the murders of Eric Lindberger and Lamar Jennings, at the same time, about ten doors away? Four: Why was Eric Lindberger killed? Five: Did it have anything to do with his links to the Arab world? Six: Is Justine Lindberger at risk, too? I'm putting her under surveillance for safety's sake. Seven: Can we find Wayne Jennings in the immigration register for 1983? Eight: The difficult and delicate question — is Wayne Jennings CIA?"

"We could always go the official route," said Arto Söderstedt, "and just ask the CIA."

"I'm afraid that if we do, we'll guarantee that he'll disappear one way or another."

"As far as I can tell from this," Chavez said, waving Hultin's summary papers, "he could just as easily belong to military intelligence. Or he could have been recruited by the opposing side or the Mafia or a drug syndicate or some nasty maverick organisation."

"Agreed," Hultin said. "It's far too early to identify him as CIA as any sort of main theory. Anything else in general? . . . No? Then to details. Arto keeps working on Lindberger, Jorge on the Volvo. Viggo and Gunnar can stay in today — take on the immigrations. Paul can go down to Frihamnen and sniff around. Kerstin can

**340**

take on Benny Lundberg. How's it going with Lindberger, Arto?"

"Eric Lindberger left behind a lot of notes, which I've checked out, and they contain no mysteries. But his calendar includes an extremely interesting entry: a meeting scheduled for the night before his death. His corpse was loaded into the Volvo in Frihamnen by Wayne Jennings at two thirty in the morning on the twelfth of September, we know that. At ten o'clock the night before, the entry for the appointment says 'Riche's Bar' — unfortunately nothing more. I went down and waltzed around Riche's yesterday afternoon, trying to find someone who had been working at the bar at ten that night. There are a lot of staff members, so it was hard, but finally I found a bartender, Luigi Engbrandt. He racked his brains to remember, but it's a busy bar. He thinks he might remember Lindberger; if he's right, he hung around the bar for a while, waiting for someone. Unfortunately, Luigi has no memory of anyone ever coming. I also checked Eric's bank account. He leaves behind a decent but not exceptional fortune, six hundred thousand kronor all together. Today I'm going to see Justine."

"Why Justine?" said Norlander. "Leave her alone."

"Discrepancies," said Söderstedt. "The large apartment, the spouses' collaboration, a few strange things she said when we last spoke. There are also some interesting items in her Filofax that I'd like her to comment on."

"OK," said Hultin. "Did you get any further with the cars, Jorge?"

"The cars." Chavez made a face. "As you know, I've set a whole fucking armada of foot soldiers to work. Soon they will have gone through all the cars. Volvos seem to be owned by dependable, average middle-class Swedes as a rule. None of the ones we've checked so far has been stolen or was loaned out the night of the murder. Stefan Helge Larsson, the small-time criminal whose car had disappeared along with him, has returned from a month-long stay in Amsterdam. The traffic cops in Dalshammar, wherever that is, caught him, quote, 'exceptionally under the influence of drugs' on the E4. He was driving the wrong way down the highway. My interest is focused more and more on the car that's registered to a non-existent business. That's what I'm going to work on today."

"I think everything else is settled," Hultin said briskly. "Let's go. We have to get him. Preferably yesterday, as stressed-out businessmen like to joke."

"What's going on in the media?" said Kerstin Holm.

"The witch hunt continues," said Hultin. "Sales of locks, weapons and German shepherds have increased considerably. Orders have been given for platters containing the heads of those responsible. Mainly mine. Mörner's too. He's in a full-time panic. Do you want me to call him down so he can give you a little morale-boosting speech?

"Better than a blowtorch in your arse," he remarked to the now-empty Supreme Central Command.

342

Arto Söderstedt called Justine Lindberger right away.
The widow was home. Her voice sounded surprisingly
upbeat.

"Justine," she said.

"Söderstedt here, with the police."

"Oh."

"Do you think I could take a peek at your diary?"

"My Filofax, you mean? It's still at my office, I'm
afraid. And I don't understand what that could have to
do with anything."

"I can pick it up there, if it's too tough for you to
go."

"No! No thank you — I don't want the police nosing
around in my desk. I'll have them send it here by
courier. Then you can come and have a peek."

"Right away?"

"I'm barely awake. It's ten past nine. How's eleven?"

"Great. See you then."

*So she has time to make a few adjustments,* he
thought slyly.

The next step was to call her bank. The same bank as
her late spouse. The same bank manager. He called.

"Hello, this is Söderstedt," he said in his sing-song voice.

"Who?"

"The policeman. Yesterday you kindly gave me access
to the deceased Eric Lindberger's accounts. Today I
need to look at his wife Justine's."

"That's different. I'm sorry, but that's not possible."

"It's possible," he sang. "I can go the official route,
but I don't have time, and if it comes out that you've

held up the most important murder investigation in modern Sweden, I'm sure your boss will be very pleased."

It was quiet for a minute. "I'll fax it," said the bank manager.

"Like yesterday," Söderstedt sang. "Thanks so much!"

He hung up and tapped the fax machine. It soon began to spit out pages decorated with numbers. While it did, he called the housing cooperative and found out about the ownership of the apartment. He called the vehicle registry, the tax authorities, the boat registry, the Ministry of Foreign Affairs and the land registry. And he called the men who were to watch Justine Lindberger.

"You'll come along with me to Lindberger's at eleven," he said. "From that moment on, you can't let her out of your sight."

Then he half danced out the door.

At eleven on the dot he was at the door intercom on Riddargatan. One minute later he was sitting on Justine Lindberger's sofa.

"Nice apartment," he said.

"Here's my Filofax." She handed it to him. He skimmed through it and seemed unconcerned, but his brain was working overtime. There had been seven mysterious characters in her uncensored agenda, which he had copied at the Ministry of Foreign Affairs: G every other Monday at ten; PS on Sundays at four; S, who showed up at various times in the evenings; Bro, who appeared every Tuesday at different times; PPP on

6 September at 1.30; FJ all day on 14 August; and CR on 28 September at 7.30p.m. He had them all in his head and was struggling to look dumb as he battled his way through the official version of the Filofax.

"What's G?" he said. "And PS?"

She looked embarrassed. "G is manicures; my manicurist's name is Gunilla. PS means parents; we have a family dinner at four o'clock every Sunday. I have a large family."

"PPP and FJ? How can you keep all these abbreviations straight?"

"PPP was a girls' lunch on the sixth, with Paula, Petronella and Priscilla, to be exact. FJ was a conference day at work, foreign journalism. Aren't you about finished?"

"CR?" he persisted.

"Class reunion," she said. "I'm going to see my old class from upper secondary."

"S and Bro?" he said.

She looked like she'd been struck by lightning. "There's nothing like that," she said, trying to remain calm.

He elegantly returned the Filofax. "S on occasional evenings, Bro every Tuesday at various times," he said with a chivalrous smile.

"You've got a screw loose."

"Those entries were in there, in ink, so you had to go out and buy a whole new Filofax to replace the pages with S and Bro. What does S mean, and what does Bro mean?"

"You had no right to go through my things," she said, close to tears. "I've lost my husband."

"I'm sorry," he said, "but actually I had every right. This is a murder case of enormous proportions. Talk to me now."

She closed her eyes. And didn't say anything.

"This apartment is yours," he said quietly. "It was purchased two years ago, and you paid 9.2 million kronor cash. You also own an apartment in Paris that's worth two million, a summer home on Dalarö worth 2.6 million, two cars worth 700,000, and all together you are worth 18.3 million kronor. You're twenty-eight years old and you earn 31,000 kronor a month at the Ministry of Foreign Affairs. In addition, you get substantial expense allowances when you're abroad. You come from a reasonably wealthy family, but none of them have the kind of money you do. Can you explain that? How did you explain it to Eric?"

She looked up. Her eyes were red, but she wasn't crying, yet.

"Eric accepted it without questions. My family is rich, I said, and he was satisfied with that. You should be, too. He was satisfied with anything that brought a little joy into this life. Well-invested money. Superior money. If you have a fortune, it works for you. Money is what earns money in this country now; people like you have to accept that, too."

"I don't," said Söderstedt, without changing his tone.

"It's best that you do!" she shouted.

"What do S and Bro mean?" he said.

"Bro means Bro!" she yelled. "Every Tuesday I met a man by the name of Herman in Bro. We fucked. OK?"

"Did that bring joy into Eric's life, too?"

"Stop it!" she cried. "Don't you think I feel guilty enough about it? He knew what I was doing — he accepted it."

"And S?"

She stared at him fiercely. Her body seemed to contract. Had he pressed too hard?

"That's when I jog," she said calmly, exhaling. "That's my jogging session. I work so much that I have to schedule my jogging."

"S as in 'jogging'?"

"S as in 'stretching'. It takes longer to stretch than to jog."

He looked at her with amusement. "You schedule stretching? And you want me to believe that?"

"Yes."

"And the money?"

"Successful gambles in the stock market. It's possible to earn money in Sweden again, thank God."

"And it has nothing to do with shady Arab transactions?"

"No."

"Excellent. Fifteen minutes ago you were placed under watch by the guard unit of the National Criminal Police. We are of the opinion that you are in mortal danger."

She glared at the crafty Finland Swede, full of hate. "Protection or surveillance?" She maintained her calm.

"Take your pick," said Arto Söderstedt, and took his leave of her.

It could have gone a *little* better, but he was satisfied.

Jorge Chavez had put one hundred cars to the side and was now concentrating on a single one. He was taking a bit of a chance. The non-existent company's name was Cafe Havreflarnet, which sounded harmless — it was named after a biscuit — and was therefore an excellent front. It was supposed to be located on Fredsgatan in Sundbyberg, but there was no fucking Cafe Havreflarnet there, just a boring old Konsum grocery.

He pored with his usual intensity over the patent office's business register and finally came upon the name of an authorised signatory, a Sten-Erik Bylund, who had been living on Råsundavägen in Stockholm when the business was established in 1955. The National Social Insurance Board showed that the firm had gone bankrupt, and Chavez was obliged to consult a large manual register and page through lists of bankrupt estates. Finally he found Cafe Havreflarnet and learned that it had gone bankrupt in 1986. The Volvo with the B number plate had been registered three years later, in 1989. So even then the practically non-existent business had been the owner of the car. Taxes and insurance were paid up, but the money didn't come from Cafe Havreflarnet.

He tracked down a current address for Sten-Erik Bylund in Rissne. Without further ado, he set out to meet force with force, but that tactic turned out to be inadequate, because the address belonged to a

**348**

long-term-care institution, and Bylund was a seriously senile ninety-three-year-old. He didn't give up; rather, he sat across from the snacking elderly man and watched him stick bananas in his armpits and pour blueberry soup over his bald skull. Perhaps the cafe was not a CIA front after all.

"Why did you register your Volvo station wagon under the name Cafe Havreflarnet, even though the business had gone bankrupt three years earlier? Who pays the bills? Where is the car?"

Sten-Erik Bylund bent towards him, as though he were about to tell him a state secret. "Nurse Gregs has wooden legs," he said. "And my father was a strict old woman who liked a quickie or two on the go."

"On the go?" Chavez said, fascinated. Could it be a code?

"Yes indeed. He ran like a bitch on heat among the mutts. Brother Kate's breasts are great."

Chavez was beginning to have his doubts, not least when Bylund stood up and exposed his genitals to an old woman, who only yawned loudly.

"It was different with my Alfons," she said to her neighbour at the table. "He was well hung, let me tell you. A real hunk of beef just hanging there jiggling. Unfortunately, it just hung there jiggling."

"Well, dearie," her neighbour replied, "one time my Oliver and I were sitting there kissing in the dark, and he reached it out to me. I said, 'No thank you, dear, I don't really feel like a smoke.' But he could go on for hours and hours until a person was really tender, you know, dearie. Even though a person had seen bigger, if you know what I mean."

Chavez's mouth was hanging open.

As he left he heard the women tittering, "Wasn't that the new doctor, darling? Why, he must be from Lebanon. The smaller the body, the bigger the member — that's what they say down there in the tropics, you know."

"I think it was Oliver. He visits me sometimes. For being dead, he's kept his backside in very good shape, dearie."

Paul Hjelm shivered. He'd crossed many borders in the past twenty-four hours, but the weather transition was the most awful. As he stood under a police umbrella, he saw LinkCoop's long row of warehouses standing out against the streaky perpetual-motion machine that was the rain. He understood what Nyberg had meant when he talked about fallen skyscrapers. A downtown skyscraper in Täby and a slum skyscraper in Frihamnen. Both had fallen over.

He passed the sentry box with his ID raised, then moved to the right along the building with its loading dock. Hell had many manifestations, he thought. He had been in a crack house in Harlem, in Lamar Jennings's dismal Queens apartment, in a torture chamber in Kentucky: so alike, yet so different. And now this dismal, grey warehouse in Frihamnen, where the only upgrade that had been done in decades was the business logo, which glimmered and flashed in spectacularly spectral spectra. Here Eric Lindberger had experienced his hell, Benny Lundberg his and Lamar Jennings his.

He peered behind the blue-and-white police tape that surrounded the door on the far right end of the long row of buildings. Beyond the curtain of rain he could see crime-scene techs moving back and forth carrying various tools. He entered and went down the stairs to the storage area — and found a set-up surprisingly reminiscent of Wayne Jennings's secret torture chamber in Kentucky. The cast-iron chair that was welded to the floor appeared to be identical, as did the cement walls and the bare light bulb.

"How's it going?" he called to the technicians.

"Pretty good," one of them called back. "Lots of organic material here. Mostly the victim's, I expect, but since the perp didn't have time to clean up after himself, we might get lucky."

Seen in daylight, Hjelm thought, the premises looked relatively harmless, defused. So this was where the confrontation had taken place, he mused. Lamar Jennings had got in with the key made from a clay imprint, stationed himself behind the boxes in the corner, and awaited his father; that seemed the most likely scenario. Wayne Jennings arrived with Eric Lindberger, who was either unconscious or not, placed him in the chair, took out the pincers and set to work. For Lamar, the sight of the diabolical father he'd thought was dead for fifteen years, performing the very actions that had given rise to the most horrifying of his mental images, was too much; he couldn't keep his cool and showed himself. Wayne heard him, took out his pistol and executed him.

So they could hardly call it a confrontation. It was more like a quick elimination, without reflection, as when you kill a mosquito without interrupting your lawnmowing. A fitting end.

Hjelm strode back over to the entrance, under the large, grotesque LinkCoop logo, and spoke to the receptionist, a tanned forty-five-year-old woman who was dressed in overalls because she was also the warehouse's organiser.

"What kind of warehouse is the one at the far end?" Hjelm asked.

"It's a resource building," she said without looking up; apparently she had already said this a few times today. "That means it's empty. If we get a larger delivery than expected, we have a little extra space. We have a few like that."

"Is there anyone who often hangs out there?"

"You don't hang out in a warehouse," she rebuffed him. "You keep things there."

He chatted idly with the warehouse workers. None of them knew anything; none understood anything. Break-in, yes, we've had those before, but murder — that's insane.

He grew tired and went home.

Home to police headquarters.

Kerstin Holm didn't feel up to holding a difficult, demanding conversation, such as one with Benny Lundberg's parents. Not only was she feeling her jet lag, she had a stressful work week behind her. She wanted to sleep. Instead she was sitting in a small apartment in Bagarmossen at the home of shocked and grieving parents who blamed her personally for their son's ill fortune.

"The police are falling apart," said the father, who kept up the resentful facade even as his every word revealed the depth of his sorrow. "If they would fight crime instead of devoting themselves to affirmative action and other shit, our son wouldn't be lying there like a fucking vegetable. Every other fucking cop is a woman. I'm just an old, fat school caretaker, but I would easily be able to get ten police birds off me and scram, believe me."

"I believe you," said the police bird, trying to move on.

"Let the men do their thing and the women do theirs, for fuck's sake."

"It was a man who assaulted your son, not a woman."

"Thank God for that!" the father yelled, disconcerted. "A man's home is his castle. Everything is going downhill."

"Stop it!" she finally had to bark. "Sit down!"

The large man stared at her, struck speechless in mid-speech, and plopped down like a chastised little mischief-maker.

"I am truly very sorry about your grief," Holm continued, "but what Benny is going to need is your help to come back, not a mercy shooting."

**353**

"Lasse would never do that," sniffled the small, shrunken mother. "He's just so —"

"I know," Holm interrupted. "It's OK, just take it easy and try to answer my questions. Benny lived here at home. He had a holiday in August. Do you know why he took time off almost immediately again?"

The father sat there, stiff. The mother trembled but answered, "He went to Crete with some friends from the military in August. He hadn't planned any more holidays. But he hardly talks to us these days."

"Didn't he say anything about why he took more holiday?"

"He had got extra holiday time. That was all he said. A bonus."

"A bonus for what?"

"He didn't say."

"How did he seem the last few days?"

"Happy. Happier than he had been for a long time. Like he was expecting something. Like he had won some money at Bingo or something."

"Did he say anything about why?"

"No. Nothing. We didn't ask, either. I was a little nervous that he was up to some sort of trouble, now that he'd finally got a proper job."

"Had he been in trouble before?"

"No."

"I'm here to catch his" — she was about to say murderer — "his tormentor, not to put him away. Tell me."

"Benny was a skinhead, before. Then he went through coastal commando training and became a new

354

person. He tried to become a career officer and applied to the police college, but his grades weren't good enough. Then he got that security guard job. It was wonderful."

"Is he on the criminal registry?" she said, cursing her own laziness; she should have found out ahead of time instead of asking the parents. Couldn't someone who was more familiar with this aspect of the case have taken care of it? Gunnar Nyberg wanted nothing more than to go out into the field, after all. She *had* just come straight from the United States, after all. *Old bastard*, she thought, thinking of Hultin.

"A few assault convictions in his teen years," the mother said, embarrassed. "But just against blackheads."

*God in heaven*, thought Kerstin Holm. "Nothing since then?"

"No."

"OK. What can you tell me about yesterday?"

"He was pretty tense. Stayed closed up in his room and talked on a phone a lot."

"You didn't happen to hear what he was saying?"

"Do you think I eavesdrop on my own son?"

*Yes*, thought Holm. "No, of course not. But you can just *happen* to hear things."

"No, you can't."

*Not her too*, thought Holm, groaning, imagining that she kept most of her groan internal. "I'm sorry. Then what happened?"

"He went out around five. He didn't say where he was going, but he seemed nervous and keyed up. Like he was going to pick up some winnings or something."

"Did he say anything that might give some hint as to where he was going or what he was doing?"

"He said one thing: 'Soon you'll be able to move out of here, Mum.'"

"Have you touched anything in his room?"

"We've been at the hospital all night. No, I haven't touched anything."

"May I look at it?"

She was shown to the door of what seemed to be a teenage boy's room. Old, peeling stickers from packs of gum covered the surface.

Once inside the room, she thanked the mother and closed the door in her face. An enormous Swedish flag covered two of the walls; it was creased in the middle, behind the bed. She lifted the fabric and peered behind it. A few banners were hidden there. She couldn't really see them, but she recognised the black, white, gold and red stripes; they were probably miniature Nazi flags. She flipped through the CDs. Mostly heavy metal, but also some white power albums. Benny Lundberg hadn't broken very radically with his skinhead past, that much was certain.

She went to the telephone on the bedside table and looked for a notepad. She found it on the floor. It was blank, but she could see impressions on the top page — something for the crime-scene techs to sink their teeth into, she thought, feeling as if she were quoting someone. She lifted the receiver and pressed redial. The speaking clock rattled off numbers in her ear. She was disappointed. The only thing she found out from this was that Lundberg had had an appointment that he didn't want to miss for any reason.

She dialled a number.

"Teleservice? This is Kerstin Holm, National Criminal Police. Do you see the number I'm calling from on the screen? Good. Can you run a quick check on outgoing and incoming calls for the past twenty-four hours and email it to Chief Inspector Jan-Olov Hultin, NCP? Top priority. Thanks."

She did a quick check of the cluttered desk. Comic books, porno magazines out in the open — what would Mum say? Company pens, military magazines, rubbish. In the top drawer were two items of interest: a small bag of pills, doubtless good old pinkies, anabolic steroids; and a small jar of keys, probably spares: house key, car key, bike key, bike lock key, suitcase key, and then a key that seemed vaguely familiar. Was it to a safe-deposit box? What could Benny Lundberg have in a safe-deposit box? A weapon? Surely there was a whole arsenal under the floorboards. No, a safe-deposit box didn't really fit the profile. She lifted the receiver of the phone again and dialled.

"Is this customer service at Sparbanken? Hi, my name is Kerstin Holm, National Criminal Police. Do you have a central register of your safe-deposit-box customers? Or do I have to . . . OK, I'll hold . . . Hi, Kerstin Holm here, National Criminal Police. Do you have a central register of your safe-deposit-box customers? Or do I have to go to each individual branch? . . . OK, excellent . . . It's Lundberg, Benny.

Spelled like it sounds . . . No, OK. Thanks for your help."

She called a few more banks with the help of directory assistance. Finally she got a nibble. Handelsbanken on Götgatan, near Slussen. Thank goodness. She took the notepad and the safe-deposit-box key with her; that would have to do.

She yanked the door open without warning. Not unexpectedly, Benny's mum was standing right outside, polishing a spot on the door jamb.

"Do you have a recent picture of Benny?" Holm asked briskly.

The mum looked for a while and found one of the whole family. Benny was standing in the middle with his arms around his parents, who looked undeniably small. His smile was wide and a bit fake. OK, that would have to do.

When she left the parents with their crippling grief — and what grief *isn't* crippling? — the father was still installed on the sofa, as if he were frozen.

She took the Metro to Slussen, a brief trip, then battled her way up Peter Myndes Hill in the pouring rain. She turned onto Götgatan, walked a few feet further, passed the ATMs, and reached Handelsbanken. She ignored the queue, resulting in audible protests from the lunchtime patrons, and held up her police ID.

"I'm here about a safe-deposit box," she said to a teller.

"That will be over there." The teller pointed to a man in a tie who was cleaning his nails in the middle of the lunchtime rush. He stood up automatically when he saw her police ID.

"Safe-deposit box. Benny Lundberg," she said briskly.

"Again?" said the man.

She gave a start. "What do you mean, again?"

"His father was just here, right after we opened, visiting the box. He had a signed power of attorney in good order and both his own and his son's IDs."

"Shit," she said. "What did he look like? Like this?" She held up the photo of the Lundberg family.

The bank employee took it but handed it back immediately. "Absolutely not. This is a work . . . a completely different type of person."

"This is Benny Lundberg's father," she said. The man's face fell. "What did he look like?"

"An older, distinguished man with a beard."

"There you have it," she said. "A beard and everything. Come along to police headquarters and help us with a composite sketch."

"But I'm working."

"Not any more. First I'll take a quick look at the safe-deposit box, which will probably be empty. Number?"

"Two fifty-four," said the man, showing her the way.

Benny Lundberg's safe-deposit box was indeed empty. Absolutely.

She took the bank employee outside and got in a taxi. Time for another composite sketch. She was starting to get tired of sketchy types.

Viggo Norlander had a headache. Gunnar Nyberg had a headache. Norlander had gathered up his things, moved into Nyberg's office and quickly taken over Kerstin Holm's spot. They were both there now, avoiding putting their clever heads together.

A thick list of data lay between them: the immigrants of 1983, gathered in one place, like an extremely compressed and thorough ghetto. The names were arranged in chronological order. Chavez, who had produced the printout, had made sure that the names of American immigrants had a star next to them.

There were thousands of names, but only about a hundred Americans. It still took time. A lot of information had to be sorted through, checking sex against age and this and that.

Norlander felt ill. He had left the hospital way too soon. The microscopic lines of text were dancing before him. That damn overzealous Chavez creep must have deliberately picked out a font that would sustain head-aches and promote nausea. He ran out and threw up.

Nyberg heard him through the open door. It was a splendid cascade, the sound waves echoing through police headquarters.

"That did the trick," Norlander said when he came back.

"Go home and sleep," said Nyberg, fingering the bandage on his nose.

"I will if you do."

"OK, let's get to it. No more breaks."

Norlander gave him a murderous look and kept working.

In the end, a list of twenty-eight people crystallised: American immigrant men who claimed to be born around 1950. Sixteen of them had been in the Stockholm area in 1983. Then they checked those names against the national registry to see which of them were currently still in Sweden and in the Stockholm region. There were fourteen.

"Are diplomats included on this list?" said Nyberg.

"Don't know. I don't think so. They aren't immigrants, after all."

"Could he have ended up with the American embassy?"

"The Kentucky Killer? Surely that's taking it a bit too far?"

"Yes. It was just a thought."

"Forget it."

"Guest researchers, then? This list isn't complete."

"I have to get out." Norlander, like a chameleon, had begun to take on the colour of his bandage. "I'll take the top half, up to — what does it say? — Harold Mallory in Vasastan. A to Ma. You take the bottom half."

Norlander rushed off before Nyberg had time to warn him against taking the car. He didn't want to find him, quote, "exceptionally under the influence of drugs" in Dalshammar.

Gunnar Nyberg studied Norlander's scratches, a transcribed list of seven American immigrants from 1983. Morcher, Orton-Brown, Rochinsky, Stevens, Trast, Wilkinson and Williams. Trast was Swedish for thrush, like the bird. Could Trast be a name? Daddy blackbird. Did it even mean the same thing in English?

Nyberg didn't really feel relieved, although he should have. To him the grunt work felt hopeless, routine. He wanted to go out and punch the killer in the face. He had worked past the shock of encountering Benny Lundberg, but he still could not digest the fact that Wayne Jennings had been allowed to knock him down.

No one knocked Gunnar Nyberg down. That was rule number one.

He went over to the wall and observed his face in the mirror. His bandage had been reduced to a nose cone, a plastic splint of the sort that heroic football players wear after the doctor stops the flow of blood. It was held in place with bizarre rubber bands around his neck. Bruises were still spreading out around the cone. He refrained from imagining what it looked like under there. Why the hell did he always have to look like a battlefield just when a case was moving towards its conclusion?

Because this case was moving towards its conclusion, right?

He returned to his desk and sank down into his chair. It creaked alarmingly. He had heard ghost stories about office chairs that had gone crazy and transformed into horrible instruments of torture, mechanisms that flew up eighteen inches through your rectum. He thought of his broken bed and rocked lightly in the chair. It actually did sound a bit murderous. *Revenge of the Office Chair IV*. The Hollywood blockbuster that played to sold-out houses. Worn-out cinema seats jubilated and shot off springs that drilled into the screen. Not a single monitor was dry. Curtains blew their noses on themselves. Office after office revolted throughout the entire United States.

*Distracted* was an understatement. There was usually a reason for his attacks of distraction. Something, somewhere was chafing, irritating him. Something was causing him not to be really one hundred per cent satisfied with the list.

He sorted the names, to come up with a suitable priority ranking. Three were in the inner city, two in the northern suburbs, one in the southern suburbs. They were probably working now. So, places of work. Huddinge, two in Kista, two at the Royal Institute of Technology, Nynäshamn, Danderyd. Order of priority: Danderyd, the Tech, Kista, Huddinge, Nynäshamn. Or Kista, Danderyd, the Tech, Huddinge, Nynäshamn. Maybe that was better.

He put the list aside and stared at the wall. He tried his voice, working his way through a scale. An ugly, nasal tone. This injury too had affected his singing voice. Something about that made him uncomfortable. Punishment? Reminder? A reminder, maybe. A commemoration.

Suddenly they were there again. Gunilla. The burst eyebrows. Tommy and Tanja's eyes, as large as platters. *Do you have to come right now?*

His past had a single redeeming feature: he had never touched the children, had never lifted a hand against Tommy and Tanja.

Was that why he always took beatings that distorted his voice? So that he would never forget why he sang?

For the very reason that it came at such an incredibly inconvenient time, he seized the opportunity.

There were two Tommy Nybergs in Uddevalla. He called the first one. He was seventy-four and deaf as a post. He called the other. A woman answered. An infant was crying in the background. *A grandchild?* he thought.

"I'm looking for Tommy Nyberg," he said in a surprisingly steady voice.

"He's not home," said the woman. She had a lovely voice. Mezzo-soprano, he guessed.

"May I just ask, how old is Tommy?"

"Twenty-six," she said. "Who is this?"

"His father," he said.

"His father is dead. Come off it."

"Are you sure?"

"Dead as a doornail. I'm the one who found him. Stop fucking with me, you old creep." She threw the phone down.

OK, Tommy wasn't necessarily still living in Uddevalla. Besides, he was twenty-four, he quickly calculated. *Fucking old creep?* he thought, laughing. Gallows humour. He had one chance left.

There was a Tanja Nyberg-Nilsson. Married. And not a word.

He called. A woman's voice answered, "Tanja." Sweet. Tranquil.

Who was he to disturb the peace? *Hang up, hang up, hang up,* said a voice. *Your bridges are burned. It's too late.*

"Hello," he said, swallowing heavily.

"Hello, who is this?"

Yes, who was it? He had tossed out the word *father* to a strange woman without thinking it over. Was it really a title he had earned?

"Gunnar," he said, for lack of anything else.

"Gunnar who?" said the woman, in a west coast dialect. It sounded like the Gothenburg dialect and yet did not. "Gunnar Trolle?" she said a bit suspiciously. "Why are you calling? It's been over for a long time, you know that."

"Not Gunnar Trolle," he said "Gunnar Nyberg."

Silence. Had she hung up?

"Dad?" she said, almost inaudibly.

Her eyes, large as platters. Was it possible to keep going?

"Are you OK?" he asked.

"Yes," she said. "Why . . ."

She fell silent.

"I've been thinking of you all recently," he said.

"Are you ill?" she asked.

Yes, it's something completely enormous.

"No. No, I — don't know. I just have to make sure — that I didn't completely destroy you. That's all."

"You promised never to contact us, Mum said."

"I know. I kept my promise. The two of you are grown up now."

"Pretty much," she said. "We never talked about you. It was like you never existed. Bengt became our dad. Our real dad."

"Bengt *is* your real dad," he said. Who the hell was Bengt? "I'm something different. I would like to see you."

"I only remember yelling and violence," she said. "I don't know what difference it would make."

"Me neither. Would you forbid me to come?"

She was quiet. "No," she said at last. "No, I wouldn't."

"You're married," he said, to hide the rejoicing inside him.

"Yes," she said. "No kids yet. No grandchildren."

"That's not why I'm calling," he said.

"Yes, it is," she said.

"How is Tommy?"

"Good. He lives in Stockholm. Östhammar. He has a son. There's your grandchild."

He received the small blows right on his nose cone, with a smile.

"And Gunilla?" he said hesitantly.

"She still lives in the house, with Dad. They're thinking about switching to an apartment and getting a summer place."

"Good idea," he said. "Well, see you. I'll be in touch."

"Bye," she said. "Take care of yourself."

He would. More than ever before. That soft Uddevala dialect. The girl who had spoken such pronounced Stockholmish. He remembered her little Stockholm-accented vowels so well. It was possible to become someone else. To change dialects and become someone else.

Then it hit him. There and then, it hit him.

There and then Gunnar Nyberg caught the Kentucky Killer.

He didn't have to be an American. It would even have been more convenient to become some other nationality. Maybe not a Norwegian or a Kenyan, but something plausible.

He paged frantically through the lists. He went through name after name after name and ignored the stars.

Hjelm came in and regarded the intensely reading giant with surprise. An enormous aura of energy was rising up above him like a storm cloud.

"Hi yourself," Hjelm said.

"Shut up," Nyberg said amiably.

Hjelm sat down and shut up. Nyberg kept reading. Fifteen, twenty minutes went by.

April, May. 3 May: Steiner, Wilhelm, Austria, born 1942; Hün, Gaz, Mongolia, born 1964; Berntsen, Kaj, Denmark, born 1956; Mayer, Robert, New Zealand, born 1947; Harkiselassie, Winston, Ethiopia, born 1960; Stankovski, B —

Gunnar Nyberg stopped short.

"Bing bang boom," he roared. "The famous Kentucky Killer. Get a photo of Wayne Jennings. Now!"

Hjelm stared at him and slunk out, suddenly immeasurably subordinate. Nyberg stood up and paced, no *ran*, around the room, like an overfed rat in a tiny hamster wheel.

Hjelm returned and tossed the large portrait of Wayne Jennings as a young man onto the desk.

"Haven't you seen it before?" he said.

Nyberg stared at it. The youth with a broad smile and steel-blue eyes. He placed his hands on the photo, letting only the eyes peer out. He had seen those eyes before. In his mind he made the hair grey and moved the hairline up. He added a few wrinkles.

"Meet Robert Mayer," he said, "chief of security at LinkCoop."

Hjelm looked at the photo, and then at Nyberg. "Are you sure?"

"There was something familiar about him, but I didn't put it together. He must have undergone some sort of plastic surgery, but you can't get rid of your eyes and your gaze that easily. It's him."

"OK." Hjelm tried to calm down. "We have to get confirmation. It would be logical for you to contact him after the Benny Lundberg incident."

"Me?" Nyberg gaped. "I'd just give him a whipping."

"If anyone else goes, he'll get suspicious. It has to be you. And it has to seem routine. Play dumb — that ought to work. Bring along some lousy, unrelated photo." He rummaged in the desk drawer for a photograph of a man, any man at all. He found a passport photo of a man in his sixties smiling serenely. "This will be good," he said. "Who is it?"

Nyberg looked at the picture. "It's Kerstin's pastor."

Hjelm stopped short. It hadn't occurred to him until now that he was sitting at Kerstin's desk. "Do you know about it?" he asked.

"Yes," said Nyberg. "She told me."

Hjelm felt a little twinge and fingered the picture clumsily. "OK. It'll have to do. We'll wipe it, and then you make sure to get Mayer's fingerprints."

"Can't we just bring him in? Once we get the fingerprints, it's over."

"We might not get that far. There are powerful interests involved. A lawyer could get him released before they even get to fingerprints. And we can't ask him — he'll run. I'll check with Hultin."

He called Hultin, who came right in, as though he had been waiting outside. He quickly got a clear picture of the situation, then nodded at Hjelm.

"OK, let's do it. Gunnar will go back to Frihamnen. Mayer ought to see it as pure chance that Gunnar and Viggo showed up in Frihamnen, which it is — he's had the idea to check the rest of the storage spaces there. He shouldn't have any idea how far we've got. Provided it doesn't leak at the FBI. I just got a report from Holm — she's on her way. Benny Lundberg had some secrets in a safe-deposit box, but they were picked up this morning, probably also by this Robert Mayer with a ridiculous fake beard. We're getting a composite sketch."

"How will we do the fingerprint checks?" said Hjelm. "There are these new micro-variants, you know."

"Can you do them?"

"No. Jorge can."

"Get him. We'll all go together. In case he tries to run when Gunnar is there."

Hjelm ran into his office and found Chavez contemplating "Nurse Gregs has wooden legs" and "Brother Kate's breasts are great". Were those children's rhymes?

"Get a laptop with fingerprint equipment," said Hjelm. "We're going to take K."

The children's rhymes dissipated. Chavez was the last one to arrive at Hultin's car and threw himself into the back seat beside Hjelm, placing the small computer on his lap. Hultin drove like a madman towards Täby. Gunnar Nyberg was in the passenger seat. He had pulled himself together and called LinkCoop, sounding perfectly blasé. Robert Mayer was there. He would be available for another couple of hours. Nyberg asked to discuss last night's incidents with him. He needed to show him a photo.

That was fine.

They turned off of Norrtäljevägen, drove past Täby's city centre, which they could vaguely see through the drizzle, and arrived on a small side street.

"This isn't good," Nyberg said. "They have mega-security. Sentry boxes at the gates. Monitoring systems. He'll see everything."

Hultin drove to a bus stop and pulled over. He thought for a moment, turned round and drove back. It was incredibly frustrating. In the garage at police headquarters, Nyberg changed cars — he hopped into his own good old Renault. Then he followed them to Täby.

Hultin's Volvo turned off into a parking spot next to an industrial building a few hundred feet before LinkCoop's gate. There it stayed, in the storm.

When Nyberg drove up to the sentry box, everything was just as it had been at his last visit. On the surface.

The twin receptionists were the same too. Although he insisted that he could find his way to Mayer's office himself, one of them walked ahead of him through the stylistically pure building; he became more convinced than ever that this was a well-thought-out marketing strategy. This time, however, his interest in the miniskirt and what it hid was minimal. Incredibly tense, he entered chief of security Robert Mayer's office with the blinking-monitor walls.

Mayer fixed him with his ice-blue gaze, Wayne Jennings's gaze, while Nyberg made the utmost effort to seem effortless. Mayer was otherwise relaxed; only his gaze was firmly focused, and it seemed to see right through him. The evening before, Mayer had tortured Benny Lundberg, beaten Viggo Norlander unconscious and broken Nyberg's own nasal bones in three places. Mayer himself seemed fresh as a daisy.

"That doesn't look good," he said, tapping his nose lightly.

"It's a tough job," Nyberg said, shaking Mayer's extended hand. He refrained from using his Mr Sweden grip this time.

"I've been looking more closely at what that building has been used for recently," said Mayer, sitting down and folding his hands behind his head. "It really has been empty — all that's there is old empty boxes. So it's been accessible to anyone at all. And apparently for any purpose at all."

Nyberg was blinded by Mayer's professionalism. "It's a horrible story."

"It really is," Mayer said sympathetically.

Nyberg felt like he was going to throw up. "Naturally, this places the break-in in a slightly different light."

Mayer nodded thoughtfully. "Yes. Benny reports a break-in in one place while at the same time the Kentucky Killer is at work nearby. Then he's nearly murdered himself in that very same spot. What do you make of that?"

"Nothing, for the time being," Nyberg said nonchalantly. "But one wonders what Benny Lundberg was up to."

"It certainly seems very strange," said Mayer. "We knew, of course, that he had a past as a skinhead, but we thought he deserved a chance at a new life. I suppose most of this would now indicate that he had something to do with the break-in."

"I don't quite understand," said Nyberg with meticulous stupidity.

"I'm not going to get involved in your work," Mayer said briskly. "That's hardly necessary. You were close to getting him, after all."

"It would be nice to have that honour, but the truth is that we were only down there doing a routine check of all the buildings in the vicinity." Nyberg took out the photo of Kerstin Holm's deceased pastor and extended it to Mayer. Upside down.

Mayer took it and had to turn it round. He glanced at it and shook his head.

Nyberg took the photo back and put it in his wallet.

"I'm sorry," said Mayer. "Should I recognise him?"

"We picked him up in a car that was leaving Frihamnen at high speed. One of the warehouse workers thought he recognised him. That he might have worked at LinkCoop."

"No, I don't recognise him."

Nyberg nodded doggedly and stood. He extended his hand towards Mayer, and they shook in a civilised fashion.

He had to check himself so that he didn't run through the corridors. He smiled at the twin receptionists and received a double dividend. His car rolled calmly out through the gates and rounded the curve slowly.

Then for the last twenty yards he stepped on it; he thought he could allow himself that much. He bolted over to Hultin's car and got in, dripping.

"Everything OK?" asked Hultin.

"I think so." He handed the photo to Chavez in the backseat.

Hjelm watched the hand over. There was something deeply macabre about the Kentucky Killer's fingerprints being on the timid, cancer-ridden pastor's face.

Wearing plastic gloves, Chavez put the photo into a little scanner fastened to the side of the laptop. Everything had been prepared in advance. Nyberg's fingerprints had been fed in, as had Jennings's. After an uncomfortably long time, the computer beeped. "Match" was blinking on the screen.

"We have a match for Gunnar Nyberg's fingerprints," said Chavez.

No one answered. They waited. The time dragged unbearably. Each second was a step towards hopelessness.

Then another ding — another match.

"Not Nyberg again?" said Hjelm.

"Match for Robert Mayer," said Chavez. "Wayne Jennings and Robert Mayer are the same person."

A silvery grey turbo Volvo in an industrial car park in Täby heaved a sigh of relief.

"We can't just storm in," said Hultin. "He'd see us at least two minutes beforehand. I imagine that ten seconds would be enough for him to disappear into thin air."

They were quiet for a moment. Their thinking could have been called brainstorming if a storm hadn't been howling as if through the skulls of the dead.

"I'll have to take him myself," said Nyberg. "I think I seemed dumb enough to have forgotten something."

"You have a concussion," said Hultin.

"That is correct," said Nyberg, hopping over to his car. He rolled down the window. "Be prepared. I'll call as soon as anything happens."

"Be careful," said Hultin. "This is one of the most experienced professional killers in the world."

"Yeah, yeah, yeah." Nyberg waved, irritated, and drove off.

At the sentry box he said he'd forgotten to ask about something; he was let in. By this point Mayer-Jennings had had him in sight for fifteen seconds; he might already be gone. He hoped with all his heart that he had given the impression of being useless, a sloppy cop. The twin receptionists smiled and announced him, and he managed to resist the dancing miniskirt; at least she wouldn't die. Ideas and plans teemed through him. How should he act? In all likelihood, Mayer would have access to a weapon within a tenth of a second. At any hint of a threat, he would immediately kill Nyberg, who wouldn't have a chance.

But he wanted to meet his grandchild. He made a decision.

Mayer stood waiting in the corridor outside his office; he looked a bit suspicious, which probably meant that he was churning with suspicions.

Nyberg lit up when he saw him. "I'm sorry," he said breathlessly, tilting his head. "I remembered that there was one more thing."

Mayer raised an eyebrow and was ready. His hand moved a fraction of an inch towards the lapel of his jacket and pulled back.

Gunnar Nyberg delivered a tremendous uppercut that tossed Mayer through the corridor. His head crunched into the wall. He didn't get up.

And that was that.

# CHAPTER
# TWENTY-EIGHT

"Brilliant plan," Jan-Olov Hultin said sternly.

"Well, it worked," said Gunnar Nyberg, grimacing. Three fingers on his right hand were broken. The cast had hardly had time to dry.

Nyberg had dragged Mayer into his office and called Hultin. They decided to keep the media at bay so as not to limit the space they had to work in. Together they came up with a strategy. Hjelm, saying he needed to get hold of his colleague Nyberg, had got into LinkCoop and followed one of the dance-happy twins through the corridor. Together the somewhat injured duo had located a handy back door, out of which they moved Mayer. While Hjelm stood guard, Nyberg walked coolly back through the corridor and left the premises in due order; his smile at the twin receptionists had been a bit forced. He drove his car round to the back of the building, and he and Hjelm loaded Mayer into the trunk. Then Hjelm, too, left LinkCoop via the reception area. The twin receptionists were indeed sparklingly lovely.

For a while they worried that Nyberg had actually killed Mayer, which might not have been legally justifiable. But the man was a professional even in that respect. In the small, sterile and nearly secret cell in the basement at police headquarters, he came to after half an hour. No one else actually knew he was there; Hultin had chosen to keep an extremely low profile, even internally. The staff doctor confirmed a concussion as well as a cracked jaw and cheekbone. In other words, no broken jaw — Mayer could speak. But he didn't.

Hultin made the first attempt. Hjelm sat on a chair behind him and to the side, while Viggo Norlander and Jorge Chavez sat by the door. Along the other wall were Arto Söderstedt and Kerstin Holm. The whole gang. No one wanted to miss this — except for Gunnar Nyberg. He bowed out.

"My name is Chief Inspector Jan-Olov Hultin," Hultin said politely. "Perhaps you've seen my name in the papers. They're demanding my head on a platter."

Robert Mayer sat, bound to a fixed table with handcuffs, and regarded him neutrally. *A competitor*, thought Hultin.

"Wayne Jennings," he said. "Or should I say the Kentucky Killer? Or perhaps K?"

The same icy gaze. And the same silence.

"So far no one seems to be missing you at LinkCoop, and we've arranged it so that the press doesn't get wind of the story. As soon as your name comes out in the papers, things will be a bit different, you see. Not even your superiors at LinkCoop know you're here. So tell us what's going on."

Wayne Jennings's icy gaze was truly unsettling. It seemed to nail you down. You felt like you were in the cross hairs of a telescopic sight.

"Come on, now. What are you up to? Who do you work for?"

"I have the right to make a phone call."

"In Sweden we have a number of controversial terrorist laws that I personally dislike, but they are actually quite useful in situations like these. In other words, you do not have the right to make a phone call."

Jennings said nothing more.

"Benny Lundberg," said Hultin. "What did he have in his safe-deposit box?"

No answer was forthcoming.

He held up a drawing of Jennings with a beard. "Why a beard?"

Nothing, not a movement.

"May I suggest a scenario?" Hjelm said from his corner. "My name is Paul Hjelm, by the way. We have an acquaintance in common. Ray Larner."

Jennings's head turned an inch to the side, and for the first time Paul Hjelm met Wayne Jennings's eyes. He understood how the Vietcong must have felt in the jungles of Vietnam. And how Eric Lindberger must have felt. And Benny Lundberg. And tens of other people who had met their death with these eyes as their last point of human contact.

"The night of September the twelfth was tough for you," Hjelm began. "Several unexpected things happened. You had Eric Lindberger, a civil servant with the Ministry of Foreign Affairs, with you in your private torture chamber in Frihamnen. Incidentally, it's very similar to the one under your farm in Kentucky. Did you bring along your personal architect?"

378

Jennings's eyes might have narrowed a little. Possibly they took on a new sharpness.

"We'll come back to Lindberger, because that's the whole point in continuing this case. Anyway, you make sure that he loses consciousness, and you fasten him into the chair. Maybe you have time to start the procedure. You drive your pincers into Lindberger's neck with surgical precision. Then suddenly the empty boxes fall down. A young man is crouching behind the boxes. You take him out immediately. Bang bang bang bang, four shots to the heart. But who the hell is he? Are the police on your trail? Already? How is it possible?

"He has no ID, none at all. You search his bag. You find — a set of vocal cord pincers and a set of nerve pincers. Maybe you even recognise your own tools. What was this? Did you know who he was even then, or did you think he was a competitor? An admirer? A copycat? We'll get back to that.

"You finish torturing Lindberger and are forced to get away from there with two corpses instead of one, and what's more, you're surprised by a coach load of drunken lawyers, so you have to leave the strange man behind. You're certain that the lawyers have called the police and reported your number plate, so you have to hurry. You drive out to Lidingö and dump Lindberger in the reeds.

"At the same time, you know that the police are going to show up and search the warehouses and find your torture chamber. This means that you have to redirect their attention. There's only one thing to do.

Benny Lundberg. In your capacity as chief of security, you call the sentry box and order him to fake a break-in at one of the other storage units. You promise him money and time off. Sure enough, the police go to the place where Benny's fake break-in has occurred and are satisfied. The corpse can be assumed to be left over from the break-in. Everything ought to be just fine.

"But Benny Lundberg has other plans. He tries to extort money from you. He has hidden a letter in some unknown place, in which he's written in detail about the night's events, as life insurance. Unfortunately, he doesn't know that your speciality is getting people to talk. You get him to do just this, right before two police officers arrive on the scene. You injure the officers, but you don't kill them. One of them gets a bit angry and knocks you out. And now you're here."

Jennings's gaze was fixed throughout the account. Wheels were turning behind the cold blue eyes. His face was swelling and colouring; it didn't seem to concern him.

"So there are two basic questions," Hjelm continued. "One, what was Eric Lindberger expected to reveal? And two, do you know who you shot and killed?"

Pause. Nothing. Nothing at all.

"The second one is a trick question," Hjelm continued. "Because it was the Kentucky Killer."

The icy eyes narrowed. Or Hjelm thought they narrowed. Perhaps it was an illusion.

"You know, of course, that there has been a copycat running riot in New York for a year. Someone got hold of your old pincers and went out on the town. You've also read in the Swedish media that he's come to Sweden; no one can have missed that. He was twenty-five years old, and he was out to get you. You shot him in cold blood. Do you know who he was?"

Jennings held him with his gaze. Was there a trace of curiosity in there? Had he really not guessed?

"You're not going to like it," said Hjelm. "His name was Lamar Jennings."

Wayne Jennings leaned backwards four inches. It was a lot in a situation like this. The icy gaze wavered, then flew up towards the ceiling. And then it returned. Steady as a rock.

"No," he said. "You're lying."

"Think about it. What happened to your pincers after you fooled Larner and went underground? You left them behind in the cellar. A striking blunder. If you were going to keep killing and put Larner away, you needed them. They had to be identical, so they would leave identical marks and prove that K was still alive. Without them, you had to manufacture new ones and make sure they were identical, with the same scratches and idiosyncrasies. That must have been pretty tricky."

Jennings stared at the wall.

"Your son surprised you one night down in the torture chamber in Kentucky. It was the culmination of several years of abuse. Why the hell did you do that to him? A child? Don't you understand what you created? A monster. He copied you. He came here to give you a taste of your own medicine, and you shot him like a dog. Bad blood always comes back round."

"It's 'what goes around comes around'," said Jennings.

"Well, now it's 'bad blood always comes back round'. You've changed a proverb."

"Was it really Lamar?"

"Yes. I've read his diary. Hellish stuff, just hellish. You murdered him twice. What did you do to him when he startled you down in the cellar? A ten-year-old, for Christ's sake! What did you do to him?"

"Hit him, of course," Wayne Jennings said tonelessly.

He closed his eyes. There was an enormous amount of activity behind his eyelids.

When they finally opened, it was as though his eyes belonged to someone else, both more single-minded and more resigned.

"I was war-weary," he said. "You can't imagine what that's like — in this country you haven't had to fight a war for two hundred years. He was a reminder of what I'd once been, just a regular weakling. He got on my nerves. I only burned him a little, with cigarettes. He became my outlet. I wasn't that much different from my own father."

"Tell us," said Hjelm.

Jennings leaned forward. He had made a decision. "You were right not to let this get out to the public. It would have been devastating. I'm the good guy. You don't believe it, but I'm actually on the right side. The uglier parts of the right side. I'm distasteful but necessary. It was all about getting enemies to talk."

"In what way was Eric Lindberger an enemy?"

Jennings fixed his eyes on Hjelm's. "Wait on that. I have to think about the consequences."

"OK. How did all this start?"

Jennings braced himself and began.

"I don't know if you can understand what patriotism is. I went to war to escape from my father. I was seventeen. Poor white Southern trash. I was a child who killed other children. I noticed that I had a talent for killing. Others realised it, too. I quickly rose through the ranks. And then suddenly I'm called to Washington and I'm standing eye to eye with the president, at just a little over twenty years old. I'm going to be in charge of an extremely secret special task force in Vietnam, one that will be directly below the president. Civilians train me to use a new secret weapon. I become an expert. Then I train the others in the group. I'm the only one who has contact with the civilians. The whole time it's just me — I don't know who they are. After the war, all they say is 'Keep yourself available' and pay my salary. It's extremely strange. I'm completely destroyed when I come back. I can't get close to my wife. I badger my son. Then they suddenly contact me. They emerge."

"CIA?" said Hultin.

Hjelm widened his eyes in surprise.

Jennings shook his head. "We'll hold off on that," he said. "In any case, I suddenly realised what was expected of me. At this point, in the late seventies, the Cold War was moving into a new phase — I can't go into it in detail, but it was truly war. There was an immediate threat — they needed information, lots of information. The same thing was happening on the other side. One by one I picked up the agents who were under surveillance. Professional spies and traitors alike. Academics who sold state secrets. Soviet agents. KGB. I got an incredible amount of vital information out of them.

"Someone got the brilliant idea that it would be handy if it looked like the work of a madman, I don't know who, so I had to play serial killer, even if it meant I got caught. And that's how I got Larner on my case. You have no idea how hard that man worked to find out about Commando Cool. He was a threat to national security.

"On the political front, the Cold War started to calm down. Brezhnev died, the Soviet Union was on its way to dissolution, and other enemies were emerging. I would be more useful in some border state between east and west, where the trade exchange of the future would take place, and in my escape I would bring down Larner, make a laughing stock of him."

"So it was time to escape. Your teeth and someone's remains were in the car."

"It took weeks of preparation. A lot of night work out there in the wilderness. Colleagues who were ready to go at any time. Rigged equipment. A perfect set of teeth. A disguised Soviet agent whose teeth had been extracted. A concealed hole in the ground that I could roll into, along with some colleagues, and stay for a day or two. Everything is possible; the impossible takes a bit longer."

Hjelm, satisfied, still had to ask, "What kind of ideal are you working towards? What does the life that you're defending with all this violence look like?"

"Like yours," said Wayne Jennings without hesitation. "Not like mine, like yours. I have no life. I died in Vietnam. Do you believe that you live this freely and with this much privilege at no cost? Do you believe that Sweden is alliance-free and neutral?"

He paused and looked at the wall, then moved his gaze towards Norlander. He met eyes filled with hate. It was hardly the first time. He ignored it.

"Where is Gunnar Nyberg?" he asked.

"Taking care of his broken hand. Why?"

"No one has ever taken me out before. And no one has ever fooled me like that. I thought he was an idiot."

"He identifies with Benny Lundberg. He sat with him as he was going through the worst of his suffering. His warmth saved Benny's life. Is that something you can understand?"

"Warmth saves more than cold. Unfortunately, cold is also necessary. Otherwise we would have an eternally cold earth."

"Is that what the Lindberger story is about — eternal cold? Nuclear weapons? Chemical or biological ones? Or is it LinkCoop? Computers, or control devices for nuclear weapons? Saudi Arabia?"

He smiled inwardly. Maybe he was even a little impressed by the Swedish police — and by Paul Hjelm. "I'm still thinking about it. I could ask you to contact a certain authority, but I don't know. There are risks."

"Are you aware that you are sitting here because you committed twenty murders and one attempted murder? That you are a criminal? An enemy of humanity? Someone who destroys all the human worth that we have spent several thousand years building up? Or do you think you can get out at any time? Do you think you can just choose the right second to get up from the chair, free yourself from the handcuffs and tear my head off?"

Jennings smiled again, that smile that never reached his eyes. "People should never make murder machines out of other people."

Hjelm looked at Hultin. Suddenly they began to feel threatened. After all, the only thing that separated them from a murder machine was a set of handcuffs.

"You don't kill police officers," Hultin said with bombproof certainty.

"I weigh the pros and cons of every situation. The alternative with the most pros wins. If I had killed that policeman" — he nodded towards Norlander — "you wouldn't have handled me this mildly today. And then we would have had a problem."

"You were counting on being caught? You're joking!"

"It was in fifteenth place in the list of possibilities. It went down to seventeenth after Nyberg's visit. That was why I wasn't on my guard. That was an excellent tactic."

Jennings closed his eyes and weighed the pros and cons. Then he made an extremely fast movement and was out of the handcuffs.

Chavez had his pistol up first. Holm was second, Norlander third. Söderstedt was sluggish, and Hultin and Hjelm sat still.

"Nice reaction over there in the corner," said Jennings, pointing at Chavez. "What's your name?"

Chavez and Norlander approached him with pistols raised. Hjelm took his out to be on the safe side. All three held Jennings in check while Holm and Söderstedt cuffed him again, considerably tighter this time.

"I've had a full month's training on handcuffs," Jennings said calmly. "And I mean a full month. We need to understand each other here."

"OK," said Hjelm. "You've made your point. So how did the pros and cons look on 6 April 1983?"

Jennings performed a quick search of his memory bank, then he flashed a smile. It passed. "I understand," he said.

"What is it that you understand?"

"That you're not a bad policeman, Paul Hjelm, not bad at all."

"Why did you write that letter to your wife?"

"Weakness," Jennings said neutrally. "A pure con. The last one."

"The episode with Nyberg, then?"

"We'll see," he said cryptically.

"We found the letter, almost completely burned up, in Lamar's apartment."

"Was that where you found my name?"

"Unfortunately, it wasn't. If it had been, Benny Lundberg wouldn't be lying half terrified to death at Karolinska right now. Why did you write your name? Surely it didn't matter to Mary Beth what you called yourself. It was really quite infantile. And it drove Lamar to come here, which killed him."

"It was a farewell to my last remnants of a personal life. The letter was supposed to have been burned immediately. She got her revenge by not burning it."

"Or else she wanted one last memory of the man she had once made the mistake of loving. It's called human emotion. For you, it's something other people have, something you can exploit."

"It was a final farewell," Jennings said.

"This final farewell killed your whole family. It made your son follow you and get killed by you; it made your wife kill herself. A cute farewell."

Was it possible to hurt him? Hjelm wondered, as Jennings looked at him with narrowed eyes. Had he found a sore spot?

"Did she kill herself? I didn't know that."

"Your deeds are never done in isolation. You can't kill someone without it having a wide array of consequences. You spread clouds of evil and sudden death around you — do you really not understand that? Do you know how many serial killers you have inspired? You have a fan club on the Internet. You're a fucking legend. There are K T-shirts, small biscuits in the shape of a K that say 'The Famous Kentucky Killer', badges that say 'Keep on doing it, K', liquorice versions of your pincers. You have actively contributed to the fact that a frightening number of serial killers are running riot in the country you think you're protecting. You're a madman who must be stopped. Stop yourself, for God's sake."

"I'm hardly alone," he said, looking up at the ceiling. "I follow orders and receive a salary each month. If I

**388**

disappear, there'll be a job opening, and a lot of people will apply."

"Are you finished thinking?"

"Yes," he said abruptly. "I'll make it short and concise — listen up. LinkCoop is a shady company. It survives on illegal imports and exports of military computer equipment; the rest is a front. The CEO, Henrik Nilsson, is a crook. LinkCoop has got hold of control devices for nuclear warheads, just as you said, Hjelm. Eric Lindberger from the Ministry of Foreign Affairs was the middleman between LinkCoop and the Saudi Islamist movement. I thought I had stopped the deal by taking out Lindberger. By the way, he's the only one who hadn't talked under pressure — I was impressed. But great sums of money have been transferred to LinkCoop's secret accounts today. This means the equipment is in the hands of the Swedish middleman, in an unknown location, and will soon be on its way to a Swedish harbour, I don't know which one, in order to be transported on to those in the fundamentalist movement."

"Perhaps Eric Lindberger withstood your torture simply because he didn't know anything. Perhaps he was innocent, and the Swedish middleman was someone else."

"I received reliable information from . . . my sources. They've never been wrong before."

"How did the message read, exactly?" Arto Söderstedt asked from over by the wall.

Jennings's head turned the necessary fraction of an inch, no more.

Söderstedt had his turn to meet the gaze. *Hard* *core,*
he thought.

"It was a coded message," said Jennings, "and it went
'E Lindberger MFA'. It was unambiguous."

"Elisabeth Justine Lindberger," Söderstedt said
coldly.

The eyes narrowed again. A tiny movement in the
corner of one of them. "Oh," said Jennings.

"Not 'O' but 'E'," said Söderstedt. "That letter
subjected an innocent person to a hellish journey into
death."

"Do you have her under surveillance?" Jennings said.

Arto Söderstedt reduced everything on the tip of his
tongue to "Yes."

"Increase it right away."

"Let me see if I understand this," said Hultin.
"You're giving us orders? One of the worst serial killers
in history has finally been caught, and he's sitting here
giving orders to the police?"

"Not me," said Jennings. "I'm not giving any orders.
I'm No One. But I can summarise the choice you have
to make in two questions. One: Do you want a nuclear
war or not? Two: Which world order do you prefer —
American capitalism or Islamic fundamentalism? It's a
globalised world these days — that's irreversible. So it's
more important than ever that there be a world order.
And you can pick — just the seven of you."

"I wonder if it's that simple," said Hjelm.

"Right now, in the next few hours, it really is that
simple. After that you can do whatever you want with
me."

"What was the authority that you were debating whether we should contact?" Hultin asked.

"It won't work now. It will take too long. There's only one possibility, and that's for you to make sure that that ship is not allowed to leave the harbour."

"Does Henrik Nilsson at LinkCoop know any of this?"

"No, he makes himself ignorant as soon as he has the money. The middleman moves the materiel to a neutral place. From there it's transported to the harbour. Both the neutral place and the harbour are unknown. The ship will leave harbour sometime today or tomorrow. That's all the information we have. Except for Mrs Lindberger."

"The ship's destination?"

"Faked. Could be anywhere at all."

"OK," Hultin said. "Gather outside."

They stood up one by one and left.

Hjelm lingered for a second and looked at Wayne Jennings. "All of this," he said, "the whole admission and confession and everything was just a way to buy time, wasn't it, to size up the situation? Get us over on your side? Is any of it true?"

"It's the result that counts," Jennings said coolly.

"And Nyberg?" said Hjelm. "What was your assessment when he came walking towards you down the corridor? Did you already see this scenario in front of you? Was there no surprise in that uppercut?"

Jennings's eyes bored into Hjelm's. Hjelm thought they were like primeval darkness, the eyes of a shark.

"You'll never know," said Jennings.

Hjelm took a step closer and bent over him. Positioned this way, Jennings could have killed him in a tenth of a second. Hjelm didn't know why he was purposefully sticking his head into the lion's mouth. Had he heard a call from the other side? A siren's song? Or did he want to sneer in the face of death?

"For the first time in my life I have some understanding of the death penalty," he said.

Jennings smiled fleetingly. It had nothing to do with happiness. "Of course as an individual I deserve the death penalty," he said. "But I'm not an individual, I'm an — authority."

Hjelm left him then and joined the others out in the corridor. Arto Söderstedt was speaking into a mobile phone.

"Is he telling the truth?" Kerstin Holm said. "Is it all about control devices for nuclear warheads? Or is he sending us off on some crap errand so he can find a way out?"

"He's the devil's right-hand man," Hjelm said grimly. "His methods are inscrutable. What the fuck is he doing with us? What kind of game is he playing?"

"Isn't this Säpo's domain?" said Chavez.

"Don't we have to take it up to the government level?" Holm said.

Hultin stood motionless. Was he thinking, or was he paralysed?

"Let's go in and kill him," Norlander suggested eagerly.

Söderstedt hung up his phone and sighed deeply. "Justine has escaped the surveillance."

392

Hultin made a face, his first sign of life in a long time. "We'll do it ourselves. Whatever Justine is up to, it's illegal. Take her. And check all planned departures from all Swedish harbours in the next twenty-four hours."

"And Jennings?" said Hjelm.

"Put him under more stringent guard. I'll arrange for it. Arto, do you still have all Justine's notes?"

"In my office."

They went. Gunnar Nyberg, contemplating the cast on his right hand, stayed behind, observing their departure sceptically.

"You've made a pact with the devil," he stated. "Watch out, for Christ's sake. I won't be a part of it."

"You're part of the team, Gunnar," said Hultin. "We have to find Justine Lindberger. We're talking about international politics here."

"Fuck you."

Hultin looked at him dispassionately.

"He's fooled you all," Nyberg continued. "Can't you see that he's messing with you? He messed with me. He let me hit him. I saw his eyes. It was all a game. I realise that now."

"It's possible," said Hultin. "But the fact is that Justine Lindberger has escaped her surveillance. We need you."

Nyberg shook his head. "Never."

"Then you're on sick leave, starting now. Go home."

Nyberg gawked at him wildly. Snorting with rage, he left the room, paused in the corridor and then charged down to the basement where the cell was. Two powerfully built officers in civilian clothes had just taken up stations outside the door. They sat on chairs in the dark corridor, with a table and a deck of cards between them. They eyed Nyberg uncertainly as he planted himself in a third chair along the wall.

"Play your game," he said. "I'm not here."

He *was* there, and he intended to stay. He had suddenly seen it all. The corridor in LinkCoop. His steps forward. Robert Mayer's eyes. The tiny, tiny movement towards his jacket. The hand pulled back. The ice-cold acceptance of the blow.

Here he intended to stay.

Meanwhile Arto Söderstedt went over to his whiteboard, which was covered with cascades of writing.

"All the notes from the Lindberger couple. Justine's on the right, Eric's on the left."

"Is there anything that could be the name of a ship or a date, today or tomorrow, or the name of a harbour?" Hultin asked. "Or something that seems to be in code?"

Söderstedt scratched his nose. "She may have met a contact code-named S now and then. That was one of the things she chose to remove from her Filofax. She claims it's her jogging session, S as in 'stretching'. Unfortunately I have no more information about that. The other thing she removed was dates with her lover Herman in Bro. I have nothing more about him. She has three friends that she seems to be close to: Paula, Petronella and Priscilla. I have their full names and addresses. Beyond that she has a relatively large family, which also seems to be quite close-knit. This should all be checked.

"We have a few things here on the board that might be something. A little piece of paper that said 'Blue Viking'. That could be code for a place — a bar, for example — but I haven't found anything. This might be something, too — I can't make head-or-tail of it. It's a small yellow Post-it that says 'orphlinse', and that's all. Then I might also mention that it was in Östermalmshallen that Justine disappeared from her mediocre surveillance team."

"We'll have to divide it up," said Hultin. "Paul will try to find Herman in Bro. Kerstin can take the friends and family — call everyone you can find. Viggo will check with the surveillance team about exactly how and when she disappeared — take them along to Östermalmshallen. Jorge will take on Blue Viking and the other note. Arto, you and I can check the harbours — we do have a few of them in Sweden. Let's go."

Hjelm discovered that Bro was a commuter town with six thousand inhabitants between Kungsängen and Bålsta. Checking various databases from his office in police headquarters, he found eight Hermans in Bro. Two were retired; the others were possibilities, between the ages of twenty-two and fifty-eight. He called them. Three weren't home; none of the others admitted to knowing Justine Lindberger, even though he impressed upon them how important it was and guaranteed confidentiality, which made one of them — Herman Andersson, forty-four — very angry. After more research, he found the workplaces of the other three and got hold of them at their jobs.

None of them knew Justine; all seemed genuinely surprised by the inquiry.

And suddenly he had nothing left to do. It made him crazy after just a few minutes, so he decided to drive up to Bro. Filled with misgivings, he left police headquarters for a tour of Uppland. At that point it was three o'clock, and rain was still pouring down.

Kerstin Holm got hold of PPP. Paula Berglund sobbed at the thought of her friend being hunted by a madman and recalled that at various times her friend had unexpectedly travelled to Västerås and Karlskrona and maybe another place as well. Petronella af Wirsén laughed aloud at the fact that Justine had fled the police and assumed she was in her apartment in Paris or her villa in Dalarö. And Priscilla Bäfwer recalled various unexplained trips to Gotland, Södertälje, Halmstad and Trelleborg. All the relatives were less responsive and demanded the heads of the entire Swedish police force on a gigantic platter. "Little, confused Justine," said the only communicative one, Aunt Gretha, whom Holm had located only by chance; "she always was the black sheep in the family, the one who wasn't interested in money and power, the one who sympathised with the poor weak lambs on the edges of society." Aunt Gretha was bewildered to hear of Justine's immense fortune; it quite simply couldn't be her own.

Jorge Chavez slaved away at Justine's notes. He mobilised all his energy and all his mathematical knowledge to decipher the two that Justine Lindberger had left on her desk at the Ministry of Foreign Affairs: "Blue Viking" and "orphlinse". After taking detours through multitudes of conceivable codes, he went the direct route and managed to find a few pubs in various parts of Sweden called Blue Viking: Cafe Blue Viking in Härnösand, Blue Viking Restaurant & Bar in Halmstad, Cafe Blue Viking in Visby, and food stands called Blue Viking in Teckomatorp and Karlshamn. Härnösand, Halmstad, Visby and Karlshamn were all harbour cities.

When it came to the other note, he cursed himself that it took him so long to stick a full stop in "orphlinse" so that it became "orphlin.se" — that is, an address for a Swedish website. It was the Swedish branch of Orpheus Life Line, an international humanitarian organisation with special focus on Iraq. The song of Orpheus, said the programme description, was so poignant and strong that he had been able to sing the dead up out of the kingdom of the underworld. This was the organisation's goal. At the moment they were engaged in the situation in Iraq after the Gulf War and the blockades and the weapon-inspector crises — it bore a frightening resemblance to a kingdom of the dead. The website listed a whole series of matters in which human rights had been disregarded. Apparently the organisation kept its members secret, so that it could work fairly undisturbed in Saddam's domain. Chavez wondered why Justine had had the Orpheus Life Line's web address on her desk. Did she have a general interest in the Islamic world, or was there some more specific reason?

Viggo Norlander arrived at Östermalmshallen along with the two rather shamefaced colleagues whom Justine had eluded. Detective Werner had been stationed in the surveillance vehicle on Östermalmstorg, keeping watch down Humlegårdsgatan, while Detective Larsson had been, quote, "glued like a shadow" to Justine. Norlander's investigation revealed that this strange metaphor had concealed a distance of fifteen yards, which was rather a lot among the aisles and stalls of a busy market. Larsson had stood just inside the entrance doors and pointed into the hall, where the most surprising animal parts hovered like defective helicopters in the aromatically complex air. Justine had disappeared somewhere on the far left-hand side. So there were three possible stalls from which she could have gone underground: a classic Swedish delicatessen, a small Thai restaurant and a cafe that served coffee in tiny cups. After doing a few routine checks that had not been performed earlier, Norlander realised that she could only have escaped via the cafe. She could have hidden temporarily in the delicatessen or the Thai restaurant, but only the cafe, via a long aisle, had direct contact with the world outside. Norlander followed the aisle, keeping his gaze on the shamefaced Larsson every moment. They emerged some distance down Humlegårdsgatan, where a wet storm wind met them. Norlander strode over to Werner in the car and gave him the same evil eye that he had given Larsson. Then he went back inside and, without a word, took the violently protesting cafe owner with him to police headquarters.

**398**

Now Fawzi Ulaywi from Baghdad was sweating in one of the interrogation rooms, as the police watched him through a one-way mirror. "He must have unlocked it for her," Norlander said. "He must have followed her into the back room and unlocked the door. He works alone in the cafe, and the door to the aisle that leads to Humlegården was locked."

"What is he?" said Chavez, studying the printout of Orpheus Life Line's website. "An Iraqi? Isn't this about Saudi Arabia any more?"

"What did we say about the harbours?" said Hultin. "Which ones have popped up several times?"

"'Several' is probably an exaggeration," said Söderstedt, "but Blue Viking and the witnesses would point to Halmstad, Gotland and possibly Karlskrona/Karlshamn, in Blekinge County. Six vessels will leave Halmstad in the next twenty-four hours, three from Visby and sixteen from Blekinge."

"I don't think we have anything that makes one more likely than the next," said Holm. "Shall we split up?"

"When is the next departure?" Hultin asked. "And where the hell is Hjelm?"

"In Bro," said Holm.

"It's four thirty," said Söderstedt. "We have a few departures left today. The next is *Vega*, departing Karlshamn for Venezuela at six o'clock; then *Bay of Pearls*, departing Halmstad for Australia at seven forty-five; then *Lagavulin*, departing Visby for Scotland at eight thirty. Those are the next ones coming up."

"We need something more, something to tilt us in one direction," said Hultin. "Just a little more testimony about one of the places. Jorge and Arto can help Kerstin. Press the relatives. Viggo, you and I will talk to our friend the cafe owner."

Hultin and Norlander went in to see Fawzi Ulaywi, who was sweating a great deal. His stubborn facial expression concealed terror, as though he had been in this situation before and was trying to avoid thinking about what had happened then.

"My cafe," he said. "My cafe is standing there completely empty. Anyone could take my things and my money."

"We have competent guards there for the rest of the day," Norlander said sardonically. "Officers Larsson and Werner." He remained by the door looking large and brutal.

Hultin sat down across from Fawzi Ulaywi and asked calmly, "Why did you help Justine Lindberger escape earlier today?"

"I haven't done anything," Ulaywi said single-mindedly. "I don't understand."

"Have you heard of the organisation Orpheus Life Line? It is active in Iraq."

Ulaywi fell silent. A breeze of worry blew across his face and left furrows behind. It was obvious that he was thinking things over, carefully. "It's been ten years since I left Iraq," he said finally. "I don't know anything about what goes on there today."

"Are these Orpheus people involved in the nuclear weapons affair?"

Ulaywi gaped wildly at him and seemed to be trying to put the erratic information together.

**400**

"You have to tell us now," Hultin continued. "It's far too important to play games."

"Just torture me. I've survived it before."

Hultin looked at Norlander, who blinked uncertainly. He wasn't planning to torture anyone — what had Hultin's expression meant?

Hultin continued calmly, "I'm going to say the names of a few Swedish harbours. Tell me what they mean to you. Halmstad. Karlskrona. Visby. Karlshamn."

Terrified that ten years of nightmares were about to be made real again, Ulaywi tried so hard to think, he creaked.

"Halmstad," he said at last. "A woman came to me in the cafe and said she was being followed by a rapist. I helped her escape. She said something about having to get away — I think she said Halmstad."

Norlander and Hultin exchanged glances. Hultin nodded, and they went out into the corridor. As they spoke, they watched Ulaywi through the one-way mirror. He was still sweating but may also have looked a bit satisfied.

"He's part of it," said Hultin. "He's somewhere in the line of smugglers. He won't say any more. We can cross off Halmstad."

"Cross it off?" Norlander burst out. "But —"

"He's trying to throw us off. Look at him. That's not a man who talks."

Hultin went to the guys manning the phones. They were spread out over three rooms, so he had to repeat three times, "Blekinge or Visby. Not Halmstad."

Then he took out his mobile phone and dialled. "Paul? Where are you?"

"Norrtull," said Hjelm from within the heart of electronics. "I've destroyed the familial peace in a number of Bro households. Never more will the wives trust their Hermans. I got a licking from an angry wife."

"No bites?"

"None of these Hermans can reasonably have had anything to do with Justine Lindberger from Upper Östermalm. It's been a complete waste of time."

"Come home quickly. We're down to possibly Visby, Karlskrona or Karlshamn. Possibly."

"OK."

Holm came running out of her room and yelled, "Aunt Gretha had a mobile phone number that didn't exist anywhere else." She held out a piece of paper with a number on it.

Hultin hung up on Hjelm and dialled the number.

"Yes?" they could hear faintly from the receiver. A woman's voice.

"Justine?" Hultin said.

"Who is this?"

"Orpheus," he chanced. "Where are you?"

Justine Lindberger was silent for a moment. Then she said, "Password?"

Hultin looked at Holm and Norlander. They shook their heads.

"Blue Viking," said Hultin.

"Fuck," said Justine, and hung up.

"Shit," said Hultin.

402

"Background noise?" asked Kerstin Holm.

Hultin shook his head. He dialled the number again. No answer.

He went into his office and closed the door. It was quarter to five. The freighter *Vega* would leave Karlshamn in just over an hour. They would miss it. The information that pointed to Karlshamn was extremely vague: just a friend's suggestion that Justine had been in its neighbour city Karlskrona, which had a bar called Blue Viking, which should perhaps be put under surveillance immediately, but then he would have to bring in the Blekinge police, and how would they explain the situation? He didn't even really understand it himself. Should he let *Vega* get away or get the provincial police on it? He remained in his room, his shoulders pressed down by an endless weight.

Meanwhile Kerstin Holm and Viggo Norlander were still in the corridor.

Everything seemed foggy. Where were Hultin's thoughts heading? they wondered.

Hjelm showed up with a black eye. "Don't ask. Women," he said cryptically.

"Bro," Kerstin said, pointing at him. "There was something on the tip of my tongue about Bro."

"*Bro, bro, breja,*" Norlander said, quoting a children's rhyme. He seemed to have given up. He threw a bitter glance at Fawzi Ulaywi. "He's sitting here, the fate of the universe resting on his shoulders, and he's not going to talk."

"Who is that?" said Hjelm.

"Isn't Bro a pretty common place name?" said Holm.

"He's the one who helped Justine escape," Norlander told Hjelm. "An Iraqi. One of the people who hide behind Orpheus Life Line, a fake human rights organisation. Presumably they're fundamentalist spies. He's our only link to the warheads."

"They're control devices," said Hjelm, "for nuclear warheads."

"Did anyone hear me?" said Holm.

"He ought to be speared on his warheads," said Norlander. "Wouldn't we be morally justified in going in there and pressing him? Hard?"

"The way Wayne Jennings does?" said Kerstin Holm. "Has he transformed us into copies of himself? So quickly?"

"What was it you said?" said Paul Hjelm.

"We've become the Kentucky Killer's puppets," she said.

"Before that. About Bro."

"Isn't Bro a pretty common place name?"

"Are you saying I was in the wrong Bro? Where are the other ones?"

"I don't know. It was just a guess."

"If Herman is a lover and they meet there every Tuesday, it can't be that far away."

"But maybe Herman isn't a lover. Arto pressed Justine, surprised her with his little photocopier trick, and she had to make something up quickly. Maybe Herman was the right name, but she covered it up with the lie that he was her lover."

404

They half ran into Holm's office and took out a road atlas. Bro in Uppland, Bro in Värmland, Bro in Bohuslän — and Bro on Gotland.

"On Gotland. Only a few miles from Visby," said Holm. "A little church village."

Norlander started up the computer and accessed the large telephone registry. There were two Hermans in the little Bro north-west of Visby.

Hjelm unlocked his mobile phone. Holm took it from him and dialled the first of the two numbers.

"Bengtsson," said a ringing Gotland accent.

"Herman," said Kerstin, "it's Justine."

It was quiet. The longer the silence went on, the higher their hopes rose.

"Why are you calling again?" said Herman Bengtsson at last. "Has something happened?"

"Just double-checking," Kerstin croaked out. "I'm on my way."

She ended the call, then clenched her fist for a second. And then they ran in to Hultin.

The helicopter took off five minutes later from the platform atop police headquarters. *Decently fast*, Hultin thought, as he sat there next to Norlander, reading through his papers. "The freighter *Lagavulin* will leave Visby harbour at twenty thirty. Right now it's quarter past five. We ought to get there in plenty of time."

"Isn't Lagavulin a malt whisky?" said Hjelm.

"The best," said Chavez. "Extremely smoky and tarry."

The last islands of the archipelago were visible below them, drowning in the pouring rain; Hjelm thought he recognised Utö. Then it was open sea, a windswept sea, almost whiter than black. The helicopter swayed and reeled in the storm. Hjelm glanced at the pilot; he didn't like the look on his face. Nor was Norlander's face particularly confidence-inspiring — he grabbed a helmet that was hanging on the wall of the helicopter and threw up into it. Hjelm was happy that he had not been the receptacle of choice.

Others were feeling ill, too. The pilot took out some plastic bags to protect the remaining supply of helmets. Arto Söderstedt's white skin developed a mint-green tinge, and what came up in Hjelm's own heave was the same colour. Only Hultin and Holm retained their stomach contents.

Just east of Visby, a mediocre collection of police officers streamed out onto the hidden helicopter platform, where two hire cars awaited them. They stood for a second, letting themselves be washed by the rain — it was surprisingly cleansing. Their facial colours returned to normal. They were alive again and ready to find out what Justine Lindberger had waiting for them down at the harbour.

They circled around Visby and glided down to the harbour along Färjeleden. They passed the large Gotland ferries and approached *Lagavulin*. The vessel lay some way out on the pier at the northern breakwater, heaving against a pile of car tyres.

*Lagavulin* wasn't really a freighter. She was too small, more like a large fishing boat. She was alone, way out there, and there was no sign of life within her. A flock of large gulls circled the ship, like vultures around a cadaver in the desert. Out on the Baltic, a large oil tanker went by, its lanterns gleaming weakly through the storm; swaying slowly, it passed like a large, cold, inaccessible sea monster. The sky felt unusually low, as though the thick rain clouds had come down to lick the surface of the earth, as though they were witnessing the great flood. Was there great, pure, sun-drenched clearness on the other side of the clouds? Or was that just a utopian dream? Was there even room any more for clarity?

They emerged from the cars, which had been parked out of the way, by the secondary school. Almost invisible in the darkness, they made their way over to the pier and ran out along it, hunching over. The scent of the sea drowned out the faint ozone odour of the rainstorm.

They were close now. There was no hint of any surveillance.

They gathered around the gangway, dripping wet.

Chavez and Norlander went aboard first, quietly, with weapons drawn. Then Hjelm and Holm, followed by Söderstedt and Hultin. All had their safeties off.

They made their way past the bridge and moved towards the stern. Everything was dark. The boat seemed deserted. Then a few faint voices rose in the storm. They followed the voices until they were standing by a door next to some windows with pulled curtains. Behind the curtains they could see a faint, flickering light.

Norlander assessed the strength of the door, then got ready, his back against the railing. Hjelm tried to turn the door handle, but it was locked. Norlander immediately kicked it in. One giant kick was enough. The lock hung quivering on the wall for a few seconds, then fell to the deck.

Inside what looked like a dining hall, five people sat around a screwed-down kerosene lamp. A young blond man in Helly Hansen clothes, three large, swarthy late-middle-aged men in thick quilted coats — and Justine Lindberger in a rain coat and trousers. When she caught sight of Söderstedt in the rear, she seemed to exhale.

"Hands on your heads!" Norlander yelled.

"It's just the Swedish police!" Justine yelled at the three men. They placed their hands on their heads.

The Helly Hansen man stood up and said in a Gotland accent, "What is this? What are you doing here?"

"Herman Bengtsson, I presume," said Hultin, pointing the pistol at him. "Sit down right now and place your hands on your head."

Bengtsson reluctantly obeyed.

"Search them," Hultin ordered.

Norlander and Chavez searched wildly. None of those present were carrying weapons. The signs were starting to add up, and they were alarming.

"You're the ones who called me," Justine Lindberger said, as furious mental activity seemed to be going on in her brain.

"Where's the computer equipment?" Hultin asked.

"What computer equipment?" said Herman Bengtsson. "What are you talking about?"

"How many more people are on board?"

"None," said Justine Lindberger, sighing. "The crew is coming in an hour."

"And the guards? You can't carry control devices for nuclear weapons without a guard."

Justine Lindberger froze. Then an idea seemed to strike her. She closed her eyes for a few seconds, and when she opened them, they were more resigned, almost mourning. As if she were before a platoon of executioners.

"We're not smuggling nuclear weapons," she said. "It's the other way round."

"Jorge, Viggo, Arto — run and search. Be careful."

They disappeared, leaving Jan-Olov Hultin, Paul Hjelm and Kerstin Holm in charge of Justine Lindberger, Herman Bengtsson and three dark men with the marks of death on their faces.

Justine spoke, as though her life depended on getting the words right. "Herman and I belong to Orpheus Life Line, a secret human rights organisation that is active in Iraq. We have to remain secret; our enemies are powerful. Eric was part of it, too. He died without revealing anything. He was stronger than we thought."

Then she gestured towards the three men.

"These three are high-ranking officers in the Iraqi army. They've deserted. They have extremely important information about the Gulf War, which neither Saddam nor the United States wants to get out. They are on their way to the United States, to be put under the protection of a large media organisation. The information will be released from there; it won't be possible to stop it. The American mass media are the only force that is strong enough to resist."

Hultin looked at Hjelm, Hjelm looked at Holm, Holm looked at Hultin.

"You have to let us be," said Justine Lindberger. "Someone has tricked you. Someone has used you."

Hjelm saw Wayne Jennings in his mind's eye and said, "You will never know." He felt like he was going to vomit, but he had nothing left to throw up.

"In that case, they're on your trail," said Kerstin Holm. "We have to get you out of here."

"Regardless, we can't let the boat depart," said Hultin. "It has to be thoroughly investigated. So we'll take you with us now, quickly."

"It's your duty to protect us," said Justine Lindberger, looking very tired. "You've led them here — now you have to protect us with your lives."

Hultin looked at her with an expression of deep regret and backed out past the broken door. He slid aside. Holm came out. Then Herman Bengtsson, the three men, Justine and Hjelm. They stood out on the deck. The wind howled. The rain poured down on them.

They moved towards the gangway.

Then it happened, as though an order had been given — as though they themselves had given it.

Herman Bengtsson's head was torn off; a cascade of blood sent him down onto the deck. The three men were flung by cascades of bullets into the wall of the ship. Their coats turned red, and down exploded out.

**410**

They collapsed as though their bodies had no joints. Kerstin threw herself over Justine; she didn't think — she was a living wall. A bullet grazed her shoulder; she saw it drill into Justine's right eye just four inches away. Justine vomited blood into Kerstin's face — in one last exhalation.

Hultin was petrified. He stared up at the town of Visby, which rose like a distant, illuminated doomsday castle far away.

Hjelm's pistol was raised. His body spun round, but he had nothing to aim at, nothing at all. He returned the pistol to his shoulder holster and suddenly realised what it was like to be raped. He placed his arms around Kerstin, who was sniffling quietly.

Bloody, rain-soaked down slowly covered the nightmarish scene in a blanket of oblivion.

Everything was quiet. Visby harbour was calm.

As though nothing had happened.

# CHAPTER
# TWENTY-NINE

Gunnar Nyberg needed to pee. He had been sitting motionless in a chair in the basement of police headquarters for several hours. Not for a second had his attention flagged. The two guards had played blackjack for a few hours, and then they had been relieved, and now a new pair of guards were sitting there playing blackjack.

In other words, the monotony was monumental. The architecture, without a doubt, contributed its share. The walls had been sloppily painted a light yellow, and the lights, covered by a faint layer of dust on top, shone a loathsome glare through the corridor. Now the urge to pee crept over him and struck in a dastardly ambush.

Food was delivered to Wayne Jennings. That was a worrying moment. The incongruous bowl of soup remained standing on the guards' table for so long that the steam stopped rising from it. Their hand of blackjack seemed to be taking years. *Isn't blackjack a relatively quick game?* his urge to pee said. *Up to twenty-one in a few puny cards, and then you're done?*

The guards looked at him sternly. Then they picked up the tray with the soup bowl, the bread and the mug of milk, and prepared to enter.

They went in. They locked the door behind them. Nyberg remained seated in the corridor. He took out his service weapon, took off the safety, and aimed it straight at the thick door with his healthy left hand. He feared what would come crawling out of there. He was sitting five yards from the door, and he would shoot to kill.

Time crept on. The guards were still gone. With every second, his conviction grew stronger. He pushed his urge to pee back into the wings.

The door slid open.

Wayne Jennings actually looked surprised when he saw Nyberg sitting there with the pistol aimed right at his heart.

"Gunnar Nyberg," said Jennings courteously. "Nice to see you."

Nyberg stood up. The chair fell with a clang that echoed through the corridor, echoing back and forth in this wild beast's cave.

He held the weapon steady, aimed at his heart.

Jennings took a step forward.

Gunnar Nyberg shot. Two shots, right to the heart. Wayne Jennings was thrown backwards through the corridor. He lay still.

Nyberg took a few steps towards him, keeping the pistol aimed straight at the body.

Then Wayne Jennings got up.

He smiled. His icy gaze did not smile.

Nyberg trembled. He was six feet away. He emptied the magazine into the Kentucky Killer's body. It hurtled back again and lay on the floor.

Gunnar Nyberg was close now.

Wayne Jennings got up again. The bullet holes shone like black lights in his white shirt. He smiled.

Nyberg shot again. The pistol clicked. He threw it aside. Then he threw an uppercut. This time Jennings would not get up.

He hit the air. There was no one there.

A terrible pain went through his large body. He had never imagined that his body could shake so violently. He lay on the floor; Jennings was pinching a point on the back of his neck. He stared up into Jennings's serious face.

"Forget me now," said Wayne Jennings. "You have to erase me from your consciousness. Otherwise you will never find peace."

He released him. Nyberg tried to sit up, but he was still trembling.

The last thing he heard before everything went black was a voice that said:

"I am No One."

# CHAPTER
# THIRTY

The rain had not ceased. Some of Stockholm's streets had been closed off due to flooding. A few historic buildings had been destroyed and had to be evacuated. It was worse in some suburbs. Entire neighbourhoods were under water. The storm had taken out electricity and phone service in parts of Sweden. Now they were approaching a state of disaster.

Police headquarters, however, was still intact. But "Supreme Central Command" had reclaimed its quotation marks. They flapped like scoffing vampires through the room.

"I should have aimed for his head," said Gunnar Nyberg. "I could have put a single shot in his head. Fuck, that was dumb."

"You couldn't have known that the guards were wearing bulletproof vests," said Hultin, "or that he had taken one of them."

"I should have stopped them from going in."

"There's a lot we should have done," Hultin said sombrely from his lectern. "And above all, there's a lot we *shouldn't* have done."

Nyberg looked like hell. In addition to his nose cone and the cast on his hand, he now had a large bandage on the back of his neck. Of course, he shouldn't have been there; he should have been on sick leave, sleeping off his double concussion. But no one could get him to leave.

Hultin's owl glasses were in place, but other than that he was hardly himself. His neutrality had been all but blown away. Age seemed to have caught up with him. He looked smaller than usual; the era of this Father of His People was at an end. Perhaps he would be able to pull himself together before he retired.

He spoke with a slow, thick, almost old-man's voice. "Both Gunnar and the guards escaped without permanent injuries. Jennings used Gunnar's police ID to get out of the building — it was found a few hours later in a rubbish bin at Arlanda. It was a little signal for us. A 'thanks for the help', I suppose."

He paused and paged slowly through his papers, then continued. "What we saw were the effects of at least three identical high-precision automatic weapons with exceedingly effective ammunition. We can assume that they followed us by helicopter to Visby, came to the harbour and took up suitable positions in the city heights. It may have been a productive collaboration between the CIA and Saddam; we'll never know. Nor will we ever know what the three deserting army officers had to reveal about the Gulf War.

"Above all, we have to forget this case. The corpses have been taken care of. As you know, we had to use Säpo — they'll take the case from here.

"Nothing has reached the media, but even if we wanted to talk to the press, what would we say? The

**416**

case will appear unsolvable; people will keep buying weapons and hiring security firms. And maybe they're right to do so. And you all know what Fawzi Ulaywi said when we released him — I'll never forget it: 'Fucking murderers!' He was right, of course. And now his identity has probably been revealed. Maybe he'll go underground and avoid being assassinated, maybe not. He, Herman Bengtsson and the Lindbergers were the Swedish branch of Orpheus Life Line. Now there's nothing left of that branch."

He fell silent. He appeared old and tired. They had solved the case, in all its aspects, but now he was going to be hung out to dry, like a failed Olof Palme-murder detective. The demands for his resignation could become loud. And they would be justified — but for completely different reasons.

"Is there anything else?" he said.

"Justine Lindberger's bank account was emptied a few hours after her death," said Arto Söderstedt. "We can only hope that the emptier was Orpheus Life Line, saving what was left of their capital. Otherwise it went towards Wayne Jennings's salary. The Lindbergers' large apartment will go to their already-rich family; Orpheus will lose its Swedish headquarters and central office, in addition to four of its most loyal members. And everything else."

Söderstedt looked up at the ceiling. He, too, seemed very tired.

"I treated her like shit," he said quietly, "and she turned out to be a hero."

"*Lagavulin* was empty," said Chavez, looking small and insignificant. "It contained no control devices for nuclear warheads. And LinkCoop is an ordinary, computer-orientated import-export company, totally legitimate. The CEO, Henrik Nilsson, was very sorry that its excellent chief of security Robert Mayer had disappeared. He took the opportunity to report it to the police."

"Benny Lundberg died this morning," said Kerstin Holm. "His father turned off the respirator. He's been arrested — he's one floor down."

Gunnar Nyberg suddenly got up and bolted from the room. They watched him go. They hoped he wasn't planning to go down and kill the unfortunate Lasse Lundberg.

Hjelm had nothing to say. He was thinking about the concept of "pain beyond words".

"We know that Lamar Jennings shadowed his father for more than a week," Hultin continued. "It can't have been too hard for him to find Robert Mayer — he's in the phone book. Lamar copied the key to the warehouse the day after he arrived in Sweden. He must have followed Wayne Jennings to LinkCoop; maybe Wayne had already committed a murder; maybe there are hordes of dead people we'll never discover. Anyway, something caused Lamar to copy the key — and something enabled him to glean the information that his father would show up on that fateful night with Erik Lindberger in tow. We don't know how — or why — Lindberger followed Jennings to Frihamnen after their meeting at Riche, and we don't know why they

418

met there. Maybe Lindberger thought it was about Orpheus; the members do remain secret, after all. In general, there's a lot we don't know."

Hultin paused, then continued in a more intense tone. "The Cold War is over. What has replaced it almost feels worse, because we don't understand what it is. The world is shrinking, and above all, we seem to be shrinking. We did fantastic police work — I suppose that can be of comfort among all the grief, but it's not enough. We made political and psychological misjudgements that show that we're not really up to par with the rest of the world. Violent crime of an international character is slipping through our fingers. This blind violence is a mirror of the goal-orientated crime. Lamar Jennings was a hall-of-mirrors version of his father. 'Bad blood always comes back round,' as they say."

Paul Hjelm laughed, filled with scorn for himself. He hadn't even got the saying right. Wayne Jennings had corrected him. "It's 'what goes around comes around'," he said, drying his tears.

They only seemed like tears of laughter.

The others looked at him for a moment. They understood how he felt, and at the same time they understood how impossible it was to ever understand even the tiniest thing about another person.

"Do any of you have anything to add?" said Hultin.

"Well, at least the United States has one less serial killer," Kerstin Holm said, smiling bitterly. "He was serial-killed by another serial killer. Once again Wayne Jennings shows us he's the good guy."

"It's the result that counts," said Hjelm. None of his words were his own any longer. Nothing was his own. Everything had been occupied. He was a little model train going round in a circle.

"Well then." Jan-Olov Hultin rose to his feet. "I have to go take a piss. We can only hope that God stops all of this soon."

They didn't really want to disperse. It was as though they needed to be close to one another. But at last they were dismissed out into the world, as alone as they had come into it and as alone as they would leave it.

Hjelm and Holm were last to go. Paul stopped Kerstin just inside the door.

"I have something of yours." He dug in his wallet, found the photo of the old pastor and handed it to her. When she looked at him, he couldn't tell what she was thinking — sorrow, pain and a strength that pushed through the darkness.

"Thanks," she said.

"Wipe it off," he said. "He has Wayne Jennings's fingerprints on his nose."

"Yalm & Halm." She smiled. "In another world we could have been a real comedy duo."

He bent forward and kissed her on the forehead.

"We are in this one," he said.

**420**

# CHAPTER
# THIRTY-ONE

Gunnar Nyberg came out of "Supreme Central Command" steaming with rage — he didn't know how he was supposed to get rid of it. Three times a filicidal murderer had inflicted bodily injury on him. Now here was another father who had murdered his son. Lasse Lundberg was now in the cell from which Jennings had escaped. Nyberg went down there. His first impulse was to let Benny's dad have everything he had failed to give Lamar's. He shook off the guards' protests and entered the corridor with the cells. He arrived at Lundberg's and peered in through the small window. Lasse Lundberg was hunched over with his elbows on his knees and his face in his hands, shaking uncontrollably. Nyberg watched him for a moment, then did an about-face, reminded of a certain other father's sins.

He set out for Östhammar, two hours north of Stockholm, in his Renault. He had a lot of time to think as he drove, but his thoughts were wrapped in the after-effects of a double concussion. This case was supposed to have been calm and easy as he awaited retirement. No personal engagement, no risk-taking, no excessive overtime. Cutting back, some time for peaceful vegetating. And what the hell had happened instead?

The road he took, Norrtäljevägen, was flooded. The road seemed more liquid than solid. Even when he was driving uphill, he met masses of water; driving downhill, he sloshed through water. It felt ridiculous.

He passed Norrtälje. He passed the exit for Hallstavik and Grisslehamn, and then he was in Östhammar, a small, peaceful, depopulated village. The Stockholmers who holidayed there were back in the city now, so Östhammar was once again identifiable as the little farming village it was.

With the help of the extremely detailed police map, he drove far out into the countryside. The rain fell incessantly. The roads were nearly impassable — his tyres dug into the mud. At one point the Renault's left rear wheel got stuck in a veritable crater. He got out, enraged, and lifted up the fucking car.

Sometime later the farm appeared over the crown of a hill. Small as the incline was, it seemed hard to conquer. He stepped on it and pushed ahead. He barely made it but finally turned the car onto the grounds.

Next to the barn he saw a tractor — its enormous back tire was half sunk in the mud. A large man with a gold-and-green cap, muddy overalls and green size-eighteen boots was crouching next to it. His back was to Nyberg, who stepped out of the car and trudged over to him in the pelting rain. The man pounded the tractor with his large fist, whereupon it sank further into the mud. Fuming, the man yelled, "Fucking tractor!"

And then he lifted the tractor out of the mud.

At that moment, Gunnar Nyberg realised he was in the right place. He took a few steps closer.

The large farmer heard him sloshing and turned to see a gigantic mummy approaching him through the deluge. The sight would have terrified anyone. But not this farmer. He stepped towards the apparition.

Soon Nyberg could discern his face. He was about twenty-five. And he looked just like he himself had, at that age. This man wasn't Mr Sweden — he was a hick. But he appeared to feel much better than Mr Sweden had.

The man stopped a few yards from Gunnar. Was it himself or his father that Tommy Nyberg recognised? "Dad?" he thundered.

Gunnar Nyberg felt a warm wave stream through him.

Tommy Nyberg stepped up to him and scrutinised him. Then he took off his work gloves and extended his hand. "Holy shit! Dad! And you're still a cop?"

Nyberg adjusted his nose cone with his healthy left hand, then extended it and managed a rather awkward handshake. He was incapable of speech.

"What are you doing here? Come on in, dammit! It's a little wet."

They plodded over the waterlogged ground, past the tractor, past the barn and past a tyre swing in a water-filled hollow in the yard; it was floating with its chain hanging slack.

"Oh yes," said Tommy. "You'll get to meet him soon."

They reached the run-down house. It was neither big nor impressive. Boards stuck out in some places, the result of makeshift repairs; the old red paint was flaking. Here and there patches of mould spotted the surface. *Patina*, thought Gunnar Nyberg; the house fitted him perfectly.

They stepped up onto the porch. The stairs creaked alarmingly, first under Tommy, then under Gunnar. They went in, straight into the dining room. A small, thin, blonde woman in her early twenties was seated at the large table, feeding a fat, blond baby in a high chair.

She tossed an unruly lock of hair over her head and stared at the giant duo in surprise. The boy started bawling at the sight of his seriously bandaged grandfather.

"Tina and Benny," Tommy Nyberg said as he pulled off his size eighteens. "This is my dad. He popped up out of the storm."

"His name is Benny?" said Gunnar Nyberg from the entryway.

"He's Gunnar?" Tina said uncertainly. "Your real dad?"

"I suppose you could call him that," Tommy rumbled, and gave Benny an audible kiss so that he stopped crying, and then he sat at the table with a crash. "After all," he added with a broad smile.

"Come in," said Tina, rising to her feet. "Don't just stand there!"

Gunnar Nyberg took off his shoes and took a seat at a respectable distance from the child. He felt ill at ease.

"Hi." Tina extended a hand across the table.

424

Nyberg greeted her awkwardly. "Hi," he said softly.

They were quiet for a moment. The silence ought to have been uncomfortable, but it wasn't. The three of them looked at Gunnar, curiously, not hatefully.

"This is your grandfather," Tommy finally said to one-year-old Benny, who looked as though this information would bring on another attack of crying. But a scoop of porridge from his mother distracted him.

"Well then," said Tommy, "where have you been keeping yourself?"

"I didn't know you lived here," Nyberg whispered. "It's been so long since we've seen each other."

"Oh well, you're here now, anyway. Would you like some coffee?"

Nyberg nodded and watched his son disappear into the kitchen.

"He's been talking about contacting you ever since we moved here," said Tina, sticking a spoon of porridge into Benny's mouth.

"Has he said anything else?"

She inspected him, as if searching for a motive. "Just that the family moved to the west coast early on, and that you had promised not to contact them. But I don't know why."

Gunnar Nyberg knitted his eyebrows. For the first time he felt distinct pain in his nose and hand. It radiated up through him, in one fell swoop. Like a vague recollection of Wayne Jennings's nerve pinching. Or rather, as though a long-acting anaesthetic had worn off.

"Because I was an extraordinarily bad father," he said.

She nodded and regarded him curiously. "Is it true that you were Mr Sweden?"

He laughed, long and noisily, and his voice seemed to return after an eternity in exile. "It's hard to believe, isn't it? I'd have been happy to have done without that, believe me."

He looked at Benny's stout little body. The child snatched the spoon from Tina's hand and threw it at him. Gunnar caught it in mid-air. Porridge spattered on his clothes. He let it be.

"Do you want to hold him?" asked Tina.

She lifted his grandchild over to him. The boy was heavy, compact. He'd probably become a strapping fellow.

*Bad blood always comes back round.*

That wasn't true. It was possible to break the cycle.

It wasn't even true that what goes around comes around.

There was such a thing as forgiveness. He understood that now.

Tommy reappeared from the kitchen brandishing the coffee pot. Suddenly, at the threshold, he stopped and took off his wet farmer's cap.

"Hey, Dad, what the hell?" he said. "Are you crying?"

# CHAPTER
# THIRTY-TWO

Paul Hjelm emerged from police headquarters and lingered at the entrance, feeling that something was wrong. He went back in to retrieve his umbrella.

He came back out again, feeling as if he had been wandering around the hold of a ship for a month. In the raw autumn night, he opened the umbrella; the small police logos beamed down at him powerlessly. The storm pummelled the rain horizontally, from all directions at once. After he'd gone just a few yards on the flooded Bergsgatan, the wind shredded his umbrella; he chucked it into a rubbish bin at the Metro entrance.

He had called Ray Larner and told him every detail of the case, without inhibition. He didn't give a damn about the consequences. Larner had listened, then said, "Whatever you do, Yalm, don't keep looking. You'll go crazy."

He wouldn't keep looking, but he would keep *thinking* — he wouldn't be able to stop; he didn't *want* to stop. The case of K would always be in his consciousness, or just under it. He hadn't yet absorbed its horrible, awful knowledge more than superficially. Knowledge was always good, after all; he was enough of an Enlightenment rationalist to be certain of that. The question was what effect one would allow knowledge to have on one's own psyche. The risk in this case, he realised, was that it would make him crazy.

Wayne Jennings had turned an apparently hopeless disadvantage into a pure victory. Hjelm felt a reluctant pang of admiration.

But who could really tell whether it had been a success or a setback? Who knew, today, what the three Iraqi officers' disclosures would have resulted in had they been able to speak to the press? Was it true that the media today were the only counterforce against military and economic might? Or were the media themselves the actual threat? And was fundamentalism the only real alternative to an unrestrained market? Nothing anywhere seemed particularly attractive.

What is the worth of a human life? What sort of life do we want to have, and what sort do we want others to have? What price do we pay for living as well as we do? Are we ready to pay that price? And what do we do if we're not?

Simple, basic questions echoed within him.

"I haven't tickled the bass in six months," Jorge had said, plucking a few strings on an imaginary double bass. "Now I'm going home to play all night, until the police come and take me away."

People had died in their arms, heads had been torn off before their eyes, other people's blood had washed over them, and no one outside their own little circle would ever know. What could they do? Play. And put

428

their whole blackened souls into it. It had to come out somehow.

He bought an evening newspaper and took the Metro for the brief stretch from City Hall to Central Station, then switched to the train to Norsborg. He read the headline: "Still no trace of the Kentucky Killer. The police defend their passivity, citing limited resources."

Mörner was the one who was quoted. Hjelm laughed. His fellow riders looked at him. It did not interest him.

Nor was he interested in the behind-the-scenes action that would follow. Right now he just felt like sticking headphones on his ears and sinking down into his train seat.

John Coltrane, *Meditations*. He stepped into that vague state between wakefulness and sleep — the privileged space of serenity.

We thought something had only just come to Sweden, he mused. The truth was that it was already here, and had been for a long time. It just had to be aroused.

He would get himself a piano. That decision ripened as he got out of the train at Norsborg and ambled through the rain. The standardised terraced houses seemed to watch him through the flying mists. He crept along slowly, allowing the rain into every pore. He needed to be thoroughly washed. Time after time.

It had been a long time since he'd seen the moon, and there was none tonight. In the United States he hadn't thought to look. He had become close to

Kerstin in a way he hadn't expected. Somewhere inside he had longed for her, but his childish wish for a hot affair on the side had changed to something different. Was he getting old? Or was he growing up?

He arrived at his terraced house. It looked grey and dreary, as impersonal as a high-rise, but disguised as a tiny rise in status. It was all fiction. Nothing was as it seemed.

Above all, it wasn't grey and dreary inside. On the inside, nothing is the same. That was something, at least. Some little trace of comfort after what he had been involved in.

He had, as Larner said, caught the Fucking Kentucky Baby all on his own. Well. The inspiration had been his own, anyway. And not just one, but two. That the other had slipped away was not his fault — it was more a law of nature. Or at least he could pretend that that was the case for a while.

Cilla was sitting on the sofa. A little candle was burning in front of her. She was reading a book.

"You can't read in that light," he said. "You'll ruin your eyes."

"No." She put down the book. "That's one of those lies that people spread. You can't ruin your eyes by reading in too little light. There can never be too little light."

He smiled faintly and walked over to her.

"Wait, don't sit down." She disappeared, then came back with a few towels and placed them on the sofa.

He sat on them. "I could have got them myself," he said.

"I *wanted* to get them," she said, "if that's OK."

There was silence for a moment.

"What were you reading?" he asked at last.

"Your book," she said, holding up Kafka's *Amerika*. "You never have time to read, after all."

"What do you think?"

"Tricky," she said. "But when you get into it, you can't put it down. You think you understand, and then you realise you don't understand anything."

"I understand," he said.

"Do you?" she said.

They laughed briefly.

Then she fingered his clothes. "You're really wet. I'll help you get them off."

"You don't need to —"

"Yes," she said, "I need to." She slowly undressed him.

He allowed himself to enjoy it, wholeheartedly.

"I'll probably have more time to read now," he said as she pulled off his trousers. "And we'll probably have a little more time together, too."

"But you haven't caught that Montana Murderer yet."

"Kentucky Killer."

"When are you actually going to catch him?"

"Never," he said calmly.

She pulled off his soaking-wet underwear and threw it onto the pile of drenched clothes on the floor. "You don't look too bad, Paul Hjelm," she said, "for a middle-aged, lower-level official."

"You don't look too bad, either," he said. "As you can see."

She smiled and started to undress.

He reached for the candle. He put it out — and burned himself. "Ow, hell."

"You're so clumsy," she laughed, lying down beside him.

He watched the wick. The glow ebbed until no light was left. "There can never be too little light," said Paul Hjelm, letting himself go.

Outside, the rain streamed down.

# The Blinded Man

## Arne Dahl

Now a major BBC TV series

Two of Sweden's most powerful businessmen have been murdered. In the face of mounting panic amongst the financial elite, a task force has been created to catch the culprit before he kills again. To his surprise, Detective Paul Hjelm, currently under investigation for misconduct after shooting a man who took an immigration office hostage, is summoned to join the team. But the killer has left no clues — even removing the bullets from the crime scenes — and Hjelm and his new teammates face a daunting challenge if they are to uncover the connection between the murdered men and identify any potential victims before he strikes again.

**ISBN 978-0-7531-9194-1 (hb)**
**ISBN 978-0-7531-9195-8 (pb)**

# Death of the Demon

## Anne Holt

In an orphanage outside Oslo, twelve-year-old Olav is
causing havoc. The institution's ageing director, Agnes
Vestavik, sees something chilling in the boy's eyes: sheer
hatred. When Vestavik is found murdered at her desk
late at night, stabbed in the neck with a kitchen knife —
with Olav nowhere to be found — the case goes to
Hanne Wilhelmsen, recently promoted to superintendent
in the Oslo police.

Hanne suspects that Olav witnessed the murder and
fled, and she orders an investigation of the orphanage
staff. But this, however, is one case where her instincts
are leading her astray.

Meanwhile, Olav makes his way to his mother's
apartment in central Oslo. When police finally catch up
to him, he will lead them on a chase that will upend all
of their assumptions.

**ISBN 978-0-7531-9288-7 (hb)**
**ISBN 978-0-7531-9289-4 (pb)**

# The Age of Doubt

## Andrea Camilleri

The day after a storm, Inspector Montalbano encounters a strange woman who expresses interest in a certain yacht scheduled to dock that afternoon. Not long after she's gone, the yacht's crew reports finding a disfigured corpse. Also at anchor is a luxury vessel with a somewhat shady crew. Both boats will have to stay in Vigàta until the investigation is over and, based on information from the woman, Montalbano begins to think the occupants of the yacht might know more about the man's death than they're letting on.

**ISBN 978-0-7531-9098-2 (hb)**
**ISBN 978-0-7531-9099-9 (pb)**

# Fun & Games

## Duane Swierczynski

Number of accidental deaths per year. By suffocation: 3,300. By poisoning: 8,600. Staged by professionals: you have no idea.

Ex-cop Charlie Hardie's latest job is guarding an isolated mansion in LA's Hollywood Hills. But it comes with an unwanted guest — a D-list actress who says she's being hunted by professional hitman.

Charlie thinks she's just high and paranoid. But he's wrong. The killers are real. They've tracked her to the house. And they're not letting anyone out alive.

**ISBN 978-0-7531-9048-7 (hb)**
**ISBN 978-0-7531-9049-4 (pb)**